SMALL RECKONINGS

KARIN MELBERG SCHWIER

Praise for Small Reckonings

**2021 National Jury Shortlist Recognition of
Literary Excellence, Glengarry Book Award**

2021 Winner, Saskatchewan Book Awards

**2019 Winner, John V. Hicks
Long Manuscript Award for Fiction**

*"Characters in this Watrous, SK-based historical novel—set
between 1914 and 1936—are exquisitely and sympatheti-
cally drawn, the plot moves, and the portrait of this small
town and its multi-ethnic pioneers rings true and clears as
wind chimes in a prairie breeze . . . This story succeeds so
well because the writer's learned the tricky art of literary
balance. As skilled as she is at penning descriptive scenes,
they never slow the pacing of this taut novel. The book's
structure is nuanced, and seemingly minor details—like a
fishhook caught in an eye —have resonance. The characters
are people we know . . ."*

— SHELLEY LEEDAHL

*" . . . intricately told historical novel (with) modern conno-
tations broaching our current conversation around trauma,
consent, and sexual assault . . . Scenes linger, resonate in the
mind."*

— HICKS JUDGES ELISABETH DE MARIAFFI
AND RABINDRANATH MAHARAJ

" . . . an excellently-rendered story to be treasured for its intense understanding of human plight and pluck, tenderness and trauma."

— SASKATCHEWAN BOOK AWARDS

"With beautiful writing that will resonate with readers who know these prairie skies, but also with readers who long to explore this country of ours, this nuanced and powerful book is a stunning exploration of love, disability, family, and loss."

— ALICE KUIPERS

"Small Reckonings is a graceful, poignant debut novel, with the strong character of Violet at its heart. Considered vulnerable by her community, she turns out to be feisty and courageous. Her story, and that of her family, unfolds against the sweep of prairie with compelling power. Karin Melberg Schwier has given us a novel to treasure."

— ANNE SIMPSON

SMALL RECKONINGS

A novel

KARIN MELBERG SCHWIER

SMALL RECKONINGS
By Karin Melberg Schwier

Third edition
Published 2023 by Shadowpaw Press Reprise
Regina, Saskatchewan, Canada
www.shadowpawpress.com

First published 2020 by Burton House Books
Revised edition published 2021 by Copestone

Trade Paperback ISBN: 978-1-989398-74-6
Ebook ISBN: 978-1-989398-75-3

Cover and interior design by Edward Willett

For Jim, Erin, Michael, Alexander,
Ben, Julia, Pearl and Dahlia.

Especially for my husband, Richard,
my most gentle, constant, and honest reader,
who said, "You can tell this story."
I believed I could; it just took a while. I owe you one.

RCMP CONSTABLE ALBERT DICKENSON

THE YUZIK FARM, NEAR WATROUS, SASKATCHEWAN, 1935

Constable Dickenson took off his Stetson in the doorway, slapped it against the sleeve of his brown serge, and waited for his eyes to adjust to the dim interior of the barn. The cows looked like they'd been bunched up out at the gate for a good while, bellering, their bony spines arched and white, hoar frost on their haunches. He breathed in as much air as the dust and stench of scours would allow and took a few steps inside.

He looked up first and saw the body, then broke his gaze when a calf bleated, a pitiful thin noise off to the left. Sick and skinny, the calf stood trembling in the pen, gaping at him with sunken grey eyes. Albert took a few more steps. With the toe of his boot, he nudged the mound of bedding bunched up on a straw pile. It looked like Nik had been bunking in the barn for a time, all his meagre provisions laid out. A milk bottle, half empty. Bucket. Tin cup, plate, knife and fork, unwashed. Remnants of beans and bread crust. A mason jar that Albert bet would smell of potato wine if he were to unscrew the lid. Long johns, undershirt, wool socks hung over the stanchion. A yellow spray of scours across the end of the old quilt was dry.

The dog's growls pulled Albert from his inventory. He moved

slowly toward the dog on guard near the milk stool, lips grinned back and a low rumble in its chest. It took Albert a moment to realize the form behind the dog was Nik's wife. Crumpled in the dirt on her knees, Hanusia had one hand clamped firmly over her mouth, the other on Nik's boot. Her grasp made the body rotate slightly, turning Nik away from Albert and toward the back of the barn. Albert reached down and lifted the woman, stood her on her feet, and told her to take the dog and go back to the house. She looked up at him with the same sick calf stare. He pressed her shoulder gently. "Go on, now," Albert coaxed. "I'll take care of him. I'll be up to the house shortly. Go on."

Her face twisted, and a moan began deep in her throat. With a trembling hand, she clawed at the dog, grabbed it by the scruff of the neck, and pulled it toward the open barn door. Albert put a hand on the woman's elbow, steadying her, and walked with her that far.

"No good. No. He is no good. *Didko*," Hanusia stammered. She pulled at the dog again and turned to look at the constable, her thin face now a storm of fury and confusion. Her free hand clenched into a fist, and she shook it at him. "No good! *Didko*! No good!"

Albert watched her stumble across the yard with the animal. By the time she was halfway, she had begun to wail and cry out, in Ukrainian, Albert supposed. No doubt she'd be on the telephone to her sister, and the neighbour women would be rubbering on the party line. Soon, every farmer for miles would be talking about it. After what had happened to the Burke girl, Albert wondered how that child's father would take this news. He turned and walked back into the barn. He moved aside the leg irons hanging from his duty belt. They were irrelevant now. He pulled the knife from the pocket of his trousers and opened the blade.

Nik didn't have the look people tend to get when they hang themselves. He didn't look scared. Not even desperate. Just ordinary, maybe a little tired, as if he was just standing there, waiting.

Albert guessed there was a good two feet between Nik's boots and the barn floor. Nik's eyes were open. Staring. All shot through with blood, of course. That's what happens. Not wild-eyed, though; more as if he'd given it some consideration and just preferred to get it over and done with.

WILLIAM

TORONTO, MARCH 1915

The Toronto of 1915 seemed so much noisier, so much more congested, than William Burke remembered it being just the year before. He found his way out of the train station and gazed away from the lake toward the city. Modern buildings with tall spires had sprung up, rows of windows and columns of bricks marching upward in towers he didn't remember being there before. It was all so *tall*. He felt he could do nothing but look up, pulled to a sky crisscrossed with a black tangle of power lines, streetcar cables, and plumes of factory smoke. It had been a year since he'd gone west to homestead, and he'd grown accustomed to the vast, empty prairie skies.

He pushed through the crowds coming in and leaving the train station and retreated to the base of one of the big pillars to set down his case. The commotion seemed to be caused by so many people rushing everywhere. Automobiles honked, wagons rolled by, there was the shrill tweet of a policeman's whistle, dust rose from the earth where machinery dug and scraped the site for the new train station. This cacophony was disconcerting. He had a pulsing headache and remembered the first few nights in Saskatchewan when he couldn't sleep for the yipping, yowling racket the coyotes made in the coulee. By the time he walked a few blocks up Yonge Street, William longed for a few minutes of prairie stillness and coyote serenade.

He felt turned around, unsure of his directions. He tipped his bowler hat to an older woman on the sidewalk when he thought he was getting close to the department store where he hoped Louise still worked.

"Pardon me, ma'am. Can you tell me where the T. Eaton Company is located?"

The woman's small poodle, old and too fat, strained forward on its leash to sniff at William's boot. "Nearly there," she said, hoisting her walking stick to point as she passed him. "Just look for the square tower and the flag pole. Just between Albert and Queen."

William tipped his hat again, thanked her, and started off in the direction the woman had shown him.

While he walked, he wondered how Louise might look now, what she would say when he stood before her. He'd not really told her he was coming, after all, so it would be a bit of a surprise. He thought of going straight to the boarding house her aunt and uncle ran, where Louise had kept a room. But it was so much farther. Just a cup of tea with Louise first, if she was there. He longed for her familiar face. It wasn't as if they had courted, unless evening walks or sitting on the porch swing with a cup of tea counted. She had been a good listener and, it turned out, a good correspondent. Her letters were more than welcome during the months he spent proving up his home-stead. Once the small house was built, he thought he might have enough to offer. Asking a woman to move across the country to live in a soddy seemed impolite. The four days on the train had given him plenty of time to think, and as the east-bound journey closed the distance between them, William made plans to just take the bull by the horns as soon as he arrived. He'd step off the train, collect his bag, and go see Louise straightaway before he lost his nerve. Just a cup of tea. Nothing too forward about a cup of tea. If nothing else, he could ask if there might be a room available with her aunt and uncle, just for a few days.

He remembered meeting her at the boarding house for the first time last year before he went west. She was not the kind of girl who would turn heads, but they got on quite well. He pushed away the fear that maybe she'd simply found someone closer at hand.

William recalled settling in at the boarding house a year ago, glad to find comfortable, affordable lodging after the trip from England. It was a roundabout way from New Zealand. His birthplace seemed a very distant memory now. The cousins he'd sailed with thought he was daft when he said he wanted to go to Canada. "There's nothing there but ice and snow and Indians."

William hadn't been long at the Engstroms' when Louise arrived to stay with her aunt and uncle. She was a quiet, plain girl. Melancholic. Her parents were dead, and she'd moved in with Axel and Freda Engstrom, her only living relatives, after what Axel once vaguely referred to as "some bad luck" up north. Freda made it clear with a rap of her knuckles on Axel's bald spot that that was the end of any talk on the matter.

Louise had worked at an institution for the feeble-minded up in Orillia for about five years, and then, she had told him, she'd needed to get away. A person could only take so much of that sort of thing; it crept under your skin if you were around it too long, she had said and then changed the subject. He supposed that was so. Something had happened to her there, maybe the bad luck Axel had implied, but she'd never told him, and he didn't want to pry. Unlike her aunt and uncle, who revelled in "the more, the merrier," Louise was quiet, kept to herself. William remembered thinking that was a source of worry and sadness for the Engstroms.

The square tower and flagpole came into view. He realized with some discomfort that he had no particular speech in mind in case Louise was indeed there. The bell tinkled when he pushed the door open and joined the customers inside.

William straightened his shoulders and tried not to think about what he was doing. He could feel some of the confidence he'd felt on the train evaporating by the second. What if the letters she had sent were just out of politeness? He should have made firmer arrangements about seeing her. What if the last of her letters, perhaps the ones telling him of other plans, had never reached him? What would he say if she'd married? If he left now, he could just walk back and get on the train: exchange his ticket, go back to Watrous. Take care of the farm. Get on with his life. Sure to be some nice prairie girl out there. They'd meet, work shoulder to shoulder, raise crops, a batch of children. Live happily ever after. Die. Plain and simple.

"Go home, you silly trout," he muttered to himself.

He set his suitcase down and clasped his hands behind his back. He pretended to be interested in the assorted shoe and boot polishes displayed in the glass cabinets. Kiwi-brand tins. The picture of the little flightless bird was somehow comforting. Maybe a good omen, he hoped. Finally, he tapped the small silver bell on the dry goods counter and waited.

The swinging door at the far end of the counter squeaked. William looked up as Louise took a few steps, then faltered. Her eyes grew wide in recognition, and she smoothed back her brown hair. A small, cautious smile played across her lips as she made her way past customers. She had an efficiency about her, although still plain and even more—how should he say?—*solid*, perhaps. Rounder than he remembered. He was suddenly reminded of the Minister of the Interior's plea for "stalwart peasants and stout wives" to settle in the west. Only a year had passed, but she had aged more than that. Still, when her smile widened, he could feel his heart beating faster.

"Well, hello, Mr. Burke. My goodness, this is quite a shock."

"Good afternoon, Louise. Miss Engstrom," William said. "I know this must be a bit of a surprise if my last letter didn't reach you."

There was a slight shake of her head. "I'm afraid it didn't. When did you arrive?"

"Just now. I've come from the station," he said, taking off his bowler and smoothing his hair. He hoped he looked presentable. "I had to get things right on the farm, and then there was some time before seeding, so I dashed off a note to say I was coming back. I must apologize for disturbing you at work, but perhaps you might have a wee break coming up this afternoon? I apologize for being so forward, but it's lovely to see a friendly face."

Strewth, you do go on, he chided himself, turning his hat in his hands. *Shut up, man. Take a breath.*

T. Eaton had just hired Louise when she'd offered to help William select provisions for his journey to Saskatchewan. It was her first job in the city, he recalled. Now Louise tugged at a grey sweater draped about her rounded shoulders. William tried to read her face. Perhaps it had been one thing to write to him, almost like a pen pal, really. Maybe she'd had doubts about what he might be presuming from her regular letters.

"I hope you didn't think I was too forward, perhaps even improper?" Louise said. "Because I was afraid you might think so, I stopped writing." Her hand fluttered at her collar. "And here you are. It is good to see you again, Mr. Burke. William. Welcome to Canada's Greatest Store." She blushed. He remembered her practising the slogan when she learned she was hired.

"How have you been keeping?" she asked. "I've thought— well, we've wondered how you were getting along out there during the winter. More than once, Auntie Freda was certain you had frozen to death."

"There were a few chilly nights, to be sure!" William's laugh sounded a bit shrill in his own ears. He wondered why he was so nervous. "But the homesteading has gone quite well indeed. The land agent says I must live on the land for six months at least for each of the first three years. Had to erect a shelter, which I have done. A man must cultivate and crop ten acres, then break another fifteen. Of course, you know all this. My letters." He paused. "A great deal of work, but it's shaping up quite nicely. Well, I know you must be busy now, but would you care for a bit of a catch-up when you're free?" He paused, a bit breathless.

Louise glanced up at the clock over the employee door. "I came in early, so I'm finished in an hour. Perhaps you can find something to do in the meantime? Or maybe you'd care to wait? I'm sure I can find a chair." She wanted him to wait. That was certainly a hopeful sign.

"Oh, I'll have a wander about. Takes some time to get used to the commotion of the city again." He tried not to sound too eager.

"Well, if you'd care to go out the Yonge Street doors, the window displays are always wonderful. We have thirty-seven, so I'm sure there's plenty for you to look at." She glanced around the store and pointed through a grand archway. "And that is the millinery department, though I don't suppose you'd want to bother with ladies' hats." She pointed in the other direction to where a small crowd stood around a bank of glass cabinets. Men with white jackets and bow ties were quickly packing small boxes, handing them out to customers. "And there, over by those white pillars, that's the candy department. People say Eaton's makes wonderful butter-and-peanut kisses. They're a specialty of ours."

"Now *that* sounds interesting," William said and raised an eyebrow. She blushed deeply. He leaned over to pick up his case.

"Why don't you leave it with me? No sense in you dragging it around the store for an hour. I'll put it behind the counter." When Louise reached for the brown leather case, their fingers brushed.

"Let me," he said. "It's a bit heavy."

WILLIAM RETURNED PRECISELY AT FOUR O'CLOCK, JUST as Louise was pulling on her coat. Suitcase in one hand, he held the door open with the other, and the bell tinkled overhead.

Louise stepped out into the afternoon. They found a table for two at Billingsley's, a small diner around the corner. He pulled out a chair for her and lightly, so lightly, with the other hand touched the small of her back to guide her to it. He sat across from her. Her fingers fluttered over the brim of her hat while she worked to unpin it.

The waitress, round and red-haired, came to the table, and William ordered a pot of tea.

"May I interest you in a slice of our ginger pear crisp?" the waitress asked. "It's wonderful. Cook just took it out of the oven. Made with last season's put-up fruit. I believe the Bosc, preserved, of course. Gingersnap crumbs, brown sugar."

When Louise put a hand on her arm, the girl faltered. "No. No, thank you," Louise said. "I'm sorry, I can't. It's just that I can't abide pears. I'm sorry."

"Oh, no," the girl said. "Do they make you ill?"

"Something like that, yes," Louise said, and the girl hurried away for their tea. When she returned, she slid the pot and two cups to the centre of the table. William reached for her cup and took up the pot. "May I?" he asked.

Louise nodded. "Now, you must tell me what Saskatchewan is like."

"Where to begin?" He sipped his tea, putting one hand on his chest. "Louise, the sky is so big out there. You can't imagine. And at dusk, the sunsets make you stop whatever you're doing just to stare. It's as if the whole sky has caught fire. And it's never the same one night to the next. And the northern lights dance across the sky. Ribbons of coloured lights. It's truly unbelievable."

"Is there a town nearby?"

"It's a boomtown, Louise. Watrous has wooden sidewalks now, and shops, and a bakery. A very decent butcher. A poolroom and barbershop. Dress shops. Three restaurants. Tom Bjorndahl's general store." William counted off the list on his fingers. "There are brilliant mineral springs, and people come from all over. Healing powers, so say the Indians. Grain elevators. A grain growers' association, only just established. Fotheringham's Furniture and Funeral Home, if you please! And there's talk of a theatre, the Majestic, for picture shows. It all rivals Saskatoon. That's the nearest big city."

"A big city, too! Who would have thought it was so civilized? I had no idea. I thought it was all just a little village—" She hesitated. "Just land, I suppose. Have you met people? Do you have friends?"

"Wonderful farmers nearby. I've had some help from a neighbour's boy, Hank. A good lad, strong, willing to pitch in and help. Poor lad's the baby of five boys, so I'm a bit of a refuge for him. Got him through a wee fishing accident, an injury to his eye, poor soul. I think he feels beholden. Still, even with all the work I ask him to do, I reckon he's glad for the chance to be out of his brothers' reach." William dropped two sugars in his tea. "His parents, George and Erna, are good folks. And there's Nik Yuzik, a Ukrainian bloke with land next to mine. Rough as guts and quite enjoys his drink. He makes it himself, out of dandelions, chokecherries, even potatoes." Louise wrinkled her nose over her teacup. "But he's always willing to lend a hand. Decent chap. Gave me a bed while I was building the soddy last spring. Lent me his oxen to get the ploughing started."

"Where are you staying while you're here in town?" Louise asked William, dropping her gaze.

It occurred to William that he hadn't really told her why he had come back to the city or how long he'd be staying. "Truthfully, I hadn't given it much thought yet," he said. "I imagine I should have a look round for a room. Perhaps the Victoria. I passed it on the way here. I'll be going back to Saskatchewan in a week or two, I expect."

"I'm still living with Uncle Axel and Auntie Freda on Gloucester. Well, of course, you remember them," Louise said.

"They are well, I trust? Lovely people, your aunt and uncle. And your aunt's cooking, the baking!" William ran his fingers down his shirtfront and patted his belly. "I'm quite certain I put on at least a stone the first month of my stay!"

"They are well, yes," Louise said. "Thank you for asking." She studied the cuff on her sleeve and the pulse that fluttered faintly at her wrist. She took a breath. "You know, as it happens, one of the boarders, Miss Piché, met a Frenchman and was married last week. She was teaching, but the school board passed some sort of rule that doesn't allow French language instruction in the province. A shame, really. I think she was an excellent teacher. She's just moved to Montreal, and her room is still empty. Uncle said he wanted to paint before he let it again, and Auntie Freda says he must give it time to air out, so he doesn't gas the next person in their sleep. Oh my, I must be rambling."

William was certain he'd never heard Louise speak so much at any one time before. He tilted his head and wondered. She usually seemed so formal and reserved, but now and then, he could see a radiance break through. A bit like the sun coming out after a rainstorm.

After a moment, she plunged ahead. "I'm sure he would be happy to let you have it for as long as you need. They'd love to see you. And you'll be wanting supper, of course. You must be starving. We could catch the streetcar. It'll be by in ten minutes or so. Just up the block there. Auntie and Uncle would love to see you."

"That's a wonderful offer," William said, relieved. "I had a feeling there was one person in this city who would look after me properly!"

He stood and pulled Louise's chair back, put on his hat, gave the top a little tap, swept her coat from the back of her chair, and draped it over her shoulders. She flinched ever so slightly, startled, perhaps, by his gesture. William retrieved his case from behind his chair.

When he offered her his right arm, he noticed a bit of cloud seem to cross her face. Her brow furrowed just for a moment. She hesitated, her hand in mid-air. It was as though she suddenly regretted her invitation. But then, to William's relief, she carefully took his arm, and they stepped out onto the street.

THE HOUSE WAS WARM AND FRAGRANT. THE FAMILIAR front foyer with the white crocheted curtains and the colourful rag rugs was exactly as it had been when he left a year ago. "Little Sweden," the boarders called it. The comforting smell of chicken fried in butter. *Lutefisk* at Christmas. Milk gravy. The aroma of freshly baked buns from the oven and the sweet scent of rosettes just pulled from hot oil wafted from the kitchen.

"Ah." He breathed. "If I'm right about what I think that is, there is a heaven."

"Auntie Freda!" Louise called, hanging her coat on the hook by the front door, taking William's to hang next to it. "Come see the surprise I've brought you."

Through the doorway, they could see the short, round woman lift her head at the sound of Louise's voice. Her face, shiny like a plum, was pink from the kitchen heat. She looked exactly as William remembered, right down to the green apron with yellow rickrack, and sturdy brown shoes. She set down a hot rosette iron on the far side of the cookstove, slung a tea towel on her shoulder, and emerged from the kitchen. A look of delight spread across her face when she saw William.

"Well, forever more! *Hej hopp i blåbärsskogen!* Oh, forever more! William Burke, *väd säger du?* I never thought we'd see you again! How nice! Look at you, look at you," she cried, patting his lapels. "We must fatten you up, that's plain to see." She pursed her lips, poking at his stomach. "*Uff da,* you've lost a whole person!"

"Ah, Mrs. Engstrom," William said solemnly. "There are just no good Swedish cooks out there on the prairies. At least, not that I've had the good fortune to meet in Watrous. A few in Midale and Livelong, but that's a long way to go. I had to make do with gopher stew. I dreamed about your pickled herring and spice cookies. Ah, *krumkake* and, oh yes, the rosettes!"

He laughed and let himself be hugged and examined. "The thought of your baking kept me warm when the snow was drifting under the door, and the mercury dropped to thirty below."

"Oh, my heavens!" She beamed, fussed, and hugged, and picked lint from William's suit. "*Inlagd sill*, you remember my *sill*! Axel! Ax-EL!" Freda hollered up at the ceiling. She patted her niece's arm and helped Louise off with her sweater. "How did you find him, Louise? This is such a treat!"

"I didn't find him, Aunt Freda," said Louise, unpinning her hat. "He found me. There he was, standing large as life at the store."

"Mrs. Engstrom," William inhaled deeply again, closing his eyes for her benefit, "you lured me back all the way from Saskatchewan with those rosettes of yours!"

Blushing, Freda's cheeks shone while she hurried to the bottom of the stairs, pulling William along by the sleeve. "Well, you come in here with me, and we'll get you all set up with some good *Svenska* food. I'll put some coffee on. Come, come!" Smoothing loose strands of hair back over the thick grey braids wound around her head, she pulled the tea towel from her shoulder and tossed it on the table. She wiped her hands on her apron and fumbled behind her back to untie the strings. Pulling it from around her waist, she flapped it like a flag up into the stairwell.

"Ax-EL, I'm calling you! *Kaffe!*" she shrieked, making Louise jump. "Enough working now, come see! Axel, you'll never guess who Louise brought home for supper! And bring another chair!"

She steered William toward the kitchen.

"The man is deaf," she muttered. "Now, we want to hear everything. *Uff da*, now you tell me you're just pulling my leg about gopher stew!"

THEY LINGERED AT THE TABLE OVER COFFEE AFTER supper. Freda put the leftover pork chop in the icebox and scraped the too-little-to-save scalloped potatoes into the pail under the sink. Louise screwed the lid back on the sealer of lingonberries.

The Engstroms had two other boarders besides the recently departed Miss Piché. One young man avoided Freda's disapproving gaze while he slipped by the kitchen and out the front door down the street. "Off to meet his friends for snooker at O'Shaunessey's," Freda muttered and clucked. "None of my business, but don't ask me to like it. Well," she said, turning to William. "We'd better open the window in your room and air it out a bit, so the paint fumes don't kill you in the night."

"I appreciate the hospitality." William reached for her hand and patted it. "That's the best meal I've had in months. In the morning, I'll finish up the painting in there for you if you like. Maybe I'll be able to move by then." He laughed, placing his hands across his belly.

"Axel will take me to the fish market first thing in the morning to get some nice fresh pieces. Walleye. Rainbow trout, maybe. I'll bet a person doesn't get much nice fish stuck way out there in the middle of the whole country," she muttered. "Gopher stew. Louise, really, did you ever hear of such a thing?"

Axel pushed back his chair and stood. He plucked two glasses off the sideboard and stooped to pull out a bottle from the cabinet. He patted his shirt pocket in search of his snus. He jerked his head toward the door, and William followed him out onto the open front porch. They stood and surveyed the sidewalk and street. It was an ordinary neighbourhood, a street lined with red and black oaks. But so much brick, William thought, and white plaster cornices and pillars, gables and dormers. Bay windows and spires. Leaded glass. He thought of the plain and practical houses in Watrous, some no more than sheds for whole families, built with the solid intention to keep out cold and dust. He thought about his own modest house made of rough lumber, chinked with manure and straw plaster. A bay window would be putting on airs. He looked down the street. The shadows were growing long. Soon, the streetlights would come on.

"You sit, *ya*." Axel planted himself in his rocker and demanded to hear all about the west. William was happy to oblige. Axel carefully positioned the bottle between the two rockers.

After a comfortable silence, he tilted his head at William. "Louise ever tell you about what happened up north?" he asked.

"At the institution?" William asked, surprised. "Well, not in detail, I suppose. I wondered why she left, but maybe she just found it a bit hard to take after a time."

"*Ya*, that was for sure," Axel agreed. He was quiet for a time and savoured another swallow of whisky. He glanced over his shoulder through the screen door, nodded at the faint clatter of dishwashing. "I'm going to tell you what happened, William. You're a good man, and I know you take to our Louise fine. As a gentleman." He sucked his teeth and leaned toward William, his voice low. "If you took it in your head to take her back out to your farm in the west, I think she just might want to go. You should ask her."

"Go on, Axel. You're daft!" William sputtered, and laughed, his voice a little shaky. "Louise? We barely know each other. Saskatchewan? Provided Louise would even consider it, of course, but homesteading out there is a hard go. It can get pretty lonely, and she seems quite happy here." He swirled the whisky in his glass and pretended the idea had never occurred to him. Had he been that obvious?

They watched a gaggle of young boys saunter by on the street, hands jammed in their pockets, kicking a tin can ahead of them. William had the feeling Axel could see right through him.

"She says you've been writing letters since you went west," Axel said simply. "The girl needs a purpose. And I knew my Freda just a month before we were joined in holy wedlock back in the Old Country. You don't have so much time, too, far as I can see now, *ya*?"

Perhaps it was the way the whisky had loosened his limbs and warmed his faculties, but William decided not to feign protest at Axel's suggestion again. There wasn't any reason why such an arrangement might not work just fine if Axel was for it. William knew he couldn't stand another year out there, especially another long cold winter, as lonely and forlorn as he'd been this last.

"Louise was always a girl who didn't mind being by herself. Freda and I get so awful worried that she will end up a spinster. She said once she doesn't want children. I think she's just a little mixed up there on that one," Axel went on. "She's my brother's girl. The only child they had. Her mother died when she was born, and Gunnar, he was killed. Car accident."

Axel lifted his chin and sighed. He looked out at the street. "*Ya*. When she was old enough, she went to look after people, you know, the sort that can't look after themselves, at the place in Orillia on Lake Simcoe. Real pretty up there. It was hard, so many people, overcrowded. But she seemed to like it fine. She sent Freda a couple of letters. At first, she'd take the train down to see us. Then she stopped. She told us she was needed there. We didn't see her for about three years or so, and after a while, not so many letters. The children, you know, some was so awful smart if a person gave them a chance, she said. She thought they could amount to something." Axel cradled his glass against his belly. "Since we're her only family and we had no little kiddies of our own, you know, we thought we'd finally go up and visit her."

"So that one fall, me and Mother—Freda, I mean to say—she was so set on going up to see Louise, we made the trip. Leaves are sure so nice at that time of year. Well, Louise, she looked so darn smart in her little nurse outfit. Not really a nurse, but almost. I thought Freda, she would just burst being so happy to see her. And then it was time to go sit and have a little lunch, and Louise says she's got someone we should meet and off she goes quick."

Axel raised his glass and looked at it thoughtfully. William sipped from his own and concentrated on the warmth as it crept down his throat. He waited.

"Well, *ya*, then here comes Louise, holding this little angel by the hand. '*Min lilla ven,*' she tells us. Her little friend. About three years old, maybe, I don't know how old she was. Freda would know. Sarah, her name was. Wasn't right in the head, poor *flicka*. Long yellow hair. Louise had it in braids, just like hers. The doctors called the little girl a, oh now, what did they say?" Axel rubbed his chin, scratching the stubble thoughtfully. "Oh *ya*, mongoloid, it was what they call her. Isn't that just a terrible ugly thing to call a little girl? *Ish da*. Terrible ugly thing."

William sucked his teeth and shook his head.

"Louise told us that the parents left her there and never came back. You know, they did that with some, just run off and never came back. *Lilla* Sarah, she took to Louise right away." Axel smiled, turning the glass in his big fingers. "Louise was always combing that child's pretty blonde hair, doing it up in braids with ribbons. Her eyes were so blue, you know, I wonder if she didn't come from Swedes? The child wasn't right in the head, but cute as a little button. Did something real good for Louise. We could see maybe it was turning her into *en liten mama*. She had never been one much for kids and being so young herself. We got a picture around here somewhere. Freda put it away after it happened."

"After what happened?" William asked.

"Well, it was in the fall. Late fall, *ya*. Was it now? Let me think." Axel sighed heavily and looked out at the street, trying to remember. "That fall before you came to stay with us. Before you went out west. You know. You had only been with us a short time before she came, you remember that? She came here not too long after it happened. Was so awful quiet, she was. Couldn't bear to stay there, she said. Never went back, and she never wanted to talk about it again. She stayed in her bed upstairs in the dark for nearly a week. Never was the same after it. Made her hard. Such a shame."

Axel sighed, then went on. "It's just something you should know, well, if things work out and you have it in mind to ask her to go farming with you. It was so awful tough on her, so her man needs to know how to take care of her. I made a real nice box, a *hoppas brostet*. What do you call it? *Hemgift*. Dowry. A hope chest, *ya*? Freda painted it real nice with flowers and red horses and blue roosters. She is ever so handy with artwork. She put such nice things, too, there for Louise when she marries. Just something to keep in mind." Axel swirled his whisky and smiled into the glass.

"Well, I don't know if—" William faltered. "I mean to say, I'm quite fond . . . do you really think she'd have me? And go out west? It's not easy, especially for a woman from the city."

"*Ya*, sure. You just think about it. Mother and I, we see how she is about you, and it sure does our hearts good, you know. After all that business. She tells Freda she will have no children, but I think so." Axel sighed, and his gaze drifted out to the street. "This is up to God. *Ya*, that's for sure."

"What happened?" William asked, then looked toward the screen door and lowered his voice to a whisper. "What was so terrible?" William pleaded, edging forward on his chair.

Axel was not a man who made his point quickly. A big supper and three glasses of whisky hadn't helped sharpen his tongue.

Axel jammed two fingers into the pocket of his flannel shirt and extracted a toothpick. "*Ya*, like I was saying, Louise told us a bit. This little Sarah had been acting scared of this one orderly. You know, one of those man nurses. Bert was his name," Axel said, lowering his voice. "Bert, *ya*, that was it. A real oddball. Any time this Bert fella was around, Louise could see he scared *den lilla flicka*. Sarah would run and find Louise and just hang on so awful tight, shaking like a leaf. There was talk he tried some monkey business with some of the nurses. *Gris*. Dirty pig. Louise told someone in charge, but nothing came of it. I think he was the brother of the big boss, so *ya*. Louise was so determined she wouldn't let anything bad happen to Sarah."

Axel reached down for his bottle and tipped a little into his glass. Some dribbled to the floor. Axel grunted.

"They were so awful close, those two girls," Axel went on. He held the bottle up, but William shook his head.

"Well, one evening," Axel continued, "there was some sort of commotion going on. Someone had a fit like they do sometimes, you know. Louise had to go help, and when she came back, Sarah was gone. If you ask me, that Bert fella. A bad egg if you ask me."

"Uncle Axel."

The screen door squeaked open behind them. Louise's voice sounded far away, though she stood there in the doorway. She absently pushed against the screen and walked out on the porch without looking at either of them.

Freda stood behind her in the doorway for a moment and then clucked her tongue. She came out and patted Axel's bald head. "Oh, now, why did you go telling this, Axel," she fussed. "It's not good for the girl to remember such awful things. Such a bad time. It's all long gone now. Now," Freda clapped her hands together. "You men come in for coffee and some nice cookies. I made some spritz just today. And rosettes." She cast a worried look at Louise, who gazed out on the street.

"It's all right, Auntie Freda. It has been a long time."

Freda tugged at a hankie that was tucked up in her sleeve and blew her nose. "Oh, *nu har du gjort det*," she said, rapping Axel's head again with a little more force.

"Ow. Stop that, Mother," he complained, ducking away and rubbing the spot. He rolled his eyes at William. "No wonder all my hair fell out."

A T. Eaton delivery wagon rattled by, the horse's hooves clopping on the street. The uniformed driver tipped his hat to Louise, and William wondered if he knew her.

William had trouble breathing. He watched Louise's profile. Her chin thrust forward slightly. Though her eyes filled with tears, not one spilled down her cheek.

Louise swallowed and pressed her forehead against the pillar.

"She disappeared when she was in my care. We searched through the night. The custodian found her in the stream the next morning. She was my responsibility."

"Fell from the bridge, they said." Axel drained his glass.

"Oh, forever more," Freda whispered. She tugged another hankie from her heaving bosom and blew her nose.

They all fell silent and the sounds of the warm evening carried on around them. Louise stood there at the railing and looked out across the street. Finally, she turned, so suddenly her skirt twirled out around her. She rubbed her face with her hands. "Oh, Auntie, you're here," she said briskly as if noticing Freda for the first time.

"Well," Freda said, "come sit for coffee and cookies, and then, William, we'll show you upstairs to your room. Perhaps tomorrow, if it's a nice day, you and Louise can take the streetcar to Queen's Park for a picnic at Taddle Creek. I have some stale bread for the ducks. Louise, that would be a pleasant way to spend a Saturday afternoon, don't you think?"

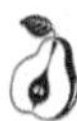

THAT NIGHT, THOUGH HE COULDN'T BE SURE HE hadn't dreamt it, William thought he heard someone cry out. He sat up and threw back the quilt, and stepped quietly across the cold hardwood to the door. He carefully turned the knob and opened the door just enough to look out. He nearly shut it again, but instead stepped out and moved down the hallway to Louise's door. He hesitated but then knocked softly.

"Louise?" he whispered as loudly as he dared.

He waited. The only sound was the ticking of the hallway clock and the usual creaks and groans of a sleeping house. But then, a slight squeak of bedsprings and Louise's voice came through the closed door. William saw the knob move and knew her hand rested there on the other side.

"William."

"I'm sorry," he said quietly, leaning forward. "I thought I heard something. Are you all right?"

"I didn't mean to disturb you." Her voice was barely above a whisper. "Just a bad dream. Thank you for your concern. I will see you in the morning. Good night."

"Good night, Louise." He turned and went back to his room.

It took him a long time to fall asleep.

LOUISE

TORONTO, SPRING 1915

When the streetcar made its final stop on the route beyond the Rosedale estates, William jumped down first with the basket, offering his hand to Louise, who gathered her skirt on the steps. They walked, pausing discreetly to look at each of the grand houses, and continued until the last was behind them. A narrow path led into a pine forest. Within a few minutes, they came to the edge of a ravine. Louise breathed deeply of the rich air softened by warm pine needles and the pungent forest floor.

William spread the blanket on the grass. There was no one in sight. A dog barked in the distance. "Let's just sit and soak it in for a moment, shall we? Here then, I'll show you how I used to waste away my time as a boy." He flung himself down on the blanket, crossed his ankles, and put his hands behind his head. He stared up at the clouds. The oak branches, some already budding, moved in the breeze, and between them, William pointed out wispy cirrus clouds skittering across the sky. "You see how the branches of those oaks are twisted? That puts me in mind of macrocarpa back home in New Zealand," he said. "The trunks grow gnarled and bent by the sea wind."

Louise held her hat brim, tilted her head back, and looked up at the trees.

"Come on, then." William patted the blanket beside him. "I promise I will behave like a gentleman. But you really must do this."

Louise smiled and smoothed down her dress. She gingerly sank to her knees, sat back, and lay down, a respectable distance between them. She folded her hands across her chest.

"Come on, girl. You're a corpse! Relax and open your eyes and ears. I used to do this all the time out in the paddocks or down by the sea." William grinned. "Don't know why we stop doing this sort of thing when we grow up. It really is quite lovely."

It truly is, Louise thought, watching the clouds through the branches. Squirrels chattered in the forest on the rise behind them, and the smell of pine was strong.

"Sometimes, it does a person heaps of good to look at things from a new angle," he said. "A new perspective. A new way to experience life, I imagine. All I know is that I feel a hell of a lot better after watching the sky for a while. I'd love for you to see a prairie sunset, Louise. Inspiring, it is. There simply aren't the right words to describe it. And at night, with no city lights to ruin it, you can see the constellations shining so brightly, it's like someone has scattered diamonds just over your head. You've got to see for yourself."

Moving her hand across the inches that separated them, Louise lightly touched his arm, brushing a pine needle from his shirt with her fingertips. The sound of the river moving down below reached them while they watched the clouds drifting across the sky.

"You've never really told me why you wanted to go west," she said. "To go all the way to England, then turn right around and cross the ocean again for Canada. It does seem like a long way to go for a bit of land."

"Seems as if I'll go to great lengths for adventure, eh?" He reached into his pocket and pulled out his leather wallet. He plucked out a bit of folded paper, soft and torn from wear, and carefully opened it. "It was this that did the trick," he said. "Once

I saw this advert, I was smitten. It was a leaflet in the *Standard*. I hadn't been in England long. Working with my cousins on the docks. I just knew. Here, have a look. In colour, too." He handed the paper to Louise and propped himself up on his elbow to watch her.

She held up the newsprint and shielded her eyes with a hand. A young farmer, white shirtsleeves rolled up to his elbows, walked behind a pair of proud, strong horses. The yellow wheat, with heads so fat they fell heavy on the ground as they were scythed, almost begged to be turned into loaves of bread.

There was a young wife in a blue dress and crisp white apron. With a baby tucked in the crook of one arm, she carried food out to the field at midday in a basket covered with a red and white gingham cloth. A banner arching across the blue sky declared, "Canada: My Land" and "The Last Best West."

"It looks beautiful," Louise said, running her finger gently across the smiling baby. "Is it really like that?"

"Near enough, although they don't mention mosquitoes or hail or the bloody long winter. But to think of all that land to be had for just a bit of hard labour."

"How much did the land cost?"

"You file for a homestead of 160 acres for ten dollars. I had that much money a few times over! If I want more land, they're selling it for three dollars an acre now." William leaned back on his elbows. "If at least thirty acres of land is cultivated within three years, and you build yourself a house, you'll have what's called proved up your homestead. Then it's yours to keep. Doesn't have to be much of a house either." He smiled at Louise. "Some blokes, mostly the bachelors, put up nothing more than a bit of a shed with a sod roof. Mine is quite presentable."

"But you're a bachelor!" Louise pointed out. "Perhaps you have greater sensibilities than most?"

"My cousins in London hauled me off to the pub on a few occasions, trying to drink some sense into me," William said. "They said the women in Canada had to always be so bundled up

I wouldn't even see what I was getting until the ruddy wedding night!" He laughed, then slapped his forehead. "Oh! I beg your pardon!"

"Was there? Was there anyone in particular? For you. In England, I mean."

"There's never been anyone before," William said, meeting her eyes. "Never anyone willing to give me a go, that's for certain."

Later, after Louise packed up the picnic basket and William shook the needles from the blanket, they walked back along the path. William held out his hand to help her navigate a fallen pine branch and held on a moment longer.

"And you?" he asked. "I mean, perhaps one or two prospects?"

Louise breathed deeply and gently took her hand from his, swapping the picnic basket to her other arm. "No," she said firmly. "No. I devoted myself to the children at the institution. I was there five years. Staff had cottages on the grounds. Most of the girls were old maids like me." Louise laughed a little half-heartedly.

They walked farther, twigs and needles crunching underfoot. A squirrel darted across the path. Louise watched it scurry up the trunk of a tree and disappear, chattering, into the branches.

LATER THAT DAY, LOUISE TOOK HER TEACUP OUT TO the porch swing. She set the cup and saucer on the wide top railing and took a deep breath. She didn't want to think about William leaving, but it was inevitable.

She closed her eyes and felt the afternoon sun warm her face. After their picnic near the cliff, something tight and curled inside her had come loose. For the first time, she felt desirable. She felt her cheeks turn warm, wondering how he could possibly see her so when she was sure no one else ever had. She had long ago resigned herself to believing no one ever would. Not after what happened at the institution in Orillia. She'd been damaged there, and no matter how hard she tried to forget it, to put it out of her mind, now and then, it crept into whatever happiness she tried to muster. The darkness that had shrouded her heart and mind for so long now seemed to lurk beneath her every movement, ready to fester if she turned her thoughts to it. Except, she realized, when she was with William.

Louise found William's courage to set off alone into the rugged unknown Canadian Northwest vaguely thrilling. He had talked to her in earnest before he set off for the west, never seeming to notice she was dowdy and too heavy for a girl in her early twenties. Since Sarah, food was such a comfort, a salve for her guilt. Even Auntie Freda, a great believer in big meals, often whispered to Louise to be careful, that maybe she didn't want to get too big and scare away a nice man. But William didn't seem to notice. There was a gentleness about him but also a confidence and a strength she longed to have herself. *And he drinks tea*, she thought. Uncle Alex did like a bit of whisky, but most men she knew drank only coffee. Not that she knew a lot of men. In fact, she really didn't know any in the proper way. Only William.

To write to William with her thoughts, the small details of her days, to open herself up in ink on paper, felt safe. It was thrilling to get his letters in return. She had imagined him at day's end, writing to her, wanting her to know everything he was doing to make a life for himself. And he had come back. She hoped he didn't feel it had been a mistake. Even though he now knew some of what had happened in Orillia, she felt a glimmer of possibility that he would understand what she had done. Maybe she could tell him the rest. She'd never been able to tell anyone, not even Auntie Freda or Uncle Axel. With William, maybe it would be all right. To him, perhaps she wouldn't be as soiled as she still felt.

The screen door squeaked, and Louise flinched. "Oh, goodness. You gave me a fright," she said.

"I beg your pardon, Louise." William leaned in the doorway.

He held the screen door, stepped out, and closed it behind him. "Didn't mean to startle you."

She smoothed back her hair and brushed a tiny moth from the long sleeve of her blouse. He took a seat beside her. She picked up her tea, but the look on his face was so intense, so dark, it made her hand tremble, and the cup clattered in the saucer. She clasped the china more tightly. Teacups seemed precarious in her hands when William was near her.

He began to speak, gathering steam, almost as if he was afraid of what he was about to do or say or afraid that he would not do it. "It's at times like these I am most grateful to Professor Hall at boys' college," William said. "He was an absolute tyrant about oratory." William held up his hand and thrust his chin out with a confident air. "'When the mind is muddled, dear boy,' he would say, 'the tongue must be able to sensibly carry on of its own accord while you sort out your point.'"

William leaned forward, elbows on his knees, and put his fingertips together. He looked at Louise. She remembered now him telling her, in one of his letters, that there had been no one for him before because he had been too caught up in chasing adventure. *Those blue eyes*, she thought. Lashes dark and so long, with such a curl. Auntie Freda whispered to her once at the kitchen sink that you could hang your apron on them.

"Right. To my point. The life I've made in Saskatchewan is a good one, Louise. It's an honest life, farming, and I feel like it needs, well, I need a wife, a family, to be complete."

Louise blinked and tried to look anywhere except into his eyes for fear he'd truly see her and would know, somehow, the truth she kept hidden.

"I don't know how I feel about children," Louise said. "My own, I mean. Since working up north, I don't know if I could shoulder that responsibility again. To have a little one need me that much is so much to bear."

William took a deep breath and said, "I find myself needing to put down roots, to feel a part of the earth again. I've seen a good bit of the world now, and I hope I can make a good life on the prairie. My father spoke of it, being part of the earth, when he worked with the stone, but I really didn't understand him then. I think I do now. It's the same to work with the soil. Do you understand what I'm on about?"

"I'm not sure," she said. "I've always been a city girl, William. Your life, the prairie, farming, it all sounds romantic. Like a tale in a book. Even though I lived in the north, I can't imagine living in a place without streetcars and shops and noise. The stillness, though, it does sound so peaceful."

"It is quite beautiful, Louise. And only eight miles to town." William continued, talking about the livestock, the house, and the barn, and his ideas about having a milk cow or two, some chickens. "A person would do well with pigs," he said. "And a milk cow. The milk separated, the cream sold, and the skim milk going to weaners. I've already got some chickens. Everything is cyclic on the farm, Louise. Everything has a purpose and usefulness. Nothing is ever wasted."

William suddenly stood, with an awkward jerk, and Louise inhaled sharply, setting her cup clattering in the saucer again. She set both on the porch railing. She pressed her fingertips to her lips when he turned and reached into the pocket of his suit coat.

He held out his hand. In his palm was a scuffed velvet drawstring bag. A long breath escaped her.

"Louise Engstrom, would you do me the honour of becoming my wife?" he asked.

She waited so long to answer that he looked worried and cleared his throat. She was certain she hadn't heard him correctly.

"I know it's terribly sudden," he apologized, turning the bag in his fingers, staring at it. "But there is a wee bit of urgency about getting back to Saskatchewan. I've left Hank, you know, the neighbour boy, a clever boy, mind you, to see to the chickens. And we mustn't delay seeding. Durum wheat is what Nik recommends." He stopped, swallowed hard. Then said, "Well, what do you say, Louise?"

William waited. She put her hand to her cheek and then to her forehead, and for a moment, she was afraid she might faint. Maybe this was her chance to push that blackness away for good. William could help her begin afresh to live a good life as a decent woman. In a voice that didn't sound quite like her own, Louise said, "I think I should see your prairie sky." Then she added, a bit breathlessly, "Yes, William. I mean to say yes."

"Strewth!" Relieved, William exhaled and tried to laugh, shaking. He pulled open the bag and carefully shook out a thin gold band. "My grandmother's," he said gently. "I do hope it's suitable."

"William," Louise whispered. "It's much more than suitable."

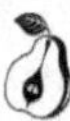

IT WASN'T A CHURCH WEDDING BECAUSE WILLIAM WAS anxious to get home. At least they were making an occasion out of it. If it had been up to Uncle Axel, Louise thought, they would have been on the train five minutes after she said yes.

Louis wore her grey wool suit, her best. "You look so pretty," Freda whispered. "A little tight, my girl, so keep still, and we won't rip a seam." Maybe it was the light, but Louise caught a glimpse of herself in the glass when William pushed open the city clerk's office door. Her face did look soft and happy. Pretty, even.

Freda's cheeks were pink with excitement, and she took turns weeping at the prospect of Louise leaving and hugging everyone within reach. "*Gudskelov!*" she cried. "Thank God! *Tack så mycket Gud för en god människa.*" She had tucked seven of her best embroidered hankies in her pocketbook, and by the time they reached City Hall, she'd gone through most of them. She wore a hat festooned with early spring garden flowers that she'd pulled, disappointed more weren't up yet. "Whoever heard of a wedding with no flowers? Oh, forever more!" She had poked a small daffodil through Axel's buttonhole, then pounced on William with a white tulip.

Now, Axel puffed out his chest and shook hands with the city clerk, smiling as if he were the one solely responsible for this turn of events.

Freda put a hand on Louise's arm and leaned forward to whisper, "I hope this is for the best. If you are as lucky as Axel and me, love will come in time." Louise felt her own cheeks grow warm as her aunt went on. "William is a good man, *en god människ*, a hard worker. Nice looking, too. Those blue eyes and such eyelashes!" Freda fluffed the ribbon around a slim bunch of tulips and daffodils. She handed them to Louise and tucked a strand of her niece's hair back up under the veiled hat. "Oh, the two of you look so nice!" Freda said. "Don't they look so nice, Axel?"

"They look scared stiff is what they look like." Axel chuckled. "Look, Mother; my flower is falling out."

Freda turned to adjust the daffodil. "Don't you think they look nice?" Freda asked the clerk and grasped his arm. "This is just so wonderful. I am just so happy for these young people. They're going by train to Saskatchewan at week's end, you know. Our William here is a farmer. Out west."

"There, Mother, you'll have to turn the poor man loose so he can do the job now," Axel said, prying his wife's grip from the man's sleeve.

Freda took Axel's arm and arranged him next to William, then she stood with Louise. She blew her nose, and her cheeks turned rosy again when the brief ceremony was over.

William touched Louise's cheek and kissed her properly for the first time. Louise felt a warmth spread through her. She held her flowers with both hands and kept her arms at her sides. Then the papers were signed.

Uncle Axel pumped William's hand. He kissed Louise on the cheek and patted her shoulder, careful not to crush her bouquet. Clearing his throat, he turned to Auntie Freda. "Well, now, Mother, maybe we should go find a smorgasbord to celebrate! A little lunch would be real good right now."

THAT EVENING, JUST BEFORE WILLIAM AND LOUISE retreated shyly to what was now—for one night, at least—their room, Freda pressed a small package into William's hands. "Something nice for your little house," she said. "It's a little wooden heart, a yellow one. You put up a nail, ya, in Louise's kitchen by the stove. You've got a stove? The yellow one by Louise's stove and the blue one by my stove." She read the words. "*Vart jag mig i varlden vander, Star min lycka i Guds hander.*" Then Auntie Freda translated for him, a little loosely, Louise noted, swapping "fortune" for "faith." "Wherever in the world I wander, my faith is in God's hands."

Later, when the house was quiet, Louise perched on the chair near her bedroom window and buttoned the collar of her nightgown at her throat. She looked around the room at the open cases packed with clothes, kitchen linens, a frying pan, wooden spoons, a lefse stick, a colourful rag rug, and the good quilt Auntie Freda insisted she take with her. The hope chest. There was even a tea kettle and the good green ceramic bowl, Auntie's best for beating cake batter.

"I apologize for the mess, William. I'm in a bit of a quandary about what I might need to take to set up housekeeping in Saskatchewan. I'm afraid Auntie Freda is determined to empty her entire kitchen into these cases."

"I can see that! We'll get it sorted, not to worry. I do have a few things, but I'd wager you'll feel better having a few familiar bits and bobs with you."

"Well, we certainly had a day to remember."

"You looked quite lovely," William said. "And Freda and Axel couldn't have been more proud. I thought a couple of his vest buttons would break away and shoot the clerk in the eye!"

Louise laughed and quickly put her hand over her mouth. "Oh, my. Do you think they're still awake?" she whispered.

"I don't know about Freda, but I think your uncle was sound

asleep and stayed that way even as she led him off to bed. All that celebration whisky." William reached for his dressing gown. "It has been a day; that's the truth." He opened the door and left for the bathroom down the hall.

Louise tried to still her heart. It was beginning to race. She crept onto the bed, reaching for the bedpost to steady herself. She smoothed the chenille coverlet with her hand. Freda had put the fancy embroidered pillowcases on, the ones with little yellow and blue flowers and red hearts. Her best ones. Louise clenched her hands together to keep them still. *This will be fine,* she told herself. *It isn't the same. William is a good man. A gentle man.* She took two breaths and closed her eyes. *Calm,* she thought. *Calm. William is a good man.*

The door opened quietly, and William came in, closing it behind him without looking at her. He trod softly across the room, pausing when the floorboards creaked. He sat on the opposite edge of the bed. For a time, they both were silent. The gingerbread mantle clock over the small fireplace now seemed extraordinarily loud. William held his hand toward her, and she reached for it. Their clasped hands rested on the soft coverlet between them.

William finally spoke. "*Du är väldigt vacker,*" he said a little awkwardly, and he gripped her hand more firmly. "*Jag är glad att du är min fru?* Sorry!" He rolled his eyes up to the ceiling. "Axel tried to teach it to me this afternoon. What I wanted to say is you are beautiful, Louise, through and through. I'm glad you are brave enough to take me on. We will have a good life together. We will."

Louise bowed her head and fought the tears that threatened to show how weak, how frightened, she was. When she couldn't stop them, she wiped them away with the sleeve of her dressing gown. Minutes passed, marked in hollow tocks from the clock on the mantle.

Finally, William gripped her hand more tightly. "Bloody hell, Louise," he said evenly. "You're my wife. If you didn't want this, then why agree to it? I've been nothing but cordial and patient. I know you've a past, that you've been hurt. I don't pretend to know, but this fellow, he's given you reason to mistrust men. But I am not him. I am your husband, and you've a duty now. I will not have this."

Louise pulled her hand from his grip and thought he couldn't have known how hard he was clenching her fingers together.

"I will not have it, dear heart," William said again more gently. "I am not that man. To think a man could treat a woman so badly makes me furious. But, dear heart, I am not him."

Louise knew what he was saying was true. But still, she trembled when he touched her cheek.

"A bridegroom has certain expectations, Louise," he said softly. "He needs to know his wife doesn't regret her decision. If we mean to make a life together, then let's begin."

Louise closed her eyes and nodded.

"Let me turn out the light," William said, reaching for the lamp on the bedside table.

She reached out and stayed his hand. "Leave the light on. I need to see you."

HANK

THE ECKART FARM, SASKATCHEWAN, MAY 1915

"Not really the kind of woman we were expecting," Hank's mother mentioned to Tensie Kramer several weeks later at the kitchen table. Erna Eckart, armed with a jar of last year's saskatoons and a loaf of that morning's bread, had been over to welcome Louise. Mrs. Kramer "just happened by" when she knew Erna would get back home. Hank slouched at the table, bit into his fried egg sandwich, and thought of Mrs. Kramer as a big doughy sponge, waiting to soak up any information she could sort through, fluff it up a bit, and turn it into gossip.

"Well, tell me," Mrs. Kramer demanded. "What's she like?"

"A little quiet," Erna said. "Serious. Solid girl. I went to give her a little hug, and she got all stiff and surprised. Seems like an odd match for William. He's such a people person, so sociable, and all those stories he tells. Such an optimistic man. She just seems an opposite, is all. Our Hank spends quite a bit of time there, helping out."

"What about her people? Are they city people?"

"I'm not sure. Swedish, they are. Engstrom is her family name."

"Hmmm," Mrs. Kramer murmured, stirring yet another spoonful of sugar into her coffee. Hank couldn't tell if she disapproved or not. "Well, if she's open to it, I'll have the Lutheran Ladies Aid lining her up with friends and projects galore before summer. And she won't have any time to be lonely with farm work. That'll be an eye-opener for her. Probably used to street cars and electric lights and whatnot." Her voice dropped to a whisper. "Swedes tend to be a bit to themselves, you know. I heard that somewhere."

But Hank thought Louise was all right. He told his mother so when Mrs. Kramer decided there were no more details to be had about William's new down-east city wife and announced she'd better be getting home. "She warms up a little once you get to know her, Ma," Hank insisted, mumbling, poking the last chunk of his sandwich into his mouth with his forefinger.

"Well, I hope so. Still, must be hard coming from the big city to end up in the middle of nowhere with gophers and coyotes as your neighbours and then not knowing a human soul."

"She knows us now," Hank said. "And William."

With a corner of her apron, Erna twisted open a sealer of dills. She inserted her fingers and pushed aside the dill head, fished around for a big pickle, and handed it to Hank. "Mmm," she said, raising an eyebrow at his bulging cheeks. "Manners, for Heaven's sake, Hank. And I believe it's *Mr. Burke.*" Erna took Hank's empty plate away and put it in the washbasin. "Well, it'll be a different life for her out here, that's for certain. It'll be hard, her being used to life in the city, Mrs. Kramer's right about that. But we can offer some help if she needs it."

Hank's mother waved another dill pickle at him. He scraped back his chair, wiping his mouth on his shirt sleeve. "Here. And you give Mrs. Burke my best when you go over this afternoon. We'll have them over to supper real soon; you tell her that."

Hank swung the bucket at his side and pushed open the screen door. He was startled to see Mrs. Kramer still there, hovering on the edge of the porch, making a big show of searching in her bag for a hankie. "Tell her the same from me. We'll want to hear how she's managing." Mrs. Kramer ruffled

Hank's hair and waved a hand over her head at Erna as she headed to her buggy. Hank flattened his hair down hard with the palm of his hand.

Hank's mother called after him through the screen door. "Tell her she's more than welcome to come by if she needs anything. And Hank, your brothers dug up that garden around the back of the house. So, you put those potatoes in before you go. And Hank?"

Hank opened the door and poked his head in again.

"That was real nice of you to plant her a little flower garden while Mr. Burke was down east. I hope she likes hollyhocks. I noticed there was a jar of my seeds missing." She smiled.

Hank grinned and let the screen door bang shut again before the flies got in.

AT THE END OF THE MONTH, WILLIAM AND LOUISE bought a couple of Yorkshire sows, four geese, some good Plymouth Barred Rock laying hens, and a Jersey cow. Except for the cow, all the livestock seemed to be black and white or red and white, Hank observed one afternoon as he pushed against the cow's hindquarters with his shoulder to get her through the gate.

"This here cow sort of looks like my old teacher," Hank offered. He tried to get better leverage on the cow's sharp hipbones. "With them big black runny eyes, she puts me in mind of Mrs. Moore. You probably seen her around, William. I mean Mr. Burke. My ma says I should call you Mr. Burke on account of you being a grownup." He smacked the cow's flank, and she squeezed through the gate with a deep belch. She swung her head around and swabbed her nose with her tongue, doleful eyes watering.

"Then Hannah she is," William said, smiling. "And, Hank, I think we can assure your mother that we've become good mates, don't you think? Call me William. Mr. Burke was my father's name. Makes me feel like an old man." William threw an arm around the boy's shoulders. "Louise was making some potato soup this morning with the spuds your mother was kind enough to send over. We'd best go see if it's good enough to eat."

Hank snatched his cap from his head as he entered the house, partly for manners but mostly because it was sweltering inside. The fire was snapping and popping its way through dry poplar in the woodstove.

"Bread," Louise explained as she stood, red-faced, her apron smudged with flour. A sweaty strand of hair had escaped from the braid she wore wound around her head, and she kept flicking it back behind her ear. "Auntie Freda gave me so many of her recipes. I just wish she were standing right beside me so I could see how she does it. Reading a recipe is just not the same as watching all her tricks."

"I'm sure it will be every bit as good, dear heart." William scraped a chair across the floorboards and sat, holding out a washcloth to Hank. "Go ahead and wash up a bit, mate. There's a bar of soap there."

Hank took the offered rag. He dipped his hands in the basin and looked around at what used to be a bare cabin. His eyes roamed the room while he scrubbed the dirt from his fingers. There was colour now, with bits of curtains, a tablecloth, and a few small, impractical fancy accessories such as tea cozies and doilies. Above the window near the woodstove was an oval frame, painted gold, that held an image of a woman in a black dress, her hair swept up on top of her head. She had kind eyes. Behind her was a sort of tree Hank had never seen.

"That's my mother," William said, following Hank's gaze. He took the rag from the boy and waved him to the table. "The management at Eaton's gave the frame to Louise as a wedding gift when she handed in her notice. We hoped to have a wedding picture done, but we didn't have time."

There was a bright yellow wooden heart nailed on the wall near the stove with some writing Hank couldn't make out. A curtain hung from a wooden rod to hide the bed set off in the far corner. A cast iron pot of potato soup bubbled on the stove. The stovetop itself had seen a good cleaning, and its black, well-oiled surface gleamed. "It just looks so different in here," Hank said. "It's like a home now. It's like a girl lives here."

William laughed, put two bowls of soup on the table, and slid a spoon across to Hank.

Dough was rising in three pans, the smooth tops glistening yellow with butter. Hank noticed that William kept a nervous eye on the chimney and wondered if he was calculating the distance he'd have to run with pails from the dugout if that dry sod on the roof caught fire.

While the men ate their soup and soda crackers and some tinned kippers, Louise slid the loaves into the oven and eased another poplar chunk into the firebox. She stepped away from the stove and frowned at the floor. "I think the dust is going to be a never-ending battle," she said. "How does your mother do it?" She reached for the broom and swept around the door.

"My ma doesn't much care for field dust neither," Hank said between mouthfuls. "She rolls up an old blanket to stop the dirt from coming in. You might want to try that. Once a week, she hangs it on the clothesline, and I have at it with a stick. You got to check which way the wind is blowing before you get going, though. I can make a real good dust storm." He reached for another cracker.

"I hope you're offering," she said.

After lunch, William and Hank dropped their kipper tins outside on the ground for the two new kittens, one a striped tabby and the other white, gifts from George and Erna Eckart. The kittens attacked the oily cans, spitting and hissing at each other.

"You got to have a couple of good mousers around here," Hank said. "My ma will be glad to know you like cats, Mrs. Burke." He watched Louise hang freshly washed flour sacks on the line strung from the corner of the house near the door to a tall post William had sunk into the ground a few feet away. "My ma says women who don't like cats don't make good housewives. We got nine." He grinned, brushing crumbs from his shirt.

"Now, Hank, you thank your folks again for their kindness. They've been so good to us." Louise tugged at the corners of the sacks to pull out the wrinkles. "I'm sure we'll have good mousers in no time." She dried her hands on her apron and propped the wash basket on her hip. She pressed a hand to the small of her back, and halfway to the house, she stopped and switched the basket to her other hip. It seemed to Hank the walk was awful long. She must be tired.

"One time, one ran clean across my mom's face while she was sleeping in her bed," Hank called after her. He leaned in toward William and whispered, "She started screaming and nearly gave my father a fit. He was sound asleep and said he just about had a heart attack on the spot. But Ma says nothing's worse than mouse dirt everywhere, especially on your pillow."

Throughout the spring, Hank hurried through chores at home to join William and carry on with the long list of jobs that needed doing to get the farm on its feet. Louise busied herself with turning the bachelor's shack into a home. A second garden patch Hank dug in the sheltered place beside the house looked like a promising site for potatoes, beets, cabbages, and carrots. A windbreak of spruce and Manchurian elm went in along the dugout and the road.

"It's so bloody treeless!" William scanned the horizon one sunny afternoon and panned his mug of tea in a wide arc. "At least we'll have these if they have it in mind to grow. I reckon I'll get used to it, but it feels like I've no place to hide. I'm afraid children here will grow up without ever climbing a single tree!"

Hank pushed his hat off his sweaty forehead and straightened up. The caragana seedlings from the federal tree nursery at Indian

Head had arrived. William and Hank were halfway through the shipment.

They surveyed their handiwork. The hedge was slowly taking shape, set down to hold back the wind from the north. "Once these take off, you'll have some trees," Hank said. "Then you won't have to look at the stones you still have to pick! I've never seen mountains, but I think I'd feel all closed in. Papa says trees and mountains just get in the way of good sunrises and sunsets."

ONE WARM MAY AFTERNOON, HANK HELD A STICK TIED with a length of twine while Louise held hers at the other end and pulled the string taut across a stretch of freshly turned earth. She jabbed her stick into the ground, and he did the same.

"My mama says to tell you to keep all the ashes from the woodstove," Hank said. "You sprinkle them on your cabbages to get rid of worms, and it keeps the slugs away, too. And coal oil is good for potato bugs. I mean," Hank corrected himself, "you drop the potato bugs in the coal oil, and it kills them. So I guess that's not really good for them at all!" He grinned.

"I've a feeling that everything we eat this winter will come out of a sealer jar or the cellar," Louise said.

"My mama's put-up peas and beans are like ambrosia in the dead of winter," Hank said. "I'm not real sure what ambrosia is, but it must be awful good 'cause that's what my papa says in February."

Hank and William spent the rest of the afternoon finishing work on a small chicken coop and nailing the wire into place around the pen. Hank looked off toward the coulee. "You suppose the coyotes are watching us right now, keeping track of where we might miss a nail? They're crafty buggers, my papa says. I like 'em, though. Out in the field, standing there like they're waiting for you to make the first move. You gotta have good eyes to spot 'em. Sometimes I can if I close my bad eye. In summer, they're the exact same colour as the land, so they can hide really good."

"Well," William corrected, pulling the chicken wire tight up around a post.

"Well what?"

"Well, as long as they leave my chickens." He took the hammer from Hank and nailed the wire securely into place.

They walked back to the house. Louise pushed open the door. "Hank, will you bring in some kindling to fill the wood box behind the stove? A good armload. There are cookies when you're done."

"Good lad," William said. "I'll go on in and wash up."

Hank picked through the pile beside the chopping block. He stacked as much poplar kindling as he could in one arm and clamped his other arm on top. He called out for help on the stoop, and Louise held the door open for him. She pulled it to and latched it before picking up the kindling he had dropped.

Hank brushed the woodchips and bark off his shirt and pulled out a chair at the table. Remembering to be polite, he took off his cap and hung it over his knee. Louise put two cookies on the table in front of him. "Oh, good! I like your snickerdoodles." He took a bite and looked around. "This place sure looks nice now."

"Well, just because a person doesn't have much money, there's no reason to live like a vagrant. My Auntie Freda—oh, I do miss her terribly—she's sending a few more things from Toronto, but, yes, it is looking a bit more homey, isn't it?"

William splashed water on his face at the washstand. Louise handed him a tea towel, and he wiped up around the basin. "But here I am, making a home for my new husband. Whoever thought I'd have a husband?" She smoothed a stray length of hair back and under a pin. "Maybe even a family one day. Maybe one day soon."

William dried his hands and winked at Hank.

Hank grinned. "Be real good to have some kids around here, Mrs. Burke. I could be sort of an uncle. I could teach 'em how to ride old Ned and catch gophers and make grass whistles. I'm real good at grass whistles. My papa taught us, so if we ever get lost, we just blow, and they can find us quick."

"Well, I don't know about *some*, Hank," Louise said. "Maybe one child would be enough for us."

LOUISE

THE BURKE FARM, AUGUST 1915

In the deepening darkness, Louise set aside the bowl of green beans and struggled to her feet. She would finish the rest in the morning. She stood with her hand on her belly and listened to night noises. The owl nesting in the tree behind the house began to prowl, and the rasp of grasshoppers in the tall grass by the garden was almost comforting. William had fallen asleep in the wicker chair, and, just for a moment, she looked down at her softly snoring husband with a pull at her heart. Louise was, she realized, content.

William had seen something in her when they'd picnicked and spent those warm evenings walking out at Rosedale and along the cliff above the river, tending Aunt Freda's roses, having their tea on the Engstroms' front porch. A lifetime ago, it seemed, though it had only been a few months. Louise hoped he saw something he might reach and still believed he would. Still grieving for Sarah, Louise had felt as if a fine dust had settled evenly on every part of her. But William had wanted her anyway. He'd built her a sound, comfortable home, a new life, perhaps believing she could be wiped clean and, like the land, restored with patience.

She had been set against having children, but now the prospect didn't seem so frightening. She had seen many damaged children. It would be good to be truly happy if she could manage a family of her own. A sound child who would grow up and make his own way in the world. A boy like Hank. It would give her purpose and help her forget.

William. Such a good man, she thought. *So patient, so optimistic. It seems he's just waiting for me to open up, to get past it, and now, I think I can. Our own land, our own home, a family. Maybe just one child. Maybe it will be all right.*

She pressed her hands to the small of her back and filled her lungs with cool night air. August days were hot and dusty, but when the sun went down in its blaze of pinks and oranges, she could count on the cool stillness to come. Standing there, she thought of Orillia, the institution, and remembered that the best time was at night. It seemed only then could she escape from grasping hands and hollow faces and the sad eyes that wanted, always wanted, something from her.

It was so much worse after Sarah died. When most everyone was asleep or at least restrained, it was the only time she could breathe deeply. At night on the ward, it was too dark to see another child occupying the bed where Sarah should have been sleeping. For a time, she was ashamed that gluttony had become a vice, offering a small measure of comfort. But it never lasted.

She sometimes asked for double shifts in the kitchen. It was painful to remember how she tried to hide the leftovers from the trays that came back from the staff dining room after mealtime. There never was anything left on the residents' trays, but on staff trays, always something: bread, pudding, potatoes. Even bits of skin on days when chicken was served. Some of it in her mouth when no one was looking. Other bits into her pocket. It wasn't long, only a couple of months, before Matron told her to get a larger uniform from the supplies cupboard.

Louise kept to herself. Being alone became her only respite, and she had drawn that solitude—and the extra weight—around her like armour, especially in those last few days before she left there for good. Although the barbs from the women were painful, it was a relief to think none of the male orderlies would cast a second glance her way.

Since coming here with William to start a new life, Louise realized, she hadn't dreamed about Sarah once. Even thinking of her now wasn't so painful. The image of the little girl in the cold stream, her yellow hair swirling in the gentle current, was fading, and sometimes Louise found it hard to conjure up her face. Louise prayed for the time when it would be gone altogether. Having a child—maybe just one—would replace it for good.

I must look forward, she thought. *No point in revisiting bad things in the past. There is nothing to be done but think of good things ahead.*

She leaned down, lifted the pipe away from William's mouth, and shook him awake enough so he could go in to bed. She remembered Auntie Freda putting down her embroidery and doing the same with Uncle Axel so many times in the evenings.

William pulled himself up from the chair, put his hand to her face, and leaned close to kiss her cheek. She handed him his cold pipe, and he let himself into the house.

Turning for a moment on the porch, Louise looked up at the dark prairie sky. The stars were out now, and the coyotes were calling in the coulee. She followed William, reached back for the door, and closed it quietly behind her.

ON A WARM MAY DAY IN 1916, DR. SPEIGHT'S BLACK buggy, drawn by his fine chestnut brown hackney, known for trotting everywhere they went, turned smartly into the Burke farmyard. It was a late spring, still cool enough for good roads but warm enough to promise good seeding weather as soon as the soil dried up.

William pushed aside the heavy blanket hanging across the bedroom doorway just enough to announce the doctor's arrival. Hanusia Yuzik, the closest thing to a midwife for farmwives in the area, held a cup of water to Louise's lips and looked up. The Yuziks lived on a ramshackle farm across the coulee, and usually, her son Andrij ferried his mother in the wagon to homesteads over dirt roads in summer and in the sleigh during winter. With no trained midwife in the area, people looked to Hanusia when the time came. With several sons of her own, she was no stranger to childbirth. Or to superstitions, as Louise and William soon discovered.

"Baby, he is boy," she announced, working through English words with pained determination. "You like salt? So he be boy! Sugar you like, is girl." She had become quite alarmed last month when Louise tried to tap a nail into the plaster beside the stove. Auntie Freda's *Star min lycka i Guds hander* heart had fallen into the kindling box. "No! No!" Hanusia had pulled the hammer from Louise's grasp and banged it down on the kitchen table. "No hammer nail!" she cried. "Baby born wrong, you do that!" Still, even with her odd ways, William was grateful for her help.

"Louise, Dr. Speight is here," he said. "I'll show him in and then tend to his horse. Hanusia, the pot on the stove is finally on the boil." William ducked out quickly, and the blanket fell back across the doorway.

Hanusia put the cup down on the nightstand, her mouth set in a pinched line. Normally, Hanusia's chin seemed defiantly and permanently thrust forward in a posture of disappointment, as if sheer will and the angular set of her jaw could keep the unwanted at bay. Louise had learned from Hank's mother that it was something she couldn't help. Her jaw had been broken when she was run over by a wagon as a child.

Hanusia was a hard, thin woman, almost as if the farm, all her children, and, not the least, her husband, Nik, had slowly chewed her up, leaving the gristle behind. Some people said she was cold, but Louise saw glimpses of kindness and was grateful for someone who knew what to do. The contractions were close together now, but for a few blessed minutes, Louise rested against the pillows.

With only the blanket in the doorway, she clearly heard the outer door open and footsteps in the kitchen.

"Good afternoon," Dr. Speight said. He paused to clear his throat. "Good afternoon, William. I see Mrs. Yuzik is here. That's just fine. I'm sure she could have handled things well enough, but it was right to fetch me. A first child can make a father anxious."

Not long out of medical school down east, Dr. Speight was a fastidious young man. He kept a tiny moustache, carefully trimmed and waxed. Erna said he practised speaking in an authoritative manner so patients would take him seriously. At the sound of the doctor's brusque voice, Hanusia snapped up a basin and rags and hurried out to the kitchen, dropping the blanket back across the doorway behind her. Hanusia had ushered in many babies in the area without so much as a word of complaint from any woman in the district. No one said much of anything, though her abrupt manner often raised the eyebrows of even the husbands when she handed them their newly swaddled infants.

Louise could hear them talking, but as a new wave of pain began to mount, the voices drifted. When she opened her eyes, she realized she must have slept for a time. Dr. Speight was at the foot of the bed. Hanusia carried in a pot of steaming water. She set it on the dresser and handed the doctor a stack of clean cloths.

The doctor busied himself beneath the sheet and soon barked at Hanusia, "I will need your help, Mrs. Yuzik. It's time for Mrs. Burke to bear down."

Hanusia put a firm hand on Louise's back, pushed her up and said into her ear, "Now you work. We finish up quick. You push when I say. I take your hand now." Louise felt Hanusia's grip, and held her breath. The pain climbed, and she pushed and pushed again, the sweat running into her eyes, blurring the room as she tried to breathe. Suddenly, when she thought it was too much to bear, she was free of pain, and the silence was filled with a lusty squall.

"A little man," Hanusia said matter-of-factly. "So quick, first baby! Much hair. Strong boy, good for farm work. Your husband, he will be happy."

Louise lay spent, leaning back against the pillows while the doctor worked, laying out his instruments on a white towel. She kept her eyes on Hanusia and the baby. Hanusia cradled the infant's head with her thin fingers. When the doctor tied the cord, she cleaned the child's shuddering body and his face with a wet cloth. The baby wailed, and Louise thought Hanusia might be a bit more gentle.

"Hanusia, please," Louise said weakly. "He's so tiny! Be careful!"

Hanusia grunted.

A boy. I prayed for a boy. Louise felt a wave of relief wash over her. But then, a nagging fear. She turned her head to the doctor. "He's all right?"

"Yes, everything is fine. Just lie back."

"Are you sure?"

"You'll have him in a moment." The doctor wrapped up his instruments and packed up his bag.

Hanusia washed the infant thoroughly, dipping the cloth into the basin of warm water. "*Dobreh.* Good. *Mama checkayeh.* Mama wait." She swaddled the baby tightly in the blue flannel receiving blanket. It was a gift from Auntie Freda, who had embroidered little bluebirds in the corners. The pink one, "just in case," had red hearts and yellow tulips. She had sent them months ago, and Louise had tucked them away in her hope chest. With a pang of tenderness, she watched Hanusia lick her thumb and forefinger and twist a little curl in the baby's fine dark hair. "There, he ready." Hanusia smiled at Louise and laid him in the crook of her arm. "Here, now is baby boy."

"Are you sure he's all right?" Louise ran her fingertips around the baby's eyes. She could feel strength spreading through her. It felt like a dipper of cool water soothing her parched throat on a dusty day.

"He's fine," Dr. Speight said yet again. "A strong boy. But if I can be frank, Mrs. Burke, it would be wise for you to consider reducing your weight." The doctor shrugged into his coat. "You're carrying a great deal for a woman of your age. It won't be easy looking after an infant and the house if this keeps up."

Carefully tucking the blanket around the baby's pink cheeks, Hanusia pursed her lips at the doctor's words. "*Chekai, chekai.* Better to have a little extra," she muttered. "Babies take all from mama." She wiped her hands on her apron.

Louise cupped her hand gently on the baby's head. "Oh, I'll worry about that later," she told the doctor. She touched the curl Hanusia had fashioned flat on his forehead. "I need to keep my milk and my strength up for the baby. A healthy, strong, beautiful dark-haired baby. John William Bystrom Burke," Louise murmured, smiling at the doctor. "Bystrom is for my mother's family."

Dr. Speight snapped his black bag shut with a loud click. "I'd best go out and tell William he has a new farm hand." He nodded at the women and went out to the front room. Louise could hear the doctor and William murmuring, but she was too spent to pay attention and leaned back against the pillow.

Hanusia patted Louise's shoulder for a moment, then put her hands on her narrow hips. Louise thought she would speak, but Hanusia stooped to gather up the soiled linens, planting the bundle on a sharp hip. "I come back to take him. You sleep now," she said. "Mr. Burke, he be happy with boy. My Nik always okay for boy, but he want girl. Just one. But we get more boys." She hoisted the bundle onto one hip and pushed the blanket aside.

She had no sooner disappeared when the blanket opened again. William let it fall back behind him and came to the bedside.

Louise caught hold of his hand. "I wish Auntie Freda and Uncle Axel could see him," she said, fighting to keep her eyes open. William leaned in close to kiss her forehead and reached out his free hand to gently touch the baby's fine hair. Louise loosened her grip on William's other hand and settled the baby into the crook of her arm. "So many times they insisted that I'd one day have a family. William, I never believed them." She looked down into the baby's face. "Yet here you are. Let me see you just to be sure you're real." Wiping tears on the sleeve of her nightdress, she loosened the flannel and kissed her son's forehead.

"I'll just pop out and get you a cup of tea, dear heart," William said. "He is lovely. A son. I can scarcely believe it."

Soon she could hear William at the woodstove, adding a chunk to the firebox and pulling the kettle across to heat. She gently worked her fingers over the baby's delicate hands, balled into little fists, and pulled the flannel back so she could examine his tiny red feet. "You're perfect," Louise whispered, her lips moving against the baby's cheek, breathing him in. "Maybe I'm even now. Surely, there is redemption in a creation such as you, my baby boy."

WILLIAM

THE BURKE FARM, SEPTEMBER 1919

When the willows and poplars turned yellow and sunsets came earlier, it was Hank's habit, after his day's chores at home were done, to whistle for Maggie the dog, climb on old Ned, and ride across the field. It was Louise and William's habit to look to the west to see if he was coming. Once John was born, Hank often came by to play a bit with his "little buddy" and, more often than not, enjoyed whatever Louise might offer him on a plate once he'd arrived.

One evening, when the kitchen was still full of the heat from the stove and of the day, Louise and William sat on the porch and watched the slow, plodding approach. When the horse and rider came around the stand of willow, William relit his pipe as he waited for the stars to flicker in the places he now expected them to be. Louise worked at his overalls, mending the rips acquired that day when he'd crawled through a barbed wire fence. The lamp was lit at her elbow. The mosquitoes weren't too bad, and John was bundled in feather ticking, asleep beside her on the bench.

Swinging one leg over Ned's neck and sliding down the corrugated ribcage, Hank draped the reins over the rail fence by the lilac bush William had planted last spring. Maggie trotted up to the porch and flung herself down at William's feet, bones knocking on the planks. Hank wandered up to the porch. It seemed to William that lately, the boy had stretched himself up taller and thinner as if he'd hung from a tree branch too long before dropping down to the ground.

"Evenin' folks." Hank grinned, propping himself up against the whitewashed post at the front step.

"It's a wonder that ancient horse can still make the trip, Hank." Louise poked the needle into the coveralls. "And Maggie, too."

"Sometimes I think that grotty old dog died last year, and someone forgot to tell her." William chuckled and reached down to tug on the dog's ear. "Is she still the best skunk killer alive?"

"Maybe if the skunk was already a goner. How's my little boy doing? Is he ready to catch a baseball yet?" Hank leaned down over the bundle. "Aw, darn it. He's sound asleep. I was hoping I could bounce him around a little bit."

"Better see if there's one or two of those baking powder biscuits left from tea," William said. Louise was already putting aside her sewing to get Hank a plate from the kitchen. "This boy's got a hollow leg."

"Hank earns every scrap of food he ever gets around this place." Louise smiled, touching Hank's shoulder as she passed him. "You sit yourself down, and I'll fix something. But if either of you wakes that boy, I'll take a willow switch to you!"

"Thanks, Louise. You know I'm always hungry. And I'll be real quiet," Hank whispered.

Louise returned with a plate and held it out. "Any of the local girls been asked to the church fowl supper by one tall, nice-looking neighbour boy?"

"Nope. I just like to ride Ned on over here. I don't worry about girls." Hank took the plate of beans with two extra biscuits and three sugar cookies, which he dropped into his shirt pocket. He smiled his thanks and sat on the straight-backed chair between William and Louise. "Girls are okay, just not very interesting.

Sometimes they act so silly." Hank shrugged. "There's one, though," he said, hunching over his plate. William raised his eyebrows and waited. "Emily Stewart. But she's got herself a boyfriend. You know their place just past the Waterhole Cemetery toward Manitou Beach? Her uncle, he works for the railway. Anyways, her father, he farms. And he sometimes wears a kilt to the Dominion Day picnic at the fairgrounds. My papa asked him once if anything gets worn under the kilt, and he said, 'No, sir, it's all in perfect working order!'" Hank grinned.

Louise drew in her breath sharply, and William laughed until he had a coughing fit. He reached for his cup of tea. "Don't know if I can top that," William said, wiping his eyes. He relit his pipe and grinned at Hank through the smoke. "Right, then. This Emily. With some folks, sometimes love grows on a person over time. Remember that. You don't just come right out and scare them off. You warm up to it. But mind not to take too long, or someone else will come along and do what you're afraid to do."

Hank tipped back his chair and leaned against the house. William knew what was coming next. The boy never tired of the stories he told about New Zealand. "Tell the story about your father," Hank prompted and wedged his plate on his lap.

"The Canterbury Plains," William began. "Sound carries so well you hear the shepherds whistling and commanding their dogs miles away. There's spiky tussock and mountain flax clinging to the cliffs. The Otago hillside paddocks are sometimes so dotted with sheep, with flocks so large, it looks like snowfall on the rolling hills that stretch out to the sea." William paused, tapping the pipe stem on his teeth. "My father never cared for sheep. Though he would not turn down a Sunday joint of mutton, mind you."

"Your father cut stone," Hank said, pulling a cookie from his shirt pocket.

"Always dusted with white powder, he was. When I was a young boy, I'd stand on a chair in the evenings before tea and blow the limestone dust out of Father's ears. He used to tell me there was something about cutting stone out of the earth that could keep a body's feet on solid ground. A wise man, my father. Must have been quite a disappointment when he worked out he was to die in the ocean." William sighed. "Their first trip. Everyone drowned."

"What terrible luck," murmured Louise. "And on their way to a wedding."

William was silent for a time, working the pipe stem. "When I was a boy," he began again, "my fancies didn't lie in cutting Oamaru limestone or the bluestone at Port Chalmers. Father said I should give farming a go with my uncles. My mates earned quite a bit of pocket money shearing with travelling mobs. None of that appealed to me. I wasn't afraid of the work. I wanted something of my own. Something different. A freezer ship could get me free passage to Britain with wages to boot. From there, I'd figure out my next step. Mother was dead set against it, but Father said if I'd made up my mind, there was no quicker way of making a boy into a man. And there were the cousins in England."

William blew a couple of smoke rings and admired them as they drifted over the porch railing. "On the night before I was to board the ship, my father took his hat from a hook by the door and turned it over in his hands. I can still picture him doing that, just turning it over and over. Small, black, a curled brim. The sort that hansom cabbies wear. That hat was as much part of his everyday apparel as his shirt and trousers. I remember he didn't really say anything for quite a while, just pinched the brim and tapped it against his leg. The limestone dust jumped up in the light. That hat was my father's favourite, his lucky hat. The crown was stiff felt, and when I was a child, he'd let me tap on it. Called it his hard knocker. He finally looked at me, and I remember seeing tears in his eyes. 'Best keep your wits warm,' he told me when he gave it to me. I said I'd look after it."

Hank nodded. "I remember when I first met you. When I got the fishhook in my eye, and you picked me up by the slough and took me home. You let me wear that hat. I'd never seen one like that before. You still wear it." Hank reached up to his left eye and ran his fingertip over the scar on the lid.

"That's the one," William said. "I do believe both my parents thought I'd be away long enough to get homesick, then be back again before they knew it. I was in England when I got word about the sinking. It was the only time they'd worked up the courage and had enough money to take a holiday. Ship sank off Cape Terawhiti. I had someone sell the house. Later, a small box arrived with some of their things. My grandmother's wedding ring. See there, Hank, that's on Louise's finger now. Some papers, some photographs, a few books, the little silver dish that sits on the table in the front room, bits and bobs of their lives."

"That doesn't sound like very much," Hank said.

"Well, true," William mused, moving his pipe to the other side of his mouth. "There wasn't much in the way of material worth, but the best thing I took with me was something of who they were. Good people, honest, gentle people. Always made the other person feel like they were worth listening to. If I got any of that, if I can live up to it, then that's a valuable inheritance."

William fell silent and sat, his pipe clicking against his teeth. He kept the mosquitoes at bay with lazy, well-aimed exhales of smoke. "I remember feeling a bit off-kilter with Orion hunting upside down in the winter and the Southern Cross gone from the night sky. You may remember when I first came, how ruddy cold that first winter was? But I feel like the prairie is home now. A good life is to be had with honest hard work. Run some livestock, grow enough grain to fatten them up. A decent and respectable living. Have a family." He reached over and rested a hand on his sleeping son. "My father would be proud."

"Yes, sir. But how come you didn't just stay in New Zealand and do the same thing?" Hank reached down to scratch Maggie's ear.

"Wouldn't have been the same thing. It would have been without adventure. Sailors back home depended on the Southern

Cross and Acrux to guide their ships. Looking for the North Star was something else altogether."

William bit on the end of his pipe and drew smoke into his lungs. He looked up at the sky. Saturn hung low on the eastern horizon. Besides the night whine of a few mosquitoes and a coyote's bark from the coulee, there was only the dog's back leg thump-thump-thumping on the floorboards when Hank's fingers wandered over just the right spot.

Louise sewed, gathering the knee of William's overalls closer so she could see, the dim lantern light glinting on her gold wedding band. It was almost buried in her flesh now. William thought she would need to see Dr. Speight about getting it cut off before it stopped the circulation. She passed the needle over and under and lifted the thread to bite it off between her teeth. She reached for another cookie from the plate set out for Hank and pulled a second pair of overalls from the pile. She found the hole in the knee and threaded the needle again.

"Well," Hank spoke softly and leaned over the sleeping boy. "I'd best be getting home, John. You be ready to play the next time I come by." He tipped his chair forward and stood to stretch his long frame. Maggie lurched stiffly to her feet and wagged her moulting tail. She padded off the porch, already headed west. "Thanks, Mrs. Burke, for the lunch. Your snickerdoodles are real good, as usual."

Louise took hold of Hank's sleeve and pressed the last two cookies into his hand. "You be careful going home in the dark. See that Ned doesn't put a leg in a gopher hole."

Hank unwound a rein from a nail Ned had managed to snag. The horse, standing with his head down and a back hoof on tiptoe, twitched awake when Hank swung himself up by a handful of mane.

"The moon's good tonight, so I can see. Besides, Ned's made the trip so many times he could do it with his eyes closed." He laid the reins against Ned's neck and turned the horse toward home. "Good night, you three."

"Good night, mate," William said.

Hank raised a hand to show he'd heard. They listened to Ned's hooves clopping on the hard dirt, fading in the distance until Hank turned off the road and headed across the field.

"He might have eyes for that girl," Louise said, settling back and folding up the overalls in her lap. "He's growing up, isn't he? Seems like he was just planting hollyhocks all around the front porch for me when you were back in Toronto. Remember when he said we needed cats so we wouldn't have mice in our bed?" Louise laughed and poked her needle into the pincushion, wound up the spool, and closed her sewing basket. "I'm going to put the boy down, and I'm off to bed. Will you be coming?"

"Soon, dear heart." William tapped his pipe on the edge of the bench. "It's a lovely night. I'll just have another smoke and wait for the coyotes. I'll be in soon."

He watched Louise slip her arms around the sleeping boy and lift him to her shoulder. "Bring my basket with your overalls when you come?" she said. "I don't want to wake this one."

He leaned to reach for the screen door and pulled it open so she could pass.

William sat alone on the porch, pulling smoke into his lungs, listening to prairie night noises. He wondered what some people thought of his wife. It didn't matter if they thought she was the least bit solitary or kept to herself. It mattered what she was to him and what he could see inside her. The baby had softened her so much. One was enough, she told him, but he hoped she'd change her mind about that.

He liked to do little things for her. Bring her dug-up prairie lilies, bulbs wrapped in his handkerchief, for her to plant by the house. Or the delicate blue halves of a robin's eggshell he'd found for her to display on the windowsill. Sometimes, he'd take her walking in the field, Louise carrying John on her hip and switching a willow branch to keep the mosquitoes away. William would spread his arms wide and tell her about the crops he wanted to plant the next spring. So she could be part of it all.

Their future would be something they were building together, and no matter what, she wouldn't feel alone anymore.

William heard the coyotes start up on the far side of the coulee, yipping and barking in the dark, and he waited to hear the reply from those on this side. Then, a flick of movement by the garden. There was enough moonlight to make out the large grey coyote, without a trace of fear, trotting across in front of the shed, a rabbit, still struggling, hanging from its jaws.

LOUISE

THE BURKE FARM, FEBRUARY 1920

During the first weeks of the new year, Louise struggled toward the end of her second pregnancy. When her legs swelled like Erna Eckart's overstuffed summer sausage, the doctor ordered bed rest. "Ridiculous," Louise said to William. "Bed rest with a four-year-old in the house? You can tell he doesn't have any children of his own to suggest something so impractical."

They sat at the table, and even though supper was finished, Louise reached for the butter dish and another thick slice of bread. Reaching for anything was an effort; she carried this child high and all out in front. John had been such an easy baby to carry; she was never even sick in the mornings with him. This one was different. There was always pressure on her bladder, and she constantly found herself pulling on her coat to trudge to the outhouse. And the hunger. She often dreamt of Auntie Freda's cooking and tried not to think about how many times other girls at Eaton's had commented about her weight. Hefty, they said. Her supervisor suggested she wear "more slenderizing clothes to camouflage, something with faux tiers," particularly when she was working in the women's department. Now the gnawing in her gut put her in mind of the coyote she saw picking at a frozen deer carcass behind the barn last winter. She was content enough and sometimes even joyful when she looked at her son, but as this second baby grew inside her belly, a feeling of disquiet grew with it.

"He doesn't want you to get overly tired, darling," William said. "Dr. Speight is just concerned about you getting enough rest. Being crook, you know, it's what we'd say back home. Sick with one child when there's another on the way isn't good. He just wants you to save your strength."

"I don't feel sick," she protested a little weakly.

She wiped a heel of bread through a bit of gravy on her plate. They couldn't afford to let good food go to waste, even though William often gently reminded her that it was never wasted when it went to slop for the weaner pigs.

John pushed through the blanket that hung in the doorway to his parents' bedroom, squealing, then disappeared into the cold darkness on the other side. Soon he was back, on his knees, pushing his cast iron toy tractor through to the warm kitchen. John crawled beneath the table, where he drove his tractor around the legs of the kitchen chairs and his parents' feet.

Louise had already devoured the bread and was absently poking through the chicken bones on her husband's plate.

William wiped the corners of his mouth with his serviette. "Lovely tea, darling," he said. "Those chooks would do well with a bit more straw in the shed during this cold spell. I'd best see to it."

Louise nodded and popped a bit of fried chicken skin into her mouth. She dabbed at the grease that dripped on the front of her apron.

William scraped his chair back, careful of the boy, and reached for his heavy winter coat on the hook by the door. "I'm off, then," he said with a tug on the boy's hair. "Mind your mama. I'll be back in time to tell you a few bedtime stories, won't I?"

ON THAT BLINDINGLY WHITE FEBRUARY AFTERNOON just after Valentine's Day, the temperature suddenly dropped and stayed down for a solid week. The occasional crack of branches splitting on the poplar and white birch down in the coulee sounded like distant gunfire. Louise tried to hold out as long as she dared, but it seemed the outhouse beckoned every hour. She refused the indignity of the chamber pot William had suggested. He even offered to go to town to find a pretty one at Bjorndahl's general store. Instead, he strung a rope from the porch so she could make her way on her own if he was out tending to the animals. There was more than one story in the area about a farmer who was lost between the house and barn during a whiteout and was found frozen just steps from the back door.

By Friday, the cold hung still and so crisp that Louise could hear Pete Dechant calling his dog across the coulee as clearly as if he was standing ten feet away. She ran her woollen mitten along the rope, and the cold air stabbed her eyes and pierced the rough scarf across her face. By the time she got back to the house, a thick white frost had built up where her breath came and went in moist, shallow pants. The time for this baby had come and gone, and everything seemed to exhaust her. The days were long.

She had barely kicked off her boots and hung her coat when she heard a horse whinny. She scratched at the frost on the windowpane and let out her breath. It was a relief to see Hanusia Yuzik arriving in the wagon with her son.

Andrij pulled the wagon up close to the porch, and Hanusia climbed down. She flicked her hand at the boy, and he slapped the reins on the horse's rump, taking the wagon into the barn. She had been coming by nearly every day for two weeks now just to check on Louise, dispensing her own medical advice. From her cellar, she brought apples poked through with a knife and instructed Louise to eat them only after they sat on the table overnight. "Iron," she said, "good for baby." William said it was just an old wives' tale.

Last October, a swallow had flown into the kitchen window

with a thump. Hanusia wailed and threw her apron over her face. She hurried outside and found the bird trembling and dying in the dirt below the window. It was true, she insisted, that "birds see future." William had taken her by the elbow and spoken sternly to her about "planting silly ideas" when she cried that "baby born wrong now." Although they had rarely spoken since Hanusia helped with John's birth, Louise was grateful to have the female company, odd beliefs aside.

There had been contractions for the last three or four days, but nothing more serious than a belly ache. Hanusia dismissed the discomfort with her own homespun explanation. "Baby, hair is growing." She wasn't a warm person, but she had a sharp efficiency about her. Quick to snap at her own children, she spoke of her husband now and then with what Louise thought was a festering disappointment.

"Always children. One more, one more," she said one afternoon when she consented to a cup of tea while she waited for her son to come with the wagon to take her home. Her voice was sharp with bitterness. "The work! He just want more children. Not care I do the work! He just drink potato wine, not listen. *Staray.*"

As the days dragged on with nothing more than cramps and no real movement from the baby, Hanusia's tone and her face grew more stern. Louise felt a rising guilt that somehow she was wasting Hanusia's time.

"No baby today?" Hanusia asked now. She hung up her coat beside Louise's on the peg near the door.

Louise shook her head.

"Too long. No good. We get up now." Hanusia reached for Louise's elbow and pulled her to her feet. "You walk around, baby think now is time. Maybe doctor, we need him."

An hour later, Louise had finally dragged out a chair at the table, pleading with Hanusia for a brief respite from walking the floor. William came in and shut the door quickly, kicking the rolled blanket back against the threshold. He stomped his feet and peeled the layers of clothes from his body. He nodded at Andrij, who held John on his lap at the window.

"Good lord, boys! What a day out there," he said. "I had to chop a hole open in the slough again to fill the trough for the cows. I must have carried twenty buckets." He held his mittens up. "John, are my hands still there? I can't feel them anymore!"

The boy nodded.

William hung his mittens on the line strung up behind the woodstove and breathed into his fists. Louise leaned over to put her own hand on the pane beside John's small handprint on the frosty glass. She realized she hadn't eaten anything since some dry toast that morning. She shifted her weight on the chair and swallowed down sudden nausea.

"We melt a spot so we see you coming in," Andrij said. "I go see to the horse. Soon we go back home. My mother says tomorrow we come back." John slid down to the floor, and Andrij gave the toy tractor a little shove with his boot. He stepped over the boy to reach for his coat. When the door closed, Louise struggled to her feet and toed the blanket roll back into place.

"I'll warm up some soup for you. I'll just need to put a bit of wood in the stove, and it won't take a minute," Louise said to William, who was still huffing warm breath into his numb fingers. "Hanusia, I'm afraid you've made another trip today for nothing."

She pushed back her chair and stood and sucked in a breath. "Oh," she said. The floor darkened around her wool socks, and Hanusia reached for her arm. Louise put her hands to her belly and grunted. "Oh, I think I need to get into bed. Help me. Hanusia, if you could. William, it's—"

Her words turned into a wail. John dropped his tractor and backed into the corner behind the chair.

"Okay, now we go," Hanusia said. "You, missus, bed now."

Louise bent over as much as her swelled belly would allow and scratched at the air, searching for Hanusia's hand. "It's all right,

John. Mother's all right," she gasped. "William, get the boy. I've got to—"

Hanusia propped the pillows against the iron bed frame, then waited with a hand on Louise's back until the contraction subsided. She helped Louise climb into bed, springs squeaking as she lay back, gasping in short, quick breaths.

William was back soon, and John appeared at his knee, clutching his tractor with one hand and William's pant leg with the other. Louise lay quietly, but her flannel nightdress was dark with sweat. Her cheeks felt flushed, and she felt angry red blotches spreading across her neck and chest.

William put his hand on the lump where her foot made a small rise in the quilt. Hanusia's mouth turned up in a small smile. Louise thought it must feel unnatural for her.

"Not to worry. Baby just take time. Good get doctor. Maybe problems go too long," Hanusia said to William, a little too brightly. She folded a cloth into a square, dipped it in a basin beside the bed, wrung it out, and wiped Louise's forehead and across her throat with long, deliberate strokes. She pointed a finger at John, who still peered from behind William's legs. "You be good boy. Help Andrij. Play quiet," she said briskly, tilting her head at the boy.

John lifted his chin and stared at Louise with wide eyes. His lip trembled.

"*Oy, yoy, yoy.* Boys, they not cry," Hanusia said, shaking her head. She grasped his shoulder and bent down, so they were face to face. John pressed back against William's leg. "We make job for you. Take tractor in kitchen. Watch window. You see Mr. Yuzik and doctor come, you come say to me. Now, you. Go."

The boy turned his head toward his mother and searched Louise's face. She nodded. He turned and pushed through the blanket hanging in the doorway. In a moment, Louise heard the chair scrape on the floorboards and the squeak of the iron toy on the windowsill.

Hanusia took William's arm and propelled him toward the

door. "William, you tell Andrij go get Father. Nik, he go. I not want Andrij go to town alone. Doctor and fancy horse not make it in so cold."

LOUISE HEARD VOICES, BUT THEY SOUNDED SO FAR away. She wanted to thank Hanusia for her kindness, for keeping John from becoming frightened. But the pain seemed to wash over her in a clenching wave when she tried to speak, sucking the breath from her body. This wasn't like it was with John. Something was not right.

She fell into fitful spells of sweaty sleep. Voices droned around her.

A distant, vague voice grew more insistent than the rest, and Louise struggled and turned away as it drew closer. She barely felt Hanusia's hand on her shoulder, and the coolness of the damp rag pressed to her forehead.

Come with us, the voice demanded. It was a rough man's voice, the one she had tried so hard to forget. *There are enough pears for two.*

"No!" Louise shouted and looked wildly around the room.

"*Shchoh*! What!" Hanusia dropped the rag she was wringing out into the basin and hurried to the bedside. She took up Louise's hand and rubbed it roughly between her own. "Doctor here soon. *Tehenko*, sit quiet—"

Her voice wobbled and faded. Then Louise's eyelids grew heavy.

LOUISE HAD NO RECOLLECTION OF FALLING ASLEEP, BUT when the fresh pain gripped and surged through her, her eyes flew open, and she tried to sit up. Dr. Speight appeared in the bedroom doorway, where William held the blanket aside. Hanusia stood by the bed, arms folded across her chest. Worry and lamp-light deepened the lines on her face. William stepped forward and took Louise's hand, and bent close. "The doctor is here now," he said.

Dr. Speight shrugged off his heavy buffalo coat and unwound his muffler. His wind-burned face was streaked with tears from the cold, and ice coated his moustache. John had been the first child he delivered when he began his practice in Watrous. In four short years, the doctor seemed to have aged, and what once was a practised look of concern had etched itself into a grim certainty that if anything could go wrong, it would.

He leaned forward, took Louise's wrist in his hand, and was silent for a moment. He straightened and spoke quietly to William. "Damn near didn't make it. The wind has kicked up, and with the blowing snow, I couldn't even follow the fence line." The doctor opened his mouth wide and worked his jaw to get some feeling back into his face. He pressed his handkerchief to his moustache and blotted the melting frost. "I think I was about a mile from town when I couldn't see my horse's rump. I just dropped the reins and let him go. I'm grateful Nik's team was leading the way. Pure whiteout. The horse just kept going on his own and pulled the hackney along. I knew we were getting close because he picked up the pace at the last. Lost sight of Nik's team again when the wind came up. Maybe they could see your light enough to aim for it."

"Come out to the kitchen. Let's put your coat by the stove," William said. "Do you have stones to put in the oven? John, you come help." John stood next to the doctor, and Louise almost laughed when the boy asked if he could ride atop the buffalo coat. "And the horses need tending. Hanusia can get you whatever you need here."

The doctor blew into his cupped hands. "Not to worry," he said. "Nik pulled the horses inside out of the wind. Let's pray no one gets lost out in this, or I'll be doing amputations or worse." He turned to Hanusia. "Mrs. Yuzik, I'll tell you what I need once

I have a better look at Mrs. Burke. Now you say the poor woman has been in labour for days. I wish you'd come for me sooner."

Louise heard the door off the kitchen open and slam shut, then heavy boots on the floorboards. Nik Yuzik filled up the doorway, bundled in his heavy coat, with a scarf wound around his face, so only his watery eyes and red nose were visible. Hanusia leaned over, shaking her head, and hissed at her husband. "Niko-lai! Look! What you do. Dirty floor. Go!"

He waved her off. The scarf was stiff and white where his breath came and went, and he pawed at it with a heavy mitten, pulling it aside so he could speak. "Warm water." He panted. "Horse. Eyes frozen shut. And some rags I can soak. Thaw them nice, slow."

"How the hell did he even see where he was going?" Speight asked.

"He don't look," Nik said, rubbing feeling into his hands. "Just listen to my horses go on ahead and follow close. Good thing you don't make trip on your own."

"Louise," William said quietly, bending close to her ear, "I'll just see to Nik and get him a pail of water. We'll be right here." The doctor and Nik left the room, and William reached for John's hand. "Come with me, my lad. We'll get you set up with that mighty buffalo." He strode across the room and dropped the blanket across the doorway.

Louise closed her eyes and tried to keep her breath steady. She clung to the sound of voices in the kitchen. Hanusia busied herself at the bedside, tucking the quilt in tightly across Louise's legs. She refolded linens and stacked them on the dresser. She muttered to herself. Now and then, Louise could make out Nik's name in a string of harsh syllables.

"Here are the stones. They're cold now, but I'll need them for the trip back," the doctor said, and she heard the oven door open. She knew William was sliding in the large stones the doctor would wrap and keep close for warmth, maybe under his boots, in the wagon. "You'd best start melting a few more pails of snow on the stove there, William," the doctor went on. "I'll need lots more hot water. Always do." Louise could hear the hiss of snow turning to steam on the hot stovetop.

Hanusia clucked her tongue and took a rag to the floor where Nik's boots had been. Now she straightened up, her jaw tight. Dr. Speight pushed aside the blanket in the doorway and stepped back into the bedroom. He set his Stanley bag on the bureau and snapped it open. Louise closed her eyes tightly against a mounting surge in her belly. Hanusia took her hand, and Louise was glad for the distraction of such a painful grip.

WILLIAM

THE BURKE FARM, FEBRUARY 1920

It eased William's mind a little to know Hanusia was sitting with Louise. She was an odd woman, bony and colourless. It couldn't be an easy life with Nik and their boys. She had a sharp tongue and strange beliefs but mostly kept her thoughts to herself. She wasn't the busybody her sister Hilda was, and she had helped with the birth of so many babies. There had only been two he knew of who had died, one along with its mother, but that was during the flu epidemic back in '18. He had heard that Hanusia herself had lost at least that many of her own. One had been still-born. He tried to put the thought out of his mind.

William gathered up John from where he sat on the floor, holding his toy, his head bobbing down on his chest. He pulled the child onto his lap and tucked the doctor's buffalo robe around him. John petted the sleeve until he finally fell asleep.

Dr. Speight emerged from the bedroom. "She's two hundred pounds if she's an ounce," he complained gruffly to William. "It doesn't make it any easier when a woman gets to be of such a size if you'll pardon me saying." He ladled some water from the tub on the stovetop into a pan. "I've spoken to her about this, but apparently, she hasn't done anything to correct it. The baby's small, I think. That'll help some."

The groan from the bedroom drew the doctor back through the doorway, and he let the heavy blanket fall behind him. John didn't stir, and William was grateful.

Nik pushed open the door, then shut it quickly behind him and shrugged off his coat. He stood awkwardly near the stove and bent down to pull off his boots. He thought better of it and straightened up. He held his hands over the stovetop and flinched each time he heard a moan from the bedroom. "Well," he said finally. "Wind, it die down a bit, and I can see to get home. I take the saddle horse. Andrij, he hook up the other one to the wagon for Hanusia in the barn. She stay until morning, I think. We come back for her. Maybe doctor, he stay too."

"Thank you for your help, Nik," William said, his voice heavy. "I appreciate everything you and Hanusia are doing. And Andrij, too, for entertaining the boy. I'm a bit at wit's end about what I should be doing to help."

"It's okay," Nik said, pulling out a chair at the table and sitting down heavily. "Hanusia, she know what to do for baby." They sat together for a time, now and then talking in hushed tones while John slept. Finally, Nik put his hands on his knees and pushed up off the chair. He pulled on his coat and his cap. "Tell doctor horses are fine. They get rubbed dry before he heads back to town if he go tonight. Their eyes okay, a bit sore, but no shooting blind horses in morning." He wound the scarf around his head and across his face and pulled his cap down over his ears.

William eased John off his lap, leaving him wrapped in the coat on the chair. He closed the door behind Nik and kicked the rolled blanket back in place. He could do nothing now but wait. He made himself a cup of strong tea and sat at the table, cradling the cup in his hands.

The woodstove had been stoked all evening, and the house was filled with warmth and the musky smell of damp woollens drying on the line behind the wood box. The light from the coal-oil lanterns threw long shadows up the wall behind the doctor as he came and went from the bedroom, and William's head snapped up at each entry, his eyes following every exit. When Dr. Speight came out a third time, William tried to keep his voice calm and steady. "Is it going all right? Louise, is she all right?"

Dr. Speight dipped a pair of forceps into the tub of boiling water on the stove. His jaw was set hard, and he only muttered, "Just a precaution, these," he said, holding the tongs up. "Shouldn't be long now." Before William could ask anything else, the doctor went back into the bedroom. William shifted on the wooden chair and folded his hands on the table. He could hear the doctor and Hanusia in murmured snippets. Louise moaned and now and then cried out.

When John opened his eyes, William lifted the boy, coat and all, onto his lap again. "The doctor says it won't be long, John," he said, combing down the boy's mussed hair with his fingers. "You didn't sleep much. Can you try to have another wee nap so you'll be wide awake when the baby comes?"

But John slid down to the floor at William's feet. He retrieved his tractor and, standing between his father's knees, he drove the toy up and down William's pant legs. He looked up and grinned. "Baby," he said, patting his father's arm. "Baby sister."

William smiled at the boy with some difficulty; his cheeks seemed too stiff with worry to make the effort convincing. Instead, he took the child's face in his hands and planted a reassuring kiss on the boy's forehead. "This baby is very lucky you're waiting here so patiently to be the big brother," William said, gathering the boy up onto his lap. "And you think it will be a little girl, then? How do you know such a thing when none of the grownups in the house know it?"

The boy buried his face in William's shirt.

"If she is a girl, her name might be Violet, just like Mama's flowers," William said, running his hand over John's soft hair. "Mama says they're really called Johnny-Jump-Ups, but that's not a good name for a girl."

"I am Johnny!" the boy protested.

"Righto, my boy," William said. "We can't have two Johnnies! Violet it is then, eh?"

After midnight, the wind died away altogether. William scraped the frost from the windowpane and held the lantern so he could see the International Harvester thermometer mounted outside on the sill. The mercury had sunk to thirty below. He pushed another chunk of wood into the stove and sat down again at the table in front of a cold cup of tea.

LOUISE

THE BURKE FARM, FEBRUARY 1920

In the early morning hours, Louise shuddered through her last push and fell back against the iron bedframe, spent, her body heaving and slick with sweat, sobs escaping her throat. The tiny infant feet came first, and the doctor's eyes quickly met Hanusia's. Louise saw the look that passed between them, and she struggled to sit up against the headboard. "What is it? What's wrong?" She strained to see around Hanusia and the doctor, hunched over the baby.

"*Tehenko*, quiet. We fix," Hanusia said without turning around. "Sometimes, the baby he get cord around the neck."

"Mrs. Yuzik, hold the child so," the doctor barked. "I need to free the cord. It doesn't seem too tight, but turn the child toward me so I can get a grip."

Hanusia held out her hands to take the infant, tiny and blue. They bent low over the baby, and with two fingers, the doctor loosened the cord enough to slip it over the head.

"Good, good. Baby good now," Hanusia said.

"That's always worrisome," the doctor replied. "We'll need to just watch for a bit to make sure things are as they should be. Can't be too careful. Very small," he muttered.

"Hanusia? Hanusia, please!" Louise implored.

"Okay now. A little girl. You wait now. We clean up."

"Mrs. Yuzik, do that quickly and get her wrapped up. It won't be good if she gets a chill. Be quick now," Dr. Speight said, wiping his hands on a clean cloth. Then he spoke to Louise. "We've seen this before, and things can go bad in a hurry if we're not quick about it. But the cord wasn't tight, so we're out of the woods." With clean hands, he took the baby from Hanusia. "Mrs. Yuzik, I need another blanket. There is a draft, and we need to keep her warm."

The infant was small, as the doctor had said; it was surprisingly tiny and loose-jointed. "A girl, just as your boy predicted," Dr. Speight said, then he muttered something under his breath. In the lamplight, Louise couldn't be sure, but something seemed odd. The baby moved a little. Hanusia brought another flannel to tuck around the child, and Louise could see a tiny arm emerge from the bundle the doctor held in the crook of his arm.

"She's breathing," Dr. Speight said. "But so very loose, like a rag doll. Now that the cord is cut, I would expect a little more—"

Hanusia washed Louise's face with cool snow water from the basin, but the smell of sweat, blood, feces, and fear hung thickly in the close bedroom air. She quickly handed the doctor clean cloths and the other blanket to wrap the baby, then turned her attention back to Louise.

"Mrs. Yuzik, I need more light," Dr. Speight said harshly. "Turn that wick up, will you?" He looked closely into the baby's face. "What do we have here." It wasn't a question. On his face was a grim expression Louise remembered from the time John had a bout of whooping cough. Louise felt as if she were staring at him from the bed like an owl, unblinking, not breathing.

"Let me see her," she said hoarsely.

Please, God, don't let her be like Sarah.

The knowing that something was wrong passed between Louise and Hanusia, and it was Hanusia who turned away. Louise struggled to sit up in bed and gripped the bedpost with one hand, her knuckles white. The baby was weak, loose. She hadn't even made a peep yet. Louise felt her ears pound with each heartbeat. Even when Hanusia turned up the lamp, so the flame burned more brightly, Dr. Speight's face looked dark and grim.

"She doesn't look good, Mrs. Burke," the doctor said.

Hanusia glanced from the doctor to Louise and seemed to want to offer some hope. But like her early cheerfulness, it seemed unnatural. "But we can't always be sure about this so soon, can we, Doctor?" Her voice was strained, and instead of feeling reassured, Louise felt a prickling at the back of her neck.

Dr. Speight laid the baby on a pink flannel. He dried the baby's head, and her soft, fine hair stood up, pale in the lamplight. Despite his concern about a chill, he peeled back the flannel and looked carefully into the baby's face, turning her slightly. "I've read about this, heard about it during my training," he said. "No doubt." He lowered his voice and took Hanusia by the elbow, steering her closer to the lamp.

Louise sat up against the pillows and leaned forward. "No, Hanusia, bring her to me," she pleaded. "Hanusia. I need to see her."

"Doctor, mother needs to have her baby!" Hanusia said sternly. She put her hands out for the child. "It is right to do."

"Taking the baby before there might be some sort of attachment is best." Speight turned his back to the bed, and Louise leaned sideways to look around him. Did he think she couldn't hear him if he turned away? "It only leads to more misery for the family if they deny the truth, if they try to pretend that somehow the child is normal. It is God's way, Mrs. Yuzik. Sometimes a baby isn't meant to live. How this one has, I don't know, but I'm quite sure it won't be for long."

"Let me see her!" Louise cried out.

Hanusia strode to the bed and propped the pillows up behind Louise's back. The doctor brought the baby closer, like a reluctant offering, and stood at the side of the bed, holding the baby out to her. Like a rag doll, the infant lay in his big hands, blinking. Her mouth worked, but she uttered no sound. Her skinny legs splayed against his thumbs. With those stick-like limbs and the doctor's thick fingers and thumbs, it seemed he was showing Louise a large pink spider. In the lamplight, Louise recognized the broad face, the flat bridge of her nose, the skin folds in the inner corners of the eyes.

The eyes, open and sombre, were shaped like almonds. It was true, then.

"This baby is not right," the doctor said firmly. As if to protest, the baby mustered a thin wail. "There are signs to look for, and if the diagnosis is what I suspect, then you and William can try again, Louise."

"I can't do this again."

"There are places for these children."

No one but William knows about Sarah. Some of it.

Dr. Speight looked at the infant more closely. He carefully opened the baby's tiny fist and showed Louise the tell-tale sign, a single crease bisecting the palm. She turned her face into the pillow.

"This sort usually has heart problems, holes. If she lives, it won't be for long, most likely. She'll be susceptible to this new Spanish influenza. It's killed hundreds too frail to fight it. The weakness, the headaches, fever. The eucalyptus masks, the mustard plasters, do no good." The doctor shook his head, looking at Hanusia over the rim of his glasses as if needing her confirmation. "And the mental faculties, if any, will never develop. The child probably won't even be able to distinguish you from other people. She'll certainly never walk or talk or even feed herself." The doctor bundled the infant in the flannel, and she was quiet.

Louise lay as if drowned, her body heavy, held down as if by some immense stone.

Hanusia picked up Louise's pale hand and rubbed it, trying to warm it between her own. Her hands were rough, her grip much too hard. Louise winced and felt her wedding band dig into the flesh of her little finger.

"You and William should try again," the doctor urged. "Right away. You can tell people this one died, and we'll handle the arrangements to send her somewhere. If she lives, which isn't likely. You've got to think of John. This wouldn't be fair to him, this burden. To be the brother of such a child—" He trailed off, shaking his head.

"Doctors not know all," Hanusia whispered, bending close to Louise's ear. She shook Louise's hand again, a little more gently. Louise wondered if it was because this was a girl. A girl was what Nik wanted, Hanusia had told her so. Is that why Hanusia seemed to be defending the baby? "Hard birth make baby head funny. You know Wetzel boy? I help his mother. He backward, now handsome boy. This baby is okay one, two days, maybe!"

Louise pulled her hand away and turned her face to the wall. She closed her eyes, shutting out Hanusia's protest. Sparks, flashes of light, flared behind her eyelids. Doors opening, figures grey and reaching.

She remembered.

THE HALLWAYS TOO GLOOMY, KEYS TURNING IN LOCKS, echoes harsh in the corridors. The smells of urine and worse, lye soap, disinfectant, and loneliness swirled, making her head throb. The whispers among the staff about pregnancies, abortions, sometimes a newborn delivered and taken away in secret. The small hands reaching, grasping at her. Vacant faces, questioning faces. Their voices.

"Do you know my mother?"

"Where's my dad?"

"Can I go home now?"

"Where's my baby?"

"Where's Sarah?"

Louise hadn't thought of it for so long. The images pushed into her mind with such sharp clarity that she felt physical pain as if each were a shard of glass. Parents standing stiffly in the lounges on the wards, some never even taking off their coats. They stood rooted to the disinfected floor, out of place in a foreign land with a foreigner before them. Their child asking to go home, pleading when they turned to leave. Some children stood with glum determination and waited for parents who never came back. Some waited for no one, for nothing at all.

The voices, Louise remembered, had been relentless. They came to her now, and she shook her head. Then she heard her own voice, angry and afraid, louder than the others. *What happened to Sarah? What did you do?*

Louise squeezed her eyes tightly and tried to think beyond her pulse pounding at her temples. There had been no bad dreams for so long, but now Sarah appeared, as real as if she stood beside Louise's bed. The child reached out and laid her fingers on Louise's arm. Her soft blonde hair was braided, looped together down her back in French braids with blue ribbons, the way Louise always did it for her on Sundays when the other children waited for their parents.

But there was someone who had an interest in Sarah. It was Bert who now stepped into her mind as clearly as if he stood at the foot of the bed, too. Louise pressed her face into the pillow. He ran his hand through his hair, taking care to arrange it just so across his forehead. He looked at Louise for a long time and then reached out, his fingers coming to rest like a whisper on Sarah's hair. He drew one finger down the side of her face and along her jaw, lightly, and made slow circles around her mouth. She giggled and tilted her head to one shoulder.

"Uncle Bert has a kitty." Sarah's mouth worked over the words.

"Come with us." Bert's lips pulled back in a smile. "Come on, Nursie. There are enough pears for two."

Just an innocent girl, Louise thought and tried to rid the memory from her mind. *They found her in the stream, down by the bridge. Floating, one bare foot caught in a tangle of fallen branches at the water's edge.* "Just an innocent baby."

"*Tak*, she innocent baby. Tank God is girl," Hanusia agreed, and Louise realized she'd spoken the words aloud. Hanusia's angular face swam unfocused before her. Her voice was almost wistful. "You lucky is girl."

Louise pressed her hand hard against her own mouth. Sarah's lips turned from blue to white, her eyes still open in the stream.

Louise realized someone was calling her name.

"Mrs. Burke," Dr. Speight said sharply. "Louise. Are you listening?"

"I can hear you," she said. "I'm just so tired. I'm so tired now." Louise covered her face with her hands.

Hanusia stood rooted to the floor by the bed with the washbasin, her mouth pinched in a tight line. "Baby, she okay," Hanusia insisted, moving the basin to one hip. "The doctor, maybe he does not know. Nobody know." She leaned over and flicked Louise's hair away from her eyes. The baby began a thin gurgling wail again as if she was insisting they tend to her. "Air now in lungs. See, pink now. Now okay. Hold her."

"I can't," Louise whispered and turned her face away again from Hanusia's touch. She tried to shut out the baby's crying by pressing her fists against her ears. Voices, long dark corridors. The clank of keys in locks. No place for a child, but what kind of mother was she if the thought of keeping her baby was so detestable?

"Mrs. Yuzik, you aren't making this easier for the woman." The doctor laid the baby in the cradle at the foot of the bed. He went out to face William alone.

Hanusia busied herself with tidying up, and Louise watched her with half-closed eyes.

"Me, it was bad with my one boy." Hansuia talked almost to herself. "Andrij good boy, not smart, but good boy. Your girl same maybe. Your husband, boy, come now. You lucky to have girl." Her words, though sparse, calmed Louise a little. Hanusia stood stiffly for a moment, put the soiled cloths in a bundle under her arm, and grasped the basin. She hurried out, flicking the blanket back across the doorway.

Then John appeared at the bedside. William tiptoed up behind him and took Louise's hand. "Darling, how are you feeling?" he asked.

"Mama!" John nearly shouted. "We got Violet! My sister! Her name is Violet!"

"John, softly, my boy." William shushed him and put his hands on his son's shoulders. "We mustn't wake the baby, and Mama needs quiet now."

"Violet," she said. "Is that it, then?"

"Your favourite little flowers, Mama," John explained, his voice a stage whisper. "You love them, and now you love Violet!"

She took a ragged breath and closed her eyes. Her need for sleep was overwhelming and tugged at her mind. She seemed to drift like a kite, with only William's voice holding her tenuously here and in the moment.

"Mama needs her rest, John," he whispered. "There's a good boy. Let's have a little peek at your sister, just for a moment, to say hello. You will need to be a big brother and take care of her. We'll all need to take care of her."

WILLIAM

THE BURKE FARM, FEBRUARY 1920

William frowned as he dipped the ladle into the soup pot. By the fifth day after Violet's birth, Hanusia's thin encouragement seemed to evaporate in the still, dark room where his wife lay. When he went in, Louise turned her face away.

"Sweetheart, you must eat something," William said, cradling a bowl of the beef and barley soup Hanusia had left. She'd stored two jars of it in the cellar. It had been simmering on the back of the woodstove for two days. "A bit of hot soup. It would do you a world of good." He moved a plate aside on the bedside table; at least she'd eaten some of the toast he'd left in the morning. He'd tempted her with a bit of saskatoon jam. "I'll just set it here for a moment to cool. It's quite hot, but you'll be pleased to know I've managed to not burn the bottom of the pot yet."

Though Dr. Speight had said Louise would be unable to nurse, Violet did fine and latched on to the breast often. William was grateful. But for Louise's part, there were no smiles or cooing as there had been lavished on John when he had nursed. Louise left the bed only to go to the outhouse. William offered to carry out a chamber pot for her, but she said no, she'd not have him doing that. It was a trip for which she did not dress but merely tugged a barn coat over her nightgown and slid her feet into William's boots.

William picked up Louise's brush. Her hair smelled of sour sweat and talcum. "John's so anxious. Might he come in to see you, even if it's just for a wee bit?" William sat on the edge of the bed and untied the strip of cloth at the end of Louise's braid. "Let me tidy your hair, and perhaps he can come in while you have your lunch. He misses you terribly, darling."

Louise sat up slowly and slumped forward while William undid the plait and carefully pulled the brush through her hair. Violet gurgled and made a sucking noise from her cradle, her tiny fingers grasping at the air.

"Looks like someone else is interested in having her tea."

William drew two fingers down through Louise's hair and carefully crossed each piece one over the other, and tied the cloth at the end. He placed it over her shoulder at the front of her flannel nightgown, and Louise leaned back against the pillow. She fingered the braid and closed her eyes.

William took her hand. "Will you see him, just a little?"

"Not today. I'm too tired," Louise said, each word an obvious effort, as though she was carrying rocks up a hill to a stone boat.

"I'll put a pan on the stove," William said. "I'll heat some water, and you'll feel better with a wash-up."

A creak in the floorboards made William turn. John clutched his blue flannel blanket, sat down just outside the room, and peered around the doorframe.

"That's a face far too serious for such a wee boy. Mother's not feeling well, my lad." He patted Louise's shoulder. "She needs her sleep, and soon she'll be good as gold. In the meantime, it's just us men, eh, to look after our new baby girl?"

William went to the boy and lifted him over his shoulder. John wrapped his arms around William's neck and looked back in time to see Louise turn over, her face to the wall.

Louise's disposition had not improved. William sat at the table, his fingers laced around his mug, and caught a glimpse of Auntie Freda's little yellow heart on the wall by the woodstove. He studied it for a moment. In his own house, with its silent kitchen and diminishing wife, William pushed his mug away and stood. "Right," William said. "This is in my hands now. Come with me, boy. We're off to town."

John waited patiently on the chair where William left him and watched William tamp down the damper in the stovepipe and check the firebox.

"Should be good for the afternoon," William said. He went through the curtain to Louise and told her that he was taking John out for a ride. "Did you hear me, Louise? We'll be back soon. I'm in need of a stop at Dykstras's shop for the carriage hinges, too. We won't be long." He paused. "Louise?"

"Yes, all right."

William leaned over the cradle and tucked the blanket around the sleeping baby.

"You'll be all right? The stove should be fine. I've seen to the girl."

"I'm fine. Yes, just go." There was an edge of irritation in her voice.

He bundled John up in woollen layers, then went outside to hook up Chub and Florie to the cutter. Then, back in the kitchen, he picked up the boy and carried him out to the wagon, stamping in the snow. After wrapping John under heavy blankets in the cutter, William turned the horses across the frozen wheat stubble toward town, the runners hissing across the hard crust of snow.

The air was biting and crisp, and William pulled a great breath into his lungs and held it. The sun was bright in a cloudless blue sky, and it turned the snow banks into sparkling drifts that hurt to look at for too long. The wind had sculpted the drifts gathered around stone piles in the corner of the fields and putting William in mind of cresting waves on a rough sea back home. He felt more hopeful as Chub and Florie fell into a rhythm as they cut across the fields. John, snugged in so tightly he could only slightly move his swaddled head from side to side, peeked out over the brown woollen scarf around his face and nodded as William pointed out the dot-dot-dash-dash of rabbit tracks.

"How are you getting on there?" William asked, leaning over to check on his son. The morning's worry suddenly lifted, and he laughed at his son's big eyes peering over his muffler, lashes already tipped with frost. "John, my boy. You put me in mind of a morepork. That's a wee spotted owl where I come from across the sea. They have big round eyes just like yours. When I was a lad, I'd hear them at night, making their funny noises. The Maori thought it sounded like *ruru*, and we thought it was *more pork*, so that's how it got its name."

John blinked at his father and mumbled something behind his muffler, and William looked off at the horizon. "There was a little song about the morepork," he said. "We used to sing it in fourth form a long time ago. A very long time indeed. How did it go, now?"

He sang out bits of a tune just above the shushing of runners on the snow.

> *"There's a queer little bird lives far, far away.*
> *So far at the back of the world.*
> *And all that queer little bird finds to say..."*

"Hmmm, humm. How did it go?" Remembering, William leaned down and sang on with gusto, belting out the lyrics to John's delight.

> *"At morn, at night, and again at midday*
> *is 'morepork,' 'morepork.'*
> *An old man with a hoarse, croaking note..."*

"And then what's the next bit?"

"There's another close by who repeats as by rote…"

"And, ah, yes…"

"And now gives his vote for more pork!"

"More pork!" John cried out from behind his muffler.

William grinned. John put his head back and looked up at his father from under the brim of the knitted cap. William drew another lungful of the cold air and held it. It felt good, this. It felt like he could draw a complete breath, as though his chest was opening up, his ribs realigning to their proper place. It was right, doing something for his wife and baby girl. "We'll get this sorted, my boy. The men of the house are up to the task," he said and gave John's muffler a tug. "Ha, Chub. Florie! Let's go!" He slapped the leather reins down on the horses' rumps, and they picked up their pace, taking the shortcut across the fields to town.

An hour later, Chub and Florie steamed in the cold air, stamped and jostled under creaking harnesses, and busied themselves with feedbags. William tossed a burlap blanket over each of them and then held up his arms to lift John down from the wagon. He carried the boy up on the porch and knocked on the district nurse's door.

"SHE JUST DOESN'T SEEM TO CARE, YOU UNDERSTAND," William tried to explain as he shrugged off his coat and unwound the scarf from his neck. "She said she didn't want any more children after John, but I thought it was just melancholy. Mind, she wasn't happy when there was to be another." William cleared his throat. "This time, it's been a fortnight since she's been right." He got down on his knee to attend to the boy.

Nelda Rees pulled a kettle from the stovetop and reached for mugs in her cupboard while William tugged and pulled, helping John struggle out of his layers of clothing.

"I believe a woman might have a better insight, and a nurse at that. I thought of having a chat with Hanusia Yuzik, but she's not the warmest of sorts, and Dr. Speight doesn't seem too approachable on the subject, so I came here instead," William explained, rubbing some feeling back into his fingers. "I don't know what else to do.

"The doctor, well, he still thinks our baby isn't quite right," William went on, turning his cap. Pins and needles were painfully creeping into his fingers. The tip of the little one he froze during that first winter would ache for hours. He laid his cap on the table and sat in the chair the nurse offered. John came to stand next to his father, grasping a fold of pant leg.

Nelda set the mug of tea in front of him, and William took it thankfully. "Ta," he said. "Lovely." He felt some relief spread through him like the warmth from a fire. She handed a small cup of milky tea and a piece of soft ginger biscuit to John, who grinned and plopped down on the floor.

"Mind your manners, John, there's a good boy," William said.

"Thank you!" John chirped, his cheeks still rosy from the trip to town.

"You're welcome, John," the nurse said. "That's one, and there's more where it came from. You just sing out when you'd like another." Nelda turned to William. "It's not uncommon for a new mother to be a little out of sorts," she suggested, pulling up her chair to face William across the table.

She was a round, soft Welsh woman with a presence that was strong and reassuring. She had big square hands, but they were quick and certain. She wound a stray bit of once-red hair back in place and jabbed a loose bobby pin back in to secure it. Her voice was firm but soothing, and William appreciated the crow's feet around her eyes. *A sign of good humour*, he thought.

"I see it now and then," she said. "Depression. It happens

after childbirth, that sort of melancholy. Usually doesn't last more than a few days. When was your girl born?"

"Just over a fortnight ago." William leaned forward. "I'm afraid my wife's just given up. There was another little girl once, you see, in her care at an institution back in Ontario. The child died. Quite tragic, really. Louise always felt responsible since the child was in her care. It wasn't her fault," he added quickly. He sipped his tea. "This baby is much like that child, you know, and I think she may feel it's too much to be reminded of it all again. I think it perhaps was more of a trauma to her than she ever realized. More than I ever knew . . ." He fell silent.

Nelda nodded and patted William's hand. "One needn't be a student of psychology to know, Mr. Burke, that a newborn and its mother want to be close. It's nature's powerful way." The nurse paused and cocked her head to the side, studying him.

William took a quick gulp of tea, frustrated and embarrassed at the tears springing into his eyes.

The nurse grasped his hand and paid no attention to the tea that slopped onto her tablecloth. "My God, if only some of the other farmers I've come across would pay this much attention to the state their wives were in after childbirth. Hang on." She tapped her forehead with her finger. "I just remembered. I have just the thing for the moment." She got up and went to the kitchen. Opening the cupboard over the sink, she took out a small flask and pulled out the cork with her teeth. When she sat down again, two small glasses pinched between her fingers, she leaned across the table and poured a healthy measure of brandy into each. "Medicinal purposes, of course." She winked. "Drink up and get some warmth into your skin. You should see the sight of your face. Come on, just a sip. It'll do you good. "

William gratefully did as he was told.

"Now, Mr. Burke, as I was saying. It's nature, and if your wife is trying to battle a force of nature by turning her back on her baby, then she won't be the one coming out on top. Whoever saw a mare and a colt at opposite ends of the pasture? What Louise needs is a honeymoon with this baby. She needs friends to come by and congratulate her. Make a fuss. You say your baby is healthy otherwise?"

William set down his glass and pulled a handkerchief from his pocket. He wiped his forehead and blew his nose. He carefully folded the cloth in quarters. "Right as rain." He suddenly felt weak, his limbs heavy. He wasn't sure if it was from gratitude or the brandy or perhaps a pleasant mixture of the two. "At least that's what the doctor says. For now. Well," William hesitated. "He wants to pay attention to her heart as she grows a bit. He mentioned a murmur, an offbeat. He suspected pleurisy. As I said, he's even suggested, well, sending the child away. But she's a beautiful wee thing, a box of fluffy ducks she is, quite strong. She has lovely blonde hair."

"Fluffy ducks," John agreed from the floor. "Her fluffy ducks."

Nelda snorted. "Then you need to love this baby fiercely, Mr. Burke, and to hell with Speight. Compassion isn't that man's strong suit. He's a young man, but he acts a hundred sometimes. You and your son here," Nelda insisted, handing John another gingersnap. She held up the flask, and William nodded. She poured. "You're what that little girl's got if she's going to amount to anything in this world. As for pleurisy or a bad heart, well, time will tell. The two of you love her, and your wife will learn to do the same once she gets over her spell. Comes the sun to the hill, don't you worry. You'll see."

Sometime later, with a near-empty flask between them, William shook Nelda's big hand vigorously, feeling better and warmer than he had in a long while. He wanted to kiss the woman. Instead, he pumped her hand so hard she began to laugh. He wound John's scarf around the boy's face, leaving a slit for his eyes, helped the boy on with his coat and mittens and buckled his galoshes. He still had the hinges to pick up, and he remembered the trace he'd taken in last week to get re-stitched at Jamieson's

Harness. If he pushed the horses, they'd be home well before teatime.

And ribbons. It suddenly occurred to him that Bjorndahl's was on the way to Jamieson's. Wouldn't Louise love a piece of velvet ribbon for her hair? Yellow, perhaps. A small gift might lift her spirits.

"Thank you, Miss Rees. I feel so much better now," William said. "A load off, I can tell you. I'm sure Louise will come 'round." He pulled his cap down over his ears. "And I'll tell her what you said about coming out to see her in a few days. I'm sure she'd enjoy the female company. And thank you for the, uh, tea. Did me a world of good. You can't imagine."

"Ah, Mr. Burke, there's nothing like a good strong cup of tea to lift the spirits." She bent down and pulled John's earflap up so he could hear. "You be a good boy, John, and look after your new sister. You have an important job there because she'll need you to help quite a bit. Can you do it?"

John's swaddled head bobbed, and he mumbled something behind his muffler.

"I will look forward to meeting her, John," Nelda said solemnly, "and it was so nice to meet you." She extended her hand and grasped his woollen mitten for a shake. "Tell your mother I'll be out to see her by week's end."

"My sister." John pulled the muffler down. "Violet."

LOUISE

THE BURKE FARM, 1920

Nelda Rees was enthusiastic about the baby, deliberately pointing out the infant's "lovely golden hair and pretty blue eyes." Louise noticed that she focused on the shape of the child's eyes and her tiny ears, the floppy limbs, but for now, at least, kept any worries to herself.

"Looks healthy as a horse, your sister," Nelda announced, carefully placing the bundled infant in John's outstretched arms. He sat ramrod straight beside Louise on the bed. "Careful now, watch her head. Her skinny little neck isn't strong enough yet to hold her head up, so I'll lay her down in your arms. There you are! You're a natural big brother, John! I've never seen anything like it. Have you, Missus?"

Nelda gathered up her things and popped them back into her black bag. "She's strong, and I think she's healthy, Mrs. Burke. We'll just have to wait and see about the heart." She snapped her bag shut. "It's just too early to tell, but it might be wise to keep the child away from others with colds or sniffles. It's not been long since that dreadful influenza, and the diphtheria before that, so any measure that could increase her resistance to respiratory problems is always a good idea." She paused. "Now, you know there are those who subscribe to the notion that Manitou Beach waters have quite strong healing powers. Dr. Speight would never admit it, but they say the medicinal properties are of a higher degree than that famous German spring. I can't quite recall the name. Anyway, it might not hurt for you and the baby to have a good soak at the beach from time to time this spring. Wouldn't a little paddle in the lake be fun, John?"

John sat straight against the headboard, gripping his sister, his rosy cheeks flushed. He nodded vigorously.

Louise had dressed for the nurse's visit, and William took her hand. Louise glanced in the small mirror on her dresser, and saw there was at least some colour in her face, too. Her eyes, though, seemed lifeless. She tilted her head to see if the grey shadows beneath them would disappear. They didn't. She fingered the end of her braid and rubbed her finger along the smooth silk of the ribbon. William had asked her to put it in her hair, and she'd only done it for him.

"John. Give your poor wee sister some room to breathe!" John's head was bowed over the baby, and he was smothering her with kisses. Violet gurgled and spit, and John giggled.

"She smell good!" John announced. "My sister smell good!"

Louise laughed for the first time since Violet's birth. The raspy sound seemed foreign; it had been so long since she'd heard it. It felt jagged and sharp in her throat. She had to swallow, and thought about shards of glass.

THE NEXT DAY, WILLIAM TOOK CONTROL.

Louise picked at a loose thread on the edge of the quilt and slowly unravelled it.

"We're a family, Louise," he said. "Violet was created for a reason, and she is who she is meant to be. Nothing more. Nothing less." He set a cup of tea on the nightstand near the washbasin. "Violet's not a runt pig we knock on the head. She's our little girl. There will be no talk of sending anyone away. We'll help her and look after one another. We'll teach her. She'll be right as rain, you'll see."

The doctor's advice to send Violet to an institution was never mentioned again. But it hung unspoken between them, like an electrical charge in the air, the sort to portend a coming storm.

Louise withdrew deeper into herself. Food had always been a comfort, but now the sight and smell nearly made her retch. She rarely went into town. In church on Sundays, she avoided the eyes of her neighbours.

"They're talking about the baby," she said to William, staring at her hands folded in her lap. "I can tell. They think it's my fault, that I did something to make her this way. It's usually because of the mother when a child is like this."

"No one thinks any such thing," William said, the baby sleeping soundly in his arms. John sat between them.

The dust of Sarah had settled on them once again.

WILLIAM LET THE COWS OUT TO PASTURE BEYOND THE slough in April. Louise, leaning in the doorway, could see him just beyond the budding willows, where he checked the eastern slope. He had mentioned he thought it must be time for crocus, and sure enough, he found a patch had sprung up almost overnight. The blue flowers pushed up from the ground, drawn by the thin warmth of morning sunshine.

Louise saw him disappear over the rise. In a few moments, he walked back toward the house. He fished a piece of twine from his pocket and tied it around a small bundle, then let himself back through the gate by the barn. She quickly stepped back out of sight into the kitchen, pulled the door to, and busied herself at the stove. She could hear him stomp the dirt from his boots on the stoop before he flung open the door and waved the crocus bouquet before him.

"Behold!" he cried and held the flowers out to Louise. "I present you with springtime!"

Louise had hoped her gloomy outlook would change now that the days were growing longer, that the trapped feeling she'd had during the cold winter would disappear. But now, she felt an unreasonable pang of anger. *How could he be so cheerful?*

John looked up from the table and waved the spoon gripped in one fist. Oatmeal plopped on the floor. "Uh oh!" he said, his mouth round. He looked at his mother, a furrow set over his eyes. "Mama is not happy again," he insisted. "Mama is not happy all the time, and Violet makes her sad."

Louise dropped the ladle into the pot on the stove and fled from the room.

"Not to worry, John," William said. He laid the flowers on the kitchen windowsill. "Eat up your porridge now, there's a good boy. Mother is all right."

William followed Louise into the bedroom, where she sat on the bed, wiping her nose with a handkerchief. He stood in the doorway.

"He's right. I can't even hide it from him. Spring doesn't change anything," she whispered. She took a breath, and the words tumbled out. "The looks, I see them," she said, a deep frown cutting across her brow. "People look at me with pity. I can tell some are disgusted that I would bring such a child into the world."

"Sweetheart, most people haven't seen you at all," William said, sitting beside her. "Not since Dr. Speight ordered bed rest for you before Violet was born."

"I've seen that look, William, the one they give children like Violet," Louise said, her voice shrill. "At Orillia, the parents, the ones who came to visit their children, milling together like strangers. They practically ran out when it was time to leave. They thought what they had created was some sort of penalty for some horrible thing they'd done." Louise felt her face grow warm and knew red blotches bloomed on her full cheeks. She stared at her husband. She knew he felt helpless, but she couldn't muster any words to reassure him when she had none for herself.

As Violet grew from baby to toddler to a four-year-old, Louise felt she was still "the baby." She rarely called her "Violet." Never "my daughter." It was confounding to her that William and even Hank didn't seem to pay any heed to how backward Violet obviously was, how deficient she seemed, especially compared to John. A nagging voice within her reminded her that Violet needed just as much love and attention as John, but whenever the voice grew insistent, Louise pushed it down into silence. It was Hank who irritated her the most. Clearly, he saw a difference in the children, but he treated them the same, and for some reason that eluded Louise, it merely fuelled her anger.

"Look at my two little shadows!" Hank called out one autumn afternoon. He'd come by to help William oil the horses' breast collars and leather laces. Louise, pinning flour sacks up on the line, turned and looked across the farmyard at John and Violet, each with their arms clamped around Hank's legs. With each child sitting on a foot, shrieking and laughing, Hank struggled around in a circle as though he was mired in mud.

At four, Violet was still unsteady on her feet and preferred to crawl everywhere. When she was with Hank, it seemed her feet rarely touched the ground. She simply held up her arms to be swept up onto his shoulders.

Louise shielded her eyes with one hand to watch as the children let go of their ride. Hank reached down beside the shed. He selected a blade of grass, pressed it between his thumbs, and brought it to his lips. He blew. With every squawk and whistle, the children squealed and giggled. Violet clapped her hands. William stepped out onto the porch and laughed, and they watched Hank's lumbering progress across the yard, the children having reattached themselves to his legs.

"That boy is as good as an uncle, that's the truth. And Violet, she is growing like a weed now, stronger every day," William said.

Louise went back to pinning clothes on the line. "How easy it is for Hank. And you," she said. "Hank can't see it, but you must realize that Violet will always be so much less than John."

William sighed and pulled on his barn coat. "I'm off to rescue him. When we get the tack sorted, we'll be moving some machinery out to the wheat this afternoon. I'll be back in time for tea."

"John!" Louise called out, and the children, still clinging to Hank's legs, looked up. "Bring your sister to the porch. It's time for a haircut."

"Do you have to?" William turned, his arm halfway into a sleeve. "I do love her hair. She'll look like such a boy with her hair short."

"Easier to look after," she insisted curtly. Softening at the look on William's face, she said, "She can't even comb it herself or keep it tidy. It's just another chore for me. Long hair is really just a bother."

"Don't tell that to Samson," William protested.

"It would be different if she would let me braid it, but she won't. She cries when I try to put it up for her. There's always a rat's nest at the back." Louise pulled the scissors from her apron pocket.

William shrugged his coat on and headed out across the yard to pry Hank loose from the children. She watched him go, and when it was clear John and Violet were paying no attention, Louise put her hands on her hips and called out to William, "Send her back to the house. I've got bread dough that needs punching down, so I want to get this over with."

She saw Violet's shoulders sag when William untangled the children from Hank's legs. He pointed at the house and bent low to kiss her cheek. She trudged back toward Louise. Her hair did look tidy, even after the roughhousing, and for a moment, Louise felt a pang of guilt. The sun brought out such a shine in it, and

William was right; the girl did look almost pretty. Maybe she could try again. If Violet would only let her comb it out when it got snarled, putting it in braids would keep it neat until bath day. The yellow velvet ribbons were still hidden away in her keepsake box. Wouldn't Violet love to have those for church one day? Louise tapped her finger on the end of the shears and slid them back into her apron pocket.

Halfway across the yard, Tom, one of the barn cats, picked its way through the grass by the fence, a deep growl in his chest and the remnants of a large grey rat hanging limp from his jaws. Violet tried to pick up the cat, but he skirted around her outstretched arms and stopped again to watch her approach.

Louise stepped down from the porch. "Here now, Violet. You leave that cat alone and come here!"

Tom growled but dropped the rat and prodded it with a paw. Suddenly disinterested, the cat walked off stiff-legged, then slid under the fence and disappeared in the tall grass. Violet squatted and poked the dead rat with her finger. "Wake up!" she cried and then picked it up, holding it to her chest. "Wake up, kitty!" she said and petted it just as Louise came around the corner of the porch. The rat was damp with spittle, the remnants of its head bloody where the cat had gnawed.

Louise ran to her, grabbed her arm, and slapped the rat from Violet's hands. "Drop that filthy thing! That's dirty, for heaven's sake!" Louise kicked the rat with the toe of her shoe, and it cartwheeled through the dirt, bits of entrails in its wake.

Violet began to shriek and tried to pull away, her cheeks flushed with anger. Violet was not prone to tantrums, but taking away a kitten or a baby chick could set her off. She cried and sagged into the dirt. Louise tugged on her arm, trying to get her to stand. "Violet, that's a dead rat. Now, do as I say!" She pulled on the girl and noticed with disgust that Violet had managed to get bits of rat guts and blood in her hair. "Well, that settles the question about your haircut today, doesn't it?" Louise said firmly, grasping the back of Violet's dress and hauling her back to the porch, where she plunked her solidly on the stool.

"Stop this fussing and stay still, or I'll end up cutting you," Louise demanded, and slung a towel around Violet's shoulders. She stood behind Violet, who was crying more quietly now, and pushed her head forward. With no time or patience to measure or make sure her cuts were straight, Louise ran the scissors around the back of Violet's neck, clipping into a snarled curl and snipping out the few gory bits of blood.

She came around to face the girl and took her chin in one hand. "You hold very still now, Violet. I need to trim your bangs." Violet's face was still crumpled with woe, and her anguish made Louise pull in a deep breath. She always found it hard to look into Violet's almond-shaped eyes. "Violet, please. When we're done, I'll give you a sugar cookie, but now you must be very still." Louise snipped a good inch above the girl's eyebrows, stood back, evened out a little on one side, and stood back again to look. Violet sniffed.

"You know that wasn't a kitty," Louise said more gently. "That was a rat, and they have lice. You don't want to get nasty lice. We'll all get them, and then I'll have to be doing a hot-water wash of all our clothes and the bed linens and picking nits out of everyone's hair." Louise swept the towel away and shook it over the porch railing.

Violet pulled at the blunt ends of her bangs and scratched at the back of her neck. She slid down from the stool.

"We're not done yet!" Louise hollered. "I must wash your hair now. All those beastly germs and muck. I won't have the pillow-cases ruined."

Violet thrust out her chin and leveled her gaze at Louise. "It was a kitty," she insisted and went inside the house.

LOUISE

THE BURKE FARM, 19

Louise knew Violet looked forward to church on Sundays, always trying to push her way in first to sit between her father and brother. If Violet didn't get into the pew fast enough, Louise would firmly sit her down and grasp her hands painfully to shush her into stillness. Violet twisted her hair, knowing a fidget would be cause for reproach and a stinging slap on her thigh. Louise had been mortified the week before when Violet, in a starched new dress, slid down the length of the pew, the bare skin on her legs making such a squeal on the polished wood that most of the congregation turned to see the source of such an ungodly noise. Time at church was to be endured quietly; she was not about to have the child become a regular spectacle.

But when Violet sat between John and William, just out of Louise's reach, she strained to lift her own voice with the congregation and clapped her hands during the hymns when the organ music nearly lifted her off the pew. People looked up from their hymnals, recognizing the off-key Burke girl, and some would smile.

"Violet. Watch now," William whispered, putting his hat over his knee, pulling Violet closer to him in the pew. "Here is the church." He folded his hands and laced his fingers, his thumbs crossed. "Here is the steeple. Open the doors." Violet pulled his thumbs away, and he opened his palms. "Where are the people?" Violet giggled, and Louise leaned forward with a frown.

"Shhhh, Violet. Try again." William leaned down until their foreheads touched, folded his hands again with his fingers inside. "Here is the steeple—" Before he could get further, Violet yanked his thumbs, and he wiggled his fingers.

"See all the people! Again!" Violet whispered hoarsely.

"Not now, Violet, my girl," William said in her ear, pressing his hands together and stealing a glance at Louise. "We're meant to be praying now."

At home, with no one to see, Violet could conduct church as she liked, singing for the chickens, for old Hannah and the other milk cows in the barn. Sometimes when Louise was tossing feed to the chickens, she could hear Violet's thin, discordant voice as she led her choir through the same verse over and over. Louise felt a pang of guilt, and as she listened, she thought she should take the time to teach Violet the proper words to the hymn.

> "Infant holy, infant lowly
> For His bed, the cows and all
> Oxen roly, roly poly
> Christ, the baby Lord and all—"

Violet was careful not to leave out the beef cattle in the pasture. They would calmly lift their heads and regard her with big glassy eyes, their jaws working rhythmically across their cud. "You are a good girl and boys. You sit nice now in church and be polite!" With their heads low to the ground while they pulled at tufts of grass, one or two would let Violet wrap her arms around their necks. Louise wondered why the cows seemed so docile around the child. It was almost as if they knew to be careful while they grazed around her.

"John, I need flowers! Come help me," Violet pleaded one afternoon.

Louise was hanging the wash on the line by the garden. "John, go with her. Keep an eye out, and don't go too far," Louise said, taking a clothespin from her apron pocket. "She seems a bit tired today."

"Okay, I have to find some leaves for my nature study and outdoor good manners project anyways." John grabbed the berry basket from its nail on the porch. At the fence, he held up the barbed wire while Violet wiggled through. When they reached the slope by the slough, Violet lay down and rolled through a patch of clover, scattering grasshoppers and cabbage moths into the air. John followed her.

"You better not get stung by a bee, Violet!" John headed toward the wolf willow by the water. "Come on and help me get some leaves. I'll let you paste some on paper for my project. "

Soon John announced he had enough poplar and wolf willow and a few perfect maple specimens. He found Violet sitting in the grass. John looked toward the house. Louise, the laundry basket on her hip now, waved him back. "I'm getting hungry," he said. "You want to go in for lunch?" John reached for Violet's handful of prairie wool, bluebells, and yellow daises. "Here, let's put those in the basket. You feeling all right, Violet? Your heart all fluttery?"

Violet nodded, tucking a purple clover blossom into the basket.

"Come on then, climb up," John said, squatting in the grass. "I'll give you a piggyback. Pull yourself up more, Violet, so I can get a grip on you. Here, grab this and don't spill out all the leaves and flowers." As he staggered to straighten up, he hoisted his sister for a better hold around her legs. "I sure hope your heart gets better soon so you can walk by your own self."

Violet put her arms around John's neck. "Ow, jeepers," he said. "Quit poking your bones into me."

"I sorry, John," Violet said. She laid her head on his shoulder.

"Come on," John shouted. "I'll give you a horsey ride! Giddy up!"

Louise waited while the children came across the yard, John

high-stepping, Violet's head bobbing, her face flushed from laughing. Louise had to smile, and she held the door open for the horse and rider.

LOUISE AND WILLIAM HAD PUT IT OFF AS LONG AS THEY could, hoping Violet would grow stronger, but finally, decisions about school had to be made. That evening, after both children were in bed, they sat at the kitchen table with their cups of tea.

William talked hopefully about the day Violet would begin school. "She'll be fine," he insisted. "Not to worry. We've been right to keep her back just a little while. She gets so out of breath. But once she's stronger, off she'll go, with John to mind her. Violet's just a little slow, but she'll be fine, darling. This fall. She'll catch up, you'll see."

Louise reached for another raisin scone and a butter knife. She recalled not wanting to ever eat again after Violet was born. Now, a warm biscuit seemed to fill, at least for a little while, that terrible emptiness that was always there in her gut.

DR. SPEIGHT HAD NOT LIKED THE SOUND OF VIOLET'S heart when he last examined the child, and he liked the blue tinge of her lips even less now.

"Pleurisy still seems like a strong possibility. A murmur, perhaps. There's something not right, you can be sure. As I've long suspected, her heart's not the best, that's certain."

Louise nodded, avoiding William's gaze as though agreeing with the doctor was a disloyalty. "She tires easily and struggles to keep up with John when they play out of doors," she said, "and even the short walk down to the slough is too much. Sometimes, John has to fetch one of us to come and carry her back. At the table, she falls asleep in the middle of her supper."

Louise had seen it often enough during the years she had worked at the institution. Bad hearts. Hearts with holes. Not enough blood circulating in the body. Or to the brain. Violet would never keep up. She would never grow up. Why was it so hard for William to accept this?

"She should be taught to make her own adjustment," Dr. Speight said over Violet's head. He pressed the cold stethoscope on her chest. "She needs guidance toward an acceptance of a life more restricted than John's or other children's. And with her mind feeble as it is, you'll have your work cut out to teach her. You need to protect her from anything that will increase the amount of work her heart has to do."

Violet pulled the stethoscope from her chest and put it to her lips. "Mooo cow!" she bellowed. Dr. Speight yanked the instrument from his ears and put it away in his bag. His frown cut a deep furrow between his eyebrows, and he cleared his throat.

"She has," he said sternly, pulling his earlobe, "unavoidable limitations."

"I THINK WHAT SHE HAS IS A SUNNY DISPOSITION," William said, pulling on his barn jacket while Louise ran a peeler around another potato. "Did you hear what Mildred Dechant said last week? Remember when you had done up Violet's hair? She said she was just like sunshine with all those pretty yellow curls and ribbons. I'm so pleased Violet lets you do it for her now. You were right about keeping it short. You can still tie it up in rags, so she's pretty for church."

"I don't like the way she's so willing to go to people, William," Louise said. She dropped a potato in the bowl of water and reached for another. "She can be polite without asking to be picked up. It's not appropriate."

"Violet likes everybody," John said.

"She is trusting, that's the truth," William said, lifting Violet into his arms. "But she's just a child. People understand that."

"She's seven. She's small, but she's really almost eight. We must be very firm with her about hugging and going with strangers," Louise insisted. "She cannot be allowed to embarrass people. All this grabbing and hugging people is unseemly, William."

"Oh, come now, Louise." William put an arm around Louise's shoulders. "She's just friendly and good-natured. Fluffy ducks, Louise. I don't want to spoil that in her. I don't want her to think liking people is naughty."

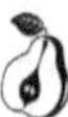

On Thursday, William drove the family into town in the buggy. John hopped out, anxious for a look around. William lifted Violet from the seat and bounced her in the crook of his arm. A rough voice that sounded like boots on gravel brought Louise out of her brooding while they strolled along the boardwalk in front of Whitmore's Bakeshop. "Hello! You, hello there!" It was Nik Yuzik, rough and loud as usual.

Sometimes Nik came by with potato wine and sat with William on the porch until well after midnight. The temperance movement in Saskatoon and Watrous had closed the bars three years ago, but they couldn't slow down Nik. More than once, she had ended up holding a bucket for William in the hours after Nik had gone home. Most recently, Nik complained as he stumbled out to his wagon that this latest batch must be *"smerdit."* Louise assumed that meant it had spoiled.

Louise hardly knew Nik's wife, despite her help with John and Violet's births. Even then, there hadn't been much warmth, and ever since Violet, Hanusia would only nod if they passed on the street in town. It was strange that she seemed so distant when they had shared something as raw and intimate as the birth of each child, but Hanusia made no effort to be cordial.

Once, when John and Violet were still small, Nik had encouraged William and Louise and the children to come along to a jitney dance on the east beach at Lake Manitou. The new dance hall had just opened and was all the rage, with horsehair burlap under the hardwood—a bouncy floor for polkas and foxtrots. Nik had quite a bit of wine even before they arrived, and during the evening, he picked up Violet and danced her around, nearly falling over a chair. Hanusia tried to pull Violet away. Violet held on and cried; the Yuziks went home after that scene. Louise had the impression the evening had not been Hanusia's idea.

"Hello, Burkes. *Dobray ranok*," Nik called now, striding toward them, his big hand already extended for a shake.

Hanusia, pinched and thin, her head covered by a pink-and-green flowered kerchief, followed her husband, baby Stefan on her hip. Louise couldn't be sure, but there seemed to be a swell in the woman's middle. *Oh, my, another child already*, Louise thought. There had been talk of another stillbirth not long ago. Louise felt a pang of sympathy and hoped for the woman's sake this one would be that girl Nik wanted.

The four older boys, topped with dishevelled black hair like their father's, sinewy and pale like their mother, trailed behind. The children, open-mouthed, fixed their eyes on Violet. Louise noticed that their mother looked at Violet in much the same way. She kept a distance, with her chin down on her chest.

It was odd to remember that it was Hanusia who seemed to protest the doctor's grim diagnosis when Violet was born. Now, it was as if whatever was wrong with Violet might be something catching if inhaled. *She told me her oldest, Andrij, was a difficult birth, and he was not so smart*, Louise recalled. *Maybe a girl was different.*

Nik grasped Violet's small hands in his big ones and winked at her. A grin crinkled his eyes, and a smile spread across his stubbled face. It was clear to everyone Nik had always wanted a daughter, something softer and more affectionate than his sharp-edged wife and five bony, colourless sons. "Hello you, little *fialka*," Nik clucked.

Violet giggled and laid her face against William's hat.

"*Dobray ranok*, Violet. Look, such a big girl you are now. How can your father carry you? You are too big for carrying."

"Moo cow!" Violet squealed and threw herself from William's shoulders toward Nik so quickly that he barely had time to catch her. Louise's cry caught in her throat, and she reached to pull Violet back. Hanusia jerked her arm out as if to keep the boys behind her. She gripped the baby so tightly against her chest that Stefan's face screwed up in discomfort and surprise.

But Violet laughed, her arms tightly wound around Nik's neck. He bounced her in his arms. "This one, she knows handsome farmer when she sees!" He poked Violet under her arm with a big finger until she squealed. "You better watch out, Hanusia. *Tse moya ni lyeepsha diwchyna*. Looks maybe like I have new girlfriend!"

A tic flicked at the corner of Hanusia's mouth.

William reached out and took Violet back into his own arms, then boosted her up over his head to ride on his shoulders again.

Andrij, the older boy, and Mihaylo begged their mother to let them run down and look at Wald's confectionery display. Mrs. Wald, round enough to be her own best customer, sold penny candies. There were bulls' eyes, jawbreakers, licorice pipes, and horehound candy sticks, all displayed tantalizingly in the front window. Louise thought Hanusia must have said there wasn't money for such things. She spoke in Ukrainian, shushing them, and the boys slumped against the bakery storefront. Ilko sat down on the boardwalk and sighed heavily.

"I come by maybe tomorrow," Nik said to William finally when the younger boys began to whine. Baby Stefan grunted and pushed against Hanusia's chest in a vain attempt to get down on the sidewalk with Ilko. "We should talk maybe about what to do with that piece of land by the coulee," Nik said.

William agreed.

"And hello to you, Missus," Nik said to Louise, touching the brim of his hat. "Bye-bye, big girl!" He reached up over William's head and patted Violet's cheeks.

"Moo cow!" Violet cried. She bounced in William's arms until he put her down and straightened her dress.

Hanusia shifted a fussing Stefan to her other hip and yanked at Ilko's hair. Ilko complained, rubbed his head, and got to his feet to follow with only a quick last look over his shoulder. He hitched up his pants. Violet waved. Ilko stared at her for a moment and stuck out his tongue before turning to follow the others.

Louise strained to hear Hanusia's whispers. She could only hear snippets of English, but she didn't need much to know what the woman was saying. ". . . that girl . . . *doornah*, feeble-minded," Hanusia hissed, glancing back over her shoulder. "Ones like that, my sister, not good she say. I help baby come in world, Nikolai, but . . . girls like that, my sister she say girls like that no good, keep away from the boys—"

Nik shrugged and waved a hand at his wife just as he would dismiss a lazy autumn fly looping around his ear.

Louise grasped Violet's shoulder and steered her down the boardwalk the other way toward the wagon. "We've got to teach Violet how to behave properly with people, with strangers," Louise said, leaning toward William.

"Nik Yuzik isn't a stranger," William protested. "He was one of the first people I met when I came here. He's a good man. Violet has known him since she was a baby. All the times he's been to the farm, to our house. He gives her horsey rides on his foot on our front porch, Louise."

"Maybe so, but it's plain that Violet is willing to go to anyone. She has no fear. You don't know what happens when people like Violet grow into their adult bodies." Louise lowered her voice as they walked past the café. "People may like kittens, but they don't like cats," she went on. "What may be cute now certainly won't be when she's older. And she's vulnerable, William. I saw it a hundred times. What's more, we can't always be with her. Someone could take advantage of her."

"Trust is not always a bad thing, Louise," William said.

Louise walked stiffly, her chin thrust out, her heels clacking a hollow echo on the boardwalk. "There are people out there who will take advantage of that trust, William. That, most assuredly, is a bad thing," Louise whispered, glancing back at the Yuziks to be certain she wasn't overheard. "Her situation invites bad types, ones who take advantage. Believe me, William, I know. You must watch people, no matter how painful it is. Anyone is capable."

"Oh, Louise," William said gently. "Hanusia Yuzik has changed a lot over the years. She is a queer old thing. I wouldn't put much stock into what she says about our Violet."

"It's not Hanusia I worry about."

LOUISE

THE BURKE FARM, AUGUST 1927

Louise was often lonely. Sometimes, such a solitary life, with only William and the children for days on end, left her longing for another adult to talk to, just a small change of pace. Today, with the children and their father away to town, she looked forward to a little female company. She listened for Erna Eckart's horse and wagon and peered anxiously out the kitchen window at every distant sound of passing car, tractor, or wagon. Erna had offered to bring by things she'd need for putting up fruit for the winter. It would be a welcome respite.

Erna had spoken about it after church the week before. "George loves peach preserves, but that's something you just don't get in this part of the country. So, we make do with what we have. Crabapples, chokecherries, saskatoons. You'll be up to your elbows in canning for the next two months. Most things come ready at once. I'll come by and help."

ERNA GRUNTED AS SHE LIFTED THE CRATE OF GLASS sealers over the side of the wagon and heaved it into Louise's waiting arms. "Have it? There's another one here. Just let me get it." She leaned back into the wagon and caught the corner of another crate. Dragging it out, she dropped a flour sack on top and followed Louise up onto the porch and inside the kitchen.

"George's cousin lives near Kaslo. Southern British Columbia." Erna stooped to put the crate on the floor beside the table. "They have a farm right on the shore of Kootenay Lake. He sent us a picture once." The glass sealer lids and metal rings clinked when she put the cloth bag on the table. "You'll want to check those lids for cracks. I just had so many. When my mother died, my father told me to take all her canning things. I was glad to make some room in the cellar."

"I don't know if it'll turn out, but I'd like to try," Louise said, wiping the dust from her hands on her apron. "My Auntie Freda sent me a very encouraging letter. She's a wonderful cook."

Louise dipped water from the barrel, poured it into the kettle, and put it on the stove. She reached into the cupboard for the tea canister. "There's a big stand of saskatoons at the edge of the coulee just past the slough. Last summer, the bushes were just black."

"Oh, never give the location of a good saskatoon patch." Erna held up a finger. "You've got neighbour women who will strip those branches bare before the birds can even get to the first ripe one!"

"Would you have a cup of tea? You've time before you have to go back home?" Louise asked. "It's good to have company."

"I'd love to have tea. And I'll write down some of these recipes while we do."

Louise, almost giddy from Erna's company, went into the front room and reached on top of the small china cabinet for the key. Unlocking the door, she reached in and took out the pale yellow porcelain teapot and the good teacups, a wedding gift from her aunt and uncle. Auntie Freda made a point to tell Louise that if William was a tea drinker by birth, he should count on that in her new kitchen. Ordinary in Toronto, the pieces seemed almost absurd here.

She put them on a tray and carried it into the kitchen. "How lovely!" Erna said, putting a small red Betty Crocker cookbook on the table. She reached into her pocket and pulled out a large square of paraffin. She set the wax on top of the bag of lids. "Do you have a bit of paper? I'll just write a few out for you. I can come by, and we can put up some jars together if you don't understand my directions." Erna touched the curve of the teapot spout with her fingertip. "I just can't keep anything nice with a houseful of boys. How do you dare use them?"

"I hardly ever do," Louise said. "Violet's such a clumsy girl, I've never had them out when she's around. They'd be a pile of splinters and shards in a minute. I wait for the times she's occupied with her father before I dare take them out." Louise softened her voice when she saw the concern on Erna's face. "But, truth be told, I don't even let William touch them, though I think he'd be afraid to." Louise poured from the kettle on the stove and put the lid on the teapot.

While the tea steeped, Erna lifted her cup carefully. "Thin as paper, this is. How did it survive the trip from Toronto?"

"Wood shavings." Louise stood and reached for a round tin on the shelf above the water barrel. She pried off the lid and placed three sugar cookies on a plate.

"I started to tell you about George's cousin and got sidetracked." Erna gently replaced her cup in the saucer and stood. "He sent us some fruit. It came on the train. There's plenty, so I thought you might like to try your hand at some jam. It's early, and they're not quite ripe enough yet, but they could just sit under a cloth for a few more days. I brought the recipe, too. I won't be a moment."

Louise reached across the table and picked up the red cookbook. She leafed through the pages, and they fell open easily at well-used recipes—the pickled jackfish, Swedish rye crisps, and ginger snaps with "Hank's favourite" or "George loves" or preferences from the other boys in Erna's hand noted in the margins. Next to the recipe for sour cream cookies were notes about poisoning gophers.

The screen door creaked, but it was the smell that reached Louise before the sound. An unbidden image leaped into her head as clear and sharp as a knife blade, thrust deep by the cloying syrup smell, the unforgettable memory clinging like burnt sugar and rotten fruit.

Somehow Erna's voice seemed too loud when she held out the pail. Louise stared at it, her knees suddenly weak.

"I can't be sure what variety," Erna was saying. "Anjou or maybe Red Clapp and too far gone now for anything but jam. George's cousin sent enough to keep us in pear and ginger jam for the winter. The recipe is in that little book, I remember now. I put a scrap of paper to mark the place just after the applesauce. Hank just loves it on biscuits. Louise?" Erna paused and leaned forward to peer at Louise's face. Startled, she set the pail on the floor and reached for Louise's hand. "Whatever is the matter? You look like you're going to be ill."

"Oh. It's nothing, really, I just can't—" Louise waved her hand over the pail and turned. Her elbow swept her teacup and saucer off the table. They shattered against the side of the woodstove.

"Oh, my goodness, no! Louise!" Erna jumped up, reached for Louise, and caught her arm. "That's my fault. I must have bumped the pail on the table and shook—I am so sorry, Louise! Your beautiful teacup!"

Louise knelt and began to pick up the larger pieces, and Erna got down beside her.

"Careful now not to cut yourself," Erna said. "The little pieces are like needles."

Louise sat back and put her hand to her mouth. Erna looked into her flushed face, trying to make sense of the disaster. "Are you cut? Let me see!"

"I'm sorry," Louise said. Erna helped her up from the floor and eased her down on the chair. "It's nothing, really. Nothing."

"It most certainly isn't nothing," Erna said. "Tell me what's the matter. Look here." Erna opened the cupboard door and took out a sturdy mug. She carefully emptied the remaining teacup into it and handed it to Louise. She set the teacup carefully in the centre of the kitchen table. "Let's not take any chance with that one." She pulled down another mug for herself, poured from the pot, and sat down on her own chair. "Now, what on earth is it?"

"It may be a relief to say." Louise pressed her hands to her cheeks. "I've carried it inside for so long. I hadn't thought of it for ages, but it's—" She pulled a handkerchief from her apron pocket and wiped her eyes. "Pears, you see. I cannot abide pears."

Erna pressed her fingertips to her mouth. "Why on earth not? Such a fuss over pears!" Erna leaned forward and patted her arm. "It's one thing to not care for something. George will not tolerate milk toast, but I've never seen him in tears about it!"

"If I tell you, you must swear never to tell another living soul." Louise looked up at Erna, who nodded.

Louise's hands trembled as she lifted the mug and took a sip of tea, the hot liquid a welcome burn in her tight throat. "Back home, I went to work in Orillia at an institution for the feeble-minded. A friend's mother worked there in the kitchen. There were hundreds of people there, some so crippled and defective that grown men and women were kept in cribs with lids so they couldn't get out. But there were others who didn't seem to have anything wrong with them at all. Maybe they just had families who couldn't or wouldn't keep them. Often, they were just poor. One young boy, Ted, just stole a bottle of milk. He'd been there four years." She swallowed, hard.

"My Lord. There's a place like that in Weyburn," Erna said. "I think it was built in the early '20s. George's second cousin worked there for a while. All sorts of awful things went on, like sterilizing them, keeping them in isolation. He said the girls were bound to become prostitutes, the boys criminals. He said a doctor in New

York opened a child's skull. The girl—an imbecile, was what he said—but after they did some sort of surgery, she woke up and recognized her mother. I really don't know if that's true. It's just what he said."

"When I first got to Orillia, I helped in the kitchen and the dining hall. I didn't mind the work, and many of the people I saw were the smart ones. Many even had jobs, though they were never paid like the real staff. We worked together during the day, but they had to return to their wards at night. One or two helped us in the kitchen. Some had been there for years."

Louise paused for a long time and gazed out the kitchen window. She watched one of the chickens scratching through the rocks at the edge of the driveway, the image distorted in the wavy glass. "I was stronger than some of the girls on staff, so when they saw that, they transferred me to the Baby Ward. There were no babies. They only called it that because most of them had to be diapered and fed. Some were violent, and we learned how to handle someone who was trying to go after us."

"Good heavens," Erna said. "How did you protect yourself?"

"Usually, we called for the male orderlies if we thought things were getting out of hand, or if the person was too wild for us to give them a shot or put them in restraints or in the Side Room. I hated the Baby Ward. It seemed we could never relax. We started seeing everyone on the ward as a threat, so we never trusted anyone who could have done with our attention. At best, we were cleaning them up, diapering, and feeding. At worst, we ended up with broken bones and black eyes. One could hardly blame them. I begged to be moved, but they said they were short-staffed. I had nightmares."

"Were you ever hurt?" Erna asked, her tea still untouched.

"Not by a patient." Louise paused and pressed her fingers to her forehead. Her throat tightened as if a fist bunched the collar of her dress.

"Go on," Erna urged.

Louise took a breath and began again. "The summer before I

planned to go back to Toronto, it was beastly hot," she said. "People died, and I'm sure it was from heat stroke, though people died now and then from suffocation. We took all the pillows away. Everyone was on edge. It seemed everyone just got angrier and angrier, staff and patients, like a pot of water ready to boil over."

"But I don't understand what all this has to do with pears," Erna said.

"Oh, I am rambling, aren't I?" Louise looked down into her mug and picked at the buttons on her collar. "This man, Bert, came to Orillia that August to work as an orderly." Saying his name aloud brought a bitter taste to her mouth. "His brother was the maintenance manager, so he pretty well did whatever he wanted to whomever he wanted. The institution was growing fast, so much construction. Nobody paid much attention to him.

"His family owned a pear and apple orchard near the lake. Not long after he arrived, we heard a rumour that he'd been in prison for doing something terrible to a young woman. They had found the girl in the orchard. She had gone missing, and everyone was searching. Her brother found her. There were rumours about this Bert, but nothing was ever proven, and the police finally said she just ran away and got lost." Louise lifted her shoulders slightly. "He seemed to almost enjoy his job more when people were upset, hard to handle. One nurse complained about him, and she was dismissed."

Erna frowned and opened her mouth, but Louise held up her hand. "I know, the pears. He always had them in his pocket. Sometimes he'd bring a sack of them for the children and dump them out on a table. Usually, they were past ripe. Sometimes there were bugs. Worms. He said this kind of child, 'dummies like these,' wouldn't know the difference. One day, I got a bucket and scooped the mess off the table so I could throw it out. I think I said what a terrible man he was, and it must have gotten back to him. There were one or two orderlies who seemed very impressed by his power."

"Well, good for you," Erna said. "Imagine letting children eat rotten fruit and joking about it, too!"

"Well, it wasn't good for me for long," Louise said quietly, looking down at her hands. She placed them flat on the table on either side of her mug to keep them still. "I had cleaned up the table, and it was after the noon meal when I took the pail to throw the mess out. There was a long corridor that led from the dining room out to a loading dock." Louise paused and looked out the window again. The chickens she had been watching before were just disappearing into the tall grass. "I was near the end when he caught me. He was very angry about what I'd done, and he grabbed the pail from me. He took my arm and pulled me into the boiler room at the end of the hallway." Louise bit her lip, and her eyes brimmed.

"My God, Louise," whispered Erna. "My God, did he—?"

"All the while, he kept reaching into the bucket, telling me he knew how much I loved pears, that he'd seen me looking at him, wanting him and—" A sob caught in her throat, and she covered her face with her hands. "On my face and hair. In my mouth. The pears, they were rotten, black. Smashed, smeared on my uniform. The smell!" Louise wiped her nose with the handkerchief. "Swear you will never tell a soul."

Erna stood and reached for the ladle. She dipped water into the kettle and put it back on the stove. "Of course, Louise. What we need is another strong cup of tea, and I'll clear these pears away. You just sit here for a moment, and I'll just whisk them out to the wagon. Then we'll compose ourselves and talk about pleasant things."

"Thank you. That would be lovely." While Erna cleared the pears away, Louise folded the handkerchief into neat squares. It was the smell, and his hands, that always came into her mind, no matter how hard she tried to forget what he did to her. What he did to Sarah.

I looked after her as well as I could, Louise thought. *I watched out for her. I watched so that Bert would never get near her if I could help it.* She straightened in her chair and smoothed her hair back away from her face, pushing it back in place with the comb that had come loose. She hadn't thought of it for so long, and yet it crept back in like a cold draft. She closed her eyes.

SHE WAS ALMOST AT THE END OF THAT DARK CORRIDOR, so close to the outside door, just past the boiler room. She had even reached into her pocket for the key. His gruff chuckle reached her first, and she held her breath. Then his footsteps grew louder as he came closer, but she still did not turn to look, as if seeing him would make him undeniable. Her skin prickled when he stopped behind her, his breath moving the hair around her ear. "Where are you off to, Nursie?" he whispered. "Maybe you been looking for me. Maybe you've been thinking about me, down here all by yourself. Don't want to share me with anyone, I'll bet. Just hoping I'd follow you. You tease."

A door slammed somewhere on the ward, and Bert took a step back. Louise strained to see over his shoulder and prayed someone would come, another nurse, a resident, a janitor, anyone. But there was no one. Bert reached out and grabbed the pail from her hand and took her roughly by the elbow. "It's time you get what you've been asking for, Nursie." He spun her around, pulled her to him, and shouldered open the boiler room door. He dropped the pail, clamped his hand painfully over her mouth, backed her into a corner behind a bank of shelves and pushed her to the floor, falling on top of her with all his weight.

Louise kicked and tried to pull his hand from her face. He held on tighter. She tried to scream. She was crying now and gulping for air. "Shut up, shut up! I've got a knife, I swear to God," Bert hissed and released her arm long enough to reach into his jacket pocket. He pulled out a jackknife, held it to his mouth and opened the blade with his front teeth, one of which was grey and dead, the colour of bruised fruit. He thrust the knife at her face and grinned. "If you don't quit squawking, you'll get some of this."

Louise jerked her head away. Bert brought his narrow face down close to hers, his thin lips pulled back over that grey tooth, close enough she could see a sharp, jagged edge and a crack across it. His breath came in bursts, hot on her cheek. He slowly loosened his grip across her mouth. He reached across her to the overturned pail, its rotten contents on the floor. He dipped his fingers into the blackened slime and brought it back to her face. "I know how much you like these, Nursie. That's why I bring them. A gentleman always brings a present in exchange for what he gets in return."

He ran the foul slop across her cheek and across her mouth, the pulp and juice dripped down her neck, and he suddenly leaned forward to lick it from the hollow of her throat. She groaned and then gagged. She turned her face away from his and tried to twist out from under his grip.

"No! No! No!" she cried, and he pinned her down with his elbow.

"You might as well relax and enjoy this," he said, licking pear mash from his fingers and then tearing the front of her uniform. Buttons scattered across the floor, sounding like tiny hailstones against a windowpane.

NOW, AN IMAGE FLASHED ACROSS LOUISE'S MEMORY OF a grey stone gargoyle she'd seen as a child on a trip to Montreal. Crouched at the apex of a cathedral window, its hollow eyes were black in shadow. Granite claws pulled its lips back to expose grey teeth bared in a gaping mouth.

The door slammed. Louise flinched. Erna bustled in, grabbed the kettle from the stove, and poured hot water into the mugs. "Out of sight, out of mind," she said. "Now. Your tea's cold, goodness me. I'll get the kettle boiling again." She put a hand on Louise's shoulder.

"I thought I would feel better somehow, letting it out, telling someone," Louise said, covering Erna's hand with her own. "I'm sorry. It's not your secret to bear, Erna. I feel sometimes I'm being eaten alive by the memory."

VIOLET

THE BURKE FARM, 1927

In the shed, Violet held herself ramrod straight on the haystack, where Hank had draped a horse blanket for her to sit on. Her hands fluttered in the air of their own accord. Sparks flew from the blade he held to the grindstone. It was her job to carefully watch for any tiny spark that might not blink out before it floated down to the dry dirt and straw under the grinding wheel. She was excited to have the weighty responsibility Hank had given her.

"Tell me again, Violet," Hank said and wiped a hot blade with a damp rag. "What is your job?"

It had really been to go fetch eggs, like Mama said. She was even wearing the old apron with the pockets in it, the one she always put on before she went into the henhouse. Father called it her egg togs. But right now, Hank's job was much more important.

"Watch for sparks!" she cried and bounced a bit on the haystack. "Not burn down the shed. Right, Hank?"

"That's exactly right," he said, reaching for the spade in the assortment of tools he brought from home. "It's good of your father to let me use the grinder. My mother has a way of finding every stone in the earth when she digs up a flowerbed. And it's good to touch up her knives. She always says a dull blade is a lot more dangerous than a sharp one."

"Spark!" Violet pointed at a bright one that arced up from the spade. Hank made a great show of stamping it out with his boot. Violet scratched her neck and fingered the ends of her cropped hair. "Hank, I got lice."

"What?" Hank took the spade from the grinder and began to wipe down the edge. "I'm quite sure you don't, Violet. What makes you think so?"

Violet was always happy that Hank truly listened, even if what she was trying to say didn't come out the way she wanted. She took a breath and concentrated on speaking slowly, just like Father said to. "Mama says. She cut my hair. When I pick up baby chooks and kittens in the barn. I pick 'em up, and they got lice, and I don't comb my hair nice. So I get lice. I miss my hair lots. See?" She sombrely bowed low so he could see the top of her head, and she nearly toppled off the haystack.

"Whoa, girl! Well, I can see how that would be a problem. I think your short hair is very pretty, too, Violet. I'll bet your mama can tie it up in rags to make it all curls." He started to pedal the wheel again and put the spade against it. "Noise now!" he yelled, turning to wink at Violet. "Do your job, and we won't –"

"Burn down the shed!" Violet hollered, thumping her heels back and forth against the horse blanket. "Don't burn down the shed! There's one, Hank!" she shrieked. Her chest felt big and round, and she grinned at Hank, who jumped up and down on a spark she knew he couldn't see because it had gone in the other direction.

When Hank said there was only the cleaning up to do, Violet left the shed and wandered back toward the house. It was a hot day, and she was sorry to leave the cool interior of the machine shed.

Uh oh, she thought, *I forget eggs*. She stopped at the chicken coop, unlatched the hook, went inside, and waited for her eyes to adjust to the dim interior. The laying hens flicked their heads nervously and started a chorus of warnings. She reached for the small basket hanging on a nail and started peeking under the laying hens. One. Two. She dropped them in the basket together and winced at the telling crack. "Be careful, dumb dumb," she said aloud to herself. She put the next one in her apron pocket.

She frowned when she saw the red hen in the laying box near the back wall. That one she didn't like. They'd had run-ins before. "You grumpy," she said, holding the basket in front of her to carefully move the chicken out of the way. The chicken cackled and hopped out onto the roost and swivelled her neck around to peck at Violet's hand when she reached for the brown egg. "Ow!" Violet cried, pulling back and dropping the egg to the floor. "You mean!" Violet said. The chicken turned its head this way and that, and Violet could see the black spot in its eye whirling bigger, then smaller, as it stepped up its frantic cackle. Violet picked up the brown egg from the dirt floor. It didn't look too bad. She put it in her pocket.

I'm a big girl, Violet thought. *Hank gives me big girl jobs. I can feed chickens, too. Mama, she see I'm a big girl.* Violet set the basket down and pried the lid off the chop pail in the corner. It was half full, but if she took the handle with both hands, she could get it outside to scatter handfuls of feed, just like Mama did.

She pulled the pail out of the henhouse, bumping it over the threshold. The pail tipped, and grain dumped out on the ground. The chickens came running from all over the yard. They scrabbled and jumped, cackling in the dirt around her bare feet. They hurled themselves at the pail, and she couldn't seem to loosen her grip on it or even get out of the way of the birds' frenzy. The birds flew at each other, squawking and beating their wings and kicking up dust.

Blinking back tears, Violet saw Hank come out of the shed, holding his hand up to shield his eyes against the sun; he started to cross the yard. She dropped the pail, the last of the chop spilling over her feet. The hens scrambled frantically, their hard beaks jabbing her bare skin and wings beating against her legs. She turned her face this way and that, feathers stuck in her hair, but still, she couldn't run. *Help me, Hank!* Her mouth opened, but she couldn't seem to make a noise.

Now the racket the chickens made was enough commotion to bring Mama from the house. Violet looked up just as Mama launched herself off the porch with a broom in her hand and thundered across the yard. Despite her bulk, she could move with a speed that sometimes surprised Violet. *Mama can run so fast.* The chickens parted and scattered when she swung the broom into the mob. Her scowl was enough to slow Hank to a walk, and Violet saw him pull up short by the granary.

Mama stooped and yanked the pail from the ground, knocking chickens away, scooping the chop back into the pail. She set it back inside the coop and pounded the lid back on it. Violet tried to gulp down tears. Mama didn't like noisy crying.

"How many times do I have to tell you? Chickens get mean," Mama barked, and she bent over to brush the dirt and grain from Violet's dress. "Let me see. You're fine." She straightened up and took hold of Violet's arm. "Didn't I say? Too close together, they tear each other up. They peck each other to death, especially the weak ones. I've told you, never let them get too bunched up like that. Throw the feed, don't just dump it in one spot. And why were you feeding them anyway? Now, where's the egg basket?"

Violet pointed at the coop.

"Well, go get it and get the rest of the eggs. And for heaven's sake, do it carefully, Violet. Can't you just once do what I tell you?"

Mama pulled up the edge of her apron and pulled Violet closer. "Look at your face, girl. Here, hold still." She gripped Violet's chin, wiping dirt and tears. Even though it hurt, Violet didn't dare pull away. She turned Violet's face from side to side and picked some pinfeathers from Violet's eyebrow. She turned and stalked back to the house. She propped the broom in the corner of the porch by the front door, and then she slammed the screen shut behind her.

Violet's mouth moved, but she couldn't make the words come out. She wanted to tell Mama she was sorry she had been bad. Her heart was thumping so fast in her temples that it made a loud noise like Mama beating rugs on the line.

Hank hurried across the yard, and all the big happy feeling she'd had just moments ago now turned into something small and tight in her chest. She stumbled toward the coop, hiccupping and wiping her face with one hand, spitting the chicken down and dust from her lips.

"Violet, here, let me help you," Hank said.

"Mama says get eggs. I do it myself," she mumbled, her bottom lip quivering. "I be careful."

"All right. I'll wait right here if you need me." Hank stood by the caraganas for a moment and then walked back to the shed.

Violet stooped and disappeared inside the henhouse. She was glad of the quiet inside the coop and didn't mind the smell. It was cool, and she took two or three deep breaths and waited for the thumping in her ears to quiet down. The red chook was still there, eyeing her suspiciously with a throaty cackle, and two or three bantams scratched in the dirt under the laying boxes. They cocked their heads and looked at Violet with blinking curiosity.

Violet looked inside and found two more eggs, one white and one brown. Mama would be pleased, and Violet felt better, but maybe it was too soon to go back to the house. Maybe Mama wouldn't be so mad after a while. Violet felt the wet in her apron pockets. It wouldn't hurt to stay a little longer.

"Want to hear a song?" Violet asked the hens. "Father tells this one to me. I like it. Listen." She avoided the red chook's glare and trilled, her voice thin and wavering,

> *"Buk buk buk, I be true.*
> *I lay lots of eggs for you."*

The red chook stretched its neck to look around the side of the box.

> *"Eww eww, be my wife.*
> *I'll lay lots of eggs for you.*
> *I be yours for my life."*

Violet sniffed and carefully put the last brown egg in the basket. "I have to go now," she said. "But next time, I sing the whole thing, okay?"

She stepped out of the coop and carried the basket against her chest, her arms carefully wrapped around it; she plodded toward the house, counting each footfall. She started over at nine, delaying what she knew might be waiting on the other side of the door. Mama would be glad of the eggs, but maybe she'd still be cross about getting the chickens all worked up and wasting chop. The two broken eggs. Afraid to go in, Violet stood still and looked back over her shoulder. The shed doors were wide open, and she could see Hank packing up his tools in the shed.

"Violet, are you there?" Mama's voice came sharply through the open window, but Violet stayed put, hearing the irritation.

"Mama!" Violet said. "Help me. The door!"

Mama held open the screen door with an elbow, wiping her hands on a tea towel. "Well? Are you coming in or are you just going to stand there? Violet, the flies!" She stepped out and grabbed Violet's arm, and yanked her closer, snatching up the basket. "Look at you. Why would you put eggs in your apron pocket? Look at this mess." Mama's fingers pressed in between her shoulder blades; she pushed her into the kitchen. Mama steered her to the sink. She reached into Violet's wet apron pocket and scooped out the crushed eggshell and yolk, and threw it into the slop pail.

The screen door opened, and John wandered in, scratching his ear. At the sight of Violet's tear-streaked face, he stopped. "What happened?" he asked, stealing a look at Violet. She retreated into the corner by the cream separator, making herself small, and started to cry again as quietly as she could. She hung her head and pushed her chin down hard on her chest.

"Where have you been?" Mama turned to look at John.

"Father told me to knock down swallow nests in the tool shed."

"Violet got it in her head to feed the chickens and ended up dumping all the chop on the ground," Mama said. "Of course, they went wild, and she just stood there."

"She shoulda waited for me," John said. "Those pails are too heavy for her. 'Member, Mama? That happened once when we fed the pigs. She wouldn't let go of the bucket and that ornery old boar we had, 'member? He knocked her down. She got awful dirty." John winked at Violet.

"I swear, I haven't got the patience for it," Mama said, the muscles in her jaw working as if she was chewing on a tough piece of meat. She dipped water from the reservoir in the stove into a basin. "Not anymore. I just don't. Not like your father does. Not like you do." She looked at John and placed the eggs in the water. They all sank but one. "You and your father, the pair of you. You don't see it. You don't—"

She broke off. She plucked out the bad egg and handed it to John. "Put this in the slop pail and take it outside before we have the smell of rotten eggs through the whole house." She lifted the remaining eggs from the water and placed them on the sideboard to dry. "She broke four eggs this morning. Four. That's twelve cents, money we won't get. Simple enough job to pick up an egg without breaking it. Don't touch these, Violet. We've got to take them into town after dinner today, and I don't want you breaking any more."

Violet seemed to grow smaller, and she touched her pocket where the wet had seeped through to her skin. She brightened when she saw the pie cooling on the sideboard. "Pie?" she asked.

"Don't pick at that." Mama pulled off her apron and hung it on a hook near the stove. "Leave it alone. It's for supper, and we'll see if you deserve any." She looked at John. "My head is pounding. I'm going to lie down."

When Mama left the kitchen, John tried to take Violet's

apron off. He pulled at the clumsy knot she had tied. "Give it here, Violet. Come on now," he said.

She held up her arms to let him pull it off, and he dropped it over the back of the chair beside the stove. He pushed her hair back and lifted her chin so she could look into his face. "Don't mind Mama," John whispered. "She's not mad at you. Sometimes when she's grumpy, you have to be extra nice."

Violet nodded her head vigorously, her bottom lip quivering. "Old red chook bite me." Violet held up her hand for him to see.

"Lemme see," John said. He inspected her hand, and Violet patted the top of his head gratefully. "I don't see nothing, Violet. But that old red hen is mean." John spit lightly on Violet's skin and rubbed it in with his thumb. "There. You're okay now."

"Mama don't like me. I get no pie." She pouted, tears welling in her eyes. Her face felt warm and itchy from dust, scratchy feathers, and bits of straw.

"Naw, she does, Violet," John insisted. "Maybe it's just easier for her to like boys. Maybe that's why she keeps cutting your hair short like mine." John ran his hand over the top of his head and scratched. Violet knew he liked to comb his hair back and make it shiny with Father's hair tonic. Father said John was getting particular about his hair. "Don't worry. She doesn't mean anything by it. Besides, what does Father always say you are?" He waited.

"Fluffy ducks. Box of fluffy ducks." Violet wiped her nose again on the back of her hand.

"Come on," John said. "Let's go outside and let her have a rest. I found something you'll like. We can show Hank, too." John ushered his sister out the door. Stepping off the porch, he leaned down to Violet and put a finger under her chin to tilt her face up. "There's a nest of baby swallows in the tool shed. I didn't knock them down. Anyway, they're too high up in the rafters. I can boost you up, and maybe you can see."

Violet reached for his hand, her mother's wrath forgotten for now.

LOUISE

THE SCHOOLHOUSE, SEPTEMBER 1927

The one-room schoolhouse squatted on the prairie within sight of Watrous. The local men had converted the house after Widow Jamieson moved into town and sold the land with the house to the school board. Louise watched the farm children untie their ponies in the stable and stuff books into saddlebags for the ride home across the fields. The ones with shorter walks home set off on foot, clusters of children swinging their books and dragging sticks in the dust along the road. A few of the older boys swooped down into the ditches in a futile attempt to catch gophers before the rodents dropped out of sight into their burrows.

Louise battled against the current of noisy children bounding down the school steps, whooping and pushing their way into the freedom of a fall afternoon. They were not used to being cooped up inside after a long summer outdoors, Louise thought. She envied the ease with which they shrugged off the burden of school as soon as Miss Scott opened the door.

John had brought home the note the day before, fished it out of his overalls pocket and handed it to Louise. "Teacher wants to see you," he said.

Louise had read the perfect handwriting. Miss Scott wanted

to see her about "a small but urgent matter" after school the next day. Louise looked at John, who was prying open the cookie tin. "What's this about?" she asked.

"Don't know. She didn't say anything except to give it to you."

The weather was fine, and William was stooking, so Hank hooked one of the plough horses up to the wagon and drove Louise the two miles to the schoolhouse. The children would have a ride home and John could help with stooking sooner than if he walked home with Violet, carrying her piggyback.

"I won't be long." Louise took Hank's hand, and he helped her down from the wagon.

"It's a good day for a little break from the field," Hank said. "Take your time." He tied a feedbag on the horse, cinching the strap behind Chub's ears. He leaned against the horse's solid shoulder and chewed on a long stalk of ripe barley.

Louise looked for the familiar sight of John towing Violet by the hand. She climbed the school steps, passing one small boy. *One of Gust and Minnie Swanson's*, she thought, *by the look of him*. Gust had ears that made him look like a Model T coupe with both doors open. *Runs in the family*, Louise thought. The boy stood banging erasers at arm's length on the bottom step, a cloud of chalk dust drifting away lazily in the afternoon heat.

Louise fingered the tether hanging from the bell. Then, gripping her purse, she pushed open the door.

Helen Scott had been to Normal School in Saskatoon and was just starting her second year in Watrous. She taught all grades except, of course, when there were no children in a particular age group. Unmarried, she looked older than she should have for her age. Maybe nineteen, twenty even. It was hard to tell, thought Louise, and she wondered if people had looked at her the same way in Orillia, thinking *old maid*.

Miss Scott was distributing clean slates to each desk for the next morning's lesson. Since the open windows faced east and the curtains were drawn over those facing west against the afternoon sun, the room was dim. Louise took a moment for her eyes to adjust. When they did, she noticed John and Violet sitting together on a bench at the back of the room between the barrel stove and a large water crock beneath the coat rack. A long piece of wire was neatly lined with clothes pegs, and Louise could almost smell the damp lanolin where, this winter, children's woollen mufflers, socks and mittens would be pinned to dry during the school day.

John leaned forward with his elbows on his knees, watching Violet make marks with a stub of chalk on a slate. Just as Louise was about to announce herself, Violet's chalk screeched, and Miss Scott straightened, frowning. She adjusted her round spectacles and saw Louise.

"Oh, Mrs. Burke. There you are. John, please bring that chair for your mother." Miss Scott rapped her knuckles on a desk and pointed. John jumped up and pulled a chair from the back of the room to the front.

Louise tried to will away the unease that was starting to roll in her stomach. The teacher, she noticed, did not sit herself but moved about behind her desk, straightening pencils and tidying stacks of paper. She picked up a small brown booklet, tapped it against her thigh, and put it down again. Violet brought her slate and chalk and sat at Louise's feet. John tried to smooth a tangle of Violet's hair at the back of her neck. She'd fought Louise when she'd tried to comb it out that morning. Rather than risk a fit of tears, Louise had let it go. Now Violet waved away John's hand and bent over her slate, rubbing her chalk in circles.

"You must realize what we're dealing with here, Mrs. Burke," Miss Scott said with a curious mixture of pity and irritation. "I'm sure you are aware that your daughter is a mongoloid, poor thing. You must also realize that these children do not make any headway in school. It can be very upsetting for them. Frankly, what she's getting out of this is hardly worth the trouble you must go to in order to get her here." The teacher nodded her head at Violet, who was still content with her chalk stub.

"I am in receipt of the *Journal of Psycho-Asthenics*, Mrs. Burke," Miss Scott said. She picked up the small brown booklet from her desk. She enunciated carefully and held up the cover. Louise thought she would sound this way if she were reading *Peter Rabbit* to the kindergarten students. "Frankly, there's no point and, what's more, there is no legal obligation. You must think me very young, Mrs. Burke, since I'm such a recent graduate of teacher's college, but I am well acquainted with all the new ideas in education. There have been many studies that show a child like Violet is beyond academic hope. This journal, for instance." She held the book up again so Louise could see the cover. "My mother's second cousin sent this journal to me from Minnesota, and it has impressed the superintendent."

Miss Scott laid the booklet flat on her desk toward Louise, pressed her fingertips on it to keep it open, and then leafed slowly through the pages. Even at an angle, Louise could make out chapter headings and some text. When Miss Scott paused at one paragraph halfway through, Louise tightened her grip on the purse she held on her lap. *Mental defect is more frequently passed down by the mother.* Louise could make out that much just before Miss Scott looked up. Louise swallowed.

The teacher took up the book and tapped the corner of it on her desk. "You see, Mrs. Burke, this journal is devoted to the care, training, and treatment of the feeble-minded and the epileptic. There are very competent doctors in the United States who study children like your Violet here. It so happens that my mother's second cousin is in the employ of the Stewart Home for persons of backward mental development in Farmdale, Kentucky. I'd be happy to write away and request literature for you if you like."

For the life of her, Louise didn't know what to say. She worked the clasp on her purse, turning it back and forth. Her tongue seemed stuck to the roof of her mouth, and she had a sudden absurd wish for the cold egg custard Auntie Freda used to make, the sort with a little nutmeg on top. It was September 12, the third day of the new school year and the third day of Violet's formal education. Louise realized that the small matter to be discussed was the fact that Violet was being expelled from the first grade. "Are you suggesting we send her away?" Louise asked finally. "Mr. Burke wouldn't hear of it. And she has John to help her learn."

At once, John scowled at the teacher. She continued more gently. "John is such an intelligent child. One of the best pupils in the sixth grade. He and Alma Pearson run neck and neck on most examinations. You and Mr. Burke can be very proud of him. But," she paused, "Violet is a needy little girl. She is, how shall I put this? Distracted. Distracting, really. She takes valuable lesson time and my attention away from the other pupils, including John. She speaks out of turn, and what she says is incomprehensible. It's quite common in these sorts of cases. She simply can't keep up."

Louise gripped her purse. She felt the September heat under her arms, and she wished she had brought a hankie to wipe the folds of her neck. That egg custard would surely soothe the tightness in her throat.

With a deep breath, she stood up and steadied herself and gripped the back of the chair. "Please, Miss Scott, I know Violet is a little backward. Because of the difficult birth. Fourteen hours, and the cord was—" Louise waved her hand vaguely across her neck, grasping for any explanation other than what was obvious. "But she will catch up in school. She must be allowed to go to school. What will become of her if she doesn't get at least some education?" There was a hint of desperation in her voice, and Miss Scott was quick to reply, even more firmly.

"Violet is a very sweet child, a little angel, I'm sure, but we cannot expect more from her than what God in His wisdom has given her. The most humane thing we can do is remove her from an environment where she has no hope of competing. You say your husband is not willing to send her to a facility of some kind. It's a shame, really, because she could be taken care of by specially trained professionals. If that's the case, then Violet must learn to do her small chores as best she can on the farm. At home."

Louise twisted the clasp on her purse, opened the pocket-book, and then shut it again with a snap. John stood at Louise's elbow and looked at the teacher. His face was dark, and he was chewing on the inside of his cheek, a storm brewing in the boy.

"In fact," Miss Scott continued brightly. She flipped open the pages in the booklet again. "Ah, here it is. There is a very prominent man, Dr. Samuel Fort, who believes sequestering the entire population of feeble-minded people out in the country is quite a good idea. It's a very modern and progressive approach to the problem. He was the president of, let me see," she ran her finger over the list of names, "the Association of American Institutions for the Feeble-Minded. In Faribault, Minnesota. *President*, no less, so I imagine he knows what he's talking about."

She stopped reading and looked up at Louise. Louise saw not only that one of the teacher's eyes was blue and the other grey but also that there was no room for more discussion. As if that was what this had been. Miss Scott went on, her tone firm. As a professional, she seemed determined that a parent must not get the upper hand. "But you must put out of your mind any notion of a normal education, Mrs. Burke. It's simply not possible with these children. A fruitless endeavour. This book says so. Now, as for Violet here, you've already made a wise decision to keep her home longer than you would have with a normal child."

"Yes, we did keep her home. She's nearly eight now," Louise admitted, "but that was really because of her heart. She tires easily. There's a hole, Dr. Speight thinks, but she's much stronger now and if she avoids too much exertion—"

The young woman held up a hand again. "She is happy at home, I'm sure, Mrs. Burke, and if you and your husband are dead-set against a facility, then home is the best place for her. Where you can keep an eye on her." She raised an eyebrow pointedly. "Surely you know what can happen if, as she gets older, she's not, well, watched," she said with a tone of finality. She leaned forward and lowered her voice to a stage whisper. "It's a commonly known fact that females with this sort of . . . shortcoming, shall we say . . . have very little control over their . . ." She paused. "Impulses." She waved the brown booklet and raised her eyebrows. "There have been *studies*."

Louise swallowed and tried to think of some sort of an appeal, someone else she could speak to. Not trusting her trembling knees, she didn't dare rise from the chair. An image swirled, a glimpse of Sarah, her sweet dimpled smile when Bert tickled her under her chin, laughing. Violet flirting with John's friend Steve. Violet, her eyes crinkled up to the point of disappearing with glee. Violet, reaching out for Mr. Yuzik, her open upturned face a picture of pure joy.

Louise shut her eyes tightly, opening them to see the teacher offering the journal to her. Miss Scott said quickly, "You might like to read it. You should know that I've already spoken to the superintendent about this, and he is in complete agreement. Violet can contribute in this life in whatever small way she can, but attendance at school is out of the question. We must be realistic. You should be quite proud that you thought of this farm life before Dr. Fort ever published his article." The teacher smiled brightly.

"But Violet is not like, well, those children. She is quite clever, and her father and John here—" Louise faltered and put an arm around John's shoulders. He shrugged it off. "John is so good at helping her learn."

"Yes, well. I'm sure that's a comfort." Miss Scott stood, and before she realized it, Louise was helped from her chair and ushered out between the desks by the elbow. John and Violet trailed behind. When Miss Scott opened the door, the afternoon sun made them all blink, and Louise reached for the railing to steady herself. Miss Scott spoke sharply to the Swanson boy, who snatched up the erasers from the step and ducked past her back through the door.

"It's not fair," John cried, screwing up his face at the teacher. "My sister's real smart. She's just little. Sometimes she just has to catch her breath. And you don't even answer her when she talks to you! You always just say, 'Be still, Violet!' 'Be quiet, Violet!' That's what you say!"

Louise put her hand against the door and held it open. "John, hush. Please, Miss Scott," she pleaded again. "If you'd try just once more. A few more days. I could assist in some way. I used to work with children like Violet."

The teacher ruffled John's dark hair, ignoring his reproach. She stooped and pulled the slate and small bit of chalk from Violet's grasp. "I'm afraid that's just not possible." Miss Scott straightened and sighed. "As I've said, the superintendent is in complete agreement. Take her home, and she'll be a comfort to you and Mr. Burke, I'm sure. There's nothing more I can do." She stepped back inside.

The door shut with a solid thud. Louise felt the last bit of strength she had left drain from her knees. She wobbled and reached for the railing to steady herself.

"I'll bring home my lessons, Mama, and we can teach stuff to Violet at home," John insisted, his face dark. He took Violet's hand, and she followed him.

Louise leaned heavily on the railing and made her way down the steps. John picked up a small rock and threw it back toward the school, sticking out his tongue. It landed with a soft puff in the powdery dirt near the base of the stairs. Violet searched for a rock, too, running her fingers over well-trodden ground. At the wagon, Hank held out a hand to help Louise, but she ignored it. She stopped, turned back to the school and then said to Hank, "Wait just a minute."

Louise pulled herself back up the steps, yanked open the door, and stepped over the threshold. Miss Scott was scolding the Swanson boy at the chalkboard—from what Louise could hear, chastising him for a job poorly done on the erasers. Louise made her way toward them, turning sideways to get by the rows of desks, her purse held tight to her chest. Miss Scott looked up, startled at first and then with some annoyance.

"Mrs. Burke, I'm afraid I've said—"

"And I'm afraid you're not one to pay much attention at all to the parents of children in this schoolhouse," Louise said, her voice gaining strength and volume now that she got started. "I realize you think Violet is beyond hope, and you won't bother yourself with teaching her even basic rudimentary lessons, numbers, the alphabet. John has already had more success in doing that than you would ever care to. You may be an educated young woman, Miss Scott, but I don't believe you have an ounce of the compassion or patience to be an effective teacher, let alone a decent human being. I hope you will remember this not as a day when you rid yourself of a problem student but one on which you failed a young child. Good afternoon."

Miss Scott's eyes were wide and unblinking. Louise thought she had lost some of the colour in her cheeks. The Swanson boy pinched his lips together with great effort to suppress a smirk that tugged at the edge of his mouth. Louise turned, strode back between the desks, and stepped out, yanking the door closed behind her. The latch shut with a very satisfying clunk. She gripped the railing and tried to calm herself. At the wagon, Louise waved off Hank's hand, and she hoisted herself up to the seat with a grunt. Hank pulled off the horse's feedbag and tossed it into the back, then swung himself up to the seat. He whistled to John and jerked his head toward the wagon.

"Violet's real smart sometimes," John reminded Louise, grabbing Violet's hand, trying to pull her along. She hung back, reaching for stones in the dirt. "Not fair she can't go to school with everybody. Not fair," he insisted, waiting for Louise to respond, to say something, anything. "Violet, come on. We have to go home now. You gotta get up there and sit down so we can go. Mind me." John climbed up and pulled Violet up after him and onto his lap.

He pressed his cheek on the top of her head and wrapped his arms around her to make her stop squirming. "Sit still, Violet. Your bones are poking me," John whispered in her ear. Violet giggled, a little twitter that John said always sounded like a chickadee.

So carefree, Louise thought. *Not a care in the world, this girl. How wonderful it would be to be without worry for the future, without a single regret about the past.*

Over the school, a crow sliced through the air, and a blackbird darted behind, pestering the larger bird as it dipped and rolled through the sky.

"Mean old dumb teacher," John muttered, casting a sideways glance at Louise. She shook her head, and he turned to look out across the field.

Louise finally caught her breath. Her voice was strained when she spoke, and she looked at no one in particular. "Stop that. You mustn't show disrespect to your teacher." Louise felt drained of any strength, as though she had been carrying heavy stones out of the field. Her voice was strained when she spoke again. "Miss Scott is trained in these things. There are people trained in these things. We know Violet is backward and she has a weak heart. I knew it the minute she was born. We should never have hoped Violet would do any more, be any more, than God intends. And the teacher is right about something else." Louise took a breath and held it until her chest ached. "As she gets older, she'll need to be watched. That much is true."

Violet grew quiet, slid off John's lap, and sat on the bench. She looked from John's face to her mother's and finally over to Hank. Louise thought she might straighten Violet's dress and pull up one slumping stocking. But the effort seemed too great.

Hank slapped the reins on Chub's backside, turned the wagon toward home, and chewed another barley stalk down to the head. John examined his fingernails. Violet pointed at the gophers standing poker straight at the side of the road until the wagon was almost on them and then making their frenzied dashes into the tall grass.

Louise looked out across the fields and wondered how she would tell William. He had been so confident that Violet would be a normal child, that she would catch up. She looked down at her children.

Violet reached for John's syrup pail and asked for a cookie. John put his hand over the lid and shook his head. Violet pointed to the black-eyed Susans bobbing along the road where they sprang up from the sand and rock. "Pick some, pick pretty!" she insisted. She twisted around and hung over the seat to watch the flowers retreating behind the wagon. She sighed and flopped down heavily on the seat. "Pick pretty flowers," she repeated with some irritation. Louise thought for a moment it would be nice to have some flowers on the table, but she said nothing.

John picked at a scab on his knee until blood seeped around its edges.

Hank slapped the reins smartly on Chub's broad backside, and the horse picked up the pace. They drove past the flour and seed mill on the edge of town, and Hank waved at two men unloading grain from their wagon. A flock of pigeons pecking at the spilled grain along the dirt road at the base of the elevator lifted into the air and circled in a great looping swarm. Violet twisted around and edged her way onto John's lap. He wrapped his arms around her, and she pointed to the sky.

"Pretty birds," she cried.

Louise followed her gaze and watched the birds swoop back to earth and settle in the dirt.

WILLIAM

THE BURKE FARM, 1927

As September days diminished, William went out to do the morning milking, his path now lit by the moon. By the time he carried the pails back to the house, morning was still only dim pink light on the horizon. Just like every other day, Violet got up early when the sun rose and tried to dress herself for school. William watched her. Her stubby fingers picked and pushed at uncooperative buttons, and she tugged her shoes onto the wrong feet. She dragged a comb through her bangs.

"Just ignore her, John, and get your books. Here's your lunch pail," Louise said, holding Violet's arm and blocking the doorway. William drank his tea and hoped Violet would give up and accept the fact she wasn't going along. She pulled away and ran to the kitchen window. It pained William to see the disbelief at being abandoned on her face. John stood grim-faced on the porch and pulled on his coat, his white knuckles gripping the syrup pail that contained his lunch. He held books to his chest and waved to Violet, crying at the window.

"For God's sake, William. Maybe she'll listen to you." Louise threw up her hands and turned back to clearing the table. "I can't seem to do anything with her, I swear. Sometimes I can't bear that everyone knows it's my fault, her being the way she is."

"Dammit, Louise. People don't think that at all. Sometimes I think you just like to torture yourself. It's not a very attractive trait, I must say." William stood and went to Violet. He gently pried her fingers from the windowsill and turned her to face him. "Sweetheart," William murmured. "Listen, now. I found a nest in the granary. Would you like to see it? Settle down now and be a box of fluffy ducks."

Alarmed, he turned to Louise. "Her lips are blue!"

"Yes, I see that. It's what happens whenever she gets all worked up like this. It's her heart. I've told you, I don't know what in the world to do about it."

"Me go to school, John! Me go! Me go!"

William nodded at John through the window and saw the set of his son's jaw. This wasn't easy on him, either. John tried not to look back, but he couldn't last. He turned to wave at his sister, her hands flat against the windowpane.

Louise stood at the screen door and hurried him along. "Don't prolong it, John," she said. "Just go. Eventually, she'll give up. She's got to learn there is no school for her. She can't do everything you do."

Violet sobbed, rooted to the spot at the window, watching John until he became a small speck in the field that finally disappeared entirely just past the stand of poplars at the edge of the slough to the south.

"In the name of God," William muttered under his breath. He looked at Louise and lifted his hands helplessly, reaching for something else to say. "I've got things to see to." He slumped his shoulders, pushed past Louise at the door, and went out to feed the steers.

NEAR THE END OF SEPTEMBER, WILLIAM WROTE A letter to the school superintendent. He didn't mention it to Louise but thought perhaps an appeal from Violet's father might have a bearing on the matter. He directed his appeal to Dr. Scharf, man to man. There must be something for Violet at the school, even just one afternoon a week? Perhaps there were other similar children in the district, too, who would benefit from even limited attendance? Violet was doing very well with the simple lessons she was learning at home. She could write her name and those of the family. Her counting was improving. Obviously, she could learn, could she not? Surely the superintendent could find it in him to reconsider.

By return post a week later, the answer from Superintendent Scharf's secretary arrived. William opened it, and his heart fell at once. Everything he feared was contained in the phrase "no legal obligation."

He folded the official-looking paper with its school board letterhead and returned it to the envelope. Then he folded the envelope, tucked it in his shirt pocket and, later that evening, put it away in his dresser drawer without showing it to Louise.

It was about the same time that Violet's morning tantrums became less frequent, then stopped altogether as if she had just cried herself out. William thought he could understand how she felt. Instead, she stood out in the yard by the caraganas most school days, like a sentry, squinting against the afternoon sun. If it rained, she was on the porch with her arms slung around the post. She watched until the speck reappeared and started waving long before there was any hope that John could see her. She often met him halfway down the lane.

One afternoon in late fall, while Louise kneaded bread dough in the kitchen, William cleaned his rifle. He twisted the cloth at the end of the long metal rod and ran it down the barrel until he was satisfied. He kept an eye on Violet, watching through the window. *Any time now*, he thought and checked the clock on the mantle over the fireplace.

John reached the bend in the lane, and Violet shrieked. As he neared the house, she scrambled down from the chair, flung open the screen door and hurried to meet him. When they came into the kitchen, Violet ran to Louise and pulled at her apron. "Look, Mama! A star!" She held up the paper proudly as if the reward on the schoolwork was her own. "And John fills the ink! Teacher says he is good boy!"

William tilted his head to catch Louise's eye and was pleased to see a flicker of a smile.

That evening, after supper and chores, John laboured over his arithmetic. Violet sat on a stool at the kitchen table beside him, feet dangling, and worked on her own piece of paper.

William poured himself a cup of coffee at the stove and tilted his head toward the children. "Louise, I believe we have the most clever children," he said. "John, you're a good man to help your sister with her letters and numbers. Just because the school doesn't think she can learn is no reason we have to believe it."

Violet grinned and bent over her work, her face just inches above the small wobbly lines, trying to copy the few letters John had printed for her.

"HOW MANY KITTENS YOU GOT THERE, VIOLET?" JOHN called out. William and John stood by the John Deere tractor and watched Violet tug the little wagon over the ruts by the gate. She was barefoot so often. William said the soles of her feet were like leather. Her everyday cotton dress, the blue one, was her favourite. Her cheeks were flushed. "John, you've done a fine job on the hand clutch. That lever will operate much more smoothly now. I think that'll do. Hand me the Symons oiler. I'll put it away if you'd like to have a look at what your sister is up to."

Violet pulled the wagon to the shade cast by the tractor and dropped the handle. John peered into the pile of straw inside. William wiped his hands on the rag and grinned when Violet bent over her mewling babies tucked beneath an old holey flour sack. "Shush, children," she soothed, carefully touching each tiny head. "Eight," she announced proudly. "Eight children. I have eight ones. Hank, he tells me good mamas like cats." Violet picked up the wagon handle with a jerk that set her babies to mewing again. "I be good mama, right, John?"

"Well, maybe so, Violet," John said, scratching a mosquito bite on the back of his neck. "But you better watch out because here comes another good mama." He pointed toward the barn at Sadie, the old tortoiseshell cat with the frostbitten ear, picking her way steadily across the yard. She was bleating deep in her throat, and her belly swung back and forth beneath her, yellow eyes fixed on Violet's makeshift doll carriage. "You better go put her babies back now, Violet, or she'll be mad. You can't just take away her babies. She gets upset if she doesn't know where they are when she wants to feed them. I'll help you, and then let's go see the new pigs. Father says there are thirteen. He's got one that's poorly in a box in the kitchen."

"I'm going in to give it a little supper," William said and headed to the house. "Put those kittens back where you found them, Violet," he called back over his shoulder. "John's right. Sadie will be yowling all night."

Once the kittens were returned safely to the straw pile by the barn, and Sadie curled herself around them, Violet and John ran to the house. They burst through the kitchen door, hung their jackets, and tiptoed up behind William, who was hunched down over the open oven door. In a wooden Gillette's Pure Flake Lye box was a tiny pig no bigger than William's hand, blinking its sombre human-like eyes. It seemed all translucent, its skin run through with spidery blue veins, its clean pink hooves delicate as shells.

"Oh, so pretty baby." Violet sucked in her breath.

"Look at his eyelashes." John touched the corner of the box with one finger. "He's so tiny." He looked up at William with a frown. "What's wrong with him?"

William got up, wincing at the popping in his knees, and sat back heavily on the kitchen chair. John and Violet crowded closer to see. William sighed and handed Louise the eyedropper and bowl of milk. "Happens sometimes, my boy. The sow laid down on two already. Too many baby pigs, and the mama can't handle them all. This one's too little and gets pushed out of the way when it's mealtime. If we can give him a chance to get a little stronger, just a wee bit bigger, maybe he'll have a crack at it. Be able to push his way in for his share of tucker."

"Let's call him Lyle," John suggested. "Look, Violet. We can just write in an L on the box where it says Lye." He pointed, and Violet ran her finger down the side of the box. "See, right there between the Y and the E."

"El. El," she said. "Lyle." She slowly reached into the box and carefully touched the piglet on the head.

"Go on, girl," William urged. "Wee Lyle could use a bit of mothering. See that he stays warm."

"All of you, don't forget to wash up before supper," Louise said. She pressed a cutter into the biscuit dough rolled out on the table. She lifted each round piece of dough and laid it on a baking tin. "I want extra soap on everyone who handles that pig."

Violet settled herself cross-legged in front of the stove, cradled Lyle in her lap, and stroked him with two fingers. He grunted and, belly stretched tight with warm milk, soon closed his eyes. She carefully pulled one of the rags over the animal, his breathing still quick even in sleep.

"His mama should love him," Violet whispered.

Louise stopped working the biscuit dough and stared at her. "What?" she asked. "What did you say?"

"His mama love him." Violet smiled, the dimple appearing on her left cheek as she turned her face up at Louise. She looked like the kewpie doll dressed in yellow and blue that sat on Auntie Freda's dresser. "Then he be all better."

William picked at a bit of chaff stuck in his shirt collar. John, too, kept quiet.

Louise turned away from her daughter's gaze, from the silence of her husband and son. She started on the second batch of biscuits, scraping the shortening into the flour, muttering when flour flew up over her apron and settled across the table. "Yes, his mama should," Louise said irritably, more to herself than the others, wiping her cheek with the back of her hand. She drew the knife through the lard with deft strokes. "Violet, put that pig back and wash your hands now. I need you to get me the other baking tin."

William cleared his throat and grasped John's hand. "Come on, John. Pull your old father up, or I'll not get off this chair. We men have got other animals to tend to. Come help me feed the rest of the lot. We'll leave these girls to get on with it, and then we'll have some of your mother's lovely biscuits with our own tea."

JOHN

THE BURKE FARM, OCTOBER 1927

"Steve is my friend, not hers, Mama," John complained the following Saturday. "She's always trying to go with us, even when I tell her to stay at the house." He pouted and folded his arms tight across his chest.

Mama started to speak, but Father put up his hand. "John, Violet's your sister. It would be good of you to include her sometimes."

"I do lots," John protested and avoided his father's eyes.

Steve Dewater was the youngest of the Dewater boys, who lived on the quarter section just off the grid road straight south of the schoolhouse. Steve and John were both eleven, birthdays only a day apart, and they'd started chumming together toward the end of the school year after they were tied together for the three-legged race at sports day. In early June, Steve began riding his horse to the Burkes' farm to catch frogs in the slough down past the barn. There was a good supply of old lumber Father had thrown into the coulee when he dismantled the original milk shed. The boys spent hours sweating under the sun, slapping at mosquitoes and black flies while they tried to build a workable raft. The visits were a source of Violet's delight and John's growing mortification. He looked forward to spending the afternoon with Steve, but Violet suddenly got as annoying as a housefly.

"Violet, you're a tag-along," John complained. It was a warm Saturday, and he was getting irritable. He'd spent an hour trying to distract her with suggestions of other things she could do and leave them alone when Steve got there.

Violet slouched in the doorway and watched Mama stir the dishrags in a pot. She added a cup of borax to boil out the hard-water stains. John hooked his thumbs on his suspenders and pouted. "Mama, she tagged along after us all afternoon the last time he came over. She stares at him, and when he says hello or even looks at her, she just starts all this girly giggling."

"It's a crush," Mama explained in disapproving tones. "She's seven."

Father shrugged, but John still wasn't happy about it. It was embarrassing.

"Violet, you can give your brother a little time to himself with his mate," Father finally said. He downed the last of the coffee in his cup. "Why don't you get your papers and pencils out and draw some nice pictures? I'm off to fix up that bit of barbed-wire fence. I shouldn't be long. Violet, you mind your mother."

Violet was only content for half an hour, and John's mood didn't improve when he noticed her start sliding down from her chair to look out the window. She dropped her pencil and ran to the door when they heard Steve's knock.

"We're going to work on our raft, and you can't come. You stay here, Violet. Leave us alone," John commanded. He stepped out onto the porch and hopped off the step. Violet crept out quietly and watched the boys stride off toward the slough. She stood still and pushed her hands into the pockets of her dress. John glanced back, then quickly pulled Steve by the arm and whispered, "Just don't look back at her. Pretend you don't hear her, and maybe she'll give up."

When Mama reached out and pulled Violet by the arm, John

felt a pang of guilt and maybe a bit of shame twist in his chest. But there was a raft to be built. Later, he'd do something nice for Violet and make it up to her.

"Violet, you come inside and get your pencils and paper out. You let the boys be," Mama said. John heard the screen door shut behind them.

His reprieve lasted half an hour. When he saw her coming, he supposed Mama had gone to lie down, and Violet took the chance to escape. She stood in the middle of the track that led down to the slough, and John tried to check on her out of the corner of his eye. Soon, she started coming their way again, her bare feet raising little puffs of powdery dust as she padded down the hill. John sighed.

Violet crouched among the cattails at the edge of the slough, her toes in the cool mud. She watched them silently for a long time and finally stood, grabbing at the skirt of her cotton dress. John knew what that meant, and he was afraid she would wet herself right there in front of Steve.

"Violet, go on up to the outhouse, for cripes sake," John hollered. "Go on now, or I'm telling!"

"My dad is taking some hay over to a farmer by Young," Steve said after Violet disappeared around the back of the house. "You can come if your folks say it's okay. My dad says we can go see the teepee rings."

"What are teepee rings?" John asked, glad to finally have some time to himself without Violet spying.

"I guess they're rocks all laid out in circles over by the lake. The Cree used to camp there. Dad says there's lots of arrowheads, too. He found three one time, just lying there on the ground when he got off his horse."

"I'll ask if I can go," John said. "And just me. Violet can't come, right?"

The boys gave up on the raft when the warm afternoon stretched out before them. They sat cross-legged on the ground near the woodshed, hunched over, peering at a small hole in the dirt. Ants emerged from the hole, and ants disappeared into it, carrying white rice-sized larvae bigger than themselves.

"I didn't think your father would let us use his magnifying glass," Steve said, turning the heavy piece of glass in his hands. The sun glinted off the metal handle. The ants scurrying back and forth on the pile of soil seemed huge.

"We gotta be real careful with it," John said. "He says if we take care of it, we maybe can take it down to the slough and look at stuff in the water."

At the end of the porch, Violet hung over the railing by the lilacs, listening to them talk, staring at Steve. "What's wrong with your sister?" Steve asked.

John felt his ears burn when he looked up and saw Violet had sneaked some of Mama's lipstick. Mama rarely used it, but John knew she kept it in her hope chest. She showed him the contents once. There was a red smear on Violet's teeth. So much mud had dried on her feet it looked as though she wore shoes.

John frowned and looked away. He squatted down in the dirt with his back to Violet. He felt a bitter satisfaction that Violet would be in big trouble for taking the lipstick when Mama found out. Still, he bristled at Steve's question. "Nothing," he said sharply, hugging his knees and handing the glass back to Steve. "What's it to you anyways?"

Steve shrugged. "I don't mean nothing bad by it. I just was asking, that's all."

John poked a twig into a few holes in the anthill. "She's just slow about stuff."

"My ma says she's a re-tar-date," Steve said, carefully breaking the word down while he turned the glass to catch the sun. A ray of light created a frenzy of ant activity. "I don't know what that means. Stupid, I guess. Ma says you should send her to Weyburn. What's in Weyburn?"

John scowled at Violet, jerking his head toward the house, but her gaze was firmly fixed on the side of Steve's face as though she was fascinated by the sound of his voice. She put her arms up over her head and laced her fingers. It was a pose she struck when she was completely absorbed in something, and John knew that something was Steve.

A spurt of anger surged through John, and he stood up with a handful of dirt. He threw it toward the porch and barked at her. "Violet, go on now! I told you, you can't be with us. Go in the house right now!"

Steve jumped up, and Violet took a step back from the railing and looked at them, confused, blinking. Her chin began to quiver, and she pulled up the hem of her dress with both hands, still rooted to the spot on the porch. As she worked her fingers along the hem, John realized with fresh disgust that she had forgotten to put on underclothes.

He ran to the porch, climbed over the railing, and grabbed her arms. John tried to stand in front of her so Steve couldn't see, and he roughly yanked down the front of her dress. He shook her and pushed her toward the screen door. "What's the matter with you, Violet? You can't even remember to put on your knickers," he hissed, his anger rising up in him until he was trembling. "I said get in the house right now!" he cried out, his voice shrill, cracking. "We don't want you around us!"

She began to sob, rubbing her arm where his fingers had dug in.

"You grumpy at me!" she wailed. She began to hiccup in loud, wet gurgles.

"Wipe your nose, Violet! Stupid! Sometimes you don't know nothing!" John shouted, pushing her again. Violet staggered back into the lilac branches. John tore off a fistful of leaves and threw them at his sister. They bounced against her dress and dropped at her feet.

"Hey, John, it's okay," Steve called out. He was standing, the magnifying glass in his hand, his arms hanging loosely at his sides.

"Jeepers, I don't care if she's with us. No kidding. Violet's okay. She's not bothering nothing."

John whirled around, his eyes brimming with shame and anger. "She doesn't have to be with me all the time!" he hollered. "I have to look after her all the time, and it's not fair!" John hurriedly wiped at his eyes with the back of his fists, his cheeks flaming.

Steve hesitated, and then he fished in his overalls pocket. He pulled out a wadded handkerchief and tried to smooth it out. Chewing on his lip, he walked up to the porch railing and looked past John at Violet. She still stood, wet-faced and hiccupping, still no closer to the screen door than when the ruckus started. Steve held the handkerchief out to Violet, leaning over the railing, stretching it toward her. She suddenly stumbled forward, breaking into giggles as if he were handing her a bouquet of flowers. She threw her arms around his neck, pinning him awkwardly over the rail.

"Oh, jeepers, Violet," John put his face in his hands. "God, you're so embarrassing sometimes. Get off him!"

"Uh, it's okay," Steve mumbled, trying to pry her arms from his neck. She sniffled into the front of his shirt. "Um, Violet, maybe you should go inside, and your mother can wash your face. Then you'll feel better, okay?"

Violet nodded vigorously, her lipstick smeared across her cheek. She ran toward the door, Steve's hankie gripped in both hands as if it were a blue ribbon like the one Mama got for pickles at the Waterhole Fair last fall.

John watched her go. "And put some underpants on, for cripes sake," he called after her as the screen door slammed behind her.

John hopped over the porch railing, and the two boys went back to squat over the anthill. Steve looked down at the red smear on his shirt and handed John the glass. John supposed Violet would be getting a hiding right then. No doubt his hollering woke up Mama.

The boys were quiet for a while. John coughed and wiped his nose on his sleeve. "She just makes me mad sometimes," he said finally, staring down at the dirt.

"Yeah," Steve said grimly. "My sister drives me nuts, too. Don't forget to ask your dad if you can come see the teepee rings on Saturday. Just you. Maybe we'll find an arrowhead for Violet."

FOR A WEEK, JOHN WRESTLED WITH HIS GUILT. HE took turns being angry at Violet, then avoiding her, and then, as remorse took over, trying to do everything for her. The night Mama served rhubarb pie after dinner, John saved the fluted edge, his favourite, and slid the crust onto Violet's plate. If his parents noticed, they said nothing.

After supper, with a flourish, Father marked in black grease pencil a large circle on the kitchen calendar in early October. "Chicken butchering day, you two!" he announced. "I need you to help, John. And Violet, too, if she can stomach it." Father reached down and pinched Violet's nose. He flicked a bit of butter from her cheek. "You might not care for the sight at the beginning, but I've seen you light up when your mother makes her fried chicken!"

While Father sharpened the axe that morning on the stone in the machine shed, John stood silently watching with his hands deep in his overalls pockets. Somehow, the scraping sounds helped John sort out the words he needed.

"What's on your mind, lad?" Father said quietly, working the axe blade across the stone. He cranked the handle with one hand and adjusted the angle of the axe with the other. Without looking up, he said, "You can tell your old father."

"It's Violet."

"Mmmmm."

It seemed a full minute passed while Father worked the blade on the stone. A spark danced up and landed on the dirt. John put the toe of his boot on it.

"She makes me so mad sometimes." He took a breath. "But I guess she can't help it. It's just that I tell her something, and she knows, and then she forgets and does the same dumb thing again."

"And that makes you cross," Father said, nodding.

"Really mad, Father. Sometimes I feel so mad I could just hit her."

"But then you don't," Father said.

John shook his head.

"What keeps you from hitting her?"

John thought a moment and shrugged. "I guess it wouldn't help. It's better to go somewhere else if you're mad. Isn't that right? Violet does a lot better if you help her when you're not mad. If you're mad, it's just your problem, and she doesn't understand that. She just gets upset."

"But sometimes it's hard," Father agreed. Three more sparks leaped up and drifted down to the dirt floor of the machine shed. John stepped on each one. Father cupped his hand and dipped it into a pail at his feet. He scooped a bit of water on the stone to slough off the grit. A stream puddled in the dust.

"You're a good boy, John." Father stopped the stone and put a hand on his son's shoulder. "Your mother and I know you've got a big responsibility with Violet. She looks up to you and tries to make you proud of her. That's a big job for her. Here, hand me that rag."

John pulled a piece of feed sack from a nail on the wall. He wiped his nose on his sleeve.

"You'll be a fine teacher one day, John. I know it," Father said, polishing the axe blade. "You've a fine mind and a generous spirit. Being a teacher is an honourable profession, helping your students discover the best within themselves. You do that every day with your sister. I am very proud of you."

John couldn't believe it, but his eyes filled with hot tears. He tried to wipe them away before his father could see. Father reached out his hand, and they shook on it.

"Let's go do in some of those tough old hens," Father said. "That'll cheer us up, eh?"

IT WAS ALMOST MIDDAY,, AND JOHN WAS STANDING IN his assigned spot, waiting for Father to lop the head off another bird. Violet, who couldn't bear to watch but couldn't bear to be too far away from the action, was hiding behind the woodpile. John could see her looking out each time the cackling died down.

"Okay, here we go," called out Father.

The axe came down with a solid thwack, and he threw the chicken in the air to bleed it clean. When the chicken hit the ground, the fact that its head was missing didn't slow it down. It reared up and made a beeline for Violet's hiding spot. With a screech, she scrambled over the wood chunks and out across the yard, zigzagging, with the chicken homing in on her every turn right at her heels. "Off me, off me, off me! John!" Violet cried. She looped back and headed straight for John, hollering with her arms open wide as if she meant to leap into his.

She hit him hard, and they both went over backwards in a heap at Father's feet. The chicken, sated from the gory chase, fell over dead in the sawdust beside the chopping block where its escape bid had begun.

Father chuckled once he realized the children were all right. Then he began to laugh, and he had to sit down on the chopping block and hold his stomach. The children watched him for a few moments, then Violet began to giggle. Soon the three of them were laughing and hooting so loudly that Mama appeared on the porch to see what the commotion was about. It was a good ten minutes and several false starts before Father could trust himself to swing the axe again.

John mulled it over for the rest of the day. The thing that

stood out in the chaos was that Violet had turned to him and expected him to protect her. He was the big brother. Just like Father said, it wasn't easy, but it was honourable.

That evening, over a supper of fried chicken, Father told the story to Mama at least twice. To demonstrate, he picked up a drumstick and waved it in circles. "The poor old hen! And here's our Violet," he said, grabbing a biscuit, rolling it across the table to bounce off John's milk glass. The three of them had giggling fits all over again.

Father finally wiped his eyes with a serviette and took his plate out to the sideboard while Mama cleared away the rest of the dishes. John brought his homework to the kitchen table. He took out a sheet of paper and a pencil for Violet. Pulling a chair up close, he held it for her while she climbed up. "Let's do our schoolwork, Violet," he said. "Come on, you're old enough to know how to spell your whole name. First, you're gonna make a V. You know that's the first letter for Violet. Burke starts with B."

"Vee, vee, bee bee," Violet chanted. "I go to school, John!"

"Yep. This is your school. And when you get your name right," John promised, "we can write the word 'chicken.'"

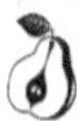

As autumn turned into winter, John rubbed Violet's small fingers over the raised letters on mason jars. He showed her a headline in the *Western Producer* and a page in a book and asked her what the letters were. He taught her to sing the alphabet. She reverently touched the smooth surface and jagged edges of the arrowhead Steve had given her while John printed the word on the paper and set the stone beside it.

They counted the sugar and oatmeal cookies they sneaked from the big glass jar on top of the cupboard. In church, unless Mama pinched them both, they counted in whispers the number of parishioners whose heads bobbed forward when they napped during the sermon. They counted the cars on the road, the plows in the field, the tomato plants in the garden, the bees on Mama's sweet peas and hollyhocks, and the number of potatoes and turnips they dug before the frost. By Christmas, Violet knew her numbers.

It was like this as the seasons changed. Sometimes, John went off with Steve and, perhaps content in knowing she would have her turn again, Violet let him have time on his own. Violet waited each afternoon in any weather for John to appear on the horizon at the end of the school day. It was his habit to sit with Violet at the kitchen table as soon as he got home. He showed her the lessons from the day. On the walk home, he thought of something she could do as they sat, heads bowed over papers, thin sun-browned arms reaching for pencils and crayons and scissors. When Mama came across a potato in the bin too far gone for eating, John cut it in half and carved snowflake designs. Dipping it in saskatoon berry juice, he showed Violet how to cover a sheet of paper with a blue blizzard and sign her name at the bottom.

"Potential," Father proclaimed over his cup of tea. "Your wee sister's got potential, eh, John? And you're the finest headmaster I've ever had the pleasure of knowing. You might give serious thought to going off to Normal School to become a teacher one day, boy."

John held Violet's hand while she made the looping cursive letters of her name. "She's smart," he agreed. "They don't know anything at that school. Especially that dumb old Miss Scott. Violet is gonna show her someday."

"John, that's no way to speak about your teacher," scolded Mama, setting down a stack of plates and cutlery in front of the children. "Now shoo, the both of you, and clear out of my way." She passed her hand lightly over Violet's blonde head and let it rest on John's dark hair.

Though John never heard her say it, even to Father when she thought they couldn't hear, John wondered if she was thankful, relieved even, that he spent so much time with Violet. He wondered for the first time whether it justified, somehow, the fact that she couldn't. He knew Mama was pretty hard on Violet. He just couldn't figure out why.

Once, late at night, he did hear her say to Father that there was just too much Sarah in Violet, and she couldn't let herself be that needed. Troubled, John couldn't get back to sleep and was afraid to ask his mother, ever, who Sarah might be to her. Some relative or friend back east, maybe, and he let it go at that.

JOHN

THE BURKE FARM, MAY 1929

John's thirteenth birthday, May 5, 1929, fell on a Saturday, fresh and sunny. The nights were still cool, and there had been a late hard frost. But John could feel spring was underway. Last week's thunderstorms seemed to be pulling the green speargrass from the ground. What had been a faint promise of life, depending on the light and tilt of the head, now suddenly had jumped up out of the soil with verdant conviction.

Father drained his teacup, pushed back his chair from the table, and announced that he might take a walk out to see when the garden plot beyond the house might be plowed.

"It's still way too wet," John said. "There's still standing water from the melt."

John thought something birthday-related must be up since Violet had been silly all morning. When John sat at the kitchen table working on his history and civics essay, she wiggled on a chair by the stove, staring at him. She giggled behind her hand, and whenever she opened her mouth, Mama frowned her into quiet. Violet settled for bouncing on her chair.

John watched her out of the corner of his eye, waiting for her to blurt out the surprise, whatever it was, but still pleased with the suspense just the same.

"I'm done with all my arithmetic problems and most of my essay, Mama. Just a little history left, and I can do that easy," he announced, pushing his papers into a stack. "Come on, Violet. Let's go out by the barn and play Anti-I-Over, maybe Simon Says," he tried, hoping to trip her up. She covered her face with her hands and shook her head. Behind them, Mama measured out two cups of flour from the bin and took down the can of cocoa from the high shelf in the cabinet.

When Father called John outside, both children, coiled like springs, leaped from their chairs and tore their jackets from the hooks at the door. Mama nearly dropped the green ceramic bowl she had taken down from the cupboard. She always made John a devil's food cake, saving the cocoa for weeks to be sure she had enough. It was his favourite. He asked for it every birthday.

John yanked open the door but pulled up short at the screen. Father stood by the edge of the garden plot, holding the bridle of a magnificent dappled grey horse. At least, it looked magnificent to John.

All the breath left him as if he'd fallen out of a tree. "Good golly," John gasped. "Look at that, Violet! We got a horse! A real horse to ride, not like Chub and Florie!"

Violet chewed on her lip. "I don't like it. Looks like dirty snow," she said.

The horse, more than sixteen hands high, threw its head up and down, nostrils flaring. It reared back, but Father held fast and spoke sharply in the horse's ear. Then he ran his free hand down the horse's neck, over and over, speaking in the same soothing voice he used to calm Violet if she woke at night with a bad dream. John saw the blue ribbon tied on the bridle.

"Is she—mine?" John squeaked, staring at Father and whirling around to Mama, who had come up behind them.

"Happy birthday, son. Yes, she's yours if you can handle her," Father said.

"Mine? No fooling? Really? My first horse," he cried breathlessly. "My very first horse, and it's big, too, not just a pony! I can handle her all right!"

He wanted Violet to touch the mare's soft nose, but she pulled back as if she wanted plenty of distance between herself and the animal.

"Stay away, John," she said and hid behind Mama.

"Slow down, boy," Father said. "Violet's quite right. The mare's got to get used to new people. Let her get the smell of you before you put your weight on her back."

"I can ride her. Just boost me up! Watch me!"

"John, now mind me," Father said quietly, stroking the mare's neck, one hand gripping the bridle. "This animal is not like Chub and Florie. Plow horses are one thing. This one is quite different. She's one of Rodger Graham's herd. She's no hammerhead, but she's been pastured all winter, so she hasn't been around people. She's got to get used to you. See how she watches you? She has to know you're the boss now, so you come here, and we'll introduce you."

"John, here," Mama said from the porch. She held a carrot, wrinkled but still good, from the root cellar. John ran back for it.

"Thanks, Mama. She'll really like me now!"

Violet backed up to the porch and stood with her arms wrapped around the post.

"This is making me too nervous," Mama said. "I've got work to do to get ready if we're to have a birthday party." She put a hand lightly on Violet's shoulder and then went inside.

The mare snorted, and her ears jerked forward when John approached.

"Talk to her, John. That's it," Father said. "Let her have a smell of you. Rodger said she takes the bridle fine in the barn. He said she was broke, but I have my doubts about how well. We'll walk her around on a longe line. She's got to be gentled out a wee bit."

John held the carrot out and took slow, steady steps. The mare reached forward and wrapped her lips around the carrot, pulling it from his grasp. John laughed as the carrot disappeared. The horse's teeth clacked against the bit, and she leaned in, snuffling for more. He tried to touch her muzzle. She threw her head up, ears pinned back against her skull.

Father held on and raised his other hand. "Calmly now, John," he said in that soothing voice. "It's exciting, your first horse, boy, but she's a bit stroppy, so you move slowly. Just walk her about the yard until you get to know one another."

John nodded and confidently reached for the lead. As he walked the horse at Father's side, he spoke in his father's soothing tone, and the horse's ears came forward. Tom and one of the other barn cats slunk quietly onto the porch at the far end and leaped up on the railing, observing through half-closed eyes.

Mama pushed through the screen door and stood behind Violet. "It makes me more nervous not to watch you, John," Mama called out. She shielded her eyes with a hand and cradled the big green bowl on one hip.

John waved. He reached up too quickly, and the horse reared back, nearly toppling John and pulling Father off his feet for an instant.

"I'm okay! What do you think of her, Violet?" John asked while Father got the mare settled down again. John looked back over his shoulder and flashed Violet a wide smile. "Can I sit on her just for a little?" John asked. "If she doesn't like it, I'll get right off."

Father hesitated, and John held his breath. Then his father nodded, leaned over and laced his fingers together. John hoisted himself up and swung his right leg over the mare's back. Once the horse felt the weight, she hopped sideways, bumping her shoulder into Father. He kept talking to the animal in a low voice.

"Stay back now, Violet," Father said when she crept down the step to get a better look. He didn't have to tell her twice. The horse was so big and noisy, snorting and swinging her big head up and down, eyes rolling up white now that John was on her back.

Spit flecked the horse's mouth as she worked on the bit, teeth clacking harder now against the metal.

There was no saddle yet. John hoped that maybe with some money from a load of barley Father was taking to the mill next week, he could have a look at the one on display at the feed store. It would take some time for this horse to get used to a saddle on her back. Bareback would have to do for now.

"John, grip with your knees," Father instructed, "and I'll lead her out to the open space in front of the house." He checked the clip of the longe line and let go of the bridle, and then took up the rope. "Careful with the reins. Gently does the trick. Keep some slack. We don't want her with a hard mouth. Heels down, John."

The horse bucked a little, and John laughed, holding the reins loosely in each hand, pressing his legs tight against the horse's sides, first one, then the other. Left, right, left, right. Soon, they were walking in wider circles, and Father, keeping a good hold on the line, backed away a few feet and let the line out more as the horse made a wider circle.

"I don't like the look of that horse, William," Mama said. "She's wild. Maybe this wasn't such a good idea."

"I can hear you, Mama! This is a great idea," John called out. "This is the best birthday present ever!"

"Not to worry," Father said. "She'll be right. My father's best mate in Canterbury used to say there's something about the outside of a horse that's good for the inside of a man. This will be good for John." He called out to his son. "I say this will be good for you, John!"

John waved at his mother. "Don't look so worried, Mama," John yelled, rubbing his palm down the horse's neck. The mare really did seem to be calmer now. "See? She likes me."

"Well, that may be true." Mama pulled her sweater across her chest. "But I don't see a great deal good about this horse yet. Look at the way she keeps laying her ears back. She hasn't been around people enough to know how to behave."

"She'll be right," Father assured her again. "John's got a good head. I was sailing the oceans when I was not much older. Surely he can handle a horse."

"I can handle her!" John said, walking the horse slowly, close enough to hear, afraid that Mama would get Father to change his mind.

"Ten dollars was a good bargain, down from fifteen," Father said. "I told Rodger we'd grub some Russian thistles for him along his lane in exchange. John will need to save up for the tack." He watched John and the horse. "Boy, heels down. You all right then?"

"I can do it. She's just getting used to me," John insisted.

John and the horse made a wider loop at the very end of the longe line, around the farmyard toward the road, then around back and up by the house, back to the barn, around and around.

The mare settled down and seemed content with John on her back and the slow walk around the yard. John saw that Violet was still sitting on the steps, her hands stuffed inside her coat sleeves, her elbows on her knees. She was keeping an eye on him, and a grim look had gathered on her face.

"I don't like that birthday horse very much," she called out. "It makes my tummy scared."

Another horse whinnied, and Hank appeared from around the back of the house, sprawled in the saddle on old Ned. Hank had the look a man gets after a long morning on horseback, and John knew he'd been down in the coulee. He waved, and Hank pushed his hat up off his forehead and leaned forward on the saddle horn. John gripped with his legs as the mare shied and pranced sideways around the yard. He had his hands full now that she had spotted Ned. Once she settled again, he dug his heels in and urged the horse a little closer to the house.

"I checked the fence lines," Hank was saying to Father. "There's still a bit of snow down where the sun can't get. No deadfall in the creek, and there's open water so the cattle can get at it." He looked up at John and winked. "Anyway, thought I'd come up to see if your father needed help giving you the royal bumps this year with you being so big now." He scratched Ned behind his ears and watched John's horse buck a little sideways.

"What do you think of my new horse, Hank? It's the best birthday present I ever got in my whole life!"

"That's a spirited animal," Hank replied. "Just about as rammy as my old Ned here."

"Maybe we could have a race!"

Hank snorted. Ned's tail twitched at the flies on his flanks, and his eyelids closed. Hank hadn't bothered with a nosebag, and long snarls of brown dry grass and fresh green rye were wound around the bit at the corners of Ned's mouth, evidence of bored nibbling at mouthfuls of dry grass snatched when he carried Hank along the fence line. Ned was as far from rammy as a horse could get, and John felt even more proud of his new mare. She'd need a good name, one that suited her high spirits. He couldn't wait to show her off to Steve.

Hank's horses had all been called Ned. Hank only ever had one at a time. Three so far. Two had been Clydesdale and one a Shire. "So's not to get them mixed up and call one by the wrong name," Hank had once explained to John and Violet. "That," he said, "might hurt their feelings."

All Hank's Neds seemed like the same horse, all big, broad, and gentle, chronically tuckered out. Born to eat, the Neds were seemingly unaware they could be anything but docile draft animals.

All of them were so wide that Hank had developed "legs so bowed you could swim through them," Father said. That always made Violet laugh. She wasn't afraid of any of Hank's horses, even to be close enough to put her face against the soft velvet of their noses and feel their hot breath puffing on her cheek in search of a treat. John's horse wasn't like any of the Neds, but he thought Violet might get brave enough for a ride.

John walked the mare slowly to where Father stood. "I think she's getting used to me now," John said, running his fingers through the mane and patting the horse's neck. Father put out his palm, and the mare snuffled at his hand. She took a nip, and Father yanked his hand away.

"That one does seem to have a bit of a streak in her," observed Hank, leaning forward in his saddle for a better look. "She from Graham's herd, that one he was running down the coulee?"

"Mmmm. Stroppy beggar," Father muttered. The horse stamped the ground and threw her head back, white froth working up in her mouth as she worked the bit. "Mind her, John. You get hold of that horse now. Don't yank on those reins. But be firm."

"Violet," John called out. She had retreated to the porch again. "When she calms down some, I'll show you how to ride her. We can share her, okay?"

Violet nodded a little but looked like she wasn't at all sure she wanted to get anywhere close enough to ride that horse. But John gave her a reassuring smile, so she stood on tiptoe and nodded more vigorously.

"Can I take her out a little bit now?" John asked. "I think she's okay now. She likes me. I'll take it real slow."

After a moment's hesitation, Father unhooked the longe line.

"I think you'd best just walk that animal for a while and just stay up here in the yard. Promise me, now," Mama warned from the porch. Her hand fluttered around her throat. It reminded John of the little bat that got into the house once and kept beating its wings against the kitchen window. Mama finally killed it with the broom. He dared not protest, or she'd have him off the horse altogether.

"Your mother's right, son," Father gripped the horse's bridle to still its head. "Let's just stay in the yard for now. Down around the barn and back. Later we'll all ride with Hank a ways, maybe all the way to his place."

"Okay," John said. "I'll stay up here close to the barn."

"Cup of tea, Hank?" Mama asked, holding open the door with a hip. She cradled the green bowl.

"That would hit the spot. Thanks." Hank looped Ned's reins

over the rail fence. He didn't bother tying them; Ned's muzzle was already resting on the top rail, and his eyes were closed.

"What shape's the fence in down at the bottom?" Father asked.

"Not too bad. Just a couple of sections where Nik's bull pushed down a post or two. Don't think he got through, though. Looks like we can pull it up without having to put any new ones in, but maybe we'll go down and have a gander." Hank took off his hat and looked up at the darkening sky to the west. "Looks like something's blowing in, though. See that? Cold, too. I thought we were done with winter."

Hank reached out and tweaked Violet's nose. The men went into the house to talk about fence mending. John waited for Mama to go inside, but the frown that had gathered on her forehead had fixed itself across her face. She wiped her hands on her apron. "Violet, run out to the coop and get me four eggs now for John's cake," she said. "You hear me? Four eggs. Take the basket and be careful not to break them. And John, you mind your father and keep that horse up here close to the house. Hank and your father will have a cup of tea, and then you can ride together."

When Mama finally went in and closed the door, he dug his heels into the horse's ribs and urged the mare closer to the porch. Violet stepped back from the railing, slid her arms around the post and peered from behind it. "Violet," John whispered, gripping the reins with one hand. "I rode plenty of horses by myself over at Steve's. It's a cinch. I'm going to take her on the shortcut down past the barn. I won't be gone very long. I'll bet I'll be back before they finish tea and are done talking, but I want to show him. Don't tell anybody, okay?"

The horse dropped its head low to the ground, and Violet's eyes were fixed on the froth around the horse's mouth. Flecks of it dropped into the dirt just off the step, and the mare blew noisy snorts, puffing up the dirt whenever John tugged on the reins. Violet shook her head.

"Violet, I told you no telling!" John said sternly. "I'll be back pretty soon. I just want to show Steve, and if I go right now, I can beat the storm. Father was saying it smelled like another thunderstorm, and if it starts to hail or something, I probably won't get to ride her for a while. I can be back before they even know I'm gone as long as you don't tell. If they do come out, say I'm just down at the slough. Okay? Promise." He tilted his head. "Come on, be a pal. I'll let you lick the icing off the whole spoon, and you can have the whole bowl by yourself, too."

Violet nodded. John put a finger to his lips. Then he tugged the reins to the side and turned the horse away. He could feel the muscles in her haunches and the heat of the animal as its sweat seeped into his jeans where he pressed his thighs against her flanks. He looked back over his shoulder and saw that Violet had taken the egg basket from the nail by the door. But instead of heading out to fetch eggs, she sat down on the step to wait.

"'I be yours, and I be true,'" he heard her sing in that funny off-key voice. Just like a little bird. "'I lay lots of eggs, I be yours for rest of my life.'" She stood up and hollered. "Four eggs, John!" She held up four fingers. "For your birthday cake! I get the spoon and bowl all myself! We sing 'happy birthday, dear John.' I blow out candles!"

He raised his arm and waved to show her he'd heard. A breeze lifted her hair from her forehead. He turned away and struggled to keep the horse to a walk until they disappeared around the back of the barn. The sky was turning a steel grey.

VIOLET

THE BURKE FARM, MAY 1929

Violet squinted one eye and reached under the red broody hen. She'd given up waiting on the step and thought she'd better get the eggs Mama wanted for the birthday cake. The sun was blotted out by dark clouds, and the morning had turned cold. The warmth was welcome on her fingers when she wiggled them under the hen's feathers. The chicken started a slow and steady cackle, and Violet knew she had to hurry. This hen was not nice, but she needed one more egg for John's cake, and the other nests were empty.

It was then Hank yelled something she couldn't quite make out. Good. That meant John was back. The wind had really kicked up, and Father had said it might even snow. So *unusual* for May, he had said at breakfast. "Unusual." She formed the word several times. John must have changed his mind about riding all the way to Steve's. She plunged her hand farther under the hen, her fingers closed on the warm egg, and she pulled it out.

But her ears filled suddenly with another sound. Mama. Screaming. It startled both Violet and the hen, and the egg smacked on the dirt floor. The hen pecked a good chunk of skin on the back of Violet's hand. She yanked her hand back and pressed it to her mouth. She looked down at the egg, its shell split evenly in two, orange yolk oozing through the dust. She knew what would come later. Mama would be mad. Thirty-six cents a dozen. Each one was precious, she was often warned. And now, not enough for John's cake. Maybe Mama was already hollering at her.

Violet sucked the spot on the back of her hand, then kicked some straw over the egg. Turning on the chicken, she stood up to the wooden box, blocking the hen's escape. Violet reached out and grabbed the bird's neck, and pushed the hen down into the straw. Trapped, it gurgled and struggled, its beak hung open, the tiny red tongue stiff in mid-air, yellow eyes blinking stupidly. Violet finally let go, and the hen, paralyzed with fright, stayed put.

"Bad chook. Can't do anything right," Violet grumbled and carefully examined her wound.

Outside, the screaming went on. Violet shivered. She squatted in the chicken coop and pulled her barn coat down over her knees. She hunkered down and peered out from the open door. She pulled up her collar to muffle the sound that had turned into some kind of wail. Maybe just the wind. But that bad feeling was twisting and turning inside her now, crawling up into her throat. Father always said singing a little song made a person feel better. Maybe one now would help.

"'Oh, won't you be my wife? Buk buk buk,'" Violet chirped softly, rocking a little and hugging her knees. "'I be yours and I be true and lay lots of eggs for you.'" Her voice quavered and broke. She took a breath. "'I be yours for rest of life.'"

Suddenly there was so much shouting and running. After a while, the chickens took no notice of her. Even the red hen, punishment forgotten, jerked out of her stupor, hopped down from the box, and went about her business. She pecked and scratched around Violet's feet, tilting her head, eyeing Violet sideways, waiting for a handful of feed. Even the smell wasn't so bad now with the cold wind coming through the cracks. It just seemed better to stay where she was.

She leaned out just far enough to look and squinted into the cold wind. Hank and Mama came up from behind the barn, and Father was carrying John. *Here I am*, she would say when they got close, but the words caught in her throat. She saw John's birthday horse running back and forth by the fence, throwing its head up and down, the reins loose and whipping across the mare's neck. Mama stumbled as if she'd forgotten how to walk straight, and Hank helped her up. Her head was thrown back, her hair wild around her head in the wind, and her mouth was wide open, but now nothing was coming out, not a sound, not even a whisper.

They passed by the coop. John's head hung down against Father's chest, a dark stain on the front of his shirt. *Why is John sleeping? He's a silly boy.* One of John's arms hung down crooked and just waggled loose, bouncing against Father's leg. They all ran up to the house. The front door slammed, and Violet was left to listen to the wind.

It seemed no more than a breath or two, and the door opened, the screen door slammed back, and Hank flew down the steps and across the yard. No jacket, either. *He'll be cold.* Ned, still standing at the porch rail, just raised his head and watched. Hank fumbled at the door of Father's truck, yanked it open, and jumped in. With a roar, the engine started, and Hank spun the wheels so fast Violet could hear dirt and stones hitting the machine shed. He was gone.

Something bad was happening.

She held her breath and tried to ignore the charley horse that bit into the back of her thigh. Her heart pounded in her ears. When sweat started to prickle around the edges of her hair, the bad feeling that filled her belly before had crawled up into her head, too. Her stomach ache was worse. Something had happened.

Violet pulled her barn coat around her and scooted back into the corner of the coop. She dug in the coat pocket. A hankie. Two hankies, old and stiff. A short piece of twine. The mitten she thought was lost. She pulled it on. It was a little warm in the coop, and the hens' clucks and gurgles sounded nice. Suddenly so tired,

Violet thought maybe closing her eyes for just a little while would fix the pounding in her chest, and that bad feeling would go away.

IT HAD GROWN SO DARK IT SEEMED LIKE BEDTIME, BUT when Violet woke, she knew it wasn't even suppertime yet. She heard the far-off growl of thunder. All the chickens had climbed into their nesting boxes, fluffed up against the wind finding its way through the cracks in the coop walls. She stretched her legs out and rubbed at the cramp in her thigh. She knew the back of her dress was getting dirty, and she thought about what Mama would say. There would be a whipping if it was bad enough.

When she heard the rumble of a car engine on the road, she leaned out just far enough to see. Father's truck pulled into the yard, and Hank climbed out. He ran around to stand in the glare of headlights. Dr. Speight's noisy Model T backfired and jerked to a stop by the porch. Father ran out and grabbed the doctor by the arm before he was even all the way out of the car. The three of them hurried inside the house.

Violet wiped her nose on her sleeve and pulled herself up into a crouch, her toes numb. She crawled out, careful not to upset the egg basket as she slid it along with her. Moments later, Hank and Mama came out onto the porch, Hank's arm wrapped around her, propping her up by an elbow. Mama couldn't stand so well, and Hank was almost carrying her to Dr. Speight's car. Mama was too big to carry, but Hank was sure trying hard. She was holding on to him, her hand grabbing at his shirt, where there was another black stain just like the one on Father's shirt. Violet wondered if Mama knew her hand might get dirty from whatever that was, but then she saw Mama's hands were already dirty, and so was her apron. Mama's shoes seemed to be just dragging along in the dirt, and she was making an awful moaning sound. She was tearing and pulling at the front of her apron as if she wanted it off, but it wouldn't come. It was her best apron, the fancy one for John's birthday.

Violet latched the gate to the chicken pen and crept to the edge of the porch. She pressed back in the shadows by the lilac. She steadied the egg basket between her feet.

"Beside herself!" Dr. Speight yelled to Father. They followed Hank and Mama out toward the car. "I've given her something. It's for the best. There's no telling what she might do in this state." Violet listened as hard as she could, but she didn't understand what anyone was hollering. She just knew it didn't feel good in her ears.

Hank put Mama in the front seat, closed the door, and ran back up on the porch and into the house. The car windows were rolled up, but Mama finally was making sound come out of her open mouth, and Violet could hear the wailing again. It wasn't so scary and loud with the window rolled up.

And John went, too, wrapped in a sheet. Hank and her father carried him out of the house, and the end of Mama's good bed sheet whipped like a flag. They put him in the back seat, where he leaned against the door and stayed so still. Violet waited for him to sit up and start laughing about scaring everyone so bad. Then he'd be in big trouble. To bed and no birthday cake. *That would fix him*, Violet thought.

"She should quiet down in a few minutes," the doctor called out, opening up the back door on the other side. "William! William, you go ahead and get in the back with your boy."

Hank was pushing on Father, steering him off the porch and toward the car. "She's just hiding from all the commotion, I'm sure," Hank yelled at Father, making his way to the car. *Who is he talking about?* "Come on now, William, she'll be all right. I'll find her. Just go."

Dr. Speight slammed the door after Father got in and put his arms around John. The doctor hurried around to climb in behind the wheel. "Hank, you come on to the hospital when you find the girl. Telephone is still out, so just get there," the doctor called out, and then he started the motor.

What girl? Violet thought hard. Maybe someone John knew at school.

Hank stood on the porch, the lantern light from the open door behind him making him all black. When the lights from Dr. Speight's car came on, Hank was suddenly white in the glare. The bad feeling lurched into her chest, and the way Hank looked made her cry. The car lurched backward, then swung round, spitting stones and dirt from the tires, and headed down the lane.

She watched the car for as long as she could, the dark, hunched figure of her father in the back window, the white of the bed sheet beside him. The white seemed to hover in the gloom until it grew so small it finally just winked out along with the taillights.

Hank went to the railing, tied Ned's reins more securely, and leaned down to put his forehead on Ned's muzzle. When Hank went to the steps, he cupped his hands around his mouth and yelled Violet's name. She put her hands over her ears and stayed still. "Violet!" Hank hollered, his voice hoarse and rough. She shrank back. "Violet! Come on out now. Come in the house. It's too cold for you to be out so long. Dammit." She heard him curse, and she pinched her lips.

Violet pressed herself back into the lilac bush, the branches poking around her collar and snagging in her scarf. The birthday horse was still running back and forth along the fence by the barn, making strange squealing noises. Ned whinnied, and Violet felt her heart flutter against her ribs. She stayed quiet even when Hank called for her again, pleading this time, reassuring.

"Please, Violet. Please come in the house now before you freeze. I need to talk to you, honey. It's all right."

She waited. Hank ran his hands through his hair. It sounded as if he was crying, but that couldn't be, Violet thought. He turned and went into the house. He was right about the snow. She looked up and felt hard flakes fall and melt on her cheeks, and she pushed out her tongue, but they were too small and dry to taste like anything. She could hear Hank going from room to room, calling her. She picked up her egg basket, crossed the porch, and pushed open the screen door. She stood in the dim kitchen, where the lantern had burned low on the wick. Setting the basket on the sideboard, Violet heard Hank's heavy footsteps, but still, she jumped when he came through the doorway.

Hank stumbled through the kitchen with Father's rifle. The 303. Violet didn't know why it was called that. Hank's face was white, his eyes dark and sunken. He was stammering, "Oh, God. Oh, my God. Oh, my—"

"Eggs. I got eggs, Hank. See?" Violet offered, her voice thin, wavering on the verge of tears. She shook snowflakes from her hair. "Dumb red chook, she make me drop it. I got three. For John's cake. Is Mama mad? I broke one."

Hank's head snapped up at the sound of her voice. He stopped and looked at her stupidly as if through a fog. His eyes looked scary, hollow and red. Violet wondered if he could see her at all.

"There you are, Violet," he whispered, swaying a little. "Where have you been? Didn't you hear me calling you?" His face crumpled, and tears slid down his face.

Violet's stomach lurched, and the bad feeling clawed at her chest. Her bottom lip trembled.

"I knew you were around somewhere," he said. "My God, I'm grateful you didn't see any of this." He waved his hand vaguely at the mess in the kitchen.

What did he mean about what had happened? What was *any of this* that she didn't see? Violet looked past him, past the kitchen chairs that were pushed back, out of place, not neatly lined up to the table like they were supposed to be. Things in the kitchen were not the way Mama liked them. Muddy footprints covered the floor. The birthday cake bowl was on the sideboard, but the cocoa was spilled on the counter. The lid was off the sugar tin. Tea things were scattered on the table, Mama's china plate still out with the snickerdoodles.

Violet stared at the sink, at the pile of dark, wet rags, dirtied like Hank's shirt. Black. Like Father's shirt and Mama's hands. The flour for John's cake was there, but it was all wet and messed like mud pies. Trying to understand, to figure it out, all she could come up with was this was wrong. This was bad. She felt sick.

"The horse was fine coming back from the field," Hank said, talking more to himself than to her. "I saw him. After coming around the slough and back toward the house, the horse was under control. John was fine until the horse saw the barn when they came up over the slope past the water. I don't think John was expecting that animal to bolt the way it did. Maybe he just got scared, I don't know."

Violet took a few steps closer. He reached out and put his trembling hand on her head, pushing her hair back from her face. Hank whispered, "John should have let go. He could have let himself fall or stopped trying to rein her in so hard. It happened so fast. I yelled for him, but the horse was too far gone by then. Out of its mind. Maybe if that horse would have taken the corner around the barn a bit wider. If only he had ducked down low and missed the eave. The sound. I can't get the sound out of my head." Hank let his hand fall away. "Like an axe coming down on wood." He sobbed. "John probably didn't feel a thing." He gripped the rifle with both hands and cleared his throat. "Your father wants to do this when he gets back. He wanted it loaded. I'm going to put the gun on the porch. That horse is tearing up the fence. It's gone crazy, Violet. I don't know, rabies maybe. The doctor thought encephalitis. From mosquitoes."

"John says make a cross," Violet said, hoping it would help. "Like this, Hank." She reached for his hand and poked her fingernail hard into his skin one way, then the other. "See, mosquito bite not itchy now. John says."

He stared down at the mark on the back of his hand and then pulled away. He gripped the rifle butt. He swallowed. "Something bad happened to John, Violet, something real bad. Couldn't staunch the bleeding, the wound. Couldn't stop." He looked helplessly around the kitchen at the blackened mess. "We couldn't —" Hank's mouth gaped again, but no sound came. He looked down at the rifle in his hands as if he wondered how it got there. "Stay here now," he said, too sharply, louder than he had ever spoken to her.

Violet began to cry. "That bad horse, Hank." Her face crumpled. "I don't like it!"

He reached down to touch her cheek. "I'm so sorry, Violet. I don't, either. Let me just put this outside, and we'll wait for your father together."

THE SCREEN DOOR SLAMMED, AND SHE WOKE WITH A start.

It took a bit to work out that she was on her own bed, the quilt pulled up over her. Hank must have put her here. She remembered crying herself out on his lap. Now, she heard voices in the kitchen. Hank and her father, loud and awful. Her head filled up with the bad thing. Something bad had happened.

She slid off the bed and opened the door. Hank gripped Father's shoulder, and in his other hand, he held a row of shiny gold, pointy things. *Pretty*, she thought. But if Hank let go of Father's shoulder, Father might just fall to the floor. Father held the rifle, the long, black end pointed at the cellar door. His head hung low, and he looked up only when Hank pressed the gold things against Father's chest and shook him as if he was trying to wake him up. "Four in the clip," Hank said, "and one in the chamber."

Violet stood in the doorway and finally, in a small voice, let them know she was there. "Where's John? Can we make his birthday cake now?"

The men turned to her, and Father let out a groan, a terrible, strangled sound. Violet remembered last year's bull calf, the one that fell down into the coulee. The coyotes had been at it overnight, and it lay there barely alive, crying, in the morning. Broke its back, Father said, and shooting it was the kindest thing. That's how Father sounded now, like that bull calf.

He grabbed the gold things from Hank and went out into the storm. The screen door banged shut behind him. Violet went to the window and watched Father head toward the barn. Once he was beyond the lilacs, the branches whipping in the wind, he was lost to view. She pulled the gingham curtains across the window and turned to survey the kitchen. Her throat was so tight it was hard to swallow, and she felt like she might be sick.

Hank sat down heavily on a chair by the table and put his face in his hands.

Father always took that rifle when he went about the business of killing a pig or a steer. Violet started to cover her ears, but instead, she carefully picked up the green bowl from the sideboard and held it to her chest, the smooth ceramic cool in her hands. Mama always made John's birthday cake in the big green bowl. Last year, Violet and John sat like hungry birds on the edge of the kitchen chairs until she scraped the batter into the pan. Then Mama let them lick the spoon and run their fingers around the bowl. Last year, John painted a chocolate moustache on Violet's top lip and then one on himself. She left hers on until Mama finally caught her before supper and scrubbed her face hard with a dishrag at the kitchen sink.

Now, Violet set the bowl back on the sideboard. She waited and watched a potato bug make its way from the blackened flour into the sugar. She wondered where it came from. It was too cold for bugs. Hank reached for her, and she crawled up on his lap, pressing her head to his chest. He tried to cover her ear, but she pulled his hand away.

The wind was rattling the windows, but she still heard the shot. And another. Another after that. Then again. Five times.

Violet knew John's birthday horse was dead.

VIOLET THOUGHT ALL THE MORNING NOISES IN THE house were louder than usual. A scrape of the chair on the floor-boards. The squeak of the hinges when Dr. Speight opened the bedroom door. The snap of dry poplar in the woodstove. Each sound made her jump.

The worst, though, was the one Mama kept making. It was a little moan, not often, but it seemed to come from somewhere else. Mama just sat on a straight-backed chair by her bedroom window, rocking ever so slightly, her fingertips pressed against her mouth. Violet thought maybe it was to keep from screaming again. So maybe the moaning wasn't so bad.

Dr. Speight put a hand on Father's stooped shoulder and led him out of the bedroom. Violet looked over her shoulder at Mama. She didn't even seem to notice they were leaving the room. "She'll sleep soon," Dr. Speight said to Father, nodding his head toward the bedroom as Violet carefully closed the door. "Too much for any woman to bear in this life. To lose such a fine child. To bear the burden of such heartache with the other." The doctor spoke to her father as if Violet wasn't standing right there in the kitchen. He always talked as though Violet wasn't there. He patted Father solidly on the back and began to gather up his bag.

VIOLET

John was buried two days later, the time it took to thaw the ground down past the frost line under a slow-burning patch of coal and straw.

The night John died, the thermometer at the town hall showed it was -10. A record low, people said. The kind of cold expected in early March but so unusual for May, when they were already thinking about gardens and seeding

It brought with it the sort of bitter winter cold that made the eyes tear up and burn. Violet's chest prickled with needles the instant she set foot outside and took a breath on the morning of the funeral. A couple of inches of snow had blanketed the fields as if it was just trying to make it all the more miserable.

Violet stomped her cold boots in the trampled snow beside her parents at Waterhole Cemetery. The pioneer graveyard was a long way from home, two section roads over toward the coulee. Her toes tingled, but no matter how she stomped and fidgeted, she couldn't get warm. It was an afternoon when there was a pale, yellow light but no sun. There were only faint purplish rings where the sun should have been the brightest. "Sun dogs," Hank told her.

A tinge of colour hung low in the leaden sky just over the

horizon, a cold blush of pink just beyond the naked caragana that made up the cemetery windbreak. Still, it hurt to look out across the white fields, and a dull throbbing soon began behind Violet's eyes. She wrinkled her nose. The sharp stink of burned coal and straw hung close in the air, a scent strangely out of place when the cold usually erased all smells.

Her good Sunday coat was a size too small and too thin to keep out the chill. It seeped through her coat and woollens and, she thought, right into her bones. The prairie wind sliced across the snow in the fields and polished to an icy finish the drifts around the headstones. The people at the funeral stood close together with their backs hunched against the wind, their breath white with crystals. Violet knew to keep her breathing shallow and quick when it was cold outside; deep breaths hurt and made her have a coughing fit.

She looked around at the small circle of people and thought she had never before seen so many people all wearing black clothes. Hank stood close to her with his girlfriend, Emily Stewart. Violet liked Emily, and she smiled up at her to show she was glad Emily had come. Talking to Emily made her feel grown up. Hank's father and mama, George and Erna, were there, and the pastor, the Lundquists, the Kramers, and the Dechants. Violet thought she saw Steve Dewater at the back of the crowd. He was shuffling from one foot to the other with some other kids who must have gone to school with John, but she couldn't see around some of the grownups.

Miss Scott was there with a tall, stern-looking man who wore a hat that had a funny crease on top. He had a moustache and a long fancy coat. Mr. Nik was there next to Father, but his wife must have stayed home with all their children. Mr. Nik was easier to say, but Mama said he was a grownup, so she should call him Mr. Yuzik. He patted Father on the back and looked sad.

Father had an arm clamped around Mama as if he didn't want her to fall over. She just hung there, and Violet knew that if Father let go, Mama would probably just sink to the ground in a heap.

The cold crept down the back of Violet's neck, where her scarf rode up over the collar of her coat. She almost reached up to straighten it, but Mama never liked it when Violet fidgeted, so she kept still and let the wind creep down her back. Not that Mama was paying any attention to what she was doing.

Violet stole a sideways look at the men who carried the box from the wagon, six large farmers who looked almost comically out of place in their Sunday suits and combed hair. Some looked like they wanted to loosen their ties, but that wouldn't have been polite. The elm trees by the gate had sprouted tiny buds, pretty now and all shiny with ice. The men passed under the branches and carefully shifted their boots from side to side, just like the horses hitched up to the cutters. Violet's stomach turned over in a moment of fright when she thought she might laugh. People weren't to laugh at funerals.

She bit down on her lip. Hank looked up then, and she gave him a tiny wave with her gloved fingertips. He smiled a little, but his chin wobbled, and Violet felt he might cry. And Emily's uncle, Bob Larson, was there. So were Rolland Nordling, Ian Hall, and Nels Dykstra, the blacksmith.

That other man was Joe something, Violet thought, but she couldn't think of his last name. She frowned and poked a little hole in the packed snow with the toe of her boot. She thrust out her chin and squinted out past the wooden gate, narrowing her eyes against the white glare. Oh, yes, he was the pig farmer, she remembered suddenly. She had ridden to his farm in the old truck with Father one morning last spring to buy two weaner pigs. It was a good remember.

The cold breeze tugged at Violet's scarf, and she shivered. She felt a little sorry for the pig farmer now, and the other men who had to carry John in the wooden box on such a cold day. That big box must be so heavy.

Chumak. She remembered suddenly. The pig farmer's name. She leaned over to Emily. "He is Mr. Chumak," she whispered, the words turning to white wisps in the cold air. "He got pigs. You 'member my pigs? Glen and Brent?"

Emily nodded briefly and squeezed Violet's mittened hand, shushing her with one gloved finger to her lips. "Hush now, Violet," she whispered back. "Pastor is talking so nice about your brother."

Pastor droned on in a soothing voice. Violet listened hard and tried to understand what it all meant. "A young life full of potential . . . taken too soon . . . who are we to know God's plan?" The pastor finally said John's soul was gone to life everlasting, and Violet wondered how that could be since Father said being dead meant he was all gone and not alive anymore. She wanted to ask but decided against it.

She looked out toward the road instead, where the horses shook themselves, tossed their heads, muzzles frosted white, and shifted against the harnesses. People began to drift off quietly, anxious to warm themselves but still wait a respectful amount of time. They began to move away, feeling the pull of evening chores.

Emily took Violet's hand and squeezed it. They picked their way through the snow past the two elm trees at the gate and out to the road to the cutters, where the horses stamped and snorted, anxious to be on the move.

Violet looked back to see Hank and Father steering Mama by her elbows through the small crowd of farmers who muttered their sympathies and shook Father's hand. Their wives clutched their collars against the cold and promised baking, preserves, and prayers. Her father waited, hollow-eyed, beside the cutter as Hank helped Mama up and settled her under a buffalo robe. Father nodded to each neighbour who reached out for his hand, his gaze always returning over their shoulders to the black box, so stark against the snow.

Violet could see that the pastor and two men had stayed behind, standing straight, heads bowed. They waited only a few solemn moments before quickly shrugging into their heavy coats and pulling on work gloves once people had turned away.

Hank took Father's arm and leaned close. "William, it's time to go. We should get Louise back to the house. She wants to lie down. And Violet needs to get out of the wind. She shouldn't get a chill."

Mr. Yuzik, who sometimes smelled like garlic and wine when he sat on the porch with Father, appeared and latched onto Father's other arm. Together they helped Father up to the seat beside Mama, who stared silently out across the snow-covered fields in the direction away from the cemetery. Father sank down heavily as if his knees gave out, and Hank drew the heavy blanket across them. Hank lifted Violet up next to Emily, who wrapped another woollen blanket around Violet's shoulders and tucked it in over her lap.

"William," Mr. Yuzik said, noisily clearing his throat and pulling off his thick mitten. "*Vybachte za vtratu.* So sorry." He pulled himself up on the runner and reached for Father's hand. "You let me know you need something. We are close by, so you just be yelling if you need something. You and your missus and little girl."

Father nodded and gripped Mr. Yuzik's hand. Mama turned slightly and stared blankly at him. Mr. Yuzik reached out to pat Violet's knees through the blanket. He took off his other glove, leaned forward, and cupped her face in his big hands. He kissed her cheek, his whiskers scratchy on her face. Violet rubbed her mitten over her mouth. "*Kveetochka moya,*" he said. Then he stepped back away from the cutter and blew his nose loudly into his handkerchief. He nodded grimly at Mama, who turned away and fixed her gaze again out over the prairie.

Bundled in so tightly, Violet could turn her head just enough to look back at the trampled place in the snow around the dark hole where John would stay. Violet wondered if he would be too cold. She thought better of asking. Father and Mama sat huddled in the cutter across from her, their knees turned outward and away from each other under the heavy robes. Father seemed old; it frightened her, and she looked away.

The cemetery was tidy, edged by last fall's brown flags of dry sorrel plumes and stalks of yellow sagebrush poking up through the snow. The elm trees arched over darkly; the bare branches seemed to reach down toward John's open grave. Most of the cemetery looked soft and white, like John's feather comforter, still on his bed at home. Maybe they should have tucked that around him so he would keep warm.

Violet heard only bits of what Emily was telling her about nice fried chicken, crackling, boiled potatoes, and a green jelly mould waiting at the house. The church ladies would have it ready for them.

Violet struggled to get a better look back over her shoulder. Mr. Yuzik still stood there, pulling on his gloves, watching them go. He waved. Behind him, Violet could see the men lowering John's box into the ground amongst the grey headstones, growing so small as Chub and Florie pulled the cutter away, the runners hissing across the new snow.

VIOLET

THE BURKE FARM, OCTOBER 1929

When John died, the corners of Mama's mouth turned down and stayed that way. Violet had watched her put the green bowl away. She never used it again. Violet wondered if she might not even take it out for her birthday.

Violet overheard her say to Father after the funeral that it was like before, that she couldn't get a decent breath of air. Violet didn't know what bad thing happened before John went away, but it worried her when she heard her mother say that this time she would never breathe properly again. Violet worried every time she looked at Mama's face.

That summer drifted by in one long stretch of silence. Except sometimes in the night, Violet thought she heard someone yelling. Or crying. In the mornings, in that warm time when Violet felt like she was floating just before waking, she thought of the things she and John would do after breakfast. When she opened her eyes, the bad feeling would knot up in her stomach.

Father always had a smile and a morning hug for her, and even though she was too big now to fit, he'd pull her onto his lap at the kitchen table while she rubbed the sleep from her eyes. But the mornings seemed to be the time of day when Mama was most unhappy. If her eyes looked dark, Violet tried to steer clear of her.

By the end of October, hard frosts had come, and people waited sullenly for winter to set in. Harvest hadn't taken long. The drought had seen to that. One evening, Violet was writing her letters, waiting for Guy Lombardo and his Royal Canadians to come on the radio. Father had brought home the gleaming Stromberg Carlson radio, that's what he called it, that summer. It cost a lot of money, Violet remembered Father saying, but maybe it would cheer up Mama. He was right. When she turned the dials, the music crackled and hissed, and she smiled a little.

Suddenly Guy Lombardo, who had just started playing, was gone, and another man was talking, too loud. Violet knew it must be something bad because Mama made a deep noise in her throat and struggled up from her chair. She reached for the doorframe and shuffled into the kitchen for some water. She kept asking Father what it all meant. Violet thought maybe if Mama took big deep breaths, just like John did when he said he could smell rain, it would help Mama. Violet could show her how. But something about the way Mama was leaning over at the sink stopped Violet from following her into the kitchen. Mama gripped the edge of the counter so hard her knuckles looked frostbitten.

When the phone rang, Father stood in the kitchen and talked so low Violet couldn't hear. Mama snatched up the dishrag from the sink. She turned around and twisted it so much that Violet thought it might rip into pieces. Violet tiptoed to the doorway and pressed herself against the wall, out of sight. She tried to quiet her breathing so her ears would hear better. She listened to her parents talk in hushed tones, words that made no sense.

"That was Hank," Father said, hanging the receiver back on the hook. "He and his folks went into Regina, you know, for the christening of Erna's nephew. He just read to me the headline in today's *Daily Star*." Father crossed the kitchen, stumbled a little on the rag rug, and sank into a chair at the table. The worried man on the radio was still talking about a crash. *A crash?* Violet thought. *Did Hank bang up his truck?*

"Well? What does the newspaper say?" Mama asked, the tea

towel finally at rest in her hands. She turned from the sink, and Violet crept forward. She waited quietly at the table. She was oddly hungry for breakfast bacon but dared not speak.

"'Near Panic Follows Slump in Stock Prices,'" Father repeated. "Front page. And the *Morning Leader* said something about stocks crumbling. Money's going to be worthless."

"What will we do, William?"

"We'll manage. You'll see. Farmers won't have it as hard as town people. Right as rain," he said, but he put his face in his hands. Violet felt her heart race.

"Right as rain? What do you mean by that?" Mama said. "Tell me how this life can get any worse. I don't think I can bear any more."

He just shook his head. Father and Mama didn't seem to notice she was even there. Violet finally went to her room and put herself to bed.

TWO WEEKS LATER, AS THE SATURDAY MORNING SUN was just beginning its pale presence in the eastern sky over the barn, Mama shook Violet awake. When Violet pulled on her flannel robe and came out into the kitchen, she saw that it must be washday. Mama had water boiling in the copper tubs on the stove. But washday was Monday. Today was Saturday. Confused, she stood in the doorway by the sideboard and tried to tidy her hair with her fingers. Mama was talking to her so fast.

"Violet, come on now," she said, turning from the stove and pointing to a few rhubarb stalks beside the cutting board. "Pull the tough strings for me. We'll just add it to what I've got here. The stove's hot anyway. Mind you don't cut yourself. Just chop the woody ends off and pull the strings like I showed you."

"Pie?"

"Yes, a pie. Why not?'

"What kind?"

"What?"

"Kind of pie?"

"Well, rhubarb by the look of it."

Two copper boilers with the good handles stood on the wood-stove, a slow roll of Sunday shirts, underthings, sheets, and Violet's Sunday pinafore. Two others on the floor, the tin ones, one ready for the bluing, the other with rinse water. Steam rolled up over the stove, curled out from under the warming shelf and swirled through the sunlight in the kitchen. The frost on the windowpanes had melted, and drips of water ran in jagged streaks down the glass. There had finally been two or three lasting snow-falls, and the nights were cold. The windowpanes would be laced with frost again by the afternoon.

"There's a biscuit there for your breakfast, Violet. And milk. Hurry now. Do as I say," Mama said absently. She stirred the clothes in one of the tubs with a long stick.

Rhubarb pie, Father's favourite. Mama was making a pie. Violet couldn't remember the last time they had pie after supper and was even more surprised that Mama had asked her to help. Rhubarb hadn't grown so well with it being dry, but there was one plant just to the side of the house where Mama always threw wash water. Mama had stooped over the plant in June, slicing her knife at the base of the red stalk, careful not to nick tender new shoots, then whacked off the big leaf without straightening up. Violet had held open her apron to gather the stalks. These few, the last in the root cellar, were tough, but Violet's lips puckered at the thought of tart pie after supper. Violet sat down on a chair in the corner of the kitchen.

The pastry was already rolled out and ready to line the pie tin. Mama cut the leftovers into little shapes and sprinkled them with sugar and cinnamon. Violet remembered how much John loved the fluted edges of Mama's pies, even if they were a little burnt. Thinking of him made her throat feel tight, but she drank her milk and brushed biscuit crumbs from her robe.

"I'm a good helper." She took up a large stalk and picked at the end with her fingernail until she could pull the tough strings away. She looked to make sure Mama wouldn't see, then bit into the end of the woody redness. She squeezed her eyes tight when the tartness bit back. Wouldn't Father be proud when he came in from chores?

"My two girls," she knew he would say. "I'm a lucky sod then, aren't I?" Times were hard, he often explained, but they were blessed with enough food to get by. Just last night, before he went out to do chores, he bent to give Violet a kiss. "There are families with only potatoes," he said. "And there are those who would be grateful for potatoes. We'll be right come spring. We'll have a fine planting and no grasshoppers this year. With a bit of luck, the predictions in *Farmers' Almanac* will be spot on, I reckon."

Mama's face was shiny, her cheeks all rosy from standing over the boiling water. A long strand of hair had come undone, pasted across her forehead. She looked as if she'd been caught outside in the rain. She wiped her face with the hem of her apron and pulled at the front of her dress to get a little breeze on her skin.

Mama went to the window with the rag and wiped the pane. She looked out into the yard. Violet frowned. Mama had her church dress on, the grey one she wore on Sunday. But it wasn't Sunday today. Couldn't be. Father hadn't shined his shoes last night.

Violet watched her mother pull pieces of clothes out of the rinse and let them drip for a while on the end of the stick. It reminded Violet of John when he fished in the slough and caught a big snarl of weeds on his hook. Mama set the stick aside and wrung each piece into fat ropes before she tossed them into the big basket. Woollen socks already hung on the line behind the stove.

"Violet, let's hurry now so I can get that pie in the oven. I've hung your father's overalls on the clothes rack in the front room. Hand me those clothespins. I've got to get these at least hung up before—" Mama looked up suddenly and walked quickly to the window. By then, Violet could hear a car engine. It didn't sound familiar.

"Mama, who is it?" Violet asked. Company for supper. That would be fun. No wonder Mama was dressed nice, and there was going to be a pie. Maybe the Dechants, or maybe Hank and Emily. She hoped it was Hank and Emily. They were here too early for supper. But if they were coming, she would know, Violet thought. Things were happening too fast. Violet frowned.

"He's early," Mama said. "Too early." She dabbed at her cheeks and forehead with the rag. She tucked her hair behind her ears and looked back at the stove. Hands behind her back, she fumbled to undo the apron strings.

"Who is here, Mama?" Violet asked again.

Mama wiped her hands on the apron. She folded it quickly and laid it on the table.

"Mama?" Violet waited but couldn't catch her mother's eye. Her mother just glanced around the kitchen, buttoning the top button on her dress.

Violet got up from the table, a rhubarb stalk in each hand, the bad feeling crawling up into her chest. Mama seemed strange, almost scared. Not the kind of scared she had been when she found the baby skunks Violet brought into her bed. More like the kind of surprise when Father brought home the orange prairie lily he dug up for her to plant in the dirt beside the front step. She had cried then, too, but Father said it was happy crying.

It was then Violet saw the suitcase on the floor near the door, almost hidden where the barn coats hung. Violet felt the bad feeling grow warm in her throat, and she tried to swallow.

"Where you go, Mama?"

"Violet, now you listen to me." Mama was suddenly at the door, pulling on her town coat and dragging the suitcase out. She wound her red muffler around her neck, picked up her purse from the sideboard and hung it over her forearm. Mama pulled a thick white envelope from the pocket of her dress. She stared at it for a moment before she set it between the salt and pepper shakers on the kitchen table. "Are you listening?" she said sharply.

Violet nodded, and her bottom lip began to tremble.

"I want you to make sure your father gets that letter, so just leave it right there. Don't touch it," Mama said, throwing a kerchief around her head and tying it under her chin. "He'll explain all this to you once he reads the letter. I have to go away. I just can't—well, you can't possibly understand this. I'm just going, that's all."

Violet felt as if she'd swallowed a large piece of bread too quickly and it stuck there. She rubbed her throat and began to cry.

"Violet, now stop. You have to be a good girl. You need to pay attention now. Don't put any more wood in the stove, do you hear me? It'll be fine until your father gets back. He's just gone across the coulee to the Dechants', and he'll be back at lunchtime. I wanted to leave him a pie, Violet. I wanted to have the laundry done, things tidy." Mama looked out the window again at the dark car idling in the snow, her eyes brimming.

Violet went to the window and peered out. She knew the car. That car came to the farm once a month. "Mr. Watkins man is here. You buy something, Mama?"

"Violet, he is giving me a ride to the train station. I'm going back to Toronto. I saved the egg money for so long for me. And John. I thought maybe he'd—well, that doesn't matter now. I'll write you a letter when I get there, okay? Maybe when you get to be a big girl, you can come on the train to see me. Maybe. Would you like that?"

Violet, uncertain, nodded. She didn't understand.

Mama grasped the handle of her suitcase. "No more wood in the stove, do you hear me? You just wait for your father. You can turn on the radio if you like, maybe practise your printing. I have to go."

"Me go, too."

This wasn't good. Violet's chest felt tight with the bad feeling.

The words didn't want to come, but she forced herself to speak. "Don't go away. Mama stay with me," Violet managed, her eyes wet and her nose beginning to run. She held up her arms toward her mother, rhubarb stalks held tightly in each hand. "Mama, stay! With me!" The rhubarb fell from her hands. She reached for the suitcase and grasped the handle. She tried to drag it back into the kitchen.

"Violet, for heaven's sake! Stop it!" Mama slapped away Violet's hand, and Violet stumbled back. The rhubarb felt like kindling under her bare feet.

"Mama stay, make pie. I help!"

"Violet, go wipe your nose now. Just be a big girl."

The door closed, and she was gone. Violet picked up the stalks from the floor and dropped them on the table. She ran to the window. The car revved in the yard and backed up before it swung around to head back out the lane. Mama's face was pale against the car window. She was looking at the house. Violet slapped on the cold glass with the flat of her hand and held it there in case Mama could see her. The car moved ahead and drove away, getting smaller against the white fields. Violet watched until it disappeared at the turnoff to the main grid road.

The house was quiet. Violet's handprint, dripping like a stain on the foggy window, seemed the only evidence of her mother's leaving.

"Not scared," Violet whispered, her heart pounding in her chest, her fingertips white as she gripped the sill. "I stay right here. Mama be right back. Father come soon. Calm down. I am a good girl."

The wash water bubbled lazily behind her on the stove, and Violet quietly sobbed at the window until she got the hiccups. She pulled a chair closer to the kitchen table and sat down. She looked at the pie dough rolled out on the table and poked her finger in the middle. It left a hole. She pulled a piece from the edge, just a little piece, and chewed it.

Violet reached out and touched the corner of the fat envelope, and pushed it just enough so she could see her mother's handwriting. She sniffed. *William.* She took a small pencil stub from her bathrobe pocket. Carefully pulling the envelope toward her, she hunched over the paper and printed one word beside her father's name. *Violet.* She tilted her head.

"Me, too," she said to the empty kitchen. She slid the envelope back between the salt and pepper shakers and wiped her nose on the sleeve of her bathrobe. She picked up the rhubarb stalks from the table and laid them across her knees. She pulled off another piece of pie dough and put it in her mouth. The fire began to die down, and the washtubs on the stove groaned and pinged. She watched her handprint on the windowpane drizzle slowly down the glass in jagged streaks. She ate another piece of dough and waited for the sound of her father's footsteps on the porch.

LOUISE

THE BURKE FARM, NOVEMBER 1929

Dear William,

I think it is better if I leave now before winter truly comes. Maybe I will feel differently in the spring, but I can't bear the thought of another winter. It's not just the cold, the harshness of it day after day for weeks and months on end. I can do the work in order for us and the animals to survive. It's not just that. What I can't bear is the relentless thought that I will always have Violet in my care for the rest of her life. For the rest of my life.

I know that sounds cruel and selfish, but you knew from the beginning that I was afraid to keep her. I was so unhappy when she was born the way she was, afraid that it would never get better. You insisted that we keep her. But it is me she is with every day, year after year, and since John died, I am without a second to myself. There is not a second in the day when she is not there, wanting something, breaking something, needing something. Always needing. You are outside, free to come and go. The farm is your respite. For me, I have Violet, the biggest chore of all.

I never told you what really happened to Sarah. I've never told you who Sarah was, not really. I told you some of it before we were married in Toronto, but only the parts I could bear to remember. I tried to believe it happened that way. When you offered me a new life, I thought I could reimagine history in a way that suited me. I was terrified that, if you knew, you wouldn't want me. But perhaps if I tell you the truth now, my leaving will not seem quite so selfish as it must appear. I hope so. I am not a bad woman, William. But I was once, and that is what you must know. It is the thing for which I cannot forgive Violet. She is the constant hold on the past, though none of it is her fault. Every day, she reminds me of Sarah and what happened to both of us.

You remember Uncle Axel and me telling you about the orderly who hurt Sarah? He didn't hurt only her. There were others. Bert always seemed to be looking at me, at a few of the other girls. I saw things that I've tried very hard to forget. It's no excuse, but I was afraid of him. Most of us were.

Late that fall, when Bert seemed to notice Sarah, I was spending time with her when I wasn't on shift. I stayed in the staff residence across an open field, and I would take Sarah to my room to fix her hair or to draw pictures with her. No one cared. But when Bert started being overly friendly with her, it terrified me. There was talk about what he did to some of the young girls. And others. I was afraid to tell for fear he'd turn on us or hurt Sarah, or worse. I tried to explain to Sarah that she should stay away from him, that he was not nice. But he could act so charming.

One day, Sarah was in my room. We were making cut-out dresses for the paper dolls she kept in a box under my bed. It was late and close to headcount on Sarah's ward, but we were almost done. Sarah didn't speak much or very clearly, but we didn't really need to talk. She was in such a happy mood. Suddenly my door opened, and Bert was standing there. Men weren't allowed in the women's residence without permission. I couldn't imagine how he got in. But then he was persuasive, and I'm sure he talked someone into lending him the key.

"I know where some kittens are, Sarah," he said. "If you come with me, I will give you one."

I jumped up and knocked all the paper doll clothes and the scissors on the floor. I told him he was a liar. Sarah just sat there on my bed, her eyes huge, looking at me and then at Bert and back again. I realized she was frightened, not of him but of me. I was the one upset, telling her she couldn't have a kitten. I was the one telling her it was against the rules. I said, "Don't listen to him."

William, this is the part where I wish I could tell you that I ran out into the hallway, screaming for help. I wish I could say I ran to the manager to tell him his brother was a monster. I could have followed them, found something, a board, a shovel, something to hit him with.

But I did none of those things. I almost cannot bear to tell you this, but I must. Sarah was his child. And mine. It had been four years since he caught me alone and forced himself on me. I discovered I was with child months later, and Matron reduced my duties as I neared the time. I was given the groundskeeper's cottage when Sarah was born. I was so ashamed and couldn't go back to Uncle Axel and Auntie Freda in Toronto. I just stayed there with the baby. We all knew there was something wrong with her. It was so ironic that we were already in the very place a doctor would have sent her had I given her up. Of course, I never told Bert about her. Perhaps he guessed, but he kept his distance for such a long time. He even left the institution and went back to work in the orchards. But he returned, and there he was now, holding her, holding his daughter—our daughter—and I was powerless.

I wish I could say I ran to the Matron and demanded she call the police. Instead, I unlocked the side door. And instead of looking at Sarah as he carried her out into the dark, I just closed my eyes. And then I shut the door behind them. And then I just waited for him to bring her back.

You know what happened next. I told you in Toronto, and that part of it was true. They said she fell from the bridge. It's what Bert told them. That was a long time ago, but the guilt has never gone away. I thought it did. Those wonderful days when you came back to Toronto, when we lay in the grass and watched the clouds, I believed I could forget. When we made our life here and then when John was born, I thought I had been forgiven. But then Violet came, so much like Sarah in every way, and I knew I never would be able to forget her. Or forgive myself.

Since John died, I've thought of nothing else.

Violet comes to me with the egg basket, or watches me at the stove, or waits for me at the table, looking so much like Sarah. She torments me, William. There have been times when I honestly thought I should just drown myself in the well. When people would talk about the healing powers of Lake Manitou, God forgive me, I thought of taking her there and drowning her, too. She makes me relive everything that happened to Sarah. She has from the moment she was born. I know that it isn't fair to her or to you, but I can't help it.

Please, let me go.

Louise

VIOLET

THE BURKE FARM, NOVEMBER 1929

"What does she say, Father?"

Violet watched her father wince and rub his neck. He was hunched awkwardly over the kitchen table, over Mama's letter, and Violet thought he might have stopped breathing. He reached up and slowly took his black hat off and put it on the table. He suddenly let out an odd sound and rolled his head from one shoulder to the other. The room seemed strangely tilted. Violet sat solidly on the chair, still gripping the rhubarb, and waited.

"Where did Mama go?" she said in little more than a whisper.

"I don't know, sweetheart," Father said, his voice raspy. "Let me work out what she says here."

"She said pie." Violet sniffed and pointed at the pastry rolled out on the table. "But she didn't make one. I can. I make one. I like pie."

"I do too, my girl." Father's voice cracked, and he cleared his throat. He looked about the kitchen as if it could help him make sense of Mama's words. His hands were shaking. He folded the letter and pushed it into his shirt pocket. "Look here. Let me get the fire built up again, and you finish your mother's pie. Mustn't waste what she started," he said, forcing a smile. "Come on, then. You get busy cutting that rhubarb and mind the sharp edge. Looks like she's got this almost ready. We'll have a lovely pie for our tea!"

Violet nodded and grasped the knife. Relief flooded her chest. Father always made things all right again. She sliced the rest of the stalks and dropped them in the bowl with butter and sugar. Violet dragged the dough over the pan and frowned when it pulled apart. She patched it with extra dough and poked it with a fork. "Like Mama does," she said, trying to trim the edge.

"Not exactly fluted, but it looks very nice. What's next?" William said, dropping some woodchips and kindling into the firebox. He poked a piece of wood into the stove. Violet dipped a spoon into the mixture. Father fingered the edge of the letter sticking out of his pocket.

"Butter," Violet said.

Father opened the icebox, set the dish on the table, and reached for a knife from the sideboard.

"Just some lumps on top when I fill it up," Violet said. She scraped the filling into the pie shell, and Father dropped a few pieces of butter from the knife, pushing them off with his finger around the top. She nodded her approval, but when she tried rolling the last of the dough for the top, it crumbled, and a good part fell to the floor. She looked at Father, and her lip trembled again. "Mama do it."

"Yes, she usually does," he said quickly, scooping the dough together and flattening it with his hand on the table. "Look, girl, this will do just fine. Not to worry, it's brilliant." He dropped the piece on the top and scraped the last bits into his hand. He sprinkled that on, too, and smiled at Violet. "I do believe this is the nicest one I've seen!" He leaned down and took her face in his hands. He kissed her nose. "Now, sweetheart, we need to wait for the stove to heat up, then we'll pop it in. Why don't you wash up and then listen to the radio for a bit, eh? There's a good girl."

Violet picked up Mama's apron from the table, wiped her hands, and disappeared into the front room. She waited for the radio to crackle and skip when she turned the dial. The reception was good tonight, and Violet felt better. She clapped as the strains of The Freshmen Quartet blared from the box.

She heard the door open and her father's footsteps over the creaking boards on the front porch. She tiptoed back into the kitchen and stood at the screen door. He'd forgotten to shut the other door, and even though it was cold to stand there, she did. She watched him sink down on the bench. He pulled the letter from his pocket and smoothed it out across his knee. The envelope with her father's name, under which she had printed her own, was still on the kitchen table.

Such pretty handwriting Mama has, she thought. Violet always had wondered how Mama could make such beautiful flowing letters when her hands were so often rough and impatient with her. Now her father mumbled something Violet could hear but not fully understand. When had her mother written the letter? Just before she left, or had she written it long ago? And then Father read the words on the pages, but only in a whisper. Violet held her breath for a moment in the hope she could hear, but the words were only sounds, faint breaths like moths fluttering their wings at the porch light. Sounds with no meaning.

She watched Father fold the letter carefully. He sat quietly and looked out across the farmyard. One of the old barn cats picked its way through the drifted snow just beyond the chicken coop. The white tip of its tail flicked as the cat came to a sudden, fluid stop. It ignored two swallows swooping and diving overhead and focused on something out of Father's sight. Violet thought he should get up and yell at the cat to get it away from whatever was doomed there on the ground. But he seemed just to slump in his chair as if his boots were too heavy to lift. Instead, he opened the letter again.

"Let me go," her father read, more loudly this time. Violet

leaned forward. He put his elbows on his knees, studying Mama's handwriting. Violet pressed her forehead to the screen and thought he looked like he might cry. This time she could hear him. "Let me go?" he said again in a ragged voice. "How can you ask us to let you go when you've already been gone so long?"

VIOLET

THE BURKE FARM, AUGUST 1932

Hank sometimes called her father "the old Kiwi." The Kiwi from New Zealand. Violet liked the way that sounded. It rolled smoothly around in her mouth and slid off her tongue in a way many words refused to do.

"I'm off for a wee bit," Father said one morning after chores. Violet straightened up at the sink and put the pieces of the cream separator on the tea towel to dry. "I come too," she said, knowing by the dark look around his eyes this morning that he hadn't slept. When he hadn't had a good night, he liked to go off alone. So she wasn't surprised when he took her face in his hands and gave her a sound kiss on her forehead. "Not this time, my box of fluffy ducks. I'll be back soon. If I come across some pretty flowers, I'll bring some back for you."

Father was weathered, and he worked hard, but Violet longed for the times when his blue eyes still twinkled. He smelled like the earth and sweet pipe tobacco, and his laughter made creases across his forehead and at the corners of his mouth. Those lines seemed deeper now.

Now Violet worried when her father went off alone like this. Sometimes it was about needing a walk down the coulee to look for the coyote den or maybe to check the fences. He did that a lot since Mama left. Violet figured the fences must be in a pretty sorry state. He just needed to have a think, to have a remember, he told her. He explained things to her in a way she could grasp. It had always seemed to Violet that Mama looked through her, just beyond her shoulder, at something else that needed doing. Sometimes when Violet had tried to give her a hug, Mama got stiff and held her away, saying she was too big to act like a child. Violet had given up trying to figure out what was wrong with being a child.

Getting worked up, Mama called it. "Violet, now hush up. Don't go getting worked up. It's not good for your heart."

It was bad to get worked up. But being happy and getting worked up seemed to sort of go together. It was hard to do one without doing the other. Instead, Violet tried to do what she was told and not make too many mistakes. That day they were boiling whites and making rhubarb pie together, it felt as if it was the only time that Mama had really thought, even for a little while, that she was a good girl, that she could help. And then Mama was gone.

Now Father, he always looked right at her and listened to what she was saying, even when she had trouble making the words come out right. They didn't talk about Mama and John much now that it was just the two of them left. Once, Father pulled out a book with stiff black pages, filled with photographs held in place at the corners with little black triangles. There was only one photograph of her grandmother, her Nanna, and it still hung over the door in a gold frame. She was Father's mother, and Mama used to take it down sometimes to dust it. The glass had cracked a little at the bottom. Someone had been careless with it, Mama had said. "That's what happens, and things get ruined," she said. Sometimes, Father looked at the picture in a way that made it hard for Violet to swallow down a sad pain in her throat. It felt like trying to swallow a bite of meat when she didn't cut it small like Father said she should.

The woman in the picture was so very pretty, with friendly eyes. Violet sighed. Even though she was all blacks and whites and greys, Nanna was so grand and dressed in the kind of clothes nobody in Watrous ever wore. They were black, and on her head was a bonnet with lace trim. The woman sat stiff and straight, her mouth set, but Violet could tell by the crinkles in the corners of her eyes that she laughed a lot. A beautiful tapestry hung in thick, soft folds behind her, and a strange plant with sharp leaves and odd flowers bent its fronds forward to her shoulder. Violet longed to unbutton the collar so the woman could breathe or at least move the leaves so they wouldn't poke her.

"That's your grandmother. Your Nanna in New Zealand," Father would say. Whenever Violet asked, he stood on a chair, reached up over the doorway and carefully took down the photograph and put it on the table for her to see. He would read to her the raised gold lettering on the back. "Rutherford Portrait Studio, Riccarton, Christchurch. That's who made the picture," Father said. "Your Nanna married my father not long after this was taken, and they shifted to Dunedin. I was born there. On a faraway island on the other side of the world."

Mama always said Violet was not allowed to hold the picture herself. It was the only one they had, and she was not to play with it, ever. Father let her hold it as long as she liked. "You are always allowed to hold onto family, Violet," Father told her. "You would have loved your Nanna. She would have been good for you and your mother."

John was dead, and Mama was gone now. But Hank and Emily were close by, and Emily sometimes came to help in the kitchen. Violet looked forward to her visits and tried hard to pay attention to do what Emily said. "Thinking of good things helps us get through hard spells," Emily told Violet. "If you are feeling sad, remember something happy, and before you know it, you'll feel better."

Since Emily and Hank had got married over in Manitou Beach last summer, Violet felt good just thinking that Emily wasn't that far away. Sometimes when Emily came by, they would have tea and cookies, just like real ladies. So when Emily said to think about good things, Violet thought of John. He was a good remembering. While she did her chores, she would think about those nights a long time ago when Father came in after evening chores, before she and John were asleep.

They were little then, small enough to fit in one bed. The door to their bedroom would creak open just a crack. A shaft of light from the kitchen had them blinking like two owls as his shape appeared in the doorway. "Anyone home?"

Sounds of Mama clattering cutlery as she set his place at the table and the aroma of his supper on the woodstove came into their room with him. Hash and milk gravy and baked beans, usually a rice pudding but sometimes even an apple crisp in the oven, mixed with smells of barn, tobacco, and the fragrant alfalfa he'd just thrown to the cows.

"Yes, Father! Here we are. We're not sleepy at all," John whispered back. "Violet's going to be still for a story, right, Violet? Hush now." John pushed against her, pressing Violet against the wall, making a place for Father at the edge of the bed.

"Shush, shush, shush," she chorused agreeably, shaking herself awake, sitting up to see over John's shoulder as Father lit the lamp. He sat down, scraped his little penknife around in the bowl of his cold pipe, and pulled from his shirt pocket a packet of tobacco. He pinched and tamped, and he always started the story the same way. "Now, where to begin, children? Where to begin?" Striking a match on his thumbnail, he sucked in smoke through his teeth, and the flame crackled in the fragrant tobacco. John edged closer to breathe it in.

The tales were always the same, but they were magical. Violet and John hung on to every word, even though they'd heard the stories countless times. Lazy smoke rings swirled over their heads in the lamplight, and their heads filled with Father's tales about escapades with his best mate Bevan Parfoot, with near-ship-wrecks and diabolical hurricanes, dreams of homesteading in the wild west, carving a farm out of the prairie and building a family. Always, as he turned down the lamp wick, Father ended the same way: "I'd do it all again if I knew it would all pay off with such lovely children," he would say. "My big John and my wee Violet."

That was a long time ago, but it was a remember she tried to think about now and then. Now it was just the two of them left, thought Violet. The family Father wanted had shrunk down small again. She struggled with a longing to still be Father's baby, his wee girl. But she was the woman of the house since Mama left. Emily and Hank said so. She had to be a big girl.

"THERE'S A DEPRESSION ON, VIOLET," EMILY TOLD HER one afternoon. Canning jars rattled in the pot of boiling water on the stove. Violet pushed another cucumber into a warm sealer on the kitchen table. "That means everyone has to work hard and try to be happy. There isn't much money for things, not for anybody, so we have to help each other. Even when the wind and dust feel like they're going to just wear away our very skin, we need to look on the bright side."

"Sometimes Father is sad." Violet poked a head of dill weed down in between the cucumbers. "He goes for walks to look at fences. He goes to town sometimes. Without me. He comes back and smells like Mr. Nik's, I mean Mr. Yuzik's, potato wine. Sometimes Mr. Yuzik, he comes here, and they drink lots of potato wine. On the porch. 'To forget,' Mr. Yuzik says." She wrinkled her nose. "But mostly, Father is happy, and he tells me stories. He says funny things."

"What's that one he says? The one he always calls you?" Emily sliced a fat cucumber and arranged the spears in her jar. "The duck one? A box of fluffy ducks, that's it! That's my favourite." When she was little, Violet liked the idea of being a fluffy duck. But she was getting older. She wasn't a baby anymore. Violet thought she was more like one of the doves that cooed on top of the barn.

"Emily, why did Mama go away?" Violet had long tried to work out an answer on her own, and when she asked Father, he said maybe someday, when she was big, she could understand it better.

"Oh, honey, I don't really know why she left," Emily said gently after a moment, leaning over to rub Violet's arm. "Sometimes we don't know why people do the things they do. Sometimes they don't know themselves. Maybe she just forgot to look on the bright side."

"I can!" Violet said.

"Then that's your job, and you can be a big help to your father," Emily said. "It's been a while now, but I'm sure your father misses her. I'm sure you do, too. But, Violet, sometimes your father needs to talk to another grown-up lady. Adults need to talk to other adults sometimes, too."

Violet jabbed another dill head into her jar. She was quiet for a time while they dropped garlic cloves into the last of the jars.

"What lady?"

"Well, I know he likes to talk to Nurse Rees. You know her. He likes to talk to her about you, how to keep you strong and healthy. Here." Emily seemed to ignore Violet's frown and held out a little blue-and-white Watkins box. "Now you take a pinch of alum and sprinkle it on the top of each jar. Just a tiny bit," she said. "Then we're ready for the hot brine. You watch how I do this, and soon you'll be making dill pickles all by yourself."

Violet took to heart Emily's words about helping her father. She tried hard to do her chores just right and remembered to rest when she struggled for breath, just like Emily told her to. But the thought of Father needing another lady to talk to made her throat tighten up, and it felt like she might cry. Wasn't she a grown-up girl now? She was a lady. He didn't need to go to town to see the nurse. He wasn't even sick. She would just have to convince him that just the two of them was all he needed.

Just us, she thought as she dumped alum into the jar.

Emily reached for the box and cried out, "Oh, Violet, just a pinch! Oh my, we'll have to fix this jar, won't we? Not to worry. Here, I should have showed you first." Emily rubbed Violet's arm. "It's all right. My, with that much alum, I'd say we'd have the crispiest pickles in all of Watrous!"

Violet laughed, worries forgotten, and she helped Emily empty out the jar and wipe the white powder off each cucumber.

THAT NIGHT AFTER SUPPER, WHEN THE CHORES WERE done, Father sat on the porch with his pipe and a cup of tea. Violet crawled up on his lap. He grunted and leaned sideways to set his cup on the bench beside his chair.

"Oh, my girl," he said. "Soon, you will be too big to curl up on my lap like a cat."

She snuggled against his soft flannel shirt and breathed deeply. "It's song time," she announced. He groaned, but she knew he was just pretending to protest.

She sang all the words of his favourites, at least the words she could remember. The one about the chickens. The one about the violets. The one about twinkle stars he used to sing to her when she was a baby. She sang so long that Father finally patted her on the arm and asked her to save some breath to cool her coffee tomorrow. Violet sat up, remembering that she needed to tell him something important.

"No nurse." She took his face in her hands to be sure he understood. "Just us."

Father looked at her for a good while, a little sadly, Violet thought. "It does seem to be so, sweetheart. You and me. It did me some good to have a grown-up chat now and then in town. But the nurse said that's all that would come of it. So yes, my girl. Just us." He began to sing softly, and soon her eyelids felt heavy. "'I fell in love with a pretty little hen,'" he crooned and hummed a melody for a while. "'I'll be yours for the rest of my life.'" He held her close and ran his fingers lightly across her cheek until she gave in and fell asleep.

AS THE MONTHS PASSED, VIOLET STRUGGLED TO LEARN all the chores that Mama had never had the time or inclination to show her. Father was a patient teacher.

"Watch me now, girl. Just little taps like this once you set the axe. See how it splits off clean? Now you try it. Mind not to lose a finger." He showed her how to get a fire started in the cook stove and how to fetch well water at the pump or from the rain barrel at the corner of the house, though it was usually dry these days. He was patient when he taught her to heat up water in one of the copper boilers on laundry day. They stood side by side at the line around the back of the house, a cold wind numbing their chapped and aching fingers, until Violet knew how to hang clothes securely so they wouldn't blow away in the first gust.

"It's important that you can look after yourself. You're a big girl now," Father said as she carefully cut up a few potatoes and dropped them into the skillet. The butter was starting to smoke, but he didn't want to rush her and have her fumble with the knife. "Fried potatoes, just the thing. A plate of that, and there's your tea! I'll show you how to make my lovely buttermilk soup with a little brown sugar and butter. We've got our garden, dry as it is, poor thing. We'll manage, and that's all anybody can do."

One evening, Father watched Violet scrape the remnants of their supper of boiled turnips, carrots and potatoes, and stewed saskatoons into the slop pail. He pulled his jacket from the hook at the door. "Lovely supper, my girl. I'm proud of you. And the chooks will be happy, too, with this lot."

"I make biscuits tomorrow," she promised. "I know how."

That would be fine, Violet. You're a clever girl. The lady of the house," he said. "You must remind me to get some wheat ground at the elevator. We're running a bit low." He turned and looked back. "We're doing all right, just us, eh?" He closed the door behind him.

"Lady of the house," Violet repeated out loud when he was gone. "Lady. A big lady." She tiptoed to Father's room and pushed open the door. He always kept the curtains drawn, and the interior, dark and cool, smelled like clean wool and pipe tobacco. She crossed the floor to the vanity where Mama used to sit and brush her hair. Violet loved to watch her. If Mama let her, she'd move one of the two side mirrors so Mama and her own face would appear over and over in the depth of the reflection.

Now, Violet smoothed her hair back from her face. She tucked a loose strand behind her ear, but it promptly fell forward again. Since Mama left, her hair was long, and Father often put it in braids to keep it tidy. Sometimes, for church or going to town, Violet tied Mama's yellow ribbons on the end of each plait. She was glad Mama had left them behind.

"Lady," Violet said again and leaned in close to the mirror. Her cheeks were flushed from the heat of the stove, and she blinked her eyes. When she smiled, the dimple in her left cheek deepened, and her eyes crinkled up. "A big lady now," she said, nodding at herself. "Lady of the house."

Violet pulled on her red sweater and joined Father on the porch after he'd shut the chickens up in their coop for the night. He pinched tobacco from the Bull Durham pouch he carried in his pocket and pressed it into the bowl of his pipe. Leaning back in his rocker, he scraped a match with his thumbnail and cupped his hand around the flame.

Violet pulled her sweater snug and crossed her arms against the chill. She wrinkled her nose at the sharp sulphur smell and waited for the sweet grass scent of lit tobacco.

Father drew in deeply. "Well, we've had a bad patch, my girl. But we've got food on the table and clothes on our backs, and that's a sight more than many. The country will turn around, you'll see. The rain can't stay away forever, so the drought has to end. But our animals are warm and fed well enough, just like us. If you don't have much, you don't have much to worry about, wouldn't you agree?"

They sat comfortably, with only the squeak of his rocker to break the silence. Not certain that he was as happy as he was saying, Violet searched his face to be sure. But there was no bad feeling in her chest to let her know he was worried. She sat back on her chair, and they were quiet together. "Show me stars," Violet finally insisted when she saw that his eyes grew heavy and his chin dipped toward his chest. "Father, now show me stars."

"Right," he said, shaking himself. "Come on, then." He held out his hand so she could make a show of pulling him up. Her arm wound around his waist, and he draped his over her shoulders. They stepped off the porch and ambled halfway out to the barn, to the spot where they always stood to look at the night sky, their backs to the light from the kitchen window. The laying chickens in the coop for the night fell silent at the sound of their footsteps but soon started their fussing again when Father and Violet stood still. Across the coulee, the coyotes were talking.

"There's Orion, my girl." Father pointed with his pipe, and Violet snuggled into the crook of his arm, pulling her sweater across her chest. "You see, right there, his belt is the three stars just across. You see?" He pointed and held his finger until she could find the spot. Violet bobbed her head up and down against his chest. "And there, if you don't look right at it, you can spot the Pleiades. And there it is, Violet. The North Star. It never moves, and it never changes. You keep an eye on that, and you'll always find your way home."

They turned and started back to the house. On the porch, Violet tugged on her father's hand. "Sing the flowers and birds song now!" Violet waited for it, and soon he began to sing. He always did when they stood out there like this before she went to bed. He always showed her Orion first and finished with the North Star, those she remembered best. She felt his deep voice rumble, and his heartbeat drummed into her head. And the words about April showers and flowers in May and raining violets. She thrilled at the mention of her name. Father sang on about clouds and daffodils and the looking for a bluebird.

HANK STOPPED BY THE FOLLOWING AFTERNOON, calling out when he opened the door and stepped inside. Violet was leaning over a large wooden bowl at the kitchen table, bent at the waist, working butter into flour with both hands, a dusting puffing up with each push and pull she made. She held her hands up for him to see. "I make biscuits today, Hank. You love them! I put them in the oven first. When they're brown, you have one!"

"I would surely like to, Violet, but I've got a sow in the farrowing pen with six little pigs born and more on the way," Hank said, leaning in the doorway, a batch of papers and envelopes in one hand. He gently rubbed his eye with his little finger and grunted. "I just brought your mail out. I'm just coming from town and better keep moving. Where's your father?"

"In the shed. He gets some wheat for the mill today. I use all the flour!" Violet said and shook some from her apron. There was white dust in her hair and some on her cheek.

"I can see that!" Hank laughed, a gleeful chortle that always put Violet in a happy mood. "Look, I'll put your mail right here. I've got to go, but tell your father to bring you over to see the baby pigs. They're awful cute."

"Maybe I can have one?"

"You never know!" Hank called, then he closed the door behind him.

Violet rubbed her hands together and picked off the biggest pieces of dough. She poked through the pieces of mail with one finger. The postcard was in the middle, a hand-tinted picture of a strange round red-domed building with a white porch that went all the way around and so many cars parked on the side street she lost count at fourteen. And people in fancy clothes, women in long dresses and hats and men in Sunday suits, strolling along a boardwalk edged by deep green grass, and little children running far ahead. Strange towers poked up high in the air. Some of the other buildings looked like little booths and stalls; they reminded Violet of the ones she'd seen at the Waterhole Sports Day and Fair last year. She had gone to Watrous with Hank and Emily and had so much fun that day. Violet looked at the postcard again. There was writing, too, and she pressed her finger down on the first letter.

"S u n n y s i d e –" she began, saying each letter aloud and then sounding out the word. She worked her way through the whole line. "Sunnyside Boardwalk, Toronto, 1931." Frowning, Violet turned the card over and at once knew Mama's handwriting. Violet's frown grew deeper as she struggled with her mother's spidery letters. She moved her fingertip over the card, and she picked out what she could.

"Doing well. I'm running the boarding house. So sorry for any pain—" Violet struggled to sound out the words and soon gave up. She searched for her own name, for at least a capital V among the loops and lines. It wasn't there. She turned it over again and looked at Sunnyside Boardwalk, Toronto, 1931.

Violet grasped the handle and dragged the lid from the stovetop just enough to drop the postcard into the firebox. She watched the edges curl, and the reds, greens, and yellows of Sunnyside turn black. She put the lid back on and went to her bowl of biscuit dough.

"We do all right, just us," she said. She pulled out a piece of dough and rolled it between her palms. She dropped it on the tray and took another.

WILLIAM

THE BURKE FARM, MAY 1935

The deal had been sealed several times after supper on William's porch. "This good deal for us," Nik Yuzik said, clacking his glass against William's and gripping his hand for yet another shake to confirm the arrangement.

"This good wine," Nik insisted, taking another swallow. "Is chokecherry. Hanusia, she find bushes, but is some big secret where they are! She thinks everyone will come steal them." He burped and pushed his black hair back from his eyes. He looked at William from under unruly eyebrows. "I think maybe she is right, and I have no more chokecherry wine!"

"I tell you, mate," William said. "This is a sight better than that bloody potato wine you brought over here last week. I'll gladly guard Hanusia's chokecherries with my life."

"Ha," Nik barked. "Ha, that is good joke. Oh!" He looked perplexed and got to his feet. "My stomach is not so good." He weaved to the end of the porch, leaned over the rail, retched and coughed.

"What did I tell you?" William called to Nik's hunched shoulders. "Still much better than your vile potato poison! Or last fall, you remember that dandelion vintage? Lovely!"

The Yuziks had about thirty Holsteins and sold whole milk to the dairy in Humboldt. Nik Yuzik coveted William's four Jerseys; they provided Nik a gallon can of rich, deep-yellow cream each week, though even it was not as good or plentiful lately, with the grass so dry and sparse. For the cream, Nik helped butcher enough chickens for the winter. And, since Louise left, it was easier for William to swap cream for a couple of loaves of Hanusia Yuzik's bread once a week rather than make it himself. Violet did all right with biscuits and had tried breadmaking but just couldn't get the hang of it. But she caught on to the new Viking cream separator William brought home. Soon, Violet knew every piece of the machinery, how to fit it together and how to take it apart.

There was also an odd piece of William's land jutting out into the coulee, and it made more practical sense just to have it in grass for Nik's cows as long as he kept the fence in good order. That was the gentlemen's agreement sealed some time ago.

Nik's shoulders shook as he propped himself over the railing. He hawked, a sound like he was shovelling a load of gravel. He straightened and turned around. "*Heemno.*" He coughed and ran a hand through his dishevelled black hair.

"You're a stronger man than I," William said.

Nik staggered back and slumped down on the bench. He wiped his mouth on his sleeve. "Must be some bird shit in that batch," he mumbled and reached around behind the chair legs for the green bottle. "Where is your girl?"

"She likes to listen to the radio before she goes to bed," William said. "She loves Guy Lombardo. Sometimes she sings along so loud you can't hear him."

Nik upended the bottle and shook out the last few drops. "*Heemno. Shlyak tehbeh trahffet.* Shit. Time to go home, my friend."

Two weeks after Victoria Day, William was out on the summer fallow with Chub and Florie, working a patch of stubborn wild mustard that was threatening to spread through the barley. Nik pulled his truck off the road and nosed it down into the ditch. William was off the plow and on his hands and knees, trying to free a stone from between the shares. Nik waded out through the spear grass and brome in the ditch. A few early grasshoppers clicked and jumped as he advanced. It was dry, wheat prices were poor, and grasshoppers threatened what did manage to grow. But still, Nik was cheerful. "*Dobray ranok,* William!" Nik called, cupping his hands. "Good morning!"

The horses swung their heads at the sound of a familiar voice, muzzles buried in the feedbags William had strapped on to keep them still while he inspected the damage.

"Probably the only bloody rock left in this part of the paddock." William crawled out and sat back on his heels. "The tractor is out of commission with no fuel to be had, so I thought I'd take the horses and plow to this patch. Bloody stone. Old Chub and Florie took me right across it. Looks like the tip's broken off." He got up, pushed his hat back, and planted one foot up on a ploughshare, glad for the break. He fetched out his water jug, hidden from the sun in the toolbox, and took a long, deep pull. He emptied a little more on a rag and wiped his face and the back of his neck.

"Now you have clean spot," Nik said. "Yep, if it is not heat, then grasshoppers, and if that is not bad enough, we can have rocks to break machinery with no money to fix."

Nik stood at the edge of the field, and William leaned on the plow. They talked in the easy way of old neighbours about what was to be done about the broken machinery, who would be the best in town at Finlay's to do the repair, and how much it might cost. They compared news on poor grain prices since the crash and how oats might fare with so little rain in the forecast.

"Nothing to it but to try," William said. "We can still feed the cows the thistle, but maybe we'll get a bit of moisture, eh?"

"We can hope so." Nik shrugged and unfolded his arms. "I got to get going. I come back later when you going home, William. I go into town, pick up some more feed at the mill this morning. I go by your place on the way back. Hanusia, she is boiling sheets today, so damn house is like oven. She has the boys churning later, so she is okay if she isn't getting that cream of yours right away."

"No, no. No sense in wasting a trip out here. You go on up to the house," William insisted. "Violet did the separating after milking this morning, so it should be all right. She was at it early, so she's probably got it put by in the cellar with the rest. Maybe a gallon and a half is all, I'll wager. Just the small cream can this time. Cows just don't produce much. Yours either, I reckon. You tell her I said it's fine for you to take it even if it's not full."

William pulled the rag from his shirt pocket. He wet it again and wiped the dirt from his lips. "You hear anything from the boys?"

Nik shook his head and pushed his hands into the sagging pockets of his grey overalls. "Not since letter from Vancouver. They say the men in relief camps are on the boxcars, go to Ottawa." Nik looked up at a cloudless forenoon sky and shook his head. "Hundreds of men, no work. At least Andrij and Mihaylo, they are together. They want to see country, so I guess they will. Better than no work at home. Riding rails. Mihaylo, he says trains like anthills, men crawling all over. They get twenty cents for work, and they want fifty. Government says no, so off they go to see prime minister." Nik sighed. "Sometimes they eat. Lots of time not."

"There's talk that Gardiner doesn't want them coming to Regina. Says if they're going to Ottawa, then they can just keep moving," William said. "I stopped in at Ling's yesterday. Duncan MacLeod was saying that boy, Matt Shaw, is doing a lot of good for the men. Finding people to donate bread, keeping everyone organized."

"Hanusia, she says boys should be here. She says Andrij, he should be here finding wife and milking cows. But it is more food on the table for the others, I tell her. She thinks that is not right thing to say." Nik shrugged and pulled his hat back on his head. "I guess she is right. I am not knowing what is right thing to say about many things." Nik reached up to his neck, pulled aside his flannel shirt, and scratched at the collar of yellowed long johns. William never understood how Nik could stand wearing them all year round.

"Your boys are clever, Nik. If there's trouble, they'll see it coming."

Both men stood silently for a moment, the heat and worry about the drought heavy on their shoulders. William knew Nik's wife was a hard woman. Louise had always said so, but it wasn't his place to ask about it. Nik was basically a good man, and it was a shame his own wife didn't think so. Not that it was any of his business.

"I better be getting to it, Nik," William finally said. "Violet's got some tea brewed. She'll fetch some for you once she gets the cream up from the cellar. You leave some for my dinner, though, you bloody sod!"

"You and your tea. In all years I know you, I never meet nobody who fuss more about goddamn tea. *Naiy tobi kachka kopnaiye.* Good strong coffee, it is good for you. Well." He paused. "Maybe some of good Yuzik wine. I got new one coming soon. I try some today, and maybe my best batch, honest to God. We have some, maybe next week."

"Tea's the only proper drink, but I will take you up on the offer one day soon." William yanked his hat back down over his brow. "Violet'll be pleased to see some company."

"She's good girl, your Violet," Nik said. "Nice friendly girl. Always happy to make best of things."

"She'll talk your ear off about King George," William warned. "We listened to that Silver Jubilee broadcast, and she's right taken with anything he says. She thinks he's speaking directly to her."

"Violet is good girl. How you say, breath fresh air!" Nik laughed, deep and gravely, from his chest. "I don't mind she is talking about George. We have good talks, Violet and me, for long time now."

"She thinks a lot of you, Nik. You're very good to her. Tell her I won't be home until teatime. If I pull that share off, I can get it in to the blacksmith, and maybe Nels can get the tip fixed by tomorrow morning. Tell Violet no need to bring lunch out, then."

William pulled his hat down over his eyes and waved as his neighbour headed back across the ditch to the truck. He called out to Nik's retreating back. "You tell your boys to watch themselves on the trains. I've been listening to the radio, and the whole business is getting pretty tense."

Nik waved a hand over his head to show he'd heard.

"Had something else to do today," William muttered to himself as he watched the dust swirl up on the road after Nik's truck. "Hank's coming to plaster up the barn," William said to the horses. Chub and Florie swung their heads toward him and flicked their ears to ward off flies. "But that's tomorrow, I'm certain." He finally shrugged and crawled back under the plow. "For the life of me, I can't recollect what it is," he said out loud, picking up a wrench. He fit it over the bolt and yanked. "Bloody machinery."

VIOLET

THE BURKE FARM, JUNE 1935

Violet was in her bedroom when she heard Mr. Yuzik's deep voice, and she grinned. She put down her father's overalls and carefully poked the needle in beside the patch she was using for mending. She plucked the loose threads from her apron and smoothed down her yellow cotton dress. She picked up the flyswatter on her way to the kitchen.

"Anybody home?" Mr. Yuzik called through the screen door. "Violet? I come for cream can. Yoo hoo? *Dorbry ranok, khtosh yeh vdoma*? Violet?" He called again. "*Khtosh tahm*? Anybody there? *Neh zhooreshia. Tse ya*. Don't worry. It's just me."

Violet tiptoed to the door with the flyswatter poised over her head. "Shhh," she whispered.

He licked the dust from his lips, pulled off his hat, and wiped the grime from his brow with the back of one hand. He nodded and pulled open the screen door, taking a step inside. As he stood taking up the doorway, three houseflies looped past him in lazy circles, so he shut the screen behind him.

It was a warm, sluggish day. Whenever the screen door opened at this time of year, Violet knew there would be flies, and she battled them all summer long. They were bad, dirty things to have around when she was separating the cream, Father said, so she planned to smack them as quickly as she could. Mr. Yuzik watched her, and his whiskery face creased into a grin, and Violet saw a bit of tobacco between his front teeth. He clapped when she carefully dropped the last dead fly into the slop pail under the sink.

She turned to him, suddenly glad she had washed her hair the night before. Mr. Yuzik always said her hair made her look like a pretty angel. "Hello, Mr. Yuzik," she said, pronouncing the words carefully, her cheeks warm. She wished there had been rainwater in the barrel behind the house for her hair. Soft rainwater from the barrel was best. Not the well water and especially not the slough water, but that's all there was and even that she had to save for washing Father's shirts and then mopping floors after that. Water had to stretch these days, Father said. It had been so long since there was a rain. Emily said if a drop fell from the sky, it would probably knock somebody out. Then they'd have to be revived with a bucket of dust. Sometimes Emily said silly, funny things.

"Good morning, Miss Violet." Mr. Yuzik bent toward her in a little bow. "Your father, he say I find you here. He say you might have some cold tea for a poor old farmer."

"For you?" Violet hesitated.

He nodded and tapped his chest with his finger. "*Tse ya*. It is me," he said.

"You hot?" she asked. "Father, he gets hot from the sun and dust. Lotsa dust. I sweep all the time. I get some tea for you. Me, too." She reached up into the cupboard over the sink for the two good cups.

Since Mama left, Father had let Violet grow her hair long, and it hung loosely around her shoulders. Golden ripe wheat, Father said. He reminded her often that clean hair made her look pretty, and Violet liked to look pretty for Mr. Yuzik.

Father also talked to her about being nice, about being polite. She was not to hug people too much. He reminded her that John's friend Steve Dewater hadn't liked it when she tried to hug him all the time. She was almost sixteen now. That was grown up. And Mr. Yuzik was a grown-up man. Much taller than Father, he was like a big growly bear, but not a bad bear. More like the nice ones in the story Father read at bedtime. She reached up and arranged her hair over one shoulder.

"Rough as guts," Father often said. "But Nik's a good bloke." He was a good provider and a good farmer, Father said. Mr. Yuzik had wild black hair and grey shadows under his eyes, and he always seemed to need a shave. Violet wasn't afraid of him. His gravelly voice intrigued her, even as a child. Sometimes, when Mr. Yuzik and Father sat out on the porch late in the evening, Mr. Yuzik's voice barked in the night air. Violet used to slip past Mama and tiptoe out to the kitchen to listen at the screen door. It was worth the risk of a slap if Mama caught her and sent her back to bed. She wasn't sure just when it happened, but lately, she looked forward to the sound of his voice and his visits even more if Father wasn't there.

"Rough as guts," Violet said.

"What was that, Violet?" Mr. Yuzik said, leaning forward.

"My ears full of dirt from field."

She blushed and put her fingers to her warm cheek. She yanked up the cellar door and disappeared, soon to pop up again, grinning and carefully cradling a mason jar of brewed tea. With one foot, she eased the cellar door shut. She spooned in some sugar and poured cups to nearly overflowing. Mr. Yuzik watched her and cried out, "Uh oh! So full!" He pulled a handkerchief from his shirt pocket, found a clean corner, and wiped at the tea that dribbled on the table.

"I see your father just now, scratching in the dirt," he said. "He is knocking down mustard when I came in. Those poor cows. Not much for them to eat now. It is just dirt, and that is blowing away, too. Dechants, they have dead cows. Too bad." He leaned over and sipped his tea down so it wouldn't spill before he picked up the cup. Violet did the same.

"I think your papa, he is ready for tea when he comes in for sure," Mr. Yuzik said, holding his spectacles up to the light from the kitchen window. "So much dirt in the air, is like big cloud today with the wind and everything. He says no lunch in field today, and I say I tell you." He held his spectacles carefully and rubbed them with a corner of the cloth.

"No lunch. Okay." Violet tucked her hair back behind her ears. Father said Mr. Yuzik was Ukrainian. Violet couldn't pronounce it, but she supposed that was why he talked the way he did.

Most times, if Father was home, he and Mr. Yuzik would talk farming. Lately, they'd been talking about his boys Andrij and Mihaylo going off to Vancouver on the train with lots of other men to find work. But if Father was doing chores or out in the field like he was today, Mr. Yuzik talked to her in his rough voice. Just her. He was big and gruff, and sometimes he was dirty from the field. But she didn't mind. He was so funny when he told her stories about when he was a boy. Those were the best visits. Sometimes she looked forward to them so much she could hardly concentrate on anything else, and she always had a happy, fluttery feeling inside when he sat with her like he was doing now. All grown up.

He seemed to like to visit her too, Violet thought, because each week when he came to pick up the cream, they stood this way in the kitchen. He sang little nonsense songs with words she didn't understand, but he made her laugh anyway.

"We do *bootz* today, Violet?" Mr. Yuzik smiled. She nodded and came to stand in front of him. It was her favourite game. He brushed his hands on the front of his overalls and reached down to cup her face.

"*Peechoo, pahpkoo, nah lopatkoo, peechoo shoo!*" He bent down until their foreheads bumped.

"*Bootz!*" He kissed her cheek and chuckled. He often smelled like potato wine, and it made her eyes water, but she liked the game, so she didn't mind. Lately, Mr. Yuzik liked to *bootz* almost every time he came to the house unless Father was home.

Sometimes he stayed so long that when he looked at the clock up over the front window, he would slap his hand to his forehead. "*Yoy, Bozhe*, look at what time is it now so soon. *Kotrah hodenah*! *Yoy*, Hanusia, she is mad at me for sure!" On those days, he'd hoist up the cream can, say his thanks for the visit, and would trot out the door to his truck.

But there had been times over the last few months, and Violet wished for them more often, when Father was out in the field or away to town, and Mr. Yuzik would come by. He would give her a hello hug and, as he was leaving, a whiskery goodbye kiss on the cheek. Sometimes he would give her a very big hug for a long time. Sometimes when he came for the cream, he asked to talk to Father. Violet thought he was funny because he would then suddenly remember that Father had gone to get barley chop at the elevator. Mr. Yuzik would take off his glasses then and pinch his nose between his eyes. "*Yoy*, my head, I forget," he would say and sigh, shaking his head. "Things fall out my ears." Violet would grab his arm and stand on tiptoe to see if it was true.

His whiskers always tickled her cheek; Violet liked that. His black hair was turning grey around the ears, and some of his whiskers were white. Sometimes he told her she looked especially pretty in her yellow dress. Sometimes he would say her green apron set off her pretty blue eyes. Once, he brought her a bunch of prairie lilies and lilac cuttings. She didn't tell him she didn't like lilacs much. They smelled like the perfume Mama had on that morning she left, so lilacs made her angry. She waited until he went home, and then she put them into the woodstove and added the kindling for the morning fire. She put the lilies in a sealer jar full of water.

Once, in early spring, he brought her a tiny pale blossom in the palm of his hand. It was a violet, he said, and told her she was a flower, too. Violet felt fluttery inside when he said those things, and her cheeks would feel warm, even on a cold day. When Mr. Yuzik talked to Violet that way, it was all she could do not to hug him.

Today, she was glad again of her clean hair, and her everyday dress was one of her nicer ones with embroidery around the collar. He leaned easily against the big wooden kitchen table. He wore his overalls despite the heat, his flannel shirt clung in dark patches, and she could see his long johns poking out his cuffs. Today, Violet could tell, was a potato wine day.

She sipped her tea and listened to him talk about his dairy herd, how the last of the spring calves were getting strong. He told her about the five little girls in Ontario born just last year and how their father put them in a zoo for people to pay money to see. Some things like that didn't make sense, and some words were ones she'd never heard before, but she didn't mind.

"You know what my boys did now?" Mr. Yuzik took another swallow of tea and set the glass on the table. He shook his head. "They do crazy things. They take potatoes from cellar. You know, old ones they think no good. Look, I show you." He moved Violet back by the shoulder and took a batter's stance by the sink. "The boys, they have big game of baseball in yard. Like so!" He swung his imaginary bat and described the potato sailing high into the air. Violet laughed. "The potatoes so old and wrinkled, some just go kaput! But then—" Mr. Yuzik raised his hands, his fingers curled into claws, and started toward Violet. "This is when Hanusia come yelling! She is hitting each boy on the head with a broom and make them go pick up pieces. So no more baseball!"

Violet giggled and covered her mouth with both hands.

"Oh, heck, I almost forgot. I bring you this little thing," he said suddenly, reaching into his deep overalls pocket. "Is nothing, honest to God. A little hobby. I think they sound so nice when they are hanging, and it makes a tune. A little nice music from heaven."

Violet sat forward on her chair, puzzled. From his pocket, he withdrew an odd little collection of spoons fastened to a round piece of metal. He held it out, and the spoons hung from his finger on a short length of fishing line. Violet looked at it, her brow furrowing.

"It is wind chime, Violet. You never see it before?" Mr. Yuzik asked. "You hang up, you know, on porch where the wind can get at it just a little bit, and it sounds like the nicest music for you. Just like angels. See, I make little hole and tie on old spoons with bit of wire." He jiggled the thing, and the spoons clinked together.

She reached out and pushed one spoon with her finger. It tinkled against the others. "Like Chub and Florie's sleigh bells," Violet cried. "For Christmastime!"

"You got it! What you think?"

She did it again, a little harder, and the spoons clinked together. She laughed and bounced a little on her chair.

"You such a pretty girl," Mr. Yuzik said. "A good girl and look after the place just as good as grown-up woman. Poor thing," he added, almost to himself. "All alone with no mother and brother, just your father now. Get lonely. I know all about that," he said. He watched her face. "Such blue eyes, like crocus."

Violet poked her finger at the spoons and watched until they stopped clinking together.

"For you, Violet. Present. You have it," he said gruffly, quickly draining his glass of tea with his free hand. "I make for you so you can listen to music when there is breeze. You go ahead. Take it. It is okay." He laid the chime in her hand.

"Mine? For me?" She couldn't believe this beautiful thing was now really hers.

Mr. Yuzik covered her hand with his and gave it a little squeeze.

"Maybe you want me to hang it up somewhere for you?" he said, clearing his throat and standing up suddenly. "Let's see if there is nail out on porch somewhere, okay?"

Violet's hand was still in his, and he led her outside. The morning sun had warmed the lilac blossoms, thick and purple, on the bush at the back corner of the porch. The lilac was so overgrown that Violet thought of that end of the porch as a secret place. Father called it "the visiting end." He and Mama used to sit there after supper. Now just he and Hank sat there in the evenings to talk when the house was still too full of the day's heat. Sometimes Father and Mr. Yuzik would talk and pour smelly wine from a jug Mr. Yuzik brought with him.

The lilac perfume drifted to Violet while she stood holding the chime, and she closed her eyes. She wrinkled her nose. It was too sweet somehow and too full of memory. If she breathed it in too much, it felt like there was something in her throat that wouldn't sit still. It felt like the start of the bad feeling.

"Violet," Mr. Yuzik said after a moment, and she pulled her hand from his and wiped it on her apron.

"Look!" She pointed to the small hook near the top of the post so he could see. "The nail Father put there for the fly swatter! Put it up there! For the music!" She clapped her hands, and Mr. Yuzik stepped up on the chair.

"Hold the chair still, Violet," he said. "You don't want me to fall down and break my neck. You know, *peechoo shoo*!"

"No, careful! No *bootz* on your head!" Violet warned, suddenly serious, afraid at the thought of poor old Mr. Yuzik hurt. She would have to run out into the field to find Father if Mr. Yuzik broke his neck. She gripped his pant leg with one hand and grasped the back of the chair with the other. "I hold chair. Don't fall," she said sternly.

He chuckled and hiccupped. He pounded his chest and then hung the chime on the nail a few inches from the post. He flicked them with his finger. For a few seconds, there was no sound at all as the spoons turned in unison with the movement, missing one another completely. Violet waited, still carefully watching, even as Mr. Yuzik stepped off the chair and stood behind her. She held her breath, her hands to her cheeks.

"Wait, Violet," he told her quietly. "It is making music soon."

Violet tilted her head back, her eyes fixed on the spoons, waiting.

Mr. Yuzik reached out and touched her hair where she had tucked it behind her ear. "So happy," he whispered. "My Hanusia, she was happy long time ago. *Kveetochka moya,*" he murmured. "Little flower. Little Violet. My Hanusia, she used to like flowers. I bring black-eyed Susans. *Bookette kvitiw.* Sometimes crocus in spring when they poke up in last of snow. Last time, she took the bunch and throw into woodstove." Mr. Yuzik put his hands on Violet's shoulders while they watched the spoons turning. "'Bugs, Nikolai!' she tell me. '*Shchoh tobee seh stalloh schoh te preniece tsyi doh khateh abeh zaraza lazla poh khati?*' She throw them in the stove. 'You have the house crawling with them,' she says."

Mr. Yuzik gathered Violet's blonde hair in one hand and let it fall, catching the light. "No more flowers," he said and hiccupped again. "No *bookette kvitiw.* She is cold, my Hanusia. She does not want—" He took a breath of air and held it for a moment, puffing out his hollow cheeks. "She is busy with boys, working from in morning to when it is dark. And the babies born dead," he whispered. "She is tired, always so tired."

"Thank you for my present," Violet said solemnly, remembering good manners.

"You are very welcome, my sweet girl," he murmured, reaching out and touching her hair again. "*Kveetochka moya.* Sweet girl."

Violet blushed, turned around, and suddenly threw herself against him, her face turned against his chest. "I love my present," she said, her words muffled in the bib of his overalls. "I love you!"

He awkwardly pulled off his glasses and rubbed at his eyes with the back of his hand. Violet wrapped her arms around him. He gently put his hand on her back. Violet held him tightly, but a whisper breathed inside her head. It was Mama.

We don't hug. People don't like that. Be a big girl now, Violet. Be a good girl. Strangers don't like hugs.

But it was such a good present with its silver spoons that glittered in the sun and made such pretty music when the breeze came. Surely Mama couldn't mean Mr. Yuzik? He was Father's friend. And it was the best present, she told him, and thanked him again and said he was a nice man. When she looked up, Mr. Yuzik put his hand on her head and closed his eyes. Violet thought again how glad she was that she had washed her hair. A girl with clean hair is a pretty girl, Father told her often.

Mr. Yuzik slowly sank down to the wooden bench and eased Violet down across his lap, and she held tightly around his neck. He murmured soothing whispers, more funny words that Violet didn't understand, and she thanked him again for her present, her best present ever. It felt good to be held. Not a Father hug, quick and safe when she was going to bed at night, but a grown-up man and woman hug that made her heart thump in her chest until her cheeks were hot.

"*Tekho, tekho*, Violet," he whispered hoarsely. "Quiet now. *Tse nyechoh*. It is nothing. It is all right." Mr. Yuzik pulled her closer. He closed his eyes and breathed deeply. He pressed her head to his chest.

Violet flinched. "Ow," she cried out and sat up on his lap. "That hurt me." She put her fingers up to her cheek and felt the sting. She looked at his overalls and saw the broken buckle, held together with a twist of wire.

"*Kveetochka moya*. Sweet girl. Let me see," he said. "I am sorry, sweetheart. This old buckle to hold up my overalls. It is broken. That's what got you, that wire. Let me see. It is okay. Okay." He took her face between his big hands and whispered. "You are okay. I would not hurt you, Violet. I will not hurt you, little girl. I kiss to make okay now."

Violet wiped her nose with the back of her hand. He kissed her cheek, and she felt the welt sting on her skin. He undid the broken buckle, shrugged his arms free of the straps, and gently pressed her face back against his damp shirt. She could feel the vibration in his chest and breathed in his sweat, sharp in her nose. Cigarette tobacco. He hummed a little song, and she felt that good fluttering in her tummy. Even her elbows and knees felt warm and wobbly.

Still rocking, Mr. Yuzik wrapped his arms around her and mumbled something into her neck. Violet couldn't hear what he said, but his whiskers were scratchy against her skin, and she squirmed. He rocked her gently and whispered again in her ear. He wanted her to do something.

She pulled back so she could hear, so she could do a nice thing for Mr. Yuzik. A nice man who brought her presents and said she was pretty. Father's friend.

"I show you how you say thank you for present," he whispered hoarsely. "A secret thank-you. Special hug. No one can know. You must not tell. Just for you. For me."

Be a good girl, Violet. Mama's voice came to her again. *Be a big girl now.*

Violet frowned. She wanted to be good. She wanted to be a big girl. Her apron and housedress were twisted, pushed up around her thighs, and when she reached to straighten her clothes, Mr. Yuzik helped her, his big hands firm, insistent. His face was sweating now, his eyes bright. She wrinkled her nose at the close smell of wine on his breath. His voice was low and steady, the way Father talked when he didn't want to spook the cows.

He hunched forward, still whispering, and took her hand. He put it on something warm and smooth, but Violet's face was pressed into his overalls, so she couldn't turn her head. He held his hand over hers. Sometimes Mama used to give her a piece of bread dough to roll back and forth on the table. What Mr. Yuzik was making her touch was like that. Violet wondered if the thing she touched was like John's thing, the one he had to take out sometimes to pee when they were playing in the woods. He told her it was private, to turn around and not look. But sometimes, she'd sneak a little peek. Maybe Mr. Yuzik had one like that? It was getting difficult to breathe, and she tried to pull away, but he held her head close to his chest with one hand, clenching his fingers over hers, moving them back and forth.

His fingers fumbled at her dress and pushed it up and pulled at the top of her undershirt. His fingernails dragged against her stomach and he pulled her underpants down. Violet grunted when he lifted her leg. That hurt, it was too rough. He gripped the back of her knee and, in the other fist, the handful of her underwear. He pulled it down her leg until it hung around her ankle.

"Ouch," Violet complained and rubbed at her belly.

"Sweet girl. Little Violet. *Kveetochka moya,*" he soothed, and his hand moved between her legs. "*Neh zhooreshia. Tse ya.*"

He said it over and over while he gripped her thighs and eased her toward him, slowly and firmly turning her, laying her down on the bench. He was pulling something, rubbing, and his mouth was pressed against her ear. His breath was warm and wet and made it hard for Violet to hear. The special hug wasn't like any hug from Father. It was a heavy hug, too heavy and too tight. It hurt.

"Quiet now," he grunted against her ear. "Shush, shush now.

Violet looked up over Mr. Yuzik's shoulder, and the wind chime tinkled. She wished Father would come home soon. She heard a dog barking far away. It was probably the Dechants' black dog across the coulee. She couldn't remember that dog's name. There had been two, but Mr. Dechant shot the bad one. The bad dog used to go after the cows in the field, biting tails, and made two cows run so hard they dropped their calves too soon last spring.

Mr. Yuzik's fingers dug into her thighs and then higher and pulled apart the place to go pee. *The private place*, Mama had said. *The not-nice place we don't let anyone see.* She squirmed, but he was so heavy.

"Such good girl. I show you," Mr. Yuzik mumbled. "Our secret. *Tse nyechoh. Kveetochka moya.*"

Over her, Mr. Yuzik was fumbling and pushing, pressing down on her, into her, hurting her, gruff, still whispering. She tried to turn her face from the smell of sweat and barn. The wine. He was too close, and her leg felt numb. He stared down into her face just once. She could see his eyes were shot with tiny red veins. His black lank hair, damp and smelly, was matted down on his forehead, and when he wiped it back, she noticed the white half-moons at the bottom of his fingernails stood out stark against the black dirt under each nail.

"Big secret," he rasped urgently, nodding as if he was trying to pry the promise from her. The rest of the words were the kind she couldn't understand.

Too heavy, she thought and tried to say it out loud. It hurt. She tried to move. The corner of the bench was poking hard into her back. That hurt, too.

A whimper came from her throat, and he shushed her, his fingers fumbling against her mouth. They smelled of tobacco. He buried his face in her neck, and the sharp smell of hair grease and sweat made her cough against his fingers.

She looked up to the wind chime, and she tried not to think of the special thank-you and how it hurt. Emily always said she should remember good things when she felt bad, so Violet's thoughts flew wildly in search of some. Just one would do.

The forenoon air was thick with the warm scent of lilacs. Their heavy lavender heads bobbed in the breeze. She gulped at the air, but it was too warm and close, and it caught in her throat.

"No more thank-you," Violet pleaded, trying to be polite, her words muffled against his chest, and she bit down on her lip. *Be a good girl, Violet. Be a big girl now.* She tasted salt. She jerked her head to the side to make Mr. Yuzik hear. Maybe she could tell him about King George on the radio. Maybe he would get up then to listen like he did when they had a nice visit.

"No more secret," she tried again more loudly. A bad feeling was crawling up her throat. "Up. Get off now!" she pleaded. Lilac, sweat, and tobacco burned her nostrils and throat. Her heart was pounding.

His fingers dug sharply into her thighs, and his body was pushing hard, making it hurt, pressing down too heavy, and his elbow dug into her arm. Then he shuddered and jerked. Her neck was sticky with his spittle, and the sharp stubble on his chin scraped against her cheek. Violet tried to hear Mama's voice, but it was gone. She strained for the sound of Father coming back with the horses.

Instead, it was Mr. Yuzik's voice, raspy, wet and muffled in her ear. Enough of these words, she knew. "Okay. Okay. Shh, little *fialka*. All done. Quiet now. *Tekho. Tse nyechoh.* A secret."

SHE DIDN'T KNOW HOW LONG HE'D BEEN GONE.

Violet sat solidly on the bench. She felt hot and sweaty and out of breath. Her heart was thumping too fast in her chest, and she knew she needed to be still.

"Stop. Stop it," she whispered, her lips barely moving. "Calm down."

But it hurt. She felt wet there, and she had a terrible feeling that she might have had a little accident. She was too old for that now. That happened once when she had been playing pioneers with John down past the slough, too far from the outhouse to risk making it back. So he showed her where to pee, keeping her underclothes out of the way while she squatted, hidden in the tall fescue. But that was a long time ago, and she was grown up now.

Violet pulled her underpants off her foot, drew her knees up, and curled in her father's chair at the visiting end of the porch. She balled her underwear in her fist and wiped her nose. She looked up at her new present, glinting while it turned one way and then the other in the afternoon breeze. Her chest stopped drumming, and she could hear horseflies droning across the front yard. Bees lumbered over the hollyhocks at the east end of the porch. A mosquito whined at her ear, but Violet found her arm too heavy to lift to wave it away. It settled on her knee, and she watched it find a spot. It was gorged with her blood by the time it occurred to her to slap it or even flick it away. She carefully pressed a fingernail hard into the bite, first one way, then the other.

Mosquito bites don't itch when you make the cross in 'em, John used to say.

She pressed her hand to her chest and listened to her heart thump more quietly now in her ears. The air and the heat were heavy on her as if she were underwater and didn't know how to break the surface.

Now and then, a faint breeze would set the spoons tinkling, and she thought about the special thank-you secret. She didn't like that kind of secret. She rubbed her hand over her stomach. She wiped between her legs with her underwear and frowned.

Father would be coming in from the field for evening tea, she realized, and she stood. He would want potatoes. Her knees buckled, and she gripped the porch railing to steady herself. There was suddenly more wetness trickling down her thighs. She shook open her underwear, wobbled a little as she stepped into them, and dragged them up over the spreading wet between her legs. She brushed down the front of her dress and patted the edges of her apron, pressing each triangle of yellow rickrack into place. She wiped her nose on the back of her hand and shuffled inside the house.

In the kitchen, she reached for a bowl on the counter and scuffed at the hole in the linoleum with her toe until she lifted the iron ring to the root cellar door. Bending over, she pulled the heavy door up with a grunt and pushed it open on its hinges. She gasped at the fresh wetness between her thighs. She turned and carefully backed down the cellar ladder, gripping the edge of the floor above to keep her balance.

The dank smell of cool, undisturbed dirt was sharp in her nose. The chill crept up under her dress and raced across her wet skin, and she shivered. She rubbed the goose bumps across her arms. She blinked until her eyes adjusted in the dim cellar. The light from the kitchen above leaked down only as far as the bottom of the stairs near the potato bin.

"Oh, no. I forget." Violet put her hand over her mouth.

The cream can. Mr. Yuzik hadn't taken it, and now Father

would be cross with her. The cream had to be tended carefully so it wouldn't spoil, and though the cellar was cool, cold even, the cream was best fresh, Father said. And now, here it was. She should have given it to him. A quiver started in her chin, and she covered it with her hand, pressing hard so she wouldn't cry. She needed to think.

Putting the bowl aside, Violet sat down on the edge of the potato bin and tried to catch her breath. "Calm down," she whispered. "Good girl."

She carefully pried up the cream can lid. A small grey spider clung to the edge, dropped to the dirt floor, then danced across the planks and disappeared up the wall by the potato bin. The cream, a deep yellow, stood thick, and a skin was starting to wrinkle and pull away from the edges of the can.

Though she knew she wasn't supposed to, Violet dipped a finger in the cream just far enough to get a taste and brought it up to her mouth. She closed her eyes. Cool and thick, it tasted of milk and the special walnuts Mama used to have for Christmas fruitcake. Just one more little bit. The thickness closed in on itself in the wake behind her finger. Violet supposed Father wouldn't be able to tell if she had another little taste. After one more, she set the lid carefully back in place and pushed it down.

Her chest finally stopped thumping so hard, and her breathing slowed. Violet cast a glance around the cellar. The wooden shelves set against the dirt walls held neat rows of glass jars of cucumber dill pickles and jam, some purple borscht, peas, and beans, mostly given by neighbours. Some of them, the dusty ones, spiderwebbed all on one side, were left from Mama's canning, and the space between those and the new clean, colourful jars marked when Mama left. Some of the new ones held things Mama never made, and Violet wasn't sure what they contained. They were prettier colours than Mama's. Maybe full of raspberries, saskatoons, blueberries, green beans. The one on the end might even be peaches, but Violet didn't know for sure. Mama never made that. The bright yellow corn relish came from

Emily last fall, and there was one of Erna Eckart's beet pickles, the ones Father liked so much.

Violet wrinkled her nose. She didn't like beets. Hank's mama sometimes made pears, and she had them at his house once, but Mama never did. Mama didn't like pears. In the dim light that filtered down from the open cellar door, Violet could make out empty mason jars lined up on shelves along the back wall, fuzzy and grey with dust and spider webs.

Violet turned a little on the edge of the bin and looked at what was left of last year's potatoes. She thought of the Yuzik boys playing baseball with their old potatoes. Thin, white vines stretched through the slats and up over the edge of the bin, blind in their search for light, pale in the dim cellar. She put a finger out to touch the end of one pale vine. It bobbed and trembled on its shrivelled base.

Why did people say potatoes had eyes? Something in the potato, Violet supposed, made them think they might see sunshine even though in the cool dark root cellar, they never would.

She eased off the edge of the bin and felt between her legs. It hurt down there, and she winced. She wiped at her eyes. Mr. Yuzik wouldn't hurt her; he was a nice man. But something had hurt her. He had promised her it would be all right. Sweet girl, he called her. He called her a special girl, a pretty girl. He liked her pretty, clean hair. He said so. He was Father's friend. But he had hugged her too tight. She couldn't breathe, and his buckle hurt her cheek.

Remembering, she rubbed it, and it stung. On her fingertips, a smear of red. And something had hurt her down there. Maybe there was blood there, too. Mr. Yuzik went home so fast that he didn't even say goodbye. Goosebumps spread across her forearms, and she trembled. She took a big breath of musty, sharp dirt air.

Remembering Father's tea, Violet picked out a few good potatoes, careful not to disturb the tangle of vines. She wondered what Mr. Yuzik was having for his supper. Maybe potatoes, too. The corners of her mouth pulled down suddenly, her chin quivered, and a little sob gurgled in her throat. She had done something bad, but she couldn't think exactly what. Father would be angry enough about the cream. She couldn't tell him or anyone, just like Mr. Yuzik said. A secret.

"Good girl. Good girl. Calm down," Violet whispered. Tears stung the scratch on her cheek. Another sob rose in her throat. She climbed the cellar steps, and she wiped her nose with the back of her hand. She looked at the smear of blood and touched her cheek. It stung.

She thought of the five little girls in Ontario Mr. Yuzik told her about. She couldn't understand why their father would let someone take them away from home, away from their father and mama. Sometimes people stared at her in town when she sat in the truck with an ice cream, waiting for Father in front of Hyde's store. She didn't like it.

She stuffed the potatoes into the pocket of her dress and climbed one rung at a time. She pulled herself up through the open trapdoor into the kitchen, squinting in the afternoon light, the goosebumps disappearing in the warmth.

"I am a good girl. A good girl. I am a box of fluffy ducks."

HANK

WATROUS UNION HOSPITAL,
SEPTEMBER 1935

Hank waited alone in the hospital hallway, an ache in his belly, thankful for his hat, so he had something to do with his hands. Pinching the sodden brim, he shifted from one foot to the other, mud dripping from his boots, a reminder of the time old Ned had kicked him square in the guts. Ned, for once in his dull existence, had taken uncharacteristic exception to being shod and laid Hank out flat in the muck for a good spell. He'd laid face-first, the sharp stink of manure pushed up his nostrils, without the wind or wherewithal to sit up. This was like that, Hank thought, his wind and wits knocked out of him and his bad eye burning.

The smell of disinfectant brought with it another recollection of a taste of ether that had lodged itself up high at the back of his throat. It had stayed there ever since, waiting, ready to be conjured up no matter how distant the memory. Hank coughed, shuddering with a sudden chill.

He was nine when he got his tonsils out. He could still feel Dr. White's dry papery hand on his throat, his face too close, probing with a flat stick at the back of Hank's tongue. The doctor's disagreeable breath smelled oddly of mothballs and was moist on Hank's cheek when the doctor peered into his open mouth. The waiting had been the worst. Hank had a vague memory of his mother sitting beside the bed with a five-cent piece, rubbing a pencil over a piece of paper until Edward VII, with his pointy beard, magically appeared. Squinting, the paper an inch from his nose, Hank could barely make out *Dei Gratia Rex Imperator*.

Now Hank paced restlessly up and down the hallway, trying to place his feet quietly on the hardwood floor. He squeezed his hat brim and remembered the blood on Violet's face that day back in the spring, the cut on her cheek, her crying. Maybe if she'd had any say about it, she would have preferred getting kicked by a horse. Even getting her tonsils out would have been a lot less complicated. He wondered what smell she'd carry with her memory. *Potato wine, most likely,* he thought and slapped his hat hard against his leg.

Hank tightened his shoulders under his damp wool jacket. That was the trouble with September rainstorms; they came up over the fields without warning out of a sky all prickly with electricity. The hair on his arms and the back of his neck had been standing up, the itching a warning, all morning. Didn't matter about the heat just days before; the hard rain chilled a person through to the bone. With the barley and wheat drying in the stooks, he hoped this would move east quickly, but now, on their third day, the sodden grey clouds with their cold rain seemed socked in.

He turned his hat again, pinching the wet brim between his fingers. He reached for the door to the room where Violet was, where the night nurse had taken Emily in to sit with her. He changed his mind and took his hand away from the knob. Em would be better at this, calming Violet down, helping her get to sleep.

Suddenly angry with himself the more the memory started to come back to him, he stripped off his clinging jacket and tossed it over the back of a wooden chair the nurse had placed against the wall for him. He set his hat on the seat, but, not knowing how to still his hands, he picked it up again, sat down, and turned it around and around. Hell of a lot of good it did anybody now to remember that day. He might have been in a position to help her then, somehow.

Now, nearly four months later, he called it up as clear as yesterday. It was early June. He went to the Burke farm that afternoon with a load of straw, looking for William. They had planned to mix up some mud plaster to seal up chinks in the barn walls. William had complained that he couldn't keep a lantern lit during milking for the draft.

"Hank, we've got to do something about the bloody barn," William grumbled. "A person can bat a cat through the holes in those walls."

So Hank had taken the load of straw over to the Burke farm. No sign of William. Hank had poked his head in the door at the house and hollered. He'd found Violet peeling potatoes in the kitchen, and Judas Priest, nearly broke his neck when he almost stepped into the open cellar. He told her right quick she needed to keep that trapdoor shut, or someone would end up a pile of broken bones down there on the dirt floor.

When she looked at him, he could see her eyes were red, and tears streaked her cheeks. He regretted his harsh words. Then saw a bit of blood on her cheek and thought that maybe she had cut herself with the paring knife.

Hank took a good look. He tried to get her to tell him. Had she tripped and fallen? Violet didn't speak. It was just a scratch, a good one, though, and a welt with it. He figured on cleaning it up and applying a little iodine. And her lip looked like she'd bitten down on it, all puffy and a little bruised.

Violet just sat there peeling the potatoes, hardly looking at him, her nose running and her eyes red and watery. Hank couldn't get anything out of her, not a word. Later, she told William, "too heavy," and her father and Hank assumed she'd struggled to bring the cream can up the cellar steps and had stumbled, bumping her face against one of the wooden treads.

But now, in the hospital all these months later, he knew. He balanced his hat on his knee and took his handkerchief out of his overalls pocket. Hard red wheat kernels came out with it and scattered across the tile floor. He wiped his mouth, trying not to think of it, trying not to imagine it, how it must have happened. But the weight of knowing was making him sick and shivery, and he needed to get outside for air. He got to his feet.

Hank looked down the hospital hallway and tried to swallow down the smell of disinfectant, feeling sorry for Orval Wetzel, Walter and Mitzie's boy. In to get his tonsils out, the nurse said. Hank wondered if Mitzie was in there, distracting her boy with a magic coin. He swung around, looking for the door. He needed a lungful of air even though the rain had picked up. Just as he was trying to decide whether to tell Emily he was stepping outside, he heard William calling out to him.

"Hank!"

William strode quickly toward him, muck splattering off his boots and leaving a trail behind him on the floor, his unbuttoned wool shirt flapping open. His undershirt—William always called it a singlet—was soaked through. Barley chaff clung like wet snow to William's hair and that hat pushed back on his head. *Why does he keep that old moth-eaten bowler?* Hank wondered. There was more hole than hat; tufts of William's hair, dark and rain-soaked, poked through a couple of holes in the hard felt near the crown. The nurse trotted along at his side long enough to point him in Hank's direction. No escape now.

Hank took a deep breath of close hospital air, dropped his hat on the chair, and squared his shoulders. This wasn't going to be easy.

"Bloody hell, Hank, what's going on?" William was panting, and Hank figured he must have run through the rain all the way from the parking lot where he had left the truck. "Where's Violet? What's happened? Tony Dechant came over to fetch me at the seed mill." William snatched off his hat and tried to catch his breath. He gripped Hank's shoulder. "What's going on? Has she been hurt? Where's Violet?"

"She's fine, William," Hank said, and William's shoulders sagged. Hank led him to a bench a few steps down the hall from Violet's closed door. "She's resting now. Emily's in there with her. Sit down here so we can talk."

Hank swept aside his hat and pressed William down onto the chair. He kept a hand on his shoulder and suddenly didn't know what to say or how to say it, and made himself look into William's face. His brow was creased with question and worry.

"Is she crook, Hank? Sick? She had a bout of flu, I think, a fortnight ago. She's been pretty quiet lately, you know, sort of forgetful, but I figured it was just a female thing," William said impatiently, "and with her mother gone . . ."

"No, she's not sick," Hank interrupted. "She had a bit of an emergency and wasn't feeling so good. She called Emily, and we figured it would be faster for me to run straight over than look for you first. We passed Tony on the way into town, so I sent him to find you."

"Well, for Christ's sake, man, what's wrong with her?"

"Well, when I got to your place, Violet was sitting by the stove, and she had her bed sheet wrapped around her, all bunched up like." Hank floundered. Emily'd be better at this. He ran his hand over his face and went on in a hushed voice. "She'd bloodied the sheet, William. It was a bit from, you know, her female parts. Not a lot, but she was pretty scared. When I came in and got down by her, trying to find out what happened, she said not to tell you. I think she thought she was going to die, you know, like John, and she was really worried about leaving you alone with nobody."

"Oh, Jesus." William shuddered. "The poor wee girl. But what's wrong, Hank? Why the hell is she bleeding?"

"Because, William, Violet, well, the nurse says it happens sometimes. Spotting is what she called it. She'll be fine. But it can happen when a woman is—" Hank lowered his voice. "She's in the family way."

"What? She's what?"

"The family way," Hank whispered. "She's pregnant."

"Go on, Hank. You're daft," William barked, his face twisted in a way that Hank found hard to look at. "You're daft," William repeated.

"Violet's going to have a baby."

"Not Violet."

"The doctor figures she's about four months gone."

"Not Violet," William repeated; his words sounded hollow. "That can't be." He blinked and stared down the dimly lit hallway. There were no windows along the corridor, so the yellow reading lamp by the nurses' desk was the only light. It could have been midday or midnight. "Not a baby," William said, searching Hank's face for a sign of mistake as if being pregnant could mean something else. "Violet? She's not a woman. She's just a girl."

Hank nodded. "A pregnant girl."

"No, Hank," William insisted, pleading. "She's only fifteen. And she's how she is. But she's going to be all right? It's not bloody possible. Sweet Jesus." William struggled to his feet, steadying himself with one hand on the wall, then he paced back and forth. "Who did this?"

Hank's head snapped up as if like he'd been slapped. The older man's voice came from the top of his throat like someone had fingers tightening around his neck. Strained, each word jagged at the edges. "Who did it?" he demanded again.

Hank swallowed hard and leaned forward on the bench. He looked into William's face and shifted so that he could meet William's blue eyes. Oddly light blue. One was bloodshot, and the other eyelid fluttered with a pulsing tic that seemed to keep time with the clicking second hand of the hospital clock. Hank raised his fingers to his own scarred eye. It seemed to be tearing up and burning in sympathy.

"Emily's in there; been trying to get at that without scaring her," Hank said quietly. "We got a little bit of it pieced together. But you got to promise me, William, you'll let Albert Dickenson handle it. This is his area. The doctor called the detachment. Promise me, William. You hear me?"

"Do they know who the bloody bastard is?" William swung around to face him.

"We don't know for sure, that's what I'm saying," Hank whispered. "The doctor already called the detachment and talked to Constable Dickenson. Got all formal about it. Said he has to report it. Official RCMP business when it's someone like Violet. Like how she is, is what he said. There's some law, Section 219, I think. Emily'll remember. It'll get him at least two years, William, and probably the lash because he knows Violet, how she is."

William swung around to face Hank. "He knows Violet?" William asked, and his voice cracked. "He *knows* her?" His voice turned into a low rumble. "Tell me, Hank. Right bloody now."

"We think it's Nik Yuzik."

William blinked stupidly. Hank knew William was thinking he couldn't have heard right. William stood up and stumbled backwards against the wall. It was as though Hank could see inside his head because he'd imagined a stranger, too, a vagrant stopping for food, for directions, and Violet happy for the company, so friendly like she is, then getting tricked. No one to hear her screaming for help. The picture was replaced by Nik's big frame leaning in the doorway, calling out for Miss Violet. Bringing her flowers. Thought it was kind of him all this time. Thought he was trying to be kind to Violet since John died and Louise ran off.

Louise's voice suddenly pressed against Hank's ear. He could almost feel her breath. *Don't let her hug people, Hank. It's unseemly. I tell William, but he doesn't believe me. Not his little girl.* Hadn't she told him? Over and over. *We can't be with her all the time. Someone, a stranger, could take advantage of the situation. She wouldn't understand.* Hank knew William and Louise had had a few rows about it before she went away, one just that week. *It's not Hanusia I'm worried about.* She was right, after all.

William let out a ragged breath and rubbed his hand across his face. He backed a few steps down the hallway, and his mouth worked a word over and over. *No. No. No.* Hank thought William might be sick on the floor. "Nik? No. No, Hank. He's my mate, my friend. My mate, for God's sake. Can't be. I would have—wouldn't—Where was I? Where the hell was I when he . . . when this—happened?" William stammered, his hands clenching, unclenching at his sides.

Someone could take advantage of the situation. Believe me, I know. A predator. Hank looked up and almost expected to see Louise leaning over William, telling him again. *Someone pretending to be her friend, and then—*

"A stranger. It was no stranger," William hissed. "He bloody well *knows* her, knows how she is."

It's like talking to a spooked horse, Hank thought. No sudden moves, or someone was going to get trampled. He stood and reached one hand out slowly, and he spoke in a hushed tone. "William, Emily asked Violet if someone did something private to her, down there." Hank spoke evenly, his hand still outstretched, palm up. He nodded down the hallway where the nurse had looked up from her desk at the raised voices. "Come on back and sit down, and I'll tell you. Please. Nobody but you needs to know this."

As if this news wasn't already festering to be told all over town, Hank thought. Everyone would know by morning that the Burke girl was pregnant. Maybe they wouldn't know who yet, but they would soon enough. Farmwives all over the district would be soaking up the gossip, rubbering on the party line, falling all over themselves to pass the news along, never admitting they got it from listening in.

William stood there, swaying a little as if he was drunk. He stood, feet apart, as if he could somehow brace himself against the blow Hank was hammering into his skull.

"At first, Violet said it was a secret, and she wasn't supposed to tell. Emily had an awful time trying to get anything out of her. But she just kept talking real soft like she does when one of our animals is sick. She does that with me, too, sometimes, but it's usually when she's thinking about a new dress from the Style Shop." Hank tried to smile. William stared at him. Hank coughed, embarrassed. "Like I was saying, finally Emily asked who touched her, you know, that way. If it was a nice man or a bad man and Violet perked right up, defending him." Hank cleared his throat. "She said Mr. Yuzik is a nice man and tells her she has pretty hair. She said he gave her a present that day. Then she started crying and said it hurt, and it was a secret, and you'd be cross about the cream can, and Mr. Yuzik went away and doesn't like her anymore because he never came back to bring her flowers or see her just by herself again."

William sat still and quiet for a long time. He closed his eyes. "Nik has been elusive these last few months," he said evenly. "Always too busy. Hanusia wasn't well; one of the boys was sick. It was always something. When I take the cream over, it's always Hanusia or one of the boys who takes it."

The damn clock seemed too loud for a hospital with its hushed voices and sick people needing some peace. Hank left William in the hallway long enough to push open Violet's door to let Emily know William had come. She stood at the side of the bed and pointed to Violet, who, Hank could see, had fallen asleep with what the doctor had given her. Just as well. Emily had pulled out the tucked-in sheet and blanket off Violet's feet. She knew Violet, who went barefoot most every day of her life, would be restless if her feet couldn't breathe. Her flat little feet, turned in pigeon-toed.

Hank quietly closed the door and returned to William, who slumped on the chair. "The wind chime," William mumbled.

"What's that, William?" Hank bent closer, his hands on his knees.

"The goddamn wind chime. Bastard," William said. "She

showed it to me when I came in for tea. She started crying about it. I just thought she was real happy with her present, but then she said she forgot to give Nik the cream, and she reckoned I'd be angry." William steadied himself with a hand on the back of the bench. "I told her it was nothing to be upset about. Now I can't imagine what she thought I meant. Poor girl. Bloody bastard. Bloody, bloody bastard."

"If only I had come by earlier that day." Hank said. "Remember? It was the day we were going to plaster the barn."

"It was the day I took the split ploughshare to town. Didn't get back until late afternoon. Son of a bitch." William closed his eyes and swayed a little where he stood. "I remember now. I thought we were doing that job the following day. I could have been there."

Hank kept talking, hoping that the sound of his voice would stem the colour that was beginning to flood William's face and make his eyes wild. The tic was beating double-time now. Hank put a fingertip to his own aching eye again and wondered if Emily might have a clean handkerchief with her.

"I passed Nik's truck on the road just out of your lane. I waved as usual, but it was as if he didn't even see me, just staring straight ahead. When I got there, looking for you, Violet seemed a bit upset. She wouldn't tell me, but I didn't think too much about it. But now, Jesus." Hank looked up. "If I had been a half-hour earlier." He faltered. "Maybe."

"I've got to go," William said suddenly, too loudly, the chair scraping back sharply. Again, at her desk, the nurse turned her head. He lurched up and stumbled down the corridor, one hand trailing along the wall for balance. Hank ran after him and reached for him, his fingers closing on William's shirt sleeve. "Hank. Leave me be," he growled, shaking off Hank's grasp.

Hank followed him down the corridor. "Don't start anything, William. Just leave it alone," he pleaded. "The constable will be here quick. I talked to Albert as soon as Violet told Emily; the doctor said it had to be done. Leave it to the law now. Don't make it worse. Don't be doing something crazy."

"Stay out of it, Hank." His eyes were dark, sunken in shadow. "Leave me be now. I've got to get out, got to think."

"Violet needs you here." William headed for the door, but Hank cut him off firmly. "William! She's going to wake up. What do we tell her?"

"You tell her it's in my hands now."

The older man's strides were longer, and Hank tried to keep up, but William broke into a run, his shirt open and flapping behind him. He threw his shoulder into the door at the end of the hallway and ran out into the dusk. The rain had picked up along with the wind, a torrent pounding on the boardwalk. Hank stepped out, holding the door against the wind, and watched William disappear around the corner. He hesitated. What if Emily needed him? What if the doctor wanted to ask more questions? Constable Dickenson would be here soon.

Hank pulled the door back against a strong gust. He stood alone in the middle of the corridor beneath the clock and wiped his wet hand on his shirt. He looked down at the mud on the floor, closed his eyes, and sighed. He turned and went back to sit on the chair outside Violet's room. He picked up William's hat, still sodden, warm from the twisting it had suffered in William's hands. He gave it two raps on the top.

Hank shivered. Unable to sit still, he walked back to the door, pushed it open and looked out into the rain. He could see that William had made it to the truck, across from the CPR station. Even with the weight of the feed sacks on the flatbed, the tires spun uselessly in the greasy muck. The downpour had turned the streets to gumbo, and Hank guessed William must have fought the wheel while the truck's tires sank up to the axles.

The truck door jerked open, and William lunged out, slamming the truck door shut. He nearly fell, then slogged through the mud to sit on the boardwalk in front of the Royal Bank.

The rain stopped as suddenly as it had started. Hank went out and trotted down the boardwalk toward the bench where William sat, hunched over, arms draped over his knees.

Nik, you sorry old bastard. What have you done? Hank thought as he got closer. William looked as though the rage had been sucked out of him, leaving his heart as heavy as his mud-laden boots. When he reached William, Hank held out the hat.

"Bloody hell, Hank. Maybe it's better I got stuck." William's voice cracked, and he ran a hand through his dark wet hair. He took the hat and held it between his knees.

"Let's go back." Hank offered William his hand. "You've got to let the law handle Nik." And then there was Violet to tend to. What were two grown men going to do about that?

"Thank God for Emily," William said.

Hank was thinking the same thing.

RCMP CONSTABLE ALBERT DICKENSON

THE YUZIK FARM, SEPTEMBER 1935

When Albert pulled the truck into the yard by the milk shed, Nik Yuzik didn't look surprised. Albert thought Nik had probably watched his slow progress on the grid road ever since the distant engine noise reached him. Maybe a glint of light off the windshield caught his eye when the truck turned in at the lane.

A dust devil on the horizon wavered in the heat and disappeared over the stooks in the field near the road. There had been no more rain. If they had clear skies now during the day and no heavy frosts, farmers were hopeful the wheat still out, such as it was, would stay in good shape until harvest was over. Nik set down the chop pails and stood there, halfway between the barn and the house.

Rascal, the latest in a long line of black, skinny, non-descript dogs Nik had brought home for the boys, waited beside him. A low rumble started in the dog's throat, and Nik flicked him sharply on the snout with his forefinger. Rascal flinched and retreated, head low, but kept his eyes on the approaching vehicle.

Nik raised a hand, and Albert wondered if he had been expecting William instead. If it were his daughter, Albert thought, a confrontation would be due, friend or no friend.

"Morning, Nik," he said, stepping off the running board and closing the truck door carefully, tucking a file of papers under his arm. "Like to discuss a matter with you."

Rascal, hackles up, circled the truck stiff-legged and peed on a tire, scratching dirt and grass behind him. Nik must know the visit wasn't a social call. Red serge was for ceremonial wear, but the brown meant police business. Albert adjusted his Stetson and set his jaw. He came around the front of the truck, and Rascal closed in, slinking behind, sniffing the heels of his high leather boots.

Albert waved the file at the dog. Rascal dodged it, skittered around the back of the truck, and watched from around the rear tire.

"Been quite a while since I been out to this part of the country," Albert said. "How are the boys?"

Nik just tilted his head. The air was still, punctuated only by Rascal's growl and a few crickets rasping in the tall grass around the porch. Nik grunted at the dog. Nik's faded blue overalls were worn, nearly white in the creases, and heavily patched at the knees. He wore no shirt, and Albert noticed one strap over his shoulder was held on by a twist of wire looped through the buckle. Nik looked as though he'd neglected to shave for some time.

A man was innocent until the truth came out, and he was proven guilty. So far, there was only some guesswork since Violet was what the law called an unreliable witness. Relying on her alone wasn't really enough to charge a man with anything legally or any other way. The truth, if there was any, would have to come from the man who did it. Which it would do soon enough, Albert thought, if Nik Yuzik was any kind of man at all.

"Albert. *Dobray dehn.*" Nik straightened his shoulders. He adjusted his glasses and slipped his thumbs under the straps of his overalls. "Good day today. Smells like fall is coming around corner," he said, inhaling noisily. "Been watching geese fly over. A cold winter coming, I think."

"Nik. There's this matter. We have a bit of a problem," Albert said, pulling the file from under his arm, placing it on the hood of the truck. He drew out a piece of paper, but he paused when Hanusia's voice carried from the house. She stepped out onto the porch, and chickens came running, scrabbling when she threw the contents of last night's slop pail into the dirt off the step. For a moment, children's voices drifted out into the yard.

"Your family's at home." It was a statement rather than a question, and Nik nodded. "Then we best stay and discuss this outside."

Nik looked off at the horizon. Albert looked up as Nik squinted at a V formation growing from faint jagged lines over the barley stubble. It soon became recognizable as Canada geese. Both men lifted a hand to shade their eyes in the sun just about the time the rusty hinge honking reached them. The sound reminded Albert of a faraway calliope at the Exhibition in Saskatoon. It was a forlorn autumn sound, one to make anyone put down what they were doing to stand still, look up and feel melancholy.

Nik kept his eyes on the flock as it passed overhead, so close they could hear the rush of air displaced by beating wings. Every one identical, the long black necks and white chinstraps, breasts that shone almost yellow in the late morning sun. Wings thrashed the air with a sound like someone beating the dirt out of a hundred throw rugs on a clothesline. The formation veered south over the coulee toward the Burke farm, and the two men watched the geese suddenly shift positions. The lead bird dropped back, and another took the point.

"All right, Nik, the thing is—"

"Geese, they do that, you know," Nik said, interrupting Albert, his voice almost sorrowful. "When one is weak, tired maybe, other one he moves in to help keep going. They never get lost that way, the geese. They all keep going together. You see that before, Albert?"

Albert placed the toe of his boot on a dry clod of gumbo and rolled it around. He gave it a kick and watched it bounce wildly off the dried tire tracks in the yard. It finally dropped into a deep rut of glossy mud, the surface sheen stretched and cracked like a skin of cream on milk left out too long. "Yeah, I guess I heard that story before, Nik. That's what geese do, all right."

Albert withdrew the paper he'd been holding with his thumb and forefinger from the file on the truck hood. "Nik. Do you know Violet Burke? You've got to answer yes or no."

"Yes, I do know Violet. Sure," Nik said, his eyes fastened on the clod of mud Albert had kicked into the puddle. "William's girl. For years now. You know that."

"Do you understand her to be feeble-minded?" asked Albert.

"*Doornah*. Sure, she's not right in head. But she is good girl."

"Okay, that's fine. Now, I need to ask you a couple more questions. But first, I want to read you something, and when I'm done, you don't have to say anything if you don't want to. If it doesn't make sense, then we'll go over it again. And you don't have to say anything. You understand? What I'm going to read may not have anything to do with you at all, and if it doesn't, I'll just wish you a good morning, and thank you for a nice visit. I'll be sorry to have taken your time, and I'll just head back to town."

Albert waited for some acknowledgement from Nik, whose bare shoulders seemed rounded, sort of hunched forward and smaller now. The white skin on Nik's upper arms seemed almost delicate where his shirt normally protected him from the sun. His forearms, matted with black hair, were tanned dark where his sleeves would have been rolled up, just like the v at his throat where his collar would be open. Grey hair poked out over the bib of his overalls, stark against his white chest. *An old man*, thought Albert. *More like two old men pieced together in a way that didn't fit*. He could see Nik's heart pulsing at the hollow of his throat.

Albert coughed and shifted his weight from one foot to the other.

Nik stared off in the direction the geese had gone.

"There's a section of the Criminal Code, Nik, that I'm going to read out loud here." Albert took a breath and put his finger on the paper. "Reading isn't my strong suit, but I'll try to get this done on the first pass. It's under Section 219. It says here anyone is guilty of an indictable offence and liable to four years' imprisonment—" He paused, his finger stopped on the word. "That's jail —who unlawfully and carnally knows," he continued, "or attempts to have unlawful carnal knowledge of any female idiot or imbecile, insane or deaf and dumb or feeble-minded woman or girl, under circumstances which do not amount to rape but where the offender knew or had good reason to believe, at the time of the offence, that the woman or girl was an idiot, or imbecile, or insane or deaf and dumb or feeble-minded."

Albert stopped and looked up at Nik. "I know this is a lot of legal talk, but does it make any sense to you, Nik?"

Nik had closed his eyes, and his head was moving up and down so slightly that Albert could not tell if it was an acknowledgement or the man was merely breathing in and out. The wad of snus behind Nik's lip slowly made its way across to the other side of his mouth. Albert was unsure how to proceed. He couldn't tell if the man understood the words, but judging by Nik's ashen face, he had the feeling in the pit of his stomach that Nik knew perfectly well what all of this was about.

"Nik." Albert said finally. "Nik, you've got to tell me what happened with Violet. Hank Eckart said he was there at the farm that day, just after you. He passed you out on the main road. You may not have seen him. She was crying when Hank got there, but she wouldn't say what was wrong. You know what went wrong, don't you, Nik?"

Albert felt some shred of reassurance might help. "Nobody has said rape, and I'm not sure she'd even understand it, being how she is and all. People who know her, her family, they could probably work it out. But you know what happened." Albert paused and gave Nik a moment to think.

"She seems more upset that you don't come around anymore to see William," he finally continued. "She thinks you're angry and staying away because of her. It wasn't violent, I don't suppose, was it? Did you hurt her?" Albert bit off the last of his sentence.

"No, no, no. It was not rape. I swear it. No. Not that—" The words escaped Nik with a sob, and his arms, ridiculously white and dark, hung limply at his sides. After a moment, he pulled a red handkerchief from his overalls pocket. "I just," he faltered. "Could not—she was—not help to, to stop it—"

The screen door squeaked open on hinges that needed attention and snapped shut. The crack was so loud it ricocheted out across the farmyard and bounced off the wooden granaries. Hanusia stood on the step, dishrag in one hand, shaking her apron free of crumbs or whatever remnants remained from the morning kitchen work, her chin thrust out, sizing up the scene before her in the yard. Rascal pulled himself up from the dirt at the men's feet and trotted to her. His tail began a slow wag, but he jumped sideways and cowered away when she flicked her dishrag at him.

Touching the brim of his hat, Albert called out, "Morning, Mrs. Yuzik. Fine morning." That was all he could manage. He faltered altogether when she flipped the dishrag over the railing, stepped off the porch, and started across the yard toward them. Rascal circled around and followed at a safe distance.

The mid-morning sun opened up harshly across her face and cut deep shadows under her cheekbones. *Severe*, Hank thought, borrowing a word his mother used to use about women who'd had a hard life leave its mark on their faces. Some women wore that look like a grim badge of honour. It seemed to Albert that Hanusia Yuzik wore it so that no one, especially her husband, would forget that her life was hard.

Hanusia put one hand up to shield her eyes. She stalked around the caragana at the side of the garden. The men stared silently at her approach. "Constable," Hanusia said, narrowing her eyes when she reached the men. "The Dykstras lose steer? *Oy yoy*, it make three now this spring. Can't you put a stop to that?" She put her hands on her hips. Her hands were red and shiny, and

Albert recognized the smell of udder balm. So many of the wives had a square green tin of it on the kitchen windowsill to heal their raw skin after the washing and bleaching and hanging sheets outside in the winter air. Albert's mother always said the little cow and clover picture on the can was cute, and the balm was so soothing.

Hanusia's voice was shrill; her chin jutted toward him. "I think hobos off train. Betty Ranstrom at Clip and Curl, she say so last week. I go for, what you call, finger wave. You know, she charge twenty-five cents now? *Yoy*. Well, you men don't know such things. But I say you know, maybe, Betty. Those people on relief, dirty, stealing. Hop train place to place, what not theirs, they take. Times tough for everybody. Work for not lazy ones, if only food. Last week for sewing club, you know we go over at Mildred Dechant's. Whole family came in Bennett buggy with all things, just crate chickens. Old cow tied behind. Want food. I am glad we far out from road, so my garden okay, not cabbage missing. Chickens missing."

"Hanusia. *Tekho*. Be still now," Nik said.

Nik had grown smaller, Albert thought, since his wife had started talking. Nik reached out toward her but never touched her. His hand just hung, still, in the air close to Hanusia's arm.

When he spoke, Nik's voice was somehow far away and not his own. "I talk to wife."

"All right, then, Nik," Albert said. He had been watching Nik's face intently, mostly so he didn't have to look at Hanusia. "But that leaves the Section 219 matter to be dealt with, and I'm afraid that's out of my hands now. You knew. It's not a question of her story or yours. The charge will be laid, cut and dried, and you'll have to answer for that before a judge."

He returned the papers quickly to the file and laid it on the hood. Albert had seen the expression now on Hanusia's face a hundred times. There was a moment every time he butchered an animal, an instant just before the animal felt the hot path of the bullet or the cut of the knife when it was simply trying to put together some sense of the situation when there was no sense to be made. Hanusia's jaw slackened and her lips parted about the same time Nik's arm fell down to his side.

"Nik, you'll need to come into town," Albert said. "I'll come back for you. The itinerant judge will be here on Tuesday, so you have a few days to get someone to look after the cows and get your affairs in order. It's a shame the older boys aren't here to take over, but I'm sure you can find someone willing to help out. I'll give you a bit of time here to talk."

Albert reached for the door handle and then remembered his papers and carefully picked up his file, slowly, as if there was some sort of bubble he was trying not to break with too much rustling. It was not a desire to linger but propriety that made him finally look at Hanusia. "I'm sorry for the trouble I brought you, Mrs. Yuzik," he said gruffly. "Just doing my job. Sometimes it's not a very pleasant one."

"It was for wind chime," Nik said to his wife. He spoke as if he'd forgotten Albert was still there.

The constable retreated to the truck, trying to avoid the domestic chasm splitting open between the two people behind him. He climbed in and sat looking at his knees, pretending the windows were rolled up tight.

"She loved it so much, the spoons. Violet, she get lonely," Nik pleaded, his voice cracking. "On her own so much like she is. I didn't mean it to happen. No fighting. No forcing. I swear to you." He reached out to touch his wife, but Hanusia shrank back as comprehension settled and twisted her face into disbelief. She crossed her arms, clutching herself, shielding herself. Her mouth opened and closed with no sound, and Albert watched from under the brim of his Stetson in case this got out of hand.

She stood in front of the truck, and Albert figured the truth, like a bullet, should just about be entering her skull now. He searched for any other place to look than through the dusty windshield and turned his gaze to the house.

The four youngest Yuzik boys—the "stair steps," the neighbours called them—had silently crept out on the porch, and all stood as if they had assigned places. The two oldest were off riding the rails. And there would have been more if there hadn't been two dead with the influenza and the stillborn girl. Nothing much was secret around here. They lined up, shortest to tallest, each wearing hand-me-down overalls like their father's and each more patched and faded than the pair worn by the next boy up in line. Ilko, who carried baby Nikolah in front of him like a feed sack, his hands clasped around the toddler's middle, wore the only pair that looked relatively new. Darker blue and already on its descent down the stairs from the absent Andrij and Mihaylo, handed down next to Ilko, Ivan, Stefan, and finally Nikolah, if there was anything left by then but the buckles and patches.

The boys stood at the edge of the porch but came no farther. All four pairs of dark eyes were riveted on their parents standing by the truck. It was almost as if they could sense an imminent catastrophe. Like lighting the fuse to a firecracker, they all wanted to watch but be well away from the blast.

Hanusia stared at her husband blankly. Her mouth still hung open, but her neck had turned a blotchy purple, and the skin and muscles of her face were beginning to work up into a fury. Her mouth snapped shut into a tight scar. The hollows of her cheeks clenched into small hard pulsating knots, and all the blood in her body seemed to suddenly flare in her face. Albert, glad for the protection of the windshield, wasn't sure whether he was seeing anger, betrayal, hatred, embarrassment, disbelief, or the whole lot of it suddenly storming in Hanusia's head like a tornado.

Her husband held up his palms to her. *What can he possibly say?* wondered Albert, watching from under his hat brim. He was suddenly afraid Nik was going to cry there in front of his wife and boys. His voice was a child's, small and sorrowful. "She was so lonely. Hanusia. I was—*Ya boo prostay tak samotnay.*"

But Hanusia was running now, back toward the house, her sweater stretched across her sharp shoulders and her thin arms beating the air around her head as if a swarm of wasps was eating her alive. "*Didko, didko!*" she choked. "Devil! *Ty nechysta sylo!*" Then she was screaming at the children before she got halfway across the yard. "*Eedeh do khateh ahboh boodoo vas beteh!*" she shrieked, snatching up the broom where it leaned against the railing. She stumbled on the step. The boys fled into the house before she got there, pushing and tripping over each other, staying clear of a sharp crack of the broomstick on the back of the skull.

The door slammed, and it was quiet.

Nik stood with his back to the truck, his head hanging so low that from behind, it seemed to Albert that it had been simply removed from the man's body.

Sowing and reaping. The thought kept crossing Albert's mind, and he wished he were anywhere else on the face of the earth.

WILLIAM

THE BURKE FARM, SEPTEMBER 1935

Violet came home from the hospital a few days later. She hadn't said much on the drive. Once she stood in the kitchen, she set her overnight case on the floor by the kitchen table and her face crumpled. William opened his arms and held his pale and confused daughter close to his chest. She was his clever, good girl. They stood by the stove, and he closed his eyes and patted her back. She cried until she started to cough.

"What's to become of us, my girl?" he whispered into her hair.

The coming days were clouded with questions that couldn't be answered, raised voices, and tears. William was left to flounder through his rage, the acid of betrayal crawling up his throat. He found himself more than once standing before the gun rack in his bedroom, eyes brimming.

"You were my mate," he muttered. It was all he could do not to pull a rifle from the rack and walk out to the truck.

Shaken by dark thoughts roiling through his head, he forced himself outside each time, away from Violet's gaze, and ended up splitting nearly half a cord of wood, aware of her watching him through the kitchen window. She went to the door and opened it enough to call to him. "Mind not cut finger off," she cried.

He swung the axe with fury until he could barely lift it from the ground and then sank to his knees, exhausted.

The Wednesday morning sky was alight with pink and orange creeping in the east over the slough, setting the frost on the kitchen window flickering like a fire. William emerged from his bedroom, already dressed for the barn, and gave Violet a small smile. She pulled her old blue chenille robe around her and poked more kindling into the cook stove.

"How about a nice cuppa before I go out, my girl?" he asked her in a voice raspy from a sleepless night. He shuffled by and patted her shoulder. "My little box of fluffy ducks." He sighed, brushing her cheek with the back of his fingers. How was he to help her understand what was going to happen in the next few months, that her body would swell with this new life? And what would become of the baby she was about to bring into the world?

The whistle of the morning kettle pulled his gaze to the stove, where Violet carefully poured hot water into his blue mug with one hand. With the other, she tenderly patted her belly. William could see where she'd fastened the robe with a safety pin, and he knew she'd done it to keep the baby warm. He sighed, and his eyes brimmed again. It wasn't the time to tell Violet that her baby was going to be taken from her, adopted out. The paperwork was already in the works at the church. That bit of bad news could come another day.

There are people who prey on the likes of Violet. Louise's voice flitted through his head. *You don't want to believe that, but I've seen it.*

This would have killed Louise. He doubted that John, who would have been past twenty now, a man, would have stood quietly by. William was thankful that the shame was not theirs but his alone to bear with Violet. He should have been there. Protected her, like Louise said.

If you love her, you'll protect her.

It wasn't just the shame of it, the anger at Nik, or his sorrow for Violet that had occupied William's thoughts these past few days. Dr. Speight wasn't pleased at all with this news, indecency and criminal charges aside. Last week, William had waited, sitting stiffly on the wooden chair in the doctor's office while Violet had her examination. When it was over, Dr. Speight came out with a scowl deepening the lines around his thin, pinched lips. "There's a lot of strain on a woman's heart when she's carrying a child, then during childbirth. Who knows what may happen," he muttered, disapproval creasing his forehead as if somehow William had been foolish enough to allow all this to happen. "Violet's heart isn't strong, William." He stuffed his stethoscope into this black bag. It snapped shut with an air of authority. "You know her heart has never been whole."

What an odd thing to say, William thought. He watched the doctor's retreating back. Violet had probably the most complete heart of anyone he knew.

William knew Violet needed to comprehend, as much as she could, what was happening to her now, what would happen very soon.

Emily. Emily could help Violet understand.

VIOLET

THE BURKE FARM, SEPTEMBER 1935

On Wednesday afternoon, Hank and Emily came by, much to Violet's delight and Father's relief. Emily hung up her coat and abruptly shooed the men outside.

"Violet and I are going to have a woman-to-woman talk, so you men go find something to keep yourselves busy for a while," she said. "Violet, I think it's time for a cup of tea, don't you?"

Violet, who had been rooted in the doorway since the Eckarts arrived, smiled broadly and sprang to get the kettle going on the stove. Violet watched the look of gratitude that flooded Father's face. He clapped Hank on the back.

"It's beyond me what you did to deserve this one. Your wife is a fine woman," Father said. "Don't you be forgetting that."

Hank grinned, and Emily waved her hands at them both, steering them toward the door.

"No reason to worry there, William. Emily doesn't let me forget it!"

"You give us about a half-hour now," Emily said. She closed the door firmly behind them and put her hands on her hips. She turned to Violet, who was setting cups on the table. "Well, Violet. You and I are going to have a talk. Seems to me this should have happened a long time ago, and I'm sorry for that, but no use crying over spilled milk." Emily patted her hand. "It's just an expression, honey. It means what's done is done, and now it's just time to get on with things. Sit down here now. I need you to listen to me carefully, all right?"

Violet often made Emily blush by telling her she was the most beautiful person she'd ever seen, with her thick reddish-blonde hair and green eyes. Violet said she was what the angels looking after John in heaven must look like. She often begged Emily to braid her hair in the same way so they could be twins. She pulled a chair so close to Emily's that their knees touched.

"Now." Emily folded her hands in her lap. "You, my friend, are going to have a baby. There's a tiny baby growing inside you right now, and around February or March, it'll be too crowded in there, and he's going to want to get out." She reached for her cup, took a sip of tea. Violet tried to absorb this information.

"He? He's a boy?"

"Well, now, we don't know that. It's always a surprise what a baby is," Emily said. "Could be a boy. Could be a girl. You never know until you have a look. Just like when the cows have a calf. You don't know if it's a heifer or a bull calf until you have a good close look, right?"

Violet had watched calves being born in the field, anxious cows dropping them to the ground, and then roughly licking the newborns to get them moving, pushing them to stand and get a dose of the first milk that Father said meant the difference between life and death.

Emily straightened in her chair. Before Violet could brood on that image too long, she reached out and took Violet's hands. "Your baby's most likely to come on out when we're in the hospital in town."

"February. But that's after Christmas. That's long to wait!"

Emily gently pulled one hand loose from Violet's grip and tucked a bit of Violet's hair behind her ear. "The doctor will be there, helping things along. Hank and I, we'll try to be there, and your dad. You'll have all of us with you."

"My baby love me, Emily. I put him in the doll carriage, and I show him the cats, and I sing to him. We sing lots of songs!" Violet bounced on her chair, pulling her hands away to clap in time with the music she imagined. "I can make porridge and eggs. Father, he make bacon, though, right? I don't like to make bacon."

Emily took hold of Violet's hands again to still them. *Was this going to be hard? And hurt?* It was hard for Violet to grasp what was going to happen during the birth, but she still knew they would live happily ever after on the farm.

"Violet, you need to listen to me now. I'm going to tell you very grown-up things, and I want you to pay attention. You are a grown-up girl, and this is very important." Emily was suddenly so serious. Violet wanted to hug her, to make it all go away. But she also wanted to understand.

"Does it hurt, Emily? To have a baby come out?" Violet thrust out her chin, pulled a hand free and rubbed her belly.

"Well, I'm told it's no picnic, but the good thing about being a woman is that we can create new life, bring it squalling into the world, and once we see that little face, that brand-new beginning of life, we just forget that it hurt at all. At least, that's what my mother tells me." She looked steadily into Violet's eyes. "If it hurt too much, you don't suppose women would keep doing it, do you? This is just how your Mama brought you into the world. It's how your brother got here. Hank. Me. It's how everyone gets here, Violet. You'll be just fine."

Violet bit the inside of her mouth and waited, thankful for a moment to think before she spoke. Violet turned her teacup around and around, trying to decide what the proper way to ask might be. "Mr. Yuzik?"

"It takes a man and a woman to make a baby, Violet. A man plants a seed, just like you put a bean or a radish seed in the ground in springtime."

"Like a potato? Or corn, too. I like corn. Not turnips."

"Right. The man puts a seed inside the woman. Right in

there." Emily laid her hand lightly on Violet's belly. "Then she grows the baby inside her, keeps it safe until it's ready. Most times, that man and woman are married and love each other. Like Hank and me. We hope we'll have a baby someday. Someday real soon, in fact."

"But I not marry Mr. Yuzik," Violet said, frowning.

"That's right. It wasn't right for Mr. Yuzik to make a baby with you because he has his own wife," Emily said. "But it doesn't mean you're bad, and nobody blames you for his mistake. He should have known better."

"Maybe he forgot," Violet offered.

Emily sipped her tea, "Yes, maybe he did. But he shouldn't have."

"It was a secret, he said. A special thank you. Because he made me music spoons."

"I know. But sometimes secrets aren't made to be kept. I don't suppose Mr. Yuzik was thinking of giving you a baby as a present. Babies have a way of getting themselves known."

Violet's eyes welled up with tears, and Emily pulled a hankie out of her pocket. "Now then," she said brightly, handing it to Violet. "Let's talk about how you're going to know when this baby's ready to come out. Then we can get those men back in here and give them a cup of tea, too. How about that?"

"And I made snickerdoodles. To have with tea. Emily? Do you think my baby will like snickerdoodles?"

Emily lifted her cup and drained the last of her tea. "This is just the first of many woman-to-woman talks we'll have," Emily said. "How about that?"

"Okay. But I know all about having my baby. And I make snickerdoodles for him too."

HANUSIA

THE YUZIK FARM, SEPTEMBER 1935

Hanusia hadn't spoken to her husband other than a few bitter exchanges since Constable Dickenson had been to the farm three days before. She knew Nik hated her silence. It wasn't that he ever enjoyed hearing her talk. But her chatter had to be familiar for him after all these years, like the house creaking in a cold snap. It was expected. The disbelief and shock of learning what Nik had done had been at her like rat poison, eating away at her until there were only holes where reason and sense used to be. She took away food when the boys were bad; not speaking to Nik was a small punishment for a man who had destroyed what little comfort she had in life. She was considering something more severe. He could live in the barn like the animal he was.

Everybody knew now. She wasn't even careful anymore when she lifted the telephone receiver to listen. Everybody was talking. She'd stopped going to town. The thought of going to the Clip and Curl was out of the question, and she could forget about any more sewing with the Pleasant Pals, who were no doubt gossiping about her even now. She imagined the women sitting there in someone's parlour, looking down at their handiwork and sideways at one another and wondering why poor Hanusia Yuzik's husband had to turn to that feeble-minded Burke girl instead of his own wife. What could be wrong with her? That's what they'd be thinking, trying not to stare at her from behind their *Life* magazines at the Clip and Curl. The women at the sewing circle, pretending to concentrate on the smocking project they had started just last week, would shake their heads. Disgusting. *Have you ever heard the like?* Smirking.

The burning sensation in her belly was the only thing she could feel. *I'm being eaten from the inside*, she thought, but it started to be a comfort. Pain and anger, at least, were getting her through the days, and she gripped the discomfort like a shield. She finally told Nik she simply felt hollow, like a butchered steer, guts pulled out. She didn't know, she told him, how she could be his wife again. And the children. How could the children hold their heads up? The older ones knew enough to see what had happened. What *had* happened?

"*Cheh teh zdoriw*, Nikolai. Have you gone crazy?"

He sat at the kitchen table, his back to her while she snatched clothes from the wicker basket. She spat the words, forgetting for a moment that she wasn't speaking to him.

"An imbecile. Everyone knows. I can't go to town and hold up my head. At school, kids make fun of the boys. Girls like that, you know they want that from men, my sister say. You supposed to be strong man to say no. To tell her father what she is like. Now see what you do. Who to help me with the farm and the boys? Thank God Andrij, he is man now, and Mihaylo old enough to look after things when they get home. And poor Andrij already has problems. What woman will have him when she knows his father do this?"

Her words seemed to cut into him. He flinched as he sat there, hunched over at the table, his hands flat beside a cup half full of cold coffee and a plate with a thick slice of untouched bread. "You leave us to clean your mess," she went on. "No one will want to know us. And there is baby soon. My God. *Teh sookay sen*. No more sense like rutting bull."

Her voice, bitter and cracked, sliced into his back while he sat slumped, silent. Though she didn't want to hear his excuses, it infuriated her when he didn't speak. She didn't make him anything to eat, and yesterday's coffee sat, cold, on the sideboard. He'd found the loaf of bread where she'd hidden it in the cupboard and cut a heel from the end. There was no butter, not since the last of the cream from the Burkes.

He finally lifted the bread to his mouth, and she winced at the tearing sound his teeth made. So loud it was she wanted to cover her ears. He chewed the dry slab of bread, and she hated the sight of his jaws moving up and down. *Like a stupid cow*, she thought and hoped he would choke. Past the point of caring, she looked at her hands, dry and chapped. Her fingernails were stained from beets, from saskatoons, from grinding pork. With mindless efficiency, she folded the children's shirts and underthings and rolled their woollen socks, each movement as if she was chopping kindling. After this, then, she wouldn't speak to him.

"The constable, he come for you tomorrow. You go to jail, to penitentiary in Prince Albert. And lash, too. The constable, he say so." She hissed so the children wouldn't hear her. "*Didko.* I don't want you in this house, under roof with your boys. I don't care where you go. Sleep in barn with other animals."

She clenched her teeth so hard she thought they might snap and crumble in her mouth. What would become of her and the children? She put a hand to her throat, unable to breathe or swallow. A smothering weight pressed down on her chest as if she were trying to pitch wet hay that wouldn't budge. What if their own girl had lived, what then?

Hanusia pushed the thought away angrily. "*Teh sookay sen.* You son of bitch. Get out. Barn is where you belong."

She grabbed up the folded clothes, turned and left the kitchen, the rest of the washing, and her husband without another word.

NIK

THE YUZIK FARM, LATE SEPTEMBER 1935

Early the next morning, Nik stood in the bedroom doorway and considered whether there was any point in saying something. It had been so cold in the barn that even sleeping in his clothes, piling up as many old blankets as he could find, and pulling some straw over himself didn't help. He'd kept his boots on.

Even now, after the walk up to the house at daybreak, the chill was lodged so deep he didn't trust his legs enough to stand too long. The bit of early light that seeped around the curtains let him see Hanusia lying stiff and sharp beneath the quilt, her back to him. He took a step, the floorboard groaned, and he saw her flinch as though she sensed his touch coming.

It was just as well. He looked at the back of his hands as if they were someone else's, heavy things, the veins like grey twigs in the dim light. He thought of his father's hands. Each of Nik's fingernails had a perfect half-moon, but he was ashamed by the black line of dirt and axle grease under each one. He had forgotten to scrape them with his pocketknife after overhauling the tractor yesterday. Such dirty hands should not touch a woman, not that there was any chance she'd put up with it.

In the dark, he hesitated for a moment longer. The early light cast a mottled pattern across the feather tick and the ridge on the far edge of the bed that was his wife.

"Hanusia. You and the boys. *Neh zhooreshia,*" he said. "Everything, it be okay. I be taking care of things."

Hanusia didn't move. Nik tried to say her name again, but the sound caught in his throat. The wooden floorboards creaked when he turned and, running one hand along the wall to steady himself, shuffled down the narrow staircase.

He shrugged on his barn coat in the kitchen. When he stepped out onto the porch, the hinge, the one he had been meaning to oil, screeched. He grasped the doorknob and gave a sharp pull past the rust, then closed the door carefully behind him. The cold morning air bit his face. A delicate layer of hoarfrost had decorated the farmyard in the night, and he looked across the yard at his own footsteps, made just minutes before on his bone-chilling struggle from the barn. The dog had accompanied him, but those tracks veered off and disappeared into the doghouse by the woodshed. The tree branches, the few sun-blanched cornstalks poking out of Hanusia's garden, the fence posts and the barbed wire itself had all grown a white, spiky coat overnight. The air was bright and painful, and Nik pulled his scarf up to cover his nose and mouth. Squinting, he saw that the weak rising sun was only a dull presence in a slate sky.

The sky was the kind of grey that made it plain that snow was coming early. There was good in that. A snow cover, if it lasted, would provide some moisture in the ground come spring to help hold what topsoil hadn't already blown away in the drought. The fresh snow made the farmyard look clean, hiding dirt, muck, and disarray.

To the east, where the sun was coming up, the milk cows were milling at the gate, jostling one another to be first into the barn, their coughs and bellows bursts of fog in the sharp morning air. The frozen mud and manure crackled under hooves as the stragglers plodded into the barnyard, steam lifting from their backs and sharp hip bones, heads down. They ambled in an undulating line, single file, toward the milk shed. He never tired of the sight, and he liked to watch until he could recognize his favourites. Zina. Taffy. Penny. Ulyana. And Hilda, named to irritate Hanusia's sister. But it didn't lift his spirits, not this morning.

Rascal poked his nose out of the doghouse and crept out, reluctantly shaking off straw and blinking in the morning light. The dog had kept him company in the barn for most of the night and Nik had appreciated the warmth. But the animal moved to the close confines of his own bed when Nik left to go up to the house. Now the dog stretched one hind leg, yawned, then stretched the other and trotted beside Nik, nuzzling his hand for the usual biscuit or bacon rind. This morning there was nothing for him.

Halfway to the barn, Nik stubbed his boot. He stopped and looked down over the rim of his glasses, already fogged with his own breath. The rope lay coiled and looped like a frozen snake in the dead grass. The boys had been fooling with it, tying each other up and playing cowboys and Indians. Was it just yesterday? Before they went to Titka Hilda's to be spared the sight of their father being taken away to town by the constable, there to be charged by the RCMP. He'd come out of the barn and hollered at them to wind that rope up and put it away when they were done. All the boys had stopped still and stared at him as if he were a stranger. Only Ilko had nodded. Guess the boys forgot to put it away. Before, someone would have got a hiding for that, leaving a good rope out to rot.

Nik bent down and pushed Rascal out of the way. The rope was cold and wet in his hands. The frost gnawed at his fingers while he slowly wound the rope around his thumb, looping it around his elbow and back again, fingers numb, forcing its cold resistance into loop after loop until the entire length was neatly taken up. He stood there, feeling the weight of the rope and the cold seeping into his shoulder.

When the door behind him squealed in rusty complaint, he winced and turned back to see Hanusia step out on the porch, grabbing at kindling and stacking it in one arm. Her robe was caught between two sticks of poplar, the cloth pulled down from her shoulder. He could see the sharp edge of her collarbone, her skin so pale. She would scrape herself on the kindling, the splinters.

She raised her head to see him watching her and stood, oddly bent forward at the woodpile with a stick in her hand. He thought, just for a moment, she would call him back to build the fire in the stove. He always did that for her. Every morning, so she would come down to a warming kitchen, just enough to take off the chill. She would start the porridge for the boys, and by the time they sat, hunched over their bowls, he would be back with the blue pitcher of milk for their coffee.

But now, he saw her jaw set. She straightened. She jabbed the stick at him, and her voice, shrill, pierced him where he stood in the yard. His banishment to the barn had not soothed her anger. "A feeble-minded girl! *Cheh teh zdoriw*, Nikolai," she shrieked, and her fury was fresh and raw again. "Now constable is coming, and you go. Maybe a year for jail. And lash. I give you lash myself!"

Nik felt rooted to the ground. Rascal, too, seemed pinned to the earth, quiet and motionless beside him.

"My God. *Tay sooken sen*. Like stupid bull, maybe pig, no more sense!" Her voice caught, ragged and broken. Nik thought for an instant, hoped, that she would cry. Instead, she slammed the stick against the kindling she clutched against her chest. "*Teh sooka sen!* Get out of my sight, you son of bitch. *A shchob tobi zaklalo!*"

The hinge squealed again. The door slammed. The silence that followed seemed a dull weight on Nik's head. It was as though the mind that told him to move his arms and put one foot ahead of the other had been crushed.

The dog nuzzled Nik's hand and whined. Nik looked down at the animal, expressionless. "I take care of loose ends, Rascal," he said. "Loose ends. I tie them up. Is okay."

The dog sprang to its feet and circled Nik, yelping a little now that the man was finally moving toward the barn and the usual warm milk that would be shot his way from a twisted teat as Nik filled the pails. The dog ran ahead, then galloped back, circling Nik and running ahead and back again, nudging him, keeping him moving.

More cows collected around the gate, leaning heavily into one another, great racking coughs forcing frosty bursts of breath in the morning air. With swollen udders, the cows turned their heads. Their watery, dark eyes watched his approach. A few began to bellow, a mournful plea that made him shut his eyes and wish himself deaf against it. Guilt coursed through him, and he looked away. To be judged wanting by lowly beasts made what he had done to the child even harder to bear.

He hoisted the rope up on his shoulder, went around the side of the milk shed, and pushed open the barn door. He waited for his eyes to focus in the gloom, but it was a more intimate place to him now. His eyes took in the makeshift bed on the straw laid out beside the pen. He had hoped for a little warmth from the calf, a selfish thought. It was so poorly, he was ashamed to take even that from a creature that had so little. It was not long for this world. It would be a kindness to kill it, but Nik couldn't summon up the will. A shaft of pale sunlight slanted down from the hayloft window and divided the dim interior neatly in two, and the calf backed away on trembling legs into the darkness.

Outside in the chill, with the coming of snow, his sense of smell seemed to have been peeled away. But inside the barn, fragrant and moist from animal heat and the insulation of straw, there was still earth, fermenting grass and hay, chop and manure. The bitter stench of calf scours mingled with axle grease and oil, and the clean scent of dry rope coiled neatly on spikes driven into the walls. The other calf, the late one he was weaning, stumbled up out of sleep, startled, and skittered through the straw in the other pen along the far wall. It pushed its nose through the slats, drooling, tongue searching, sucking at the air in anticipation of the milk bucket.

Nik breathed deeply and rolled his head painfully from one shoulder to the other. The heavy rope made his neck ache. Pain shot across his chest. Up to the other shoulder. He winced as the vertebrae in his neck popped and cracked. He put a hand to the back of his neck and pressed his fingers deep into the sore muscles along his spine. He was so cold.

Nik looked up at the rafters. The barn swallows had nested along the rough beams. Even though the boys climbed up into the loft regularly during the spring and summer, armed with rakes or sticks to knock the nests down to keep the bird shit out of the hay and chop, the swallows persisted. As fast as the boys worked, the birds went back to singled-minded rebuilding.

Nik took the rope off his shoulder and gripped it, testing its weight against his palm. He swung his arm back and forward past his thigh, underhand, with an effort that forced a cry from his open mouth when he heaved the rope's length up over the centre beam. The swallows, startled, whirled around the loft in a flock of one mind, tiny wings fluttering like his heart. He put his hand over the front pocket of his overalls and tried to feel it, but he could not. He thought about its will to go on, even when it did not deserve to keep beating. He reached for the small stool, the one he used when he sat to hold the milk bucket for the calf, and pulled it closer.

Barn cats cowered and streaked for the shadows in the loft when the rope slapped across the beam, the end just flicking the edge of the loft before it fell to coil at Nik's feet. Rascal leaped and snapped at the birds circling above him. When Nik threw the end back up over the beam a second time, the swallows lifted again, dipped, and swooped out through the wide door into the white morning. He worked methodically, looping the rope, twisting and testing. His mouth still open, he struggled. His breath came and went in ragged catches. In. Out. In. Out. His heart was present now, the pulsing in his ears so loud he wondered if the dog might even hear it.

He pulled the scarf from his neck, folded it loosely, and placed it on the top plank of the empty hayrack. He removed his spectacles and placed them on top of the scarf. Quickly now, he moved to the rope and stood up on the stool, swaying a bit before he steadied himself. The cats appeared again, cautiously, silently expectant, and peered down over the edge of the loft. The weak sunlight broke and flickered where it sought its way in through knotholes and cracks in the barn siding.

Rascal whined and crept to the stool, circled his tail once, and curled up beneath the tips of Nik's boots. *A good dog*, Nik thought. *Hanusia must remember that he likes a bit of the leftover oatmeal with some bacon drippings. Smalats.* He'd need some fat to stay warm this winter. Nik told her so often, but she didn't like the dog and threw the table scraps to the chickens.

A loose tuft of yellow straw, set loose by a cat or the air disturbed by swallow wings, tipped and fell from the loft. It floated down through the dusty shaft of muted light from the hayloft window and swam through Nik's blurred vision. He raised his eyes to the white light of the open doorway.

"*Bozhe proshchai menyi,*" he whispered. "God forgive me."

HANUSIA

THE YUZIK FARM, LATE SEPTEMBER 1935

Hanusia lay cold under the covers, regretting getting up when she knew Nik hadn't lit the stove. She concentrated on the sharp sick feeling of jealousy that twisted in her belly. She hadn't felt that sting, she realized, since she was a schoolgirl. Hanusia had been just a youngster when she fell from the wagon, the wheel crushing her jaw. She was nine when her friend—what was that girl's name?—told her she had a new best friend now, someone prettier.

Hanusia had crawled back into bed without bothering to light the stove. Seeing Nik hunched there halfway to the milk shed seemed to strip her of any reason to even build a fire. Now she stared up into the corner of the bedroom ceiling and waited for her body to warm the sheets. A cobweb hung there, hairy with dust, and the spider, a black dot, sat waiting just at the edge, where the yellowed wallpaper peeled away from the plaster.

She fought tears and felt she betrayed herself when they welled and threatened to spill. She pinched furiously at her cheeks until the skin was hot and red and willed the bitter anger to rise again in her chest. When it did, she felt strong enough to get up. She tapped her feet on the cold floor and let her toes search for her slippers. She pulled them on, reached for the worn green robe she had thrown across the bed, and, rising quickly and moving fast now, silently descended the stairs, puffing warm breath into her cupped red hands.

With the boys gone to her sister's, the house seemed too big, too cold and quiet. In the kitchen, she scraped up some wood chips and bark from the box she kept beside the stove. She tore some pages from last year's Eaton's catalogue, twisted them, and poked them into the firebox. There was only the bit of kindling she had brought in earlier. She'd meant to make Ilko chop some before the younger boys went to her sister's. She couldn't bear the idea of the boys watching the constable take their father away. After they left, it was too much of an effort to ask her husband for anything. She'd have to do it herself later. On a Sunday yet. Talking to him about filling the kindling box seemed absurd, too ordinary, and too normal in the shadow of all of this. She wondered if she'd be expected to offer the constable coffee or tea when he came for Nik. She decided she would not.

Hanusia gripped the stove lid handle, feeling the cold metal while she waited for the wood scraps to catch. When she clattered the lid back over the hole, she turned the damper and saw that the handle had left its impression, a spiral pressed on her palm. She stared at it until she finally clenched her fist over it, her nails, stained dirty red from peeling beets for borscht the day before, cutting into her skin.

Last night's coffee sat cold in the pot, and she pulled two mugs from the cupboard. Habit. Nikolai always liked a strong coffee, heavily sugared, before breakfast, as soon as he came in from the milk shed. Sometimes, they'd sit together before she got up to ladle out the oatmeal for him and the boys. He always brought her the blue pitcher filled with milk straight from Taffy, the only cow with some Jersey in her, and by the time he got to the house, the cream had already risen to the top. She tried not to think about the cream can from the Burkes.

There would be no fresh cream this morning. The empty pitcher was on the table. So he'd forgotten. She opened her hand

and, with a finger, traced the brown hairline crack that had crept from the spout all the way around to the handle. Nikolai had done that, too. Taffy had kicked, and the pitcher was knocked from his hand. Clumsy man. Her best pitcher, ruined now. She put Nik's mug back in the cupboard.

The weak morning sunlight began to creep into the corners of the kitchen. She realized the muffled noise she was still hearing was the cows bellowing. She looked out the kitchen window at the cows bunching up along the corner of the fence, their distress more insistent. Why was he not letting the cows into the milk shed?

Hanusia hooked the handle into the stove lid and dragged it aside again. The bark and chips snapped and popped; the twists of catalogue blackened and flamed at the edges. She dropped in a few more chips and one piece of split log and stared at the fire. A trace of dull realization dragged itself into her mind. Suddenly, she jerked the handle and scraped the lid back over the hole.

Hanusia tore her black kerchief from the hook by the door and quickly tied it under her chin with shaking hands, her face still tender where she had pinched herself. She winced when the scarf brushed against her cheek and quickly plucked out a piece of straw embedded in the cloth. She pulled open the door, ignoring the rusty squeak, and took her black barn coat from the hook in the porch.

She pulled the door closed behind her and paused by the woodpile. The split poplar that Nikolai and the boys stacked close enough to the door to have it within reach smelled strong. Hanusia tried to fill her lungs with the pungent air, this little pocket of summer smell that survived as winter drew closer. Odd that she would notice it now when the uneasy weight in her chest couldn't be displaced. Even the scent of barn, cows, and chicken coop that clung to her kerchief couldn't move it, not even when she pulled a handful of cloth over her nose.

She stepped off the porch and shielded her eyes from the white glare of the morning's frost. The panic began to beat in her chest. She began to run, her slippers scuffing through the first lasting snow, which lay in white fingers across the dead grass. She'd forgotten her boots. She'd forgotten to button her coat, and it flapped around her. Now that the sun was up, the brilliance of the hoarfrost stabbed at her eyes until they watered and the barn blurred. But she could see the barn door was open.

"*Shchtoh teh robbish doornay?* What are you doing? Don't you do this to me!" Her words beat in time with her footsteps and shallow gasps as she crossed the frozen ground. "*Ni, ni, ni.*" The panic was crawling higher in her throat. She sacrificed air to swallow it down, coughing while she ran.

By the time she stumbled over the straw pile in front of the chicken coop and reached the barn, her blood was pounding in her ears. She clawed at the edge of the open door and heaved it wide, revealing what she knew she'd see. Still, it took a moment for her to comprehend. Then she screamed, her dry lips cracked, and she tasted blood.

"*Naiy tebeh didko vozhmeh,*" she shrieked. "Nikolai, you do not do this to me. *Teh tak yak lys, te mene toot leshew tak yak sered moreh!*"

Swallows exploded into the air, circling the loft in a frenzy of beating wings. Hanusia's legs crumpled beneath her, and she sank to the dirt and straw.

The barn interior spun, and Hanusia squeezed her eyes shut, her bloody lips working soundlessly. She covered her face with her hands and rocked back and forth. "You leave me here in the middle of the sea! You go to hell!" She threw her head back, clenched her fists, and wailed. "*Ni, ni! Teh ne mozhes zrobete tze doh mene!* You cannot do this to me!"

VIOLET

Violet heard the truck when it was still out on the grid road and knew Hank was on his way, so familiar was she with the sound of the periodic backfire that heralded a visit from her favourite neighbour. She hurried to the window and peeked through the kitchen curtains just as Hank nosed the International up in front of the house and shut off the engine. He sat there for a moment, and she flicked the curtain back, giggling behind her hand. She looked out again. Hank stepped out near the lilacs and strode to the house.

Violet threw open the door, pushing out the screen as far as she could. "Hi, Hank!" Barefoot in a pink cotton dress, with her mother's green apron tied high around her waist, she tried to look grown up, at least a little older than fifteen. "Come see what I have, Hank! Father says I can care for him." She pulled at his hand. "He's in a box behind the stove. I keep him warm. Come on!"

"Well, show me then," Hank said, looking past her into the kitchen. "Listen now, where's your father? I need to talk to him for a little bit."

Something in his voice made Violet frown, and she let go of his hand. Hank pulled his straw hat from his head and carefully rubbed his bad left eye. His voice softened, and he grinned. "It's all right, sweetheart. Just something about the cows."

"Over for the plow to Dykstra's farm, and he puts it in the shed. He is coming back soon for his tea," Violet said, relieved. "How is your scratchy eye today?" she asked, just as she had for years, every time Hank came to visit.

"Same as always," he said.

She reached for his hand again and pulled him farther into the kitchen. Violet used to make him tell the story about getting the fishhook in his eye the day he first met Father and Mr. Yuzik. Now she was content with the short answer.

"See, Hank!"

Hank stood turning the brim of his sweat-stained hat with the tips of his big fingers. Violet pushed past the kindling box and bent down behind the woodstove. There was some scuffling and a weak growl. Violet stood and turned to show Hank her patient. It was Tom, one of the old barn cats, looking beyond worse for wear. A chewed left ear hung in tatters, and the hair on the side of its head and neck was still matted with dry blood, spittle and dirt. Tom opened one eye.

"See, Hank! I am a nurse."

"For heaven's sake," Hank said with some alarm. "What in the world happened to him?"

Violet beamed, and she clutched the cat against her chest. It hung limp like a piece of burlap sack. "Coyote," Violet said, pursing her lips. "Bad coyote. Father said Tom almost was supper, but he got away. He cried at the door, and I bring him in to be all better. He has some milk, and he gets better. I take care of him."

Father's boots thumped on the front porch. The screen hinges squeaked, and the door snapped shut. Hank turned to greet his neighbour.

"Father! Hank is here to see Tom," Violet cried.

Father hung his barn coat on one of the pegs at the entryway, swept off his black bowler, placed it on top of the water barrel and stood for a moment drumming the hat with his fingers. Violet smiled. He always did that.

"I reckoned as much when I saw his truck, my girl. A chilly one out there this morning. G'day, Hank," Father said, extending a hand for a shake. "I see you've met Violet's infirmary patient. I do believe that cat has used up a good many more than nine lives."

"I care for him and make him better," insisted Violet. She cooed into the cat's remaining ear. Hank chuckled when the cat actually started purring. She bent down and gently put the cat back in the box of rags behind the stove reservoir.

"I was going to dispatch old Tom when I saw the state he was in, but Violet found him up on the porch and insisted we bring him in to fix him." Father smiled and rubbed the back of his neck. "One look at her face, and I couldn't say no. I've been indulging her quite a bit lately with, well, with what's gone on." He trailed off and nodded at Violet, who stood by the stove.

Hank turned the brim of his hat again and scuffed at the metal ring on the root cellar trapdoor with the toe of his boot. He looked so serious. "Guess if you were over at Dykstras' this morning, you've heard," he said.

Violet saw Father's jaw tighten. She didn't like that.

"Violet, sweetheart, would you make two old men a nice cuppa tea? I see that kettle's been on the boil, and I need a bit of warming up, too, just like your Tom," Father said brightly. "Hank," he said more quietly. He tilted his head toward the front room. "Let's step out for a moment and leave Violet to it."

The men moved through the doorway to the sitting room, and Violet crept closer and strained to hear Hank's hushed words.

"When she said you were at Old Man Dykstra's, I figured you would have heard," Hank said. "Word like that travels real fast. I'll bet the phone lines are already hot with it. That gossipy wife of his will be more than happy to supply the news. Emily says his missus listens on the party line so much it's like she's the operator."

"Bloody hell, Hank," Father growled, keeping his voice low,

but Violet knew he was angry. "I don't know what to think. I was right pleased he was going to prison, but this. Who expected this?"

"Albert said Hanusia had banished him from the house," Hank whispered. "Said it appeared he'd slept in the barn last night."

"Who slept in the barn?" Violet stepped into the doorway. She looked at her father and then Hank. Suddenly, her belly didn't feel good. That happened when something bad was going on. She was a grown-up lady now, and Father should tell her what it was.

"Emily is right," Violet said when they didn't answer. "Remember, Hank? Emily say, 'Violet understands things if you tell her straight out.' That's right, Father? What's matter?"

The men stepped back into the kitchen and stood by the table. Father nodded at Hank and then took a breath. "All right, then, my girl. Listen to me now," Father said. "Nik—Mr. Yuzik is dead."

Violet bit down on her lip. Her throat tightened, making it hard to swallow. She thought for a moment, and then she had to push the words out. "I know already, but not for sure," she said finally, her voice small. She felt her cheeks grow warm. "Mr. Yuzik, he die. He go to Heaven."

"Violet, sweetheart." Father pulled a chair out from the table and sat down. He put his hands on his knees and leaned forward. "How do you know about Nik?"

"Telephone. I not supposed to listen." Violet pointed, avoiding his eyes, afraid her father might be cross. "You say, 'Violet, that's nosy rude.' But I can lift up real careful so there's no click, and I heard her say. This morning. I thought it was just a pretend." Violet felt that bad feeling in her belly begin to twist. She backed up beside the stove and pulled the kettle over the hotter part. She had to do something, to keep her hands busy, to think. Her lips moved, repeating the words to herself, trying them out to see if they made more sense. Her mind slowly filled with the truth. She sat down heavily on the green wooden chair by the cook stove and rubbed her stomach absently where her apron stretched too tight.

"I got seven eggs this morning. Seven," she said, looking out the window. "I count. One broke. One is too dirty, and I wash it in the rain barrel."

Hank cleared his throat and took a step toward her. Father put his hand out to stay him.

She pulled the kettle across the stovetop, and water sloshed from the spout, hissing as it evaporated on the black iron surface. She gripped the handle. Father stepped forward and put his hand over hers, rubbing her fingers until she let go. He led her to the table, and the three of them sat side by side.

Dead, she mouthed. Her lips worked the word. She worried it, turned it sideways and backward. *Dead*.

"He is dead," she said. She looked up into Father's face. He closed his eyes, and she knew it really was true. *Dead means never coming back*. "Dead like John," Violet said quietly.

"Yes. Just like your brother."

The three sat in silence until the kettle sputtered and steamed, then whistled. Tom let out a thin yowl from under the stove. Startled by the noise, Violet stood and smoothed her green apron with two slow downward sweeps the length of her thighs, carefully running her fingers along the yellow rickrack and over the clumsy patch she'd sewn over the hole in the pocket. She so often dropped the peeler in there when she did potatoes, it finally gave way, and the knife would drop to the floor. She had found her mother's sewing basket and hunched over her work for hours.

She opened the cupboard again and took out her father's blue mug and a brown one for Hank. The inside of her father's was stained with rings from his strong tea like a tree trunk cut crosswise. She pried the lid off the Bell tea tin and filled the metal infuser, hung it on the edge of Father's mug, and carefully poured water from the kettle. She carried the mugs to the table. Another yowl from Tom made her hurry to the stove, where she bent down around the back. The cat stared up with a half-closed eye, and as she carefully stroked his head with a finger, Father and Hank began to talk in hushed tones.

"Just not right, William," Hank said. "All the business before, and now Nik does this thing." Violet backed out from behind the stove, careful not to touch the hot surface. Hank lifted his mug and then set it back on the table untouched. After a few minutes, he cleared his throat, "Violet, I—" he began.

"Will we put him in the ground like John?" Violet asked quickly, cutting Hank off.

"I expect they will, sweetheart. The very same thing."

Violet knew Hank and her father always waited to hear her out, even when her words got jumbled. They didn't rush her, or worse, get cross and walk away. Hank was a good friend. He was like a brother, really, since she'd known him all her life. It seemed the only people left who could understand her well enough to get by were her father, Hank, and Emily. So many words seemed to fill up her mouth and get crisscrossed. It took so much effort just to figure out what to say, form the words, and get them said.

She often heard people wondering out loud, "why William doesn't put her somewhere," and while she didn't know exactly what that meant, she didn't feel good when they talked like that. Violet liked to talk to people. It kept her thinking, Father said, and made her feel a part of things. She didn't like people hovering over her too much, though. It made her feel like a child, and fifteen was almost a grown-up lady. But leaving her alone, it was clear, hadn't been good either. Father said that, too.

"Hanusia says he fell from the hayloft and broke his neck.

"Guess it's easier for her and the children that way," Hank said.

"A *bootz*," Violet whispered, patting her forehead. "A *bootz* on the head. That's what Mr. Yuzik says when he bump his head." She reached over and lifted the infuser from Father's mug and hung it on the rim of Hank's. "You want more tea, Hank?"

Hank pressed his fingertips over his bad eye and shook his

head. Violet knew a headache would come soon. He said it always felt like a sliver of barley chaff was in it, and by the way he was rubbing it, she knew today it must hurt a bit worse than usual.

She followed his gaze when he looked down at the chipped edges of the yellow linoleum around the cellar trapdoor. Countless cream cans had been hauled up out of the cool dugout under the kitchen and dragged across the floor along a well-worn path. She remembered the time he'd nearly gone headfirst down the steps. She hadn't dropped the trapdoor back down over the hole like she was supposed to. If only he'd come to visit a little earlier that day, she thought. Hank would have told Mr. Yuzik to stop.

Hank picked up the mug and stood. He stepped carefully over to the sink. Bits of straw and barley chop spilled out of his overalls cuff and scattered on the floor.

"Sorry, Violet. I should have cleaned up a bit before coming over. I know you keep the house real clean," Hank said. Then he turned to Father. "I had a talk with Constable Dickenson, and then I went out to the chop shed. I knocked down a few swallow nests. You know how they get in there and mess on the grain." Hank looked out the window, talking quietly. "Gave me a little time to try and work out what Nik must have been thinking. Guilt maybe. I hope. It couldn't have been quick the way he just stepped off the milk stool."

"Bloody coward." Father spoke so sharply that Violet winced. "God damn him. I hope to hell he was full of guilt and had a good deal of time to think about it." He stood up and banged his mug down on the kitchen table. He leaned forward, gripping the edge of the table, his head hanging between his outstretched arms.

Violet felt her bottom lip tremble. Father was rarely loud and angry, and it frightened her. When John died, he was very angry and sad, too, but this was different. He shouldn't be mad at Mr. Yuzik. Mr. Yuzik was a nice man, mostly. She wanted Father to think of something else, to be more like himself. Kind and happy.

"Funeral, like John?" Violet asked suddenly. She would wear a nice dress. Father always said she looked so pretty when she put on her good dress and combed her hair, so that would make him happy.

"On Wednesday, but I don't think it's a good idea," Father said sharply. He let go of the table and straightened up.

"Mr. Yuzik go to Heaven now. He likes that nice music there," she said. She felt her bottom lip trembling hard now. "I like church."

"Listen now, Violet. This is real important." Father cleared his throat and began again. "It'd be best if we stayed home from the funeral. You can say prayers for him, though, if you want. How does that sound?"

"Not go? Not go to church?" Violet stared at him. That couldn't be right. "I go, too. I go with you. And Hank and Emily. I sit with Emily. I love Emily." She looked at him, blinking hard when she felt hot tears welling up. She didn't like Father's troubled face, and Hank's didn't look nice either. She put her hands flat against her chest and felt her heart pounding.

"I don't expect your father will be going to the funeral, either," Hank said. "You know he and Mr. Yuzik didn't really have much to do with each other anymore."

"No, I am going, too," she said. "I not stay home. Mr. Yuzik, he likes me. I am going to church."

"Violet, it's out of the question. I'll hear no more about it." Father pushed his mug away. "Hanusia and the kids will be there," he said more gently. "You don't want people to stare at you, dear heart." He reached for her hand.

"No!" Violet pulled away and jerked her arm back, knocking her mug from the table. The three of them watched it arc into the air and explode against the side of the stove. Violet felt her cheeks flush. She balled up her fists and stared at the two men. Then the tears came. "I go too!" she cried, pressing back against the sideboard. "He is nice to me. He says my hair is pretty. I am a good girl!" She was crying now, and her nose began to run. Violet wished there hadn't been any talk about the funeral. Maybe Hank should just go home now.

"Violet, calm down. Jesus." Hank reached for her again. "Here, sit down and don't work yourself up. You know how you get. Come on. Please," he pleaded and took her hand, frowning. Hank frowned like that when she got "worked up," so Violet knew her cheeks must be red and blotchy, and her heart felt too fast. He pulled his handkerchief from his overalls pocket.

"I tell him no," she sobbed, wiping her nose on the apron. "I say no, thank you, and I'm polite." She looked to Father for confirmation. He'd told her so over and over. She saw his face soften. In two strides, he was to her and gathered her into his arms.

"It isn't your fault, Violet." Father had said it before, and now he said it again. He cupped his hand over the back of her head and smoothed her hair. She pressed her cheek to his shirt, the flannel soft and smelling of outside, hay, and pipe smoke. It made her feel better. "Come on now. Sit for a minute. Your heart's going to take off on you the way you're carrying on," he said, leading her to the bench by the cream separator. He took the metal spouts from the seat and set them inside the bowl. "Not everybody should go to the funeral, my girl. I'm not going. Hank's not going, Emily's not going."

She sat on the bench, shoulders slumped, and the happiness she felt when Hank arrived completely disappeared. She sniffed loudly. She mopped her face with the apron and breathed in two raspy gulps of air. "Because of me?" she asked. "Mr. Yuzik is mad. At me. I forget his cream can."

Tears welled in Hank's good eye. Father looked at the floor. "It wasn't the cream can. You didn't do anything bad." He looked up. He reached out and rubbed her arm. "Come on, now. Sit still for a minute and catch your breath."

Hank cleared his throat again and took a good hard look out the window at his truck in the yard. Violet wiped her eyes on the back of her hand and tried to pay attention to what Father was saying.

"Hanusia and the boys have had enough grief. Look here now,

Violet. You haven't had any tea. I'll make you a cup. You'll feel better with a good cuppa. We can talk about something else."

"No," Violet said and shook her head. She pulled up the edge of her apron, looked for a dry spot, and wiped her nose. "I am so tired now."

She turned and left them there in the kitchen and carefully closed the door to her room. She leaned her forehead against it and tried to calm herself so she could listen. Father said it was nosy rude to listen, but that was on the party line. Maybe this was different.

Hank spoke first. She could make it out if she held her breath.

"Albert said a long drop was humane if that's what you were after, and this didn't look like he'd even struggled. Still, a high collar will hide the bruising on his neck at the funeral. Albert must have arrived not long after he did it. Hanusia was fit to be tied."

"I almost wish Louise was here," Father said. Violet hadn't heard him mention her mother for a long time, not since she went away. "Lord knows I don't know what to do, how to help Violet now. I never confronted him, Hank. I meant to. Many times, even though I was afraid of what I might do. Maybe I'm the coward." That edge to Father's voice brought fresh tears to her eyes. Her chest felt so tight. Violet pressed her ear to the door. There was another silence before Hank spoke again.

"At least the boys had been packed up and sent to Hanusia's sister before Albert got there to take Nik to prison. So they wouldn't have to see their father hauled away in leg irons."

Violet heard the floor creak and knew Father and Hank had gone into the sitting room. She couldn't hear anything else.

She crawled into her bed and curled up, her hands pressed against her belly. She thought of poor chewed-up Tom under the stove. She would take care of him, and Father, too. Everyone would feel better soon. She was the lady of the house now.

WILLIAM

William peered at his reflection in Louise's bureau mirror. The backing was peeling away in black spots, and the surface of the glass was streaked and foggy, making his face and torso appear wobbly and off-kilter. He swallowed, and shrugged into a clean shirt, then cinched his belt.

The clunk from the kitchen when Violet dropped a wood chunk into the stove made him blink. He waited, with his black bowler in his hand, until he heard the springs in Violet's mattress squeak. She'd be back in bed again, under the covers, until the kitchen warmed up, and he could get out without having to explain where he was going. He wouldn't be gone long. She might go back to sleep for an hour or two. She had been sleeping so much lately, and he was glad of it, especially today. He could get back and be at the breakfast table with a cuppa, checking grain prices in the *Western Producer,* before she came out to cook his eggs. He crossed the kitchen, reached for his town coat on the peg, opened the door and stepped out onto the porch, holding the screen door so it wouldn't bang shut behind him.

He was confused by something that seemed lodged somewhere in his chest, and it compelled him to at least be near the church when Nik was buried. He couldn't decide if he wanted to be sure the bastard was dead and buried or if he longed to say farewell to the old friend Nik once was. Of course, he wouldn't go close, not being sure what sort of welcome there would be, if any. It would pain Hanusia and maybe the boys, so he'd just stay in the truck. Keep his distance.

There had been a heavy snowfall since Albert cut down Nik's body that day. William drove carefully, making sure he kept the narrow tires well between the ditches. For most of the way, the Ford made new tracks in the snow.

Hoarfrost had decorated the landscape during the night again, lacing the willows bunched at the corners of fields. William squinted at the stark whiteness of the prairie. It looked so pure, so clean, and he wished he could see it without thinking of the dirt and decay beneath it.

The morning sun glinted off the silver dome of the Holy Trinity Orthodox church. William spotted it on the horizon long before he could identify the building. It put William in mind of a lighthouse, flashing its beam out across a sea of snow-covered fields, alerting farmers about what lay ahead, warning of hidden rocks in the field, the sort that would break a ploughshare or cause a horse to stumble and break a leg. There was not one cloud he could see anywhere, but the sky was a soft grey, and he knew it would snow again before the afternoon was out. The frost, spikey on the cattails in the slough beside the road, would be gone soon as the sun warmed the day.

Holy Trinity was the only building on the prairie for miles around, with its little ball and cross on top. Nik helped build that church, he had once told William when they were coming back this way from the seed mill. The fact of Nik's hanging became the fiction of Nik's fall from the hayloft by the time the story reached town. Because people believed that Nik fell from the hayloft, Nik could be buried here. Taking one's own life was a sin to the believers in Nik's church.

The story of Nik's fall was efficiently spread, as so many stories were, by Stewart Macleod. "Broke his neck, poor old bugger," Stewart had muttered over his coffee at Ling's Café. "Wife found him. She figured it was odd that the cows still hadn't been milked. Damn shame, leaving all those kids and the farm. Poor old bugger."

People didn't question the story, at least not in public. The bit of deception was why Nik would lie buried here at his own church cemetery rather than at the Farmer's Independent Cemetery after a shameful send-off in the United. That was the practice for people who killed themselves. But Nik had been the one who worked with the blacksmith to fashion the wrought iron railings going up the front steps beneath the round window, and the angled cross at the top. And people did feel some compassion for Hanusia and the boys.

"Curlicues and *khresteh*," Nik had said many times. "Ukrainians, we love curlicues and *khresteh*."

At a big stand of poplar and wolf willow just before the turnoff to the church, William carefully pulled over to the side and cut the engine. Getting stuck here, now, wouldn't do. There were cars, maybe two, and a few sleighs and cutters already by the spruce and poplar trees in front of the church. A few men steered women by the elbow up the steps, and children trudged along behind. It was less than a quarter mile, but it was too far away to make out who anybody was. William did recognize Joe Chumak's green Ford. The International Harvester truck that Dr. Speight used for the hearse was up along the front step, and William could see a few figures in long black coats milling around at the back.

This was close enough. The cemetery was between him and the church, and he could see where they'd made Nik's plot ready with the black hill of dirt beside the hole. Digging must have been a hard go, William thought, what with thawing a layer, then scraping down. Just as they had done for John.

He remembered John's funeral, how he'd been so grateful for the effort the men put in to dig when the ground was still frozen. Such a late spring that year. Not easy for anyone, dying any time after the first hard frost or before the ground warmed up in spring. Nik told him once, after a day of cutting oats and more than a few sips from the flask out on the porch, that he figured freezing people, sharpening their feet, and pounding them into the ground would be a lot easier. "Leave hell of lot more land for farming," he said. They had a good laugh over that one, so Nik had another pull on the flask and told it again.

Mad bugger, thought William. Nik had always been a joker. William's jaw clenched, and he felt the old surge of anger course through his chest. He rubbed his hand roughly over his face, swallowed. *God damn him.*

The headstones and the spears of yellow grass poking up through the snow glinted with hoarfrost. Nik's stone would wait until spring. If this winter was going to be anything like the last, the stones would be completely covered with snow by mid-November and wouldn't show themselves again until the very last of March, maybe into April. The earth over Nik would sink, freeze, thaw, and sink a little more in the spring until it settled enough to bear the weight of a stone. William thought of the soil, the worms, bugs. The gophers, burrowing down to where Nik lay. Nik wouldn't mind. He always said that after he died, his soul had to wander for forty days anyway.

William cranked down the window just enough to keep his breath from fogging up the windshield too much. His throat was dry, making it hard to swallow, like the start of a cold, but he knew it wasn't that. Having the window down gave him a chill, but there was some perverse comfort in being uncomfortable. As his moist breath escaped out the window, he didn't have to run his palm over the windshield quite as often.

If he held his breath for a moment, he could hear the cantor, just faintly. The hymns seeped out of the church walls as the congregated few began to sing. He imagined Hanusia and the six pale, skinny sons filling up an entire pew at the front, all the boys staring at the wooden box that contained their father. He could just see them holding the braided bread, careful to be still so the candle flame wouldn't go out. William wondered if they really knew how he died and why.

Behind Nik's family, there would be lots of room for people who wouldn't come. Stewart Macleod's version of the events aside, some would refuse to attend. Not just because he'd hanged himself; the other scandal Nik had left behind with Violet would be more than reason enough to stay away.

William put his hand inside his coat pocket and pulled out the folded square of newsprint he'd cut from the *Watrous Signal* yesterday. He'd read it so many times already the paper was torn. Creased, too, from when he'd crushed it in his fist and then, last night, retrieved it from the wood box and smoothed it out at the kitchen table. He could practically recite the funeral notice from memory now. This was a church service, after all. You were meant to be holding something solemn in your hands. There was a black headline that read, "Death Calls a Pioneer Farmer, His Earthly Pilgrimage is Ended." The print beneath was tiny.

Nikolai Mihaylo Yuzik, a pioneer farmer in the Watrous area, died at his home in the early morning of Monday, September 30, 1935, and hence was 53 years and eight months. He fell to his death in the barn during morning chores.

Mr. Yuzik was born in Donetsk, Ukraine and was married in that country to Hanusia, the wife who now survives him. They came to the Yorkton area and then a homestead in the Watrous district, where they have lived ever since.

Mr. Yuzik was a quiet, peaceable and kindly man and an industrious and successful farmer. Through hard work and good management, he developed a fine farm. He was always an attentive and appreciative listener to the word of God at the services in the church.

William paused and reached forward to press his palm against the fog creeping over the windshield despite his efforts. The churchyard was quiet. He leaned his ear to the open window as the faint strains of a second hymn started up. He read that last line in the notice a second time. "Attentive and appreciative listener to the word of God," William read out loud. Wishful thinking on the part of the priest, who was no doubt the writer of the piece, he decided.

"You would have liked that one," William said into the stillness. He leaned forward to the windshield and vigorously wiped away the creeping fog that was beginning to again obscure his view.

The notice went on, and William realized, painfully, he was clenching his teeth. He opened his mouth and worked his jaw. He read on.

He held that the only loss no one can afford is the loss of friend or family. He was a devoted family man and lived his Christianity both inside and outside the home. He is predeceased by his parents, Galina and Khoriv, a brother, Olexander, two sons in infancy, and a daughter who was stillborn. He is survived by his devoted wife, Hanusia, and six sons.

"Nik, you bastard." William pulled his handkerchief from his jacket pocket. He stared out toward the church, where Nik's body lay in his Sunday suit. Nik hated wearing a suit, and it was a rare occasion when he took it out of mothballs. Even then, he kept his long johns on. Strangled him, he said. Wearing it once a year was too often, and he did it only when Hanusia threatened him. *With what?* Willliam wondered now. And today, William imagined, Nik wore his suit with his shirt collar buttoned up high, though curious eyes would be drawn to it.

As William pressed the handkerchief to his own eyes, pictures flooded through his head. The two of them laughing together on the porch, smoking their pipes. Nik listening, nodding, eyes closed in reverence, while William told him about the Canterbury Plains and his boyhood. Nik and William on stools at Ling's Café, drinking coffee and rolling their eyes at Stewart MacLeod's latest whopper.

Nik, climbing down from the wagon at the house, an armful of black-eyed Susans for Violet he'd picked from the ditch just past the coulee, then sweeping off his hat and bowing when she opened the door, offering her a trinket that made music in the breeze. She giggled. Nik touched his baby's face.

"Bloody son of a bitch!" William cried out and threw his shoulder into the door and wrenched open the handle. He lurched out and onto the road. Faint chanting reached him through the clear air, and he knew they were nearing the psalm of repentance. They would be asking for God's compassion and gracious mercy, for cleansing and forgiveness. "You were my friend, you goddamn old bugger!" he yelled toward the church, his shouts cutting down the grid road through the cold air at nothing but the cars, cutters, and horses stamping in the snow. "You could have just given her the bloody spoons. You could have turned around and gone home. To your wife. Easy for you now, but we have to live with what you did. There's been enough trial in my family, you son of a bitch!"

William kicked at the snow on the road and slammed the truck door. He yanked it open and slammed it again and again until the truck shook, and the window rolled down inside the door, rattling like it could shatter. On the last yank, the handle came loose in his numb fingers. Spent, gasping in the cold air, he hung by his arm, draped over the open window frame. He tossed the handle onto the seat.

"You could have let her be." William coughed, the crisp air catching in his throat. He leaned his forehead against the cold doorframe. "She's a child, for Christ's sake. Her life is hard enough." He scrubbed his hand through his hair. Tears pricked his eyes, and he rubbed them away on his coat sleeve. With effort and an arm heavy as wood, he reached through the open window and felt for the handle inside and opened the door. Sweating beneath his coat, he pulled himself in and slumped behind the steering wheel. He pulled the door shut.

"You could have let her be," he said again, his voice catching in a sob. He wiped his nose on the back of his hand and rubbed his handkerchief over the windshield to clear it. He stared across the cemetery at the pile of freshly dug earth. "They talk about my girl.

A fallen girl, Nik, for God's sake, that's what they say. 'What can you expect from the likes of that Burke girl?' They don't think I hear it. She doesn't know what the whispers are about, Nik. But she can tell what's in people's eyes."

William leaned back and took a ragged breath, thinking of the last trip they'd made into town. It seemed as if people just stopped talking when they saw Violet. Men visiting at the post office clammed up and stood aside. Tensie Kramer backed away on the boardwalk by Ling's Café, and Cliff Chalmers' wife turned on her heel in the dry goods store.

Picking up the bit of newsprint from the seat, he smoothed it as much as he could and read aloud the rest of the obituary.

> *"Though here pains wrench this mortal frame,*
> *and men are sick and weak and lame,*
> *In that fair land awaiting me,*
> *I shall from ills and pains be free.*
> Vichnaya Pamyat."

William sighed and held the paper out the window, looking again across the cemetery at Nik's waiting pile of earth, the dark centre in an expanse of white snow. William heard the cantor's clear voice in funeral song. The crumpled bit of newsprint left William's fingers and settled on the road. He watched it flutter to the wet gravel like a dry leaf. A breath of wind lifted it, and the paper slid off the road into the ditch and caught in a patch of wolf willow. William wondered if it would be stuck there until spring. He cranked the window shut, grateful it was still intact after the abuse.

He started the engine, turned the truck around back the way he'd come, and drove home.

He parked the truck at the side of the house, blew his nose again and walked heavily up to the porch. A breeze scattered frost from the bushes. William shivered and hunched up his shoulders, then stepped up onto the porch. A faint tinkling sound caught his ear. He stopped and turned toward it. Down at the end, hanging from a nail in the rafter, was Violet's wind chime. It tinkled again and was still.

"How did that get back up there?" he whispered, clearly remembering how he had torn it down and thrown it into the burning barrel behind the house. Had she seen him do it?

William glanced through the kitchen window. Violet was up, and he knew she had the radio on. Her back was to him. She poked at the wood in the firebox and blew on her hands, holding them over the warm steam lifting from the oatmeal she'd started for breakfast. She lifted the wooden spoon and tasted, nodding to herself.

He crept past the window and walked the length of the porch, stepping wide around the warped plank that always squealed at the slightest footfall. William could just reach the chime on tiptoe, and he closed his fist around it quickly to keep it quiet. How had she managed to hang it back up there by herself? Maybe she thought he wouldn't see the chime at the far end; maybe he wouldn't hear them.

He held the spoons hard, and the cold metal bit into his bare skin. There was black soot from the burning barrel in the holes Nik had drilled, but William could see how Violet had tried to clean them. What had she been thinking? It was better, he'd felt sure, if there was nothing left to remind her of what happened that day.

He held the spoons for a time, feeling the cold course up his arm. He looked up, past the frost-covered caragana hedge to where the edge of the coulee fell away well back of the chicken coop. Skunks, coyotes maybe, coming up to hopefully inspect the coop for a door left unlatched, had made a narrow grey path through the snow. William stepped off the porch and followed it, careful not to let the spiky thorns hook his trousers as he picked his way around the dry stickseed and blue burr flagging the trail.

The coulee had slowly been advancing on the house for a few years now, and even though the buildings were in no danger, William was surprised and a little startled to see how much more of the bank had crumbled away. He must remember to tell Violet not to go near the edge; the ground seemed solid on top, but as he leaned forward and looked both ways, he could see deep fissures in the sandy banks where pieces of land jutted out. He recalled the calf that had gone over the edge and had to be shot. It was worse now. One step and a person would go with the slide all the way to the bottom.

He used to tether Hannah with her calves out here to keep the grass short, which had cut down on the mosquitoes each spring. But the topsoil was only a few inches deep. With no trees to hold the soil in place, the coulee was relentlessly becoming a few inches wider each year. By next fall, part of that old barbed wire fence behind the chicken coop could be dangling in mid-air, and it wouldn't be too long before the back end of the coop would do the same. He'd have to see to that come spring.

A sharp stab of cold ran up William's arm, and he looked down at the spoons still gripped tightly in his hand. He looked at them for a long time, and then, with one fluid motion that would have made his childhood cricket mates proud, William hurled them with such force they whistled as they passed his ear. William dropped his arm. Twisting, the wind chime rose, arced, tinkled, glinted in the morning sun, and then disappeared against the black stretch of spruce on the far bank and into the coulee below.

He felt an odd, sudden peace course through him. A deep breath came easier, pushing aside those hateful thoughts about Nik, the violence of a vengeance imagined, the repentance he dreamed of extracting from the man. The final words from Nik's obituary came into his head unbidden. Perhaps he'd had held the thought at the back of his mind all morning. "In that fair land awaiting me," William whispered, "I shall from ills and pains be free."

He stood for a moment near the edge of the coulee, then he turned and made his way back through the drifts toward the light in the kitchen window. He crossed the porch and opened the door to a warm kitchen and the comforting smell of fried eggs and the grey paste that was Violet's porridge. Violet was singing with gusto along with Rudy Vallée on the radio. She looked up and, even as she missed a few words here and there, sometimes adding her own. William sang too.

> *"You must nemember this,*
> *A kiss is still for kiss,*
> *A sigh is just for sigh.*
> *Time goes by, and you can sure rely!*
> *We still say I love you,*
> *And you are welcome, please and thank you, too,*
> *When time goes by."*

Sitting down at the table in her blue robe, she surveyed her handiwork. She'd set the table for two and had cooked the eggs and already arranged them, now cool and rubbery, on the plates. She beamed at him. "You do bacon," she said, pointing at the skillet, which was smoking slightly. "It spits at me all the time." She had made toast, too, and a cold stack was piled on a plate at his place. She folded her hands carefully across her belly and waited.

Rudy continued to croon, and William turned down the radio. He looked out the kitchen window. He wondered when or if she would ever notice the wind chime was gone. He cut four thick slices of bacon and laid them carefully in the hot grease.

"Lot of people gone now. Right, Father?" Violet asked suddenly, her voice small as she slid his blue mug toward his place across the table. She hadn't asked him where he'd been. She usually assumed that whatever he did was the right thing to do. He was Father.

He knew it must seem to her that people were always dying, always going away. "That surely would appear to be the truth, Violet. You're right about that, and we miss them all. But we'll be right, you and me. Right as rain."

"You and me," she nodded. "Two box of fluffy ducks."

For the second time that morning, tears burned in his eyes. He bent over the skillet and poked a fork at the bacon. The two of them were quiet for a while and listened to Rudy and the bacon snapping in the pan.

Violet got up and held out their plates. William shook off the extra grease and laid the hot bacon across the eggs, hoping to warm them up a little. He took his plate and gave her a kiss on the cheek. They sat down, and Violet took up a forkful of egg. He reached out and cupped her cheek with one hand. "We've got some sorting out to do, my girl. But I've cast off a few things today, and I do feel a good sight better now."

Violet put the forkful of eggs into her mouth. William did feel better, but nothing would ever be the same again.

HANK

THE ECKART FARM, OCTOBER 1935

Hank sat at his own kitchen table, the newspaper spread open before him, his coffee cold, forgotten.

"I'm just going out to see if there are any eggs," Emily said, pulling on her barn coat and tying a scarf under her chin. "I can manage. I think I'll toss more straw to the chickens, too." She picked up a pail and stood for a moment with her hand on the doorknob. "You all right?"

"Yes, sure. I'll come help," Hank said, looking up. "Let me get the pitchfork from the barn. I'll be right out."

"All right. No hurry." Emily smiled and closed the door behind her.

Hank read Nik's obituary again and absently ran his thumb along the gouge on the edge of the table. He'd always meant to sand that rough spot, but he never seemed to get around to it. Emily said it snagged her tablecloth. But he liked to remember how, in the fall after pigs were butchered, his mother would clamp the meat grinder to the table and stand there cranking the handle, feeding chunks of meat into the hopper. He remembered feeling that edge when they held him down on the table to pull that hook. Over twenty years ago now.

Hank lifted a finger to his left eye. The scar was hardly visible, just a thin white line, but the hard knot of jagged tissue on the underside often made him tear up. His vision was never right. Sometimes he'd just keep the left eye closed and depend on the other. Emily often said it made him see things more clearly. The blurred view was a constant reminder of the day he took his fishing pole to the slough, nearly blinded himself, and met William Burke and Nik Yuzik together for the first time.

THE SLOUGH NEAR THE ECKART FARM, JULY 1914

The sun was straight overhead when Hank groped and stumbled his way through the poplars back up to the road beyond the slough where he'd been fishing. Gulping back tears and trying to see through his uninjured eye, he made his way to the road. He was desperate to wipe his nose on his sleeve, but he was scared to move the fishing pole. Any jiggling tightened the line and jerked the hook embedded in his left eyelid. The slightest movement sent searing pain into his skull. He could hear Maggie barking now, somewhere beyond the slough. She had followed him and nosed around his legs, whining, getting in his way when he was fishing, so Hank was relieved when the dog caught a scent and bounded away through the brush. The lure of rabbits in the woods and gophers on the other side of the road had taken her off for a good hour.

Eleven-year-old boys do not cry, he thought, but every time he blinked, a piercing pain in his eye made his knees go wobbly, and he had to bite hard on his lip to keep from hollering. If he didn't blink, it hurt, and hot tears coursed down his cheeks. He couldn't tell which was worse, keeping his eye open so he could get through the brush or trying to keep it closed. He settled on keeping his good eye open just enough to get to the road.

Just that morning, his father had told him there were no good fish to speak of in that slough anyway. How would he explain a fishhook in his eye? He didn't know. The last thing he remembered was hauling back on the line with a good yank after it caught on a snag among the cattails. Then the burning in his eye, which felt just like the wasp sting he got last summer.

Not daring to breathe, Hank put two trembling fingers to his left eyelid. He let out a ragged breath at the sight of blood on his fingertips. The end of the hook wasn't poking out, but he could feel the tip just under the skin. "Please don't twist around and go into my eyeball," Hank pleaded. His mother would be so angry if he lost his eye.

It might be okay to cry for a little while, at least until he got to the road. Sobbing, he came out of the poplars and into the ditch above the slough. The dog burst through the willows just up ahead and, tongue lolling, bounded back toward Hank. "Get away, Maggie!" Hank yelled. "Go on now! Go home!"

The dog skidded to a stop and circled around, cowering, then fell in behind Hank. Soon, she began to bark again, and Hank turned as much as he dared, stiffly, keeping the rod tight to his chest. Through a blur of tears, he could make out a horse and wagon headed toward him. The driver might be Nik Yuzik with his white horse, Beely. As it drew closer, Hank was certain it was him, judging by the dairy farmer's wild black hair. But as he tried to get a better look, more tears and probably blood blurred the image, and he couldn't tell anything about the other man with him.

"Hello, *dobray dehn*, kid," Nik called out, pulling the wagon alongside and hauling back on the reins. "Which one you of George's boys?" He leaned forward, draping the reins over his knees.

Hank wiped his nose and drew in a whiff of cow manure and tobacco, a smell that clung to Nik Yuzik even when he cleaned up for town. The movement sent a fresh cascade of tears down Hank's face, and he hiccupped.

Nik grunted. "*Yoy! Isus Khrystos*, what did you do, kid?"

"Got a fishhook in my eye." Hank croaked.

"How in hell you do that?"

"I don't know." Hank sniffed and let out a shudder. Crying in front of grown men. Cripes.

He was doubly embarrassed to see the man with Mr. Yuzik was a stranger. Hotter than the dickens today, yet he was dressed in a Sunday suit, of all things. He wore a strange black hat that, for just a moment, took Hank's mind off the burning eye. The stranger's face was friendly, and his eyes were the light blue of spring ice. He swung down from the wagon, smiled, and dropped down to the ground on one knee. Hank liked him immediately, forgetting his pain and embarrassment for the moment.

"It looks as though you could do with a bit of assistance," the man said. He poked the brim of his hat up and looked closely into Hank's face.

Nik put down the buggy whip, wrapped the reins around the stand, and pulled the brake. With a loud grunt, he jumped down and came around in front, patting Beely's muzzle. He put his hands on his knees and leaned down for a closer look. He bared his teeth and inhaled, making a wet, sucking noise as he examined the large hook caught in Hank's eyelid. "*Khrystos*, you do got fish hook in eye!"

Hank sniffed and licked the dust from his lips. He could taste blood. "I know."

Nik reached into his overalls pocket. He pulled out a pocket knife. Hank let out a squeak and took a step back.

"Not to worry, lad," the other man said. "I think we might just give that line a bit of a snip, so it doesn't pull. You'll be right as rain."

Hank winced. "Ow." *Right as rain? What a funny thing to say.*

"My name is William Burke." He squatted beside Mr. Yuzik, who gathered a loop of fishing line close to the pole. Hank tried to watch, but Mr. Burke kept getting in his way. Then Mr. Yuzik stood up with the pole, the length of fishing line hanging free. He put the knife back into his pocket. Hank could feel the slack in the line now that the pole wasn't attached, and he was grateful the pain was more bearable.

"We don't rip eyeball out. But you still got big goddamn hook in there. *Yoy, yoy.* You sure catch big fish, kid." Nik climbed up onto the wagon, took the reins, then said, "Come on, get up here. We go see your mother."

"My mama will be real angry if I lose my eye."

"We'd best get you home now." Mr. Burke held out a hand.

"I left my father's tackle box down by the slough. I'm going to get a hiding."

"Why don't we stick your fishing pole right here so when you come back later," Mr. Burke said, "you'll know straight away where to cut through the trees to get down to the water."

Hank felt himself lifted into the wagon. Then Mr. Burke leaned the fishing pole against a wolf willow shrub beside the track. He trotted back to the wagon, swung himself up, and sat down beside Hank. Mr. Yuzik yanked on the hand brake and snapped the reins on Beely's rump. "*Pospishaty! Hup, hup!*" Beely snorted, and the wagon jerked forward.

Maggie bounded in front of the horse and cut across the field, yelping as she streaked across the stubble for the farmyard.

By the time the wagon pulled into the lane, Hank's parents, already alerted by the dog, were standing on the porch.

"Whoa, Beely," Mr. Yuzik called to the horse. He pulled back on the reins and yanked the brake on, though Beely was already content to stand still. He climbed down and patted the horse's rump.

Hank's left eye felt on fire, but he wished he could talk to Mr. Burke some more. He wiped his nose again on his sleeve. "I like your hat," he said.

Mr. Burke swept the hat off and perched it on Hank's head, settling it back so it wouldn't slide down over the fishhook. "That's my hard knocker," he said. "It's a lucky hat."

"Lucky for you, kid, I tell you!" Mr. Yuzik laughed. The sound rasped like boots on gravel. He pinched his cigarette between his thumb and forefinger, coughed, and spat on the ground. "*Yoy*," he said. "You got some big luck for fishing!"

Hank frowned and wished he'd stop saying that, but Mr. Yuzik was taken with his joke, and his rough chuckle started up again each time he repeated it. Mr. Yuzik reinserted his cigarette at the corner of his mouth and clamped his lips down on it. He carried Hank to the porch as if the boy was a dog that had tangled with a skunk. He set him on the porch in front of Papa and Mama, who did not look happy at all. By the look on their faces, Hank thought his problem might be a bit worse than he feared. His mother, her mouth set in a hard line, plucked the hat from his head and steered him inside by his shoulder. Mr. Burke and Mr. Yuzik followed them in.

There were urgent introductions and handshakes, and after some discussion about where to put him for the best light, Mr. Yuzik hoisted Hank up on the kitchen table, a swift bear hug that left Hank breathless. Hank's mother took him by the shoulders and pressed him back down until he was lying flat. She lifted his head and put a rolled tea towel under his neck. She didn't even take the tablecloth off, so Hank hoped he wouldn't bleed too much.

"Under the window there, so we can see," Mr. Burke said. "Mr. Eckart, if you'd be so kind to keep the boy's head still and we'll have a bit of a look." He smiled down at Hank. "A bit of a tidy-up, and you'll right as what?"

"Right as rain," Hank whimpered.

Papa cradled Hank's head in his hands. Mama stood by and scowled when Nik pulled a flask from his overalls and waggled it at Papa.

"All right," Papa said. "Just one or two small ones. Medicinal." He sat Hank up a bit. Mr. Yuzik tipped the flask to Hank's lips and poured a few generous sips. The potato wine burned Hank's throat, and the fire seemed to go up his nose. It took his breath away, and he coughed, but it did seem to take his mind off his eye. He leaned toward the flask for another sip.

"All right, all right. Hank, that's enough!" Mama said.

"Good for courage," Mr. Yuzik insisted, talking around the cigarette still planted at the corner of his mouth.

Papa eased Hank back down on the table.

"We need to push it through so we can snip the barb, then back it out the way it went in," Mr. Burke said quietly. Hank didn't like the sound of the plan and moaned. He tried to shake his head. "Mr. Eckart, might you have small wire cutters? Tin snips, perhaps?"

"No, don't do that. It hurts enough already!"

"Erna, the small ones," Papa said. "In the grey metal box."

Mama, her hand pressed hard across her throat, hurried from the kitchen to the front door, and Hank heard her rummaging through Papa's tools. Hank worked out what they were going to do and pleaded harder. "No, Papa! Don't!"

Hank's father grasped Hank's head firmly between his hands. "Steady, boy. You jump around, and you could well lose that eye. Almost there now. I've got you, but you hold still."

Hank, ashamed of the fresh tears that spilled down his cheeks, gulped and tried to nod his head to show his father he understood, but his head was gripped so tightly between his father's big hands that he could only manage a small tilt of his chin. Mama returned and held the tin snips within reach. Mr. Yuzik tipped the flask to splash a little wine over the tool.

Mr. Burke leaned over Hank and grasped the hook, and with one quick motion, thrust it through the eyelid far enough to get at the barb with the cutters. Hank jerked against his father's grip, cried out. "Ow, it hurts! It hurts!" Hank shrieked. "Mama! It hurts!"

Mr. Yuzik leaned across Hank's chest with all his weight and gripped Hank's arms, pressing him down hard on the table. Hank's fingers clutched at his mother's tablecloth, bunching it up in his fists, and he felt the gouge in the table edge where she always clamped down the meat grinder when she made sausage. He ran his thumb back and forth across the rough wood, anything to think of other than the searing pain in his eye.

"I've got to make sure there isn't a jagged end to it," Mr. Burke said softly. "If there's even a tiny shard of metal at the end or a loose bit, it may work its way into the eye when it comes back out."

Mama moaned and handed Mr. Burke a clean cotton cloth. Hank was surprised by the strength of her grip on his arm. Mr. Burke carefully laid the snips against Hank's eyelid. Hank could feel the cold metal, a blade on each side of the hook.

"Keep your eye closed," Mr. Burke said firmly. "You mustn't move. I don't want to cut you along with it."

Hank bit down on his lip and felt the snips take hold.

"Be still. You don't think I'd hurt my best mate, having just met him?"

Hank could feel Mr. Burke's breath on his cheek when he leaned forward to examine the tip. Hank opened his good eye wide. Mr. Burke suddenly winked, grasped the end of the hook, and then with a swift motion, slid it out the way it went in. The eyelid burned every bit as much as Mr. Yuzik's potato wine had burned his throat.

"Is it out?" Hank yelled, keeping the ravaged eye shut. "Is it okay? Is the hook out? Is it?" He lifted his head and saw Mr. Burke holding the hook between his thumb and forefinger, the length of line dangling down his arm.

"We're done!" he announced.

"Thank the Lord." Mama's shoulders relaxed, and she opened a drawer, pulling out another clean cloth. She carried a basin and the teakettle to the table. The men lifted Hank and sat him on a chair, and she poured the hot water over the cloth. She held his chin firmly and ran the cloth over his face, carefully dabbing around the left eye. She dropped it back into the basin, and he could see the water swirl red.

"*Shlyak tehbeh trahffet*! Such a big hook. You think you catch a whale?" Mr. Yuzik said, removing his cigarette and pinching it between his thumb and forefinger. He reached for his flask with his other hand. Mama scowled, and he seemed to think better of it. "Maybe later," he mumbled.

"Do you want to keep it?" Mr. Burke asked.

"Yep, I want to show the kids at school." Hank took the hook carefully and examined it with his good eye. He wiped his nose on his sleeve. He flinched as his mother folded a clean cloth and dabbed a little bit of Mr. Yuzik's wine on the wounded eyelid.

She wet the cloth again with a dipper of cool water from the barrel. Wringing it out in the basin, she folded the rag again and handed it to him. "I wish I had some Watkins tincture, but I'm out. That wine will just have to disinfect that eyelid for now. Hank, I want you to go lie down and keep this on your forehead," she said, turning him around by his shoulders. She pulled another rag from the drawer. "And put this on your pillow so you won't ruin my feather ticking if you bleed. You have a lie-down for a few minutes, and then I think your father needs to get you into town to see the doctor. If we don't have you looked at, I don't know what might happen to that eye."

"*Neh zhooreshya, Meesus. Nai boodeh.* Okay, okay. It's good now. We get it out okay," Mr. Yuzik said, reinserting his cigarette stub, shrugging. Hank saw Papa shrug in agreement until he saw the set of Mama's jaw.

"Not another word," she said. "George, you hook up that horse. I don't want to take any chances with the boy's eye. I want the doctor to have a look. Hank, go on now. I'll let you know when your father's ready to go."

Hank started toward the door off the kitchen, the hook held out in front like a prize. He stopped and turned around. "The tackle box. It's by a big rock and a wolf willow."

Mr. Burke put up his hand. "Not to worry. If Mr. Yuzik would be so kind, we'll pop back to where we left the pole, and we'll find it." He picked up his black bowler from the table. "You see, Hank. I told you this is a lucky hat. I trust our next encounter will not be quite this exciting."

Hank pressed the cloth to his head. "Thanks, Mr. Burke. It was real nice to meet you. I think I'm going to have a whopper of a headache now."

Now Hank folded the paper and held it in his hands for a few moments while he looked out the kitchen window. Emily had been to the shed for the pitchfork, and she'd already disappeared into the chicken coop.

The doctor had told them there would be scarring and that Hank's sight would never be good in that eye again. The hook had scratched the cornea. A traumatic cataract might develop, or the eye would wither. Hank was always plagued by the wind and cold, and the bothersome dry eye was a reminder of his ill-advised fishing trip to the slough. But it also marked the day he met Mr. Burke. And now he realized there was more to Nik than his abrupt manner and harsh humour.

Hank sighed. He reached for his cup, downed the cold coffee, and stood, scraping the chair back. For years, his mother called William and Nik the angels who saved her boy's eyesight. He was lucky, just as his mother so often said. Over the years, he'd told William and Nik so himself, and Nik Yuzik never failed to clap Hank on the back and call him a big ugly fish.

As for Nik being an angel, Hank figured no one was ever purely good. Or purely evil.

VIOLET

ON THE ROAD TO TOWN, OCTOBER 1935

"The outside feels big today." Violet stepped off the porch, holding Father's hand, and then hugged herself as they made their way out to the truck. She watched her feet as though they belonged to someone else, bound up tight in her town shoes. She had her good town clothes on, too, and carried her mother's old pocketbook in one hand. She bunched the hem of her dress up in her fist, kicking stones.

Father looked up at the sky. "It does feel big, like something is looming up there behind the big white clouds. With the warm weather last week, we need snow, or we'll have a brown Christmas this year."

To Violet, the air felt the way it did just before a thunderstorm came to a head and finally let go of all the rain it had worked up. Last week, she'd heard Hank say that if chinook winds from Alberta had come earlier, it would have been easier to bury Mr. Yuzik. She wasn't sure what that meant.

Yet, it was a good day to go to town. Violet's grocery list was tucked in her purse. She liked making lists. She had laboured over this one after breakfast and presented it to Father when he shaved. Her spidery printing proudly declared they were in need of *tea, flower, fanila, lyle soap, and pressant for Violet.* He kissed her cheek and said she was brilliant.

"Don't let me forget now, Violet," Father said as he climbed in behind the wheel. "I've got to pick up the mastitis salve for that one cow. I've had to milk her out separately for the past few days."

"Harriet," Violet said, settling herself on her seat. "Harriet is sick."

"Right, it's medicine for Harriet. And I need to stop at the hardware store and see if they've got a hinge for the barn door."

It had been a while since they'd been into town. Violet had only been once or twice since the hospital. Father had gone in for a few groceries at the Trading Company, but he said he thought people seemed uncomfortable and "a bit formal," so he told her they would just stay home on the farm for a bit until people forgot about things.

For years, trips to town meant perching on the vinyl stools to shoot the breeze at Ling's Café next to Bjorndahl's on Main. Sometimes, Father had taken John and Violet with him to sit in a booth and eat chocolate ice cream, stirred hard with a spoon so they could pretend it was soup. Violet grinned, thinking about it now. Maybe Father would buy some ice cream today.

While he drove, Father talked a lot about the men on coffee row, gossiping worse than women, smoking, playing the perpetual checkers game, drinking the strong sludge Sam Ling kept pouring from the coffee pot. "Remember Stewart Macleod? He was always perched on the same stool at the end of the lunch counter. Sam put the spittoon in the corner so Stew wouldn't be spitting across the flow of traffic, remember?"

Violet nodded.

"Stew usually had an update on his cousin Rollie's chain of hardware stores spreading across Canada and bragged that Rollie got his start right in Watrous. Stew always seemed to be suggesting he had something to do with it. Everybody knew that Stewart was only twelve when Rollie moved to Winnipeg, but nobody mentioned it." Father wrapped his arms around the steering wheel. "Your mother would be off doing the shopping. She didn't like Stewart's spittoon."

Father was talking a lot, Violet thought. Mama used to tell him that he talked too much when he had something on his mind, and he didn't want to come right out and say it. It was irritating, Mama said. Violet plucked at her dress over her lap and thought she understood how Mama must have felt.

Father turned the truck toward town at the end of the lane. They drove quietly for a while until he suddenly reached over and took her hand. She was alarmed that the big smile on his face, there just a moment ago, was gone. "Violet, dear heart. You can't keep the baby."

Why would he say such a thing? Violet's eyebrows furrowed, and she squeezed her lips tight.

"Sweetheart, I'm sorry." Father put his hand on her forehead and tried to smooth out the wrinkles that happened when she got angry.

"Mine." She tightened her grip on Louise's old black purse and tilted her head away from his hand. "A boy. Emily said."

"I know," Father said. "It'll be a fine baby. But we can't keep him. A baby is not like finding a stray dog, dear heart. Taking care of a runt pig you push around in your doll carriage is one thing. A baby needs a mother and a father, young people who are married and can look after a child properly." He looked sideways at Violet, and she could tell he wanted her to answer him. She clutched Mama's purse and sat straight. He plunged ahead, gripping the wheel and starting to sound cross. "It's a very big job, and we have all our other chores to do."

Violet's frown deepened, and she looked at Father out of the corner of her eye as they drove. Now and then, a rock flipped up and pinged against the undercarriage. She felt a deep anger burning in her stomach, and she didn't like it at all. She had to explain to Father so he would understand.

"You do chores," she insisted after a while. "I can take care for him."

"No, Violet. We simply can't," he snapped, and she flinched. She folded her arms across her chest.

"Yes." She thrust her chin at the windshield. "My baby. *My* baby," she whispered, more to herself than to him.

Father glanced over, and she turned away, working the words over again, forming them silently. "Violet, I need you to understand. I know this is difficult. It's taken care of already. There's a couple who can't have their own children. The husband is Melsie Waldner's cousin. Remember Melsie? The nice church secretary?"

Violet tried to make his voice stop. She put her hands over her ears, but he kept on talking.

"You will mind me now, Violet. They're good, decent people aching for children. So all this is a blessing, really, and the adoption papers are all ready to sign."

Violet pressed her hands harder against her ears. "Mine," she insisted and looked out the window and across the field.

WILLIAM

William steered the truck around potholes and thought it best to let Violet be for a while. Her anger seemed to radiate like heat from the woodstove. She sat bunched up close to the door. Just as well. He didn't trust his voice, and he still hadn't worked out how he was going to make her understand. This was not going well.

The church was handling everything, all very quietly. The birth certificate would be blank where the father's name was supposed to be, even though it was common knowledge now whose name should be filled in.

One or two members of the Ladies' Auxiliary at the church had acted so superior when the arrangements were being made. Emily had stayed with Violet for the afternoon when he went to town to deal with the paperwork. It seemed to William that one of them, Bea Ranstrom, Betty's sister, looked like there was a faint stink just under her nose the entire time they were filling out the forms. William had been about ready to say to Bea that it was also common knowledge that her husband Bud spent years pickling his own liver, only to fall over dead one Thursday afternoon at the beer parlour in the company of a woman who sure as hell wasn't Bea. But what was the point?

People seemed to be on a slow boil just under the surface, judging by the looks he got on the street in town. Some of the people who didn't meet his eyes or know what to say were the same ones who used to pat Violet's head in church or stop on the street to remark about how big she was getting. Joe Chumak used to dig deep in his pants pocket for old Scotch mints, one for John and one for Violet. William remembered how Louise tried to hold her breath when Joe was near. The ammonia smell of his pigs, she said, clung to him like a shroud. But he'd hold his palm wide to pick the mints out of an assortment of coins, wheat kernels, toothpicks, buttons, bits of tobacco, and lint. Louise always waited until Joe had moved on down the sidewalk before taking them away from the children and throwing them into the street. That always set Violet to howling.

But now, Joe Chumak only glared when they saw him. William couldn't be sure, but standing behind Joe at the post office one day, he thought the man mumbled something about putting the likes of Violet away. But Joe's false teeth didn't fit properly, always sliding in and out, so he was hard to understand. If he did say it, William supposed, it was probably because Joe's wife, Hilda, and Hanusia were sisters, and family loyalty ran deep and mostly silent.

People like kittens. They don't like cats. Louise's voice came in a whisper, her lips against his ear. He shifted on the seat and gripped the wheel. It had been all right when Violet was little, but as she got older, some people grew uncomfortable. William hadn't been back to coffee row since word got around. Besides Joe, he'd seen a couple of the men at the post office and the seed mill. Their greetings were gruff, and there was always something suddenly more interesting to look at on the toes of their boots.

William remembered some people had been like this when John was killed and later when Louise left. Some people just didn't know what to say. The difference now, though, was the idea that this was Violet's fault somehow, as if she asked for Nik to do what he did, or she trapped him, if you could imagine. Led him on. *Those kind of people, you know how they are. That's why they put them away and lock them up.*

William hunched over the wheel and rolled his head to one shoulder, then the other. Most people, aside from Joe, didn't say anything to his face out of respect, but the gossip was chewing its way around town. William could pretty well see inside people's heads when they turned to look at Violet. As bad as it was for him and Violet, William's stomach turned at the thought of what these weeks must be like for Hanusia and the boys. He didn't care for her with her strange ideas, never had, but still, she must be suffering.

William fell short of thinking about Nik. It was best if he didn't think about Nik at all.

"*My* baby." Violet interrupted his thoughts. She had both hands on her stomach and patted the swell gently. "You *not* give him away."

"Violet, my girl, I'm sorry," William said sharply. "It's got to be."

"No. Mine!" Violet cried.

Her stubbornness, and maybe the unfairness of the whole situation, seemed to be prodding his heart into a gallop; it knocked against his ribs.

"Violet," he barked, more loudly than he intended. "You mind me now."

He breathed deeply and tried to calm down. He had expected this would be a tough sell, and a tiny part of him was grateful to see Violet had a mind of her own. He tried to think of a time when she had stood up to him before. The doctor told William Violet probably didn't understand anything that Emily said about having a baby. William knew different, though. And he knew enough to see that Violet was quickly becoming a mother. She noticed babies in town, and at church on the rare occasions they still attended. She fussed over where the baby would sleep when he was born. She told him she'd thought of a good name, but it was going to be a surprise. He wasn't sure if there was anything to be done about that, anything that could dissuade her from all the nesting she seemed to be doing. But taking the baby away when it was born in February wasn't something he looked forward to in the least. He wasn't at all sure what it would do to Violet. His heart ached, but he had to make her understand. The sooner she accepted the fact, the sooner she'd get over the loss.

Now he tried to keep an eye on the road, and, with his left hand on the wheel, he reached for her with his right hand. His fingers closed around her wrist. She simply had to understand this, and he would make her hear him.

Violet tried to pull free and William tightened his grip, his heart pounding. He felt her anger rise up to match his own. His face grew hot, and he pulled at her wrist harder when she resisted, much harder than he intended. "Bloody hell, Violet! I'm your father, and you will do as I say!" Blood pounded in his ears. "You must stop thinking we can keep this baby. We will not. That's all there is to it!"

"NO NO NO!" she bellowed and tore away from his grip. Surprised at the ferociousness of her objection, he let her go. Tears spilled down her face, and she pulled away from him, pressing herself against the door.

William's mouth was dry, and he was shaking as he eased the truck to a stop just off the gravel. He waited for a moment for his heart to stop racing, and he tried to gather his thoughts together, then turned to her. But Violet held her fists clenched in her lap and stared ahead. When he reached to pull her to face him, Violet cried out, and his stomach clenched, remembering how Louise had been rough with the girl for so many infractions, real and imagined. He let go. Violet turned away and clawed at the handle, shouldered open the door, and stumbled out, nearly falling into the ditch.

Some scraggly alfalfa stalks with faded purple blossoms that clung to the end of the season had emerged since last week's thaw. A few skiffs of dirty snow hid in shadows under clumps of grass and willow dotting the ditch, and the soil had turned to mud.

Violet struggled across to the rise, her shoes sliding into the soggy earth. When one foot sank into the muck, Violet grunted and tried to pull one foot free, then the other. Finally, she leaned over, pulled the laces, and stepped out of the shoes, leaving them behind like stubs of black fence posts. Panting heavily, she climbed up the other side of the ditch barefoot. She hadn't bothered with stockings. On the edge of the field, she yelled across the ditch. "My baby! Everybody all gone. John and Mama. My baby. Stay here. I keep him!"

William slid across and out her side of the truck and stepped into the alfalfa.

She stared at William, her hands on her hips, her face twisted, and her mouth pulled down at the corners. She looked so angry, so sad, the mixture of both so heartbreaking, and William held out his arms to her. She glared, her chin thrust forward and her chest heaving.

Suddenly. she sat down in the alfalfa, her good town clothes forgotten, and put her face in her hands. "*My* baby," she pleaded, her voice shrill. "You be father!" she sobbed. "I be mama and you be father."

It would be impossible. A baby and Violet both.

He could think of nothing to say that would make anything better. He closed his eyes for a moment, hating himself for laying a hand on her in anger. Hurting her. He decided, finally, the only thing to do was retrieve her shoes. He pried them out of the mud, put them in the truck box, and wondered if they'd ever come clean.

He climbed back in the truck and sat behind the wheel. He knew if he waited long enough, she would come back. She would finally do as she was told.

Eventually, Violet stood, crossed the ditch, and pulled herself up into the cab. She dragged the door shut and leaned back against the seat, wiped her nose on the back of her hand, and hiccupped. William studied her for a moment and took a deep breath. He gripped the wheel to keep his hands steady.

"I am so sorry," William said. "For everything." He swung the truck around and, after a few minutes, turned back into their lane. Violet sniffled and coughed.

"Use a hankie, sweetheart," William said. He no longer had the energy to face anyone else today. "We'll go to town another time. I think we'll both feel better after a nice cuppa, don't you think?"

"I need to wash my feet," she said in a small voice.

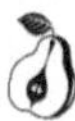

THAT NIGHT, WILLIAM REMEMBERED THE SALVE FOR the cow. Maybe Hank was going to town and could stop at the vet's for him. William picked up the phone just in time to get an earful from Hilda Chumak, who was describing her version of events to Marj Bjorndahl. Hilda was talking so intently that she didn't even hear the click when William lifted the receiver.

"Well, you know it's a known fact that people like that Burke girl can't control themselves in that department," Hilda was saying. "They flirt and throw themselves at men. It's a fact. That's why they send them to the asylums in Battleford and Weyburn. Why they didn't send that girl there, I don't know. I'm sure Nik didn't know what hit him. If my Joe ever—"

William carefully replaced the receiver and went out to sit on the porch. He felt so heavy; his elbows and knees seemed thick and solid, unable to bend or bear his weight if he stood. He thought of his pipe and tobacco on the kitchen table, but he felt welded to the chair, too heavy to go back inside to get it. The image of Violet's muddy town shoes in the ditch came into his mind, and he felt as hollow and stuck as they had been.

VIOLET

WATROUS UNION HOSPITAL, FEBRUARY
1936

Violet felt the spreading warmth and gently pushed the sleeping cat off her lap.

This morning's bellyache was better after the cold biscuit she had eaten for lunch. The tea helped, too. At first, she wondered if the milk was off. When milk goes off, Father always said, a person can tell by sniffing it. She had, and it seemed fresh, the same way milk always smelled.

The cat protested. It helped to have her feet up on the stool near the warm stove, and Tom took advantage of a place to nap. He wasn't supposed to be in the house. Cats belong outside, Father always said. But Violet had felt sorry for Tom ever since the coyote almost ate him. The old cat had been dozing with half-closed eyes while Violet darned the heel of one of William's wool socks. Now, relegated to the cold floor, the cat flicked his tail and squinted at her with a sullen look, the remnants of his mangled ear hanging down over one eye.

"You are too hot," Violet scolded, squirming in the rocker. She set aside her darning and lifted her dress to cool herself, then stared at her lap. Her dress was dark and wet. "Tom. Bad cat," she cried. "You pee on me." She stamped her foot, and the cat slunk away to glare at her from under the cook stove. She struggled to her feet, pushing herself up from the rocker, pulling her dress straight around her swollen belly.

On the kitchen floor, water puddled around her feet, soaking her socks. *An accident,* she thought wildly. No, no. Emily had said. Emily told her. Emily said there was going to be some water. Water was all right. Not a mess. Not a bad mess. A good mess. Emily said to tell Father right away. But he had gone down into the coulee to mend the gate so the Yuzik bull couldn't get through.

Violet's mind juddered over what to do, the warm wet wicking up her socks. *So much water.* She needed to get dry socks and her town shoes. She needed her father. Emily had shown her how to call in case anything happened. Violet steadied herself with a hand on the kitchen table, stepped over the water on the floor, and reached for the telephone. She listened to see if it was busy with any neighbours and then put her finger in each of the holes she had memorized for the Eckart number, one after another.

"Do as you're told now, Violet," Emily said firmly, her lips inches from Violet's ear. "It's almost over but not just yet. One or two more big pushes, and then you're done. Remember, we said this was like climbing up a big hill. We'll do it together."

Violet finally understood why the cows bellowed when they were dropping calves in the spring. *Think about good things,* she thought, *and do what Emily says.* She heard the doctor talking, but he sounded as if he was standing on his head in a rain barrel. Sweat was running into her eyes, and she was glad when the nurse —or was it Emily?—wiped her forehead with a cool cloth.

"Too much blood. The heart has to work too hard—" The doctor's voice wobbled as if from inside the barrel.

Emily's voice cut through the rainwater. "Dr. Speight, she

understands more than you think, so I'd ask you to kindly not talk like that right now. She hears everything you say."

Was she sleeping? It was like coming to the surface of the slough. She'd fallen off the raft once and gone under, John bent over, arms waving, rippling at the surface, her hands grasping slimy weeds, her mouth filling with stinking green water. Her face pushed through the surface, her mouth wide, gagging.

Then Emily's voice, bright and cheerful in her ear: "Violet, honey. Do as I say, and we'll get this baby born. One more little push right now."

And suddenly, it was over. Emily, as usual, was right about these things. "You're all done, Violet!" Emily was laughing and crying at the same time. She wiped Violet's nose, and the nurse ran a cool cloth over Violet's face.

"Come on, lift up your head a little now, and you can see!" Emily said. "See what you did."

Violet, gasping, blinking tears, gripped Emily's hand and struggled to sit up to see the baby while the nurse roughly wrapped him. A tiny red hand clutched the air, and a few tentative whimpers grew to lusty wails.

"It's a baby!" Violet cried. "Emily, he's waving to me! He is crying. He's not happy?"

"That's a good sound, Violet. It's very good for babies," the nurse said. "It helps him get some air into his little lungs."

Emily tried to ease Violet's grip, but Violet held firm. With her free hand, Emily arranged the pillows. Violet strained to see her baby, but the doctor took the bundled infant and hurried out the door.

"See my baby," Violet cried. "He is waving! He sees me!"

"All right now, Violet, you just calm down. Lean back, there's a good girl," the nurse said, turning her attention to the cleanup at hand. "Just lie back and be still. We're not altogether done yet. Let's get your breathing steady. You'll soon be all comfy and cozy. The doctor is going to make sure the baby is all cleaned up now." The nurse worked swiftly. "And we're not quite finished yet."

"My baby waved at me," Violet said again, dreamily, her eyelids suddenly too heavy to keep open. She turned her wet face to Emily, who pushed back the damp hair from her forehead.

"I know, Violet. Hush now," Emily said.

"Did you see my baby, Emily?"

"Yes, I sure did, Violet. You did a good job, didn't you?" Emily said. "Just settle down now. You worked really hard, and now you can relax." Emily smiled, wiping the back of her hand across her own damp forehead. "That old heart of yours needs to have a rest." Emily pulled the chair closer to the side of the bed. She sat down heavily. "I think we could all use a little rest after that!"

The nurse laughed, and it sounded like wind chimes, gentle and tinkling. Violet struggled to open her eyes. The nurse brought a basin of water and a cloth.

"He loves me, my baby." Violet sighed.

The nurse lifted Violet's chin and ran the cloth around her neck and chest.

"What's your name again?" she asked the nurse suddenly, fighting the drowsiness.

"Doris," the nurse said, rinsing out the cloth. She lifted Violet's hair at the back of her neck and then washed her arms. The sponge bath felt so good, but Violet continued to struggle against sleep. She opened her eyes wide. "Doris?"

"Yes, Violet."

"Was he a baby boy or a baby girl?"

"He's a beautiful little boy. Shh, now, Violet. I want you to calm yourself down and try to just breathe easy for a little while."

"He really is beautiful, Violet," Emily said. "He has a good strong cry, and he looks just fine."

"He is," Doris said. "He's just fine. No problems."

"A boy. A baby boy," Violet said, lying back against the pillows.

Doris worked a lever to raise the foot of the bed. "It will help slow the bleeding to get her feet up," she said.

Violet still held Emily's hand, but her grip was weaker now. "I knew it was a boy. His name is John," she decided firmly. "He can be John. My brother's name is John, too. Do you think my brother would like that? I do!"

"What about the middle name, Violet?" Doris asked. Violet felt her firm hand on her stomach. "I need to push a little here, Violet, so the delivery of the afterbirth is easier to bear. It'll be over in a moment. You're doing so well."

"Ow, ow." Violet winced. "My tummy ache hurts." She turned to Emily. She thought for a moment and bit her lower lip. She fingered the cuff of the gown. Finally, it felt better, and she reached for the nurse's arm even as Doris moved between her legs, washing and drying.

"Guess what!" she said. "I already think of it. He will be John and William. John is my brother, and William is my father."

She looked at the nurse. "Father, he is from New Zealand." She pronounced the words carefully. "He was a baby, he was born there. Far away. And there is lots of sheep. And a little bird that can't fly."

"Well, then, John William is a wonderful name, Violet," Doris said. "Your brother and your father will be very proud. All right now, Violet, let's get you all tidied up."

Emily gently pried Violet's hand from her own. Before Violet knew it, Doris and Emily had rolled her on her side, removed the soiled bedclothes, and slipped a blanket and a dry sheet on the bed. Another blanket went on top, and Doris wrapped up the soiled linens.

Emily helped Violet into a clean nightgown. It felt warm and dry, and Violet thought she might like a good sleep. Doris tucked a flannel around a hot water bottle, tested the plug, and slipped it under the sheets next to Violet. "You hang on to that now, dear," Doris said. "You'll most likely get a bit chilly, so you keep this close. See here, now there's a little basin right here in case you feel a little sick."

"My brother is in Heaven," Violet explained while the nurse

moved efficiently through the last of the cleanup. "I miss him. He fell off his birthday horse. I don't like that horse. Father shot it lots, so we don't look at it no more."

"John would have been so proud of the good job you did today, Violet," Emily said. "And now you're all ready for a good nap. You just try to sleep a little now. You've done a big job, and your heart must be tired. We'll just rest now and be quiet for a while. I'll sit with you right here. That'd be all right, wouldn't it, Doris?"

The nurse stood at the door with a tightly wrapped ball of linen in her arms. "That would be just fine," Doris said. "After a little sleep, you'll have a cup of broth, Violet. Maybe some nice buttered toast and a glass of milk. Would you like that?"

Violet smiled, her eyelids drooping even as Doris spoke. The nurse stood for a moment, and Violet tried to keep her in sight, even as she drifted into sleep. She could still hear the nurse and Emily talking, or was she dreaming it?

"In God's name," the nurse said to Emily. "What could that man have been thinking? If he wasn't already dead, I would put the rope around his neck myself."

Violet was too tired to stir or even comprehend, but it was a comfort to hear their voices, knowing they were close.

"Mr. Burke has gone on home to do the chores. Poor man. Breaks my heart. He said he didn't want to disturb Violet, but he'll be back in right after chores. And you look like you could use a cup of tea."

Violet mumbled. A cup of tea sounded nice. The three ladies could have a cup of tea.

"I could use a lie down if you've got a bench someplace. Hank's holding down the fort at home," she heard Emily say. "She had to do all the work, but I'm tuckered out. I guess I know what I'm in for." She patted her own belly.

Violet tried to open her eyes wider, but they felt so heavy.

She closed them, content to listen to their murmuring voices. "Really?" Doris put a hand on Emily's shoulder. "That's wonderful. Your first? Look, there's a cot in the laundry. Come on, I'll show you. You can stretch out there for a bit. I'll come and get you if she wakes up, dear soul."

"She'll be all right, with her heart and everything, won't she?" Emily asked.

"The doctor will give her a good once over to be sure, but she seems to have come through all this just fine. It's amazing, really. She lost some blood, and she may bleed for a while yet, but the pregnancy may have actually helped build up her reserves. In an odd sort of way, she had more to lose."

"You can say that again," Emily said.

"I'll go back after a few minutes and check on her. Think I'll stay pretty close by because of the ether. The other nurse will come by in the morning, and we'll keep Violet in for several days. Don't worry, though. She'll be fine. She's a bit like one of those bumblebees. You know, nobody's told them they can't fly, so they go ahead and do it anyway."

Violet fought to open her eyes as Emily tiptoed to the bed and leaned down. Violet felt her cool hand on her forehead.

"Fluffy ducks," Violet murmured. "I'm a box of fluffy ducks."

"Violet. Wake up now. We must be quiet."

It was dark. Violet woke with a start, confused about the strange bed, blinking and squinting as she tried to make out the figure beside her. Doris's hand was firm on her shoulder. Violet rubbed her eyes, then looked to the window near her bed and watched Doris pull back the curtain. The dark-purple sky to the east was tinged with the palest pink of early sunrise. The moon was full and cast a pale grey light across the room. Doris was holding something that was making soft gurgling sounds.

"For just a minute before I go home," Doris whispered. "I was charting his blood pressure and the rest, and I thought, well, I could get in big trouble, Violet, but it's just not right." Her words tumbled out, and Violet frowned, trying to wake up and understand. She wondered if it was morning. "He's your baby, and you should at least see him just this once. He's your boy, Violet." Doris came closer, and with her free hand, she quickly wiped her eyes. "It's not right a woman can't see her own child. Here now, sit up and hold out your arms and be careful."

"They won't let me." Violet winced at the wash of pain in her belly. The nurse laid the baby in the crook of her arm to cradle his head. "They told me I can't have him," Violet said. "Father said some nice people, they take him and be his mama and father."

"I know, I know. Shush, not so loud," whispered Doris. "That's the way it's going to be, but you brought him into this world, and you should at least have a minute to say hello." Doris pulled a handkerchief from her uniform pocket and wiped her eyes. She stepped quietly over to the basin. "We have to be careful, so he doesn't get sick," she said, busying herself with soap and water.

"I want Emily. Where's Emily?"

"She's asleep. Having a little rest just down the hall."

"Did Emily see him? Did you show her John?"

"Yes, she saw."

Violet kissed the soft down of her son's unruly black hair, almost blue in the moonlight from the window. She inhaled the newness and cleanness of him and felt him move against her. She looked into the little red face. "Doris, he's a wrinkly potato!" Violet whispered. Her fingertips trailed lightly over the baby's head, his whorls of hair, and they explored his face. "My baby," she murmured. "Pretty baby." She carefully touched his tiny fingers, afraid to break him, afraid to make him cry. "Can I look, Doris?" she whispered.

Doris came back to the bedside and unwrapped the infant so that he lay across Violet in his diaper. "Just for a moment, Violet. We mustn't let him get cold."

The baby was small and red, and the diaper looked like it was two sizes too big. "You are a funny boy," she whispered, her fingers moving over him again. Gently placing her palm flat on the baby's back, she smiled. "You are box of fluffy ducks."

"Just let him lie there for a minute, Violet," said Doris. "I just want to have a quick look at you." Doris took a moment to check Violet's wraps. The bleeding had stopped. "Here, let's turn him over so you can see his face." Doris wrapped the baby and settled him in the crook of Violet's arm again.

Violet cooed and kissed and smelled her son.

Doris checked her watch. "I have to take him now, Violet," Doris whispered, glancing at the door. "The doctor and the other nurse will be in soon. It's nearly morning, and someone could come. I told you I could just only bring him for a little bit."

Violet's laid her hand on the baby's head. "He's warm."

"They're a real nice family, Violet, the ones adopting him," Doris said. "They can't have kids of their own. You're giving them a new life, Violet. You made him, and that's a wonderful thing to give somebody who can't do it themselves."

"I give them a present. Father said I have to mind him. That's the end of it, he says."

"Yes, Violet," Doris said. "That's just it. The best present they could get."

As Doris began to tuck the baby's flannel into place and leaned down to take him, a thought occurred to Violet. Something she had to know first, and her hold on the baby tightened. "Do they got chooks?" asked Violet. "Chickens," she corrected herself. Chook was one of Father's words.

"What? Chickens?" whispered Doris, confused. "Who? Oh, I don't think so, Violet. They live in the city. Why?"

"They got to show him how to get the eggs right, Doris, if they got chickens," Violet insisted, her brow furrowing with determination. "Mama says do it careful. And show him to throw chop in a circle. Not dump it, 'cause mean chickens hurt little ones." Violet paused, trying to think of any other things that she had so little time to give her son, trying to stretch the time a little longer. Doris waited nervously and started to pull slightly on the bundle again. Violet blinked, the idea breaking free from inside her head. "Oh, Doris. A grass whistle. That's a good thing to know how to make, and then he never get lost."

"I'll tell them, Violet. You gave this boy a good start, Violet. A real good start. That's something to be proud of," Doris whispered, easing the baby away.

"He is a good boy. John William." Violet touched the baby's downy hair again with her fingertips and kissed his forehead. "I wish I could show him, Doris. I wish I could show him the grass whistle. I know how. Hank showed us, John and me."

The nurse carefully took the baby from her arms. Violet wiped her eyes with the sheet. She touched her tender breasts, but she knew there would be a pain far behind that, far inside, that wouldn't go away for a long time.

"Tell him is lots of practice," Violet said firmly, trying not to cry. "But he just try to learn."

"All right, Violet. Hush now and have a sleep."

"It hurts. Doris. It hurts."

"I know, but we all forget the pain in no time. You'll feel a little sick from the ether for a while. But it'll pass. You'll forget. I promise." With the baby bundled in the crook of her arm, Doris reached for the hot water bottle, turned it over, and pressed it against Violet's stomach. "You hold on to this," Doris said, and she brushed her hand over Violet's forehead. "You'll soon forget how much it hurts. You'll see. Just have a good sleep now."

"But it hurts my heart," Violet protested, touching her chest, wanting to explain that it wasn't just a hurt where the baby came out. It was worse than that.

"I've got to take him now."

"Bye, baby John William."

Doris and the baby were gone. Somehow Violet didn't think what Doris said could be right. Forget? She'd never forget John, her little baby boy, his tiny red hand waving at her. The noises he made. His soft hair. She wanted to remember all that. She'd never forget because this ache, Violet was certain, could never go away.

Her chin quivered, and she put her hands to her flushed face. The baby's new smell clung to her hands, and her skin was still warm where he had been across her chest, and she breathed him in. She tried to find a comfortable position on the hard bed. Father told her once that he had a broken heart when John died. Now she knew what he meant. The ache spread through her like a crack in an eggshell, spidering outward from her chest until every part of her was just fragile, broken pieces.

Lying on her side, she drew her knees slowly up toward her chest and clutched the hot water bottle. Violet curled her body over the emptiness in her belly where the baby had been.

AT FIRST, SHE DIDN'T KNOW IF IT WAS A DREAM OR A remember. Nurse Doris would have said it was the ether. Sometimes it was hard to tell, Father always said, if something is a story you make up in your head or if it is real life. Where does one end and the other begin? Maybe this was a bit of both. Even though she was too tired to open her eyes, it made her happy when it came into her head, whatever it was.

Violet thought she heard Emily, her voice soothing and faraway, and felt her father's touch on her cheek. She sank further into the healing escape of the remember dream, and she watched herself running barefoot down by the slough with her brother. Long before anyone went away.

It was a hot summer day, and grasshoppers clicked and scattered away through the dry grass. John wanted her help to work on the raft, and it was cool down by the water, so she followed him to the edge and waited for him to tell her what to do. They had found the old chicken coop door William had tossed on the junk pile over the edge of the coulee behind the barn. John and Violet spent most of an afternoon struggling to get it back up the bank, then hauling it through the pig pasture to the slough.

"Let's go ask Father about making the raft so it floats right," John said. "He'll know. He knows things about boats."

Violet nodded, not really understanding but wanting him to think she did.

Father was sawing boards for a new step off the front porch. He whistled while he worked, shirt open but dark and wet across his back, the sweat beaded on his forehead. Beside him was a pile of weathered grey wood, dry-rotted and crumbled, and a coffee can into which he tossed another rusty bent nail.

"Boat!" Violet announced when John told him they were building a raft.

"You children carried that door up out of the coulee?" he asked, grinning and wiping his face with his blue handkerchief.

"I was careful with Violet," John insisted. "I done the heavy work, and she walked ahead and told me where to put my feet when I couldn't see."

"Well, I'll be. It's a sorry excuse for a seafaring vessel, but I don't see why it shouldn't float well enough. There are a couple of fence poles behind the barn for the bottom. You'd have to saw the ends off to fit, but she'll be right. There's binder twine up in the hayloft, too."

John grabbed Violet's hand and started for the barn. "We can make a sail so the wind will push us around, Violet. And maybe we can get some biscuits and have a picnic lunch out in the middle of the slough."

"Hang on," Father called, holding out the coffee can of old nails. "Violet, you look after these for John and keep in the shade, girl. You'll have to find the straight ones in there for him. That will be your job. Just don't drown yourselves," he warned, blowing a puff of yellow sawdust from the end of a plank.

Mama poked her straw-hatted head up from amongst the tomato plants. "You two stay right there." She struggled toward them, shuffling sideways between the rows. She wore one of William's long-sleeved cotton shirts to discourage the sun and the mosquitoes, and her face was sweaty and flushed from a morning's pruning and weeding. The children waited, hand in hand, and watched her approach.

The forenoon sun was doing its job of baking the seedpods on the caragana bushes. The air was alive with snapping and cracking as dry pods burst and flung their tiny black beans as far away as the other end of the porch. That's how the caragana hedge got itself all the way around the house and even down into the coulee, John said.

Mama was nearly out of the tomatoes now, pulling off her straw hat, sending a cascade of caragana seeds into the garden. She frowned. "There's a garden here with carrots sorely in need of a good weeding and some thinning," she said. "Potatoes aren't going to hill themselves. And there are worms on the cabbages that could do with some coal oil. And John, you know Violet shouldn't be getting worked up in this heat."

Father held up his hand. "Louise, there's always time for chores," he said. Something in his voice made her pull up short. She stood with one hand on her hip and gripped the brim of her hat with the other, fanning it to get a breeze on her hot face. "When I was young, almost thirteen years old like our John, I had a boat," Father said, his eyes on the horizon. "It was a grotty old rowboat full of holes. So full of holes I had a tin to tip out the water with one hand while I rowed with the other. There was a little bit of seawater at one end of our land, an inlet probably no more than ten feet at its deepest. Sometimes, if the water wasn't coming in too badly, I'd lie on my back and look at the sky and wonder if other people in the world saw the sky the same way. Do you remember so many years ago, sweetheart? In Toronto. That pine forest we found beyond Rosedale? Can you picture it?"

Mama nodded and put her hat back on her head.

Father sometimes had a way of making Mama nicer. It was good to see Mama, Violet thought with some surprise now. It was good to have everyone together, a family again. Everyone was where they were supposed to be.

"I figured I could sail around the world in that boat I had

when I was a boy," Father went on. "It was the first time I knew I could do something if I only began the job and held fast. What a shame if one's life is spent only in safe harbours. Sometimes chores can wait." He pointed his hammer at John. "We all could do with a wee bit of exploration."

He winked at Mama and tilted his head at the children. Father could take the edge off Mama. He could make her happy before John was gone, and even sometimes after, he could still make her smile. At least until she was gone, too.

"John, mind your sister, then," Mama said. "But those cabbage worms will be calling your name before supper tonight." She turned and walked back into the garden through the tall tomato plants until Violet couldn't see her anymore. But Violet could hear her when she started to hum. Father joined in, singing the April showers song in a booming voice.

> *"So keep on looking for a bluebird*
> *And list'ning for his song*
> *Whenever April showers come along."*

She heard her mother laugh, a light, tinkling sound carried to her on the warm breeze.

Violet wondered if he was thinking of Mama as the girl who listened to him go on for hours about having a farm on the prairies. How she'd reached out to touch him with just the tips of her fingers as they watched the clouds pass overhead, and how she had agreed to be his wife. Father told Violet the story so often after Mama left as if he wanted Violet to remember her as he chose to.

At the edge of the slough, Violet flicked away flies with a willow. She stood with a handful of bent and rusty nails, handing them one at a time to John while he hammered an unlikely assortment of scrap lumber crosspieces to the backside of the door. Two fence posts and a pile of grey, knotted twine lay at the water's edge.

"So it's not so wobbly," he explained, lashing another board down with a length of twine.

John sat up and pulled off his shirt, and Violet could see his ribs. He carefully set the saw into the first pole and dragged the teeth across the wood. He was hot from his labour and excitement, his face flushed, his hair plastered down wet to his forehead. He squinted against the sun and held up the saw to shield his eyes.

"Hey, Violet, can't you hear your name?" John said, talking around the nails he carefully pinched between his lips, just like

Father did. He pointed up toward the house. "Look. Mr. Yuzik is up there. I think he wants to talk to you."

Violet looked beyond the slope toward the house. Nik Yuzik stood by the snapping caragana, dressed in a Sunday suit, but Violet knew he would rather be in his overalls. She wondered if his wife got him a new pair or if she fixed the buckle on his old ones. He called out. A gust of wind swept through the willows by the water just then, and Violet heard caragana seeds popping in the hot sun. He waved and called out again, but she only heard the music spoons that hung on the porch, clinking against each other. She waved her willow switch with one hand so he could see her.

She wanted to tell him about her brand-new baby boy. Mr. Yuzik would be happy about that, even with six boys of his own. He had hurt her that day, but maybe if she tried hard to remember only his nice visits, it would be all right. She could tell him so. But he turned away, and then he was gone.

Father, Hank, and Emily waded through the tall grass down toward the slough. Emily was carrying something in her arms, and Violet knew it was Hank and Emily's own baby, a boy just like hers. She turned to look for her brother.

The raft floated lightly on the slough, a length of twine securing it to the old stump at the water's edge. Ducks bobbed on the water all around it in the cattails. The raft could carry them anywhere.

"Violet, wanna try again?" Almost invisible in the tall grass, John sat cross-legged on the slope beside the slough and sorted through the tall rye. He selected two flat, wide blades and pinched them carefully from the stalk. He held one out to her. "Here, Violet. You remember how Hank showed us. The grass whistle." He brought his hands together as if he was praying, pressed his blade between his thumbs and held his hands up to his mouth. "If you get lost, you just blow like this, and we'll hear you. I have to teach you how to do it yourself before my birthday."

A shadow crawled across John, and the dark swallowed him just when he took a deep breath and blew. A clear, lasting whistle. Violet looked up. Overhead, huge white clouds drifted across the sun, across the endless prairie blue. The blue of her brother's eyes and her father's. And the colour of her own.

IN HER HOSPITAL BED, VIOLET TURNED HER FACE TO the window and opened her eyes just as the pale light of morning crept across the frosted pane. *It was a good dream*, she thought, *a good remember*. Violet saw the bundle of dry crocus beside her water jug, tied with a yellow ribbon. She knew her father had been close by.

Doris couldn't have it right, Violet thought. A good mama would never forget her baby. She promised herself she never would, not any of it.

Outside, in the soft morning light, the snow lay drifted across the stubble fields in wind-sculpted peaks and grey hollows. The hint of sunrise cast a weak pink on the horizon, and there was no way to guess where the prairie ended and the sky began.

Acknowledgments

Small Reckonings is inspired by true events; however, the story and all characters are fictional. A special thank-you to farmer Henry "Hank" Buck of Abbey, Saskatchewan. What a gift to be given the seed of a story that simply would not let itself go untold. Violet would not be here without you.

Evidently, it takes a village to raise a novel, and I am blessed to live in a flourishing arts community, a place where a writer finds herself buoyed by wonderful mentors. At the risk of name-dropping, I owe many for their support. First, I am eternally grateful to Byrna Barclay, my *Svensk goda fé*, who waved her magic rosette iron over this story. Burton House Books released the first edition of this novel in the spring of 2020, and the second printing was sold out by the end of the year. A revised edition was released by Copestone in 2021. My utmost admiration for Sandra Birdsell, who tackled the substantive editing with a deft and gentle hand. May violets always grow in your garden. My thanks to Guy Vanderhaeghe and my creative writing classmates at the University of Saskatchewan, who read very early bits. My appreciation, Guy, for the rope and for your office hours, to which I availed myself to the point of stalking. I am pleased the story came full circle with Margaret Vanderhaeghe's ethereal painting on the cover of the first edition.

The Writer in Residence program at the Saskatoon Public Library is a godsend for writers and poets. Thank you to Yann Martel and Alice Kuipers, first as Writers in Residence and in years since for ongoing encouragement. Particular thanks to Alice for her good grace and willingness to tackle an awkward early version. My affection to Anne Simpson, also a Writer in Residence, for her wise counsel, helpful guidance, and good humour.

Thanks to Ron Marken, Leona Theis, Brenda Baker, Art Slade, Marina Endicott, Nicola Schaefer, Geoffrey Ursell—writers all—for kind words and helpful suggestions along the way. My appreciation to the Saskatchewan Writers' Guild and Joanne Gerber, my guide during our SWG mentorship many years ago. For various measures of cheerleading, reading, fact-finding, and translation services, thanks to Marc Alexander, the late Baba Pearl Andrich and Yvonne Brown, Marilyn Canitz, Violet Erskine Elliot, George Grassick, Baba Mary Leonty, Earl and the late Linda Misanchuk, Darlene Gulas-Bomok, James Nobel; Saskatoon Public Library Local History, Nelda Priddle, Doug and Jocelyn Richardson, Bernice Shawaga, and Bill Waiser.

I am indebted to the Watrous and District History Committee for the book *Prairie Reflections: Watrous and District History* (1983). It provided rich detail for the story. Any resemblance to real people or incidents is not intended and entirely coincidental. My thanks go beyond Saskatchewan to the staff of the Aotearoa/New Zealand Centre archives department, Canterbury Public Library, Christchurch; Dr. Ian and Kate Hall; and Gavin McLean, historian, Ministry for Culture and Heritage, Wellington. Even though much of the New Zealand back story was trimmed, it helped me know William much better. As well, Christopher Anderson, Music Access Coordinator, National Library of New Zealand, went above and beyond to find the lyrics to an obscure children's song from the early 1900s, "The Morepork."

Some of the teacher's dialogue was taken directly from the *Journal of Psycho-Asthenics: Devoted to the Care, Training and Treatment of the Feeble-minded and of the Epileptic*, Vol. 1, No. 1. Association of American Institutions for Feeble-Minded: Faribault, Minnesota (September 1896).

William sings a few lyrics of a New Zealand children's song to

John. The song is "The Morepork," words and music by A.E. Maud, which—we believe—was created in the early 1900s.

When Violet is in the chicken coop, she often sings bits of a folksong called "Love in a Fowlhouse." This song was written by New Zealand country music artist Garner Wayne.

Violet mangles the lyrics to the song "As Time Goes By," lyrics and music by Herman Hupfeld, 1931.

William sings a snippet of "April Showers" to Louise in the garden. Music by Louis Silvers, lyrics by Bud De Sylva, 1921.

The cover image is a photograph I took of a soddy in the *Winning the Prairie Gamble* exhibit at the Western Development Museum in Saskatoon, and is used with the generous permission of the WDM.

I gratefully acknowledge the Saskatchewan Arts Board for its ongoing support of emerging writers and artists and for financial assistance in the initial creation of this novel.

Special thanks to my parents, Fred and Doris Melberg, and my late parents-in-law, Fred and Mary Schwier, for their childhood memories of farm and town life during the Depression. Their recollections have not only shaped the time, place, and people of this novel but are now a cherished record of our own family history. In particular, I am grateful to my father-in-law. At ninety-two, he had "given up on reading. No more staying power." But my sister-in-law Sue brought him pages, a few at a time, and he read an entire early manuscript. It took him back to his childhood on the farm in Indiana, he said, and rekindled memories long forgotten. I couldn't have asked for a better critical review or a better father-in-law.

Last but not least, thank you to Edward Willett and Shadowpaw Press Reprise for giving Violet a chance to meet lots of new readers. She is happy about that.

About the Author

Photo by Heather Fritz

A freelance writer, editor and illustrator, Karin Melberg Schwier contributes to *Saskatoon HOME* and *Prairies North* magazines. She began her career as a reporter for a northern Alberta weekly newspaper while still in high school. Her series of profiles on pioneers of the Peace River country was published as a book, *Yesterday's Children*, when she was nineteen. In Saskatchewan, she has spent more than twenty-five years in communications work for an advocacy organization for people with intellectual disabilities and produced an award-winning newsmagazine.

Karin has written and co-authored six non-fiction books and two illustrated children's books exploring the lives of people with disabilities and edited several others. Other creative non-fiction has appeared in anthologies in Canada and the U.S. In 2013, Karin received a YWCA Women of Distinction Award (Arts, Culture and Heritage) for her writing on disability issues.

Small Reckonings, first published by Burton House Books in 2020 and released as a revised edition in 2021, is her debut novel. It received the John V. Hicks Award for Fiction in 2019 and won a Saskatchewan Book Award in 2021. In December 2021, the novel was selected by a national jury to be given the Glengarry Book Award Jury Short List Recognition of Literary Excellence. She is currently working on *Inheriting Violet,* the sequel to *Small Reck-onings.* The manuscript was awarded the John V. Hicks Award for Fiction in October 2022.

Website: karinschwier.ca

Dollybird by Anne Lazurko

The Ghosts of Spiritwood by Martine Noël-Maw

Let Us Be True by Erna Buffie

The Crow Who Tampered With Time

Backwater Mystic Blues

by Lloyd Ratzlaff

The Shards of Excalibur Series

The Peregrine Rising Duology

Spirit Singer

From the Street to the Stars

by Edward Willett

The Legend of Sarah

The Empire of Kaz Trilogy

by Leslie Gadallah

Canadian Chills

Return of the Grudstone Ghosts

Ghost Hotel

Invasion of the IQ Snatchers

by Arthur Slade